AQUARIUS TRILOGY BOOK THREE

OLYMPUS
Of Gods and Men

Sequel to
WALL
Love, Sex, and Immortality
and
PLUTO EFFECT

I0566378

An almost post-apocalyptic novel by

Stan I.S. Law

BY INHOUSEPRESS, MONTREAL, CANADA

ISBN 978-1-987864-02-1

For Bozena, my Ambrosia,
With gratitude

cannot recommend "Olympus – Of Gods and Men" strongly enough; it's definitely a must-read!

...fantastic finish to the trilogy. ...I found myself contemplating some of the ideas in the book long after finishing it. A must-read...

Author Stan I.S. Law delivers a gripping, enchanting, and unforgettable look at an intriguing future. ...Law's grasp on the esoteric, science, religion, spirituality, history, the metaphysical, family, and love is astounding. ...Stan I.S. Law has become one of my most favorite authors of all time. Unforgettable!

Unbelievable!! ...it's rare that I'm at a loss for words but 'blown away' comes to mind. This trilogy is as inimitable as they come. ...it will be a long time before I experience anything quite like this again. A fantastic read!

...Olympus is strange, exciting, heartbreaking, and last, but not least, inspiring. It is one of the best books in Stan's prolific bibliography and deserves to be enjoyed by anyone who loves book that makes them think about what happened long after they've made it to the last page.

"Live a good life.
If there are gods and they are just, then they will not care
how devout you have been, but will welcome you based on the
virtues you have lived by.

If there are gods, but unjust, then you should not
want to worship them.

If there are no gods, then you will be gone, but will
have lived a noble life that will live on in the
memories of your loved ones."

Marcus Aurelius
26 April 121 AD – 17 March 180 AD

CONTENTS

Epilogue to Pluto Effect
Prologue
PART ONE—FIRST 40 YEARS

PART TWO—SECOND 40 YEARS

PART THREE—THIRD 40 YEARS

PART FOUR—FOURTH 40 YEARS

BIBLIOGRAPHY

EPILOGUE of PLUTO EFFECT
Part Two of the Aquarius Trilogy

Olympus

Apparently we have remained on Milos for a number of years. The worst turmoil had passed us by. We knew that our vacations, our days of rest, were rapidly drawing to a close. Apparently, manipulating the passage of time was not outside the Olympians' sphere of influence. Probably nothing was in this reality.

In this illusion of reality?

Once awakened, we used our time to strengthen our internal fortitude, as well as our psychic skills. Mama told us that in the Tibet sanctuary they have identified Maitreya. He'd remained incognito until now. There must have been a reason why he revealed himself.

At a personal level it came to me as a shock to realize that Amadeus looked, and was, a young man of twenty. He turned into a handsome broad shouldered man, not unlike his grandfather Papa.

Athena, as was to have been expected, grew up as beautiful as we'd all expected her to be.

As for Mavis, she gave an impression that she was rapidly losing her shyness. About time, I might add.

Yet when I looked at Mama and Papa, not to mention Ambrosia or even myself, I have not noticed any evidence of the passage of time. Could it be that just for the few of us time had stood still. And if so, why?

And then I looked at Jerry and Tom. They haven't aged by a single day. At least, not in my eyes. There had to be an explanation for all this but, as I like to say lately, that's another story.

At least, this is what I think had happened.

But all this came to me later, over the course of a few days. For a while, I'd remained a bit groggy. My memories needed sorting out, slowly, over time.

***

Prologue

As I mentioned in the Epilogue to my last report of this contentious period in our lives, time seems to have stood still for some ten years, though not in the world at large. There it must have accelerated to an absurd velocity, resulting in global changes that, according to archeologists, in the past would have taken hundreds if not thousands of years. While all this happened, the Island of Milos remained protected under the aegis of the gods. I could but wonder if Zeus and Athena had something to do with it.

PART ONE

The First 40 Years

*"...and name that sat on him was Death,
and Hell followed with him."*

*The Revelation
Of Saint John the Divine*

1
First Awakening

Perhaps **I should go back** a few years to recap the events that took place not so long ago.

I remember that day as though it were yesterday: the absolute silence, the incredible stillness. But most of all, I recall the incomprehensible serenity that had surrounded us to the total exclusion of awareness of either time or space. We had all been suspended somewhere between heaven and earth—in no-man's land. Perhaps we have been outside the confines of time. Perhaps, I thought at the time, this was the difference between being and becoming, where or when all is still, yet perception of all is heightened to a level unattainable in the state of becoming. In the state of constant convoluting change.

Is this where gods have their being, I wondered? Stillness? Absolute stillness?

I used the word convoluting because for a while there, wherever 'there' was, while hardly conscious of my own existence I was acutely aware of all that was taking place around me. I actually perceived individual atoms whirling in wild abandon, forming patterns of intricate, one might say fractal complexity, yet as orderly, though still incomprehensible, as the first breath is to a child after leaving the protective aegis of a mother's womb.

And that was, in a way, how I felt when facing the orderly complexity of the universe, apparently reduced, or was it miniaturized, to my present ability of perception. I saw both mega and microevolution of patterns, as though gods directed me through the first steps of universal ABC of phenomenal reality.

Up there, hovering above me, were the seemingly divine figures suspended on a cushion of the air. Hovering yet also in perfect stillness.

It was later, long after I became aware of them, (although I had no perception of the passage of time), up there, in that eerie stasis, that apparently I opened my eyes to see Ambrosia looking down at me with an expression halfway between worry and amusement. By some nook or crook I found myself again on the terrace, although I distinctly remember going indoors. No matter, here I was and gorgeous Ambrosia was here with me. The rest did not matter. Or so I thought.

"Darling, are you alright?"

Her voice was music to my ears, yet I wondered why do people invariably ask such an inane, redundant question of people who obviously are not in the least bit all right. Dumbfounded, flabbergasted, discombobulated, but definitely not all right.

"Yes," I replied with equal absurd equanimity, lying my head off.

She continued staring at me. I was everything but all right. Perhaps she was not inquiring about my mental health? Physically I seemed all in one piece. For all I knew I was dead and have been well on the way to the never-never land.

"Of course I'm alright," I repeated, adding insult to injury.

As I mentioned above, we had all been sitting on the terrace of the Milos villa. Just the family. At least, I thought my family was there. Mama, Papa, and of course, Ambrosia. The rest of the special guests evaporated into thin air.

And talking of air, for a while it continued to shimmer, as on occasion one can see it shimmering over hot asphalt towards the end of a sunny day. A little later the contours of furniture, then the close-by houses, rocks, olive trees, finally the clouds above and the distant horizon reasserted their sharpness. I took a deep breath. Slowly, still in disbelief, I turned my head towards Ambrosia.

I felt my eyes opening wider, just to make sure.

There were no giants floating in the air. No mysterious gods, neither Greek nor Chinese, nor any other; no strange events taking place. I was reclining on the deckchair, as were Mama and Papa.

All was normal. Absurdly normal. Coming out of the house was a young lady, possibly hired help unknown to me, carrying a large carafe of red liquid. Probably wine or Sangria. She walked with a step of such grace that it could be easily mistaken for a lyrical dance.

Suddenly I noticed that the children were missing. Both, Athena and Amadeus were nowhere to be seen. It was then that I heard a giggle. The maid put the tray on the table and turned to face me. She smiled at me from afar.

"You don't recognize me, Dad?"

I was staring at a very beautiful young lady, in her late teens, perhaps early twenties, whose face reminded me of...

"Athena...?" I sat up, refusing to accept the evidence of eyes. "Athena?" I repeated in utter disbelief. For a brief moment I wondered if I was still dreaming after all.

I've learned from my own lectures I'd given at McGill University, it seemed like only yesterday, that one cannot rely on the evidence of ones eyes. Ever since Ernest Rutherford proposed that atoms are almost completely empty space, the theory backed up by another giant of physics, Sir Arthur Eddington, I experienced considerable difficulty reconciling the evidence of my senses with reality.

Ten years had passed. At least Mama had said so. She, the young lady, now indisputably my daughter, was beautiful. Very beautiful. Like her mother? The next moment I remembered that Ambrosia and I had adopted both our children. And yet...? The laughter in Athena's eyes seems to have multiplied, grown, as to become contagious.

"Athena?" I repeated for the third time. Yet I couldn't help smiling, if in disbelief.

And for the second time since opening my eyes I remembered that ten years had passed since I sat on the terrace to witness the meeting Mama had called for us, and all her special guests. Ten years would have accounted for the change in Athena. For a moment I wondered if Amadeus…

"Yes, Dad. I also moved on in years…"

A mature, slightly rasping voice reached me from behind. More like an old man's yet there was something familiar in its tone.

"We all get raspy with age, Dad," he said.

As I turned I saw a broad shouldered young man, smiling from ear to ear. He stood, stooping, as though an old man, tottering on the edge of maintaining his balance. His announcement was greeted by a salve of laughter from Mama, Papa, Ambrosia and Athena. It seemed that my grown-up son was quite an actor. Or was it a comedian? As he straightened up, he looked a good six feet tall.

With the exception of my children, no one else seemed to have aged. Or matured? Or changed in any way. For a moment I was worried that Papa would come over and crush my ribs. I was spared his expression of joy, and, for once, my ribs remained intact.

"Nor have you, Dad," Amadeus assured me.

Only then I remembered that virtually all people present could read my mind. My next thought, which I quickly dismissed but not before some giggles and chuckles reached me from all sides, was the desire to look at myself in a mirror.

"Trust me, darling, you haven't aged a day," this was Ambrosia who continued to stare at me with that dualistic mixture of expressions. "Well, a week, anyway," she added, glancing at Mama, who reacted with a vague, enigmatic smile. Those ladies knew something I did not.

It was time to get up.

As I pushed myself from the *chaise longue*, my head spun, forcing me to sit down again.

"Easy, my boy," Papa was on his feet ready to catch me. "Just take it easy for a while. Your body must remember…"

I wished they would stop talking in riddles. I looked up, waiting what he had to say.

"You haven't walked for close to ten years, son. Your body knows how, but it must remember."

That was supposed to be complete explanation.

"Well, not exactly," Papa was evidently forced to admit. "For the phenomenal world outside this island, and other sanctuaries, indeed ten years have lapsed. But, as you know, time is a flexible commodity. It has to do with speed and distance and all sorts of other things."

I stared at him, none the wiser for the proffered explanation.

"Well, my friend…"

Papa's voice became monotonous, which, I suspect, must have been to place his listeners, or at least me, into alpha state. I wondered if he did it on purpose, as often Mama did.

I had an almost palpable feeling that time was slowing down again. Quickly, using much less of the commodity so precious on earth, the commodity of time, I heard Papa's words, or rather thoughts or images, directly in my head.

The concept of flexibility of time is not new. St. Thomas Aquinas proposed three types of time. Tempus concerned the "temporal" or earthly time. It measured the duration of changes taking place on earth. The second type of time Aquinas called "aevum", or time affecting changes in or of mental processes. It did not concern material changes but rather changes in mental states. It also applied to all that is incorporeal, to angels and to states of consciousness. The third type of time Aquinas called the "aeternitas". It concerned the divine.

Papa smiled as though sharing a joke. Each time he felt the idea representing a Latin word anchored in my mind, he signaled inverted comas in the air with two fingers. Then he smiled knowing that he had connected.

While it was the domain of God, it also embraced our ability to experience infinity or immortality in a single instant. It is the time that permits the present and infinity to be one. To coexist.

I remained still, motionless. Papa looked down at me, making sure I was keeping up with his images.

In science, Aristotle and Newton measured time unambiguously as the duration between two events. They believed it was "absolute time". Then Einstein destroyed the misconception that time is absolute. In his theory of relativity he married the concept of time and space into a single idea of space-time.

Papa smiled, undisguised satisfaction painted on his kind features. Then he looked up at Ambrosia who took it as a sign for her to take over. I could sense that it was she who was now passing on the knowledge.

According to the physicist Stephen Hawking, the distinction between space and time disappears completely when using "imaginary time"; time measured using imaginary numbers.
Quite a choice...

Although thoughts arrived at my awareness in what I can only describe a neutral orientation, there was an aura of emotions that accompanied them that were distinctly my wife's.

The expression on Papa's face was nothing short of triumphant. He looked at his daughter to finish the lecture. For once, I was on the receiving end.

"Once science broke down the rigidity of time," darling husband, she continued out loud, "the universe became fluid, relative. So did we. We can no longer claim the privilege of age. Someone might ask us how old we are in conformal, subjective, entropic, *aevum,* biological or absolute time, to mention just a few..."

She smiled seeing Papa's gray head nodding.

"Frankly," she went on, "I no longer believe there is such a thing as *real* time. It would probably be just somebody's vision of reality. Yours and mine might be different. Let us make sure we know the answer to the question regarding our age. Or we may have to learn to enjoy the privileges accorded senior citizens because of our contribution to society. Not because we are old."

"Alternatively," Mama put in, "we might choose to live in the present."

I had a lot to learn.

Until Ambrosia began talking out loud, as 'normal' people do, Papa's and then my wife's direct communication through what is normally referred to as telepathic communication, could have lasted no more than three or four seconds. I recall that because I was in the process of putting down my glass on the table and it hadn't arrived there until Papa and then his daughter had finished conveying their thoughts to me. It couldn't have been longer than that.

I was blessed with a most extraordinary family.

I often wondered what made me deserve them. Yet, in spite of their combined efforts, I still had no idea what happened to me during those ten years. Perhaps, I mused, perhaps I shall find out in time.

This last thought of mine brought an avalanche of laughter. *Find out in time...* reverberated in my head.

"That's a good one, Dad." Amadeus' laugh cascaded from the back of his throat, with something approaching *basso profundo*. A young *basso profundo*. It was also the loudest. My son now sported a big powerful chest. Powerful laughter seemed becoming to him.

I had no choice. I shrugged my shoulders, sat up a bit straighter, and joined the cavalcade. We all roared for quite a while. Myself, for the first time in ten years. I had a lot of catching up to do. I suspect that this explosion of merriment served to dispel the atmosphere of tension that my awakening may have created. Perhaps they were worried about me. Perhaps not all people wake up after ten years of hibernation.

I am back, I thought, looking almost triumphantly all around me. All I saw were smiling faces and a great effluence of love that seemed to engulf me, and made me feel warm all over. I guess I was a very lucky man.

Later that day Ambrosia persuaded me to take a gentle walk down to the beach. We walked slowly, as I gathered confidence. With each step I was regaining stability. By the time we got down, I could stand easily on my own. I even hopped up and down a few times, just to make sure, or perhaps to show off to my wife my newly found prowess.

"A dip?" I asked.

"But, Sir, I have no bathing suit," she replied, desperately pinching her cheeks to invoke a blush.

Only then I felt sudden weakness. As she removed her dress, years of abstinence caught up with me. My newfound energies have deserted me. I felt weak in the knees. Slowly and carefully, I lowered myself to the sand.

"Do you mean to tell me that for ten years, for ten whole years, we didn't make…"

"No, darling. Not for ten whole, long years…"

"But you were awake all the time… weren't you?"

"Yes, darling. I was. And I missed you."

Ten years without making love to Ambrosia. How on earth did I survive? How on earth did *she* survive? Then a thought struck me.

"Do you think my body remembers?"

She was looking down at me, her eyes wandering below my waistline.

"I am sure, Simon, that some things bodies never forget. After all, surely, if they did, the human race would have never survived to this day."

We spent the next hour or so watching our bodies perform the ancient art of remembering. It was wonderful. It was exactly as I remembered it ten years ago. Only better. Perhaps a little slower but definitely better. It was like a first meal after a long fast. Which it was.

Luckily for us the beach was deserted. Except for the usual Terns, one or two Common Sandpipers, and a Little Ringed Plover, which must have stopped over on its way to the wetlands scattered all over the Aegean Islands. But none of them seemed to mind.

Three days have passed during which I have been fed a diet I wish to forget. The only members of my family who have not greeted me yet were Mavis, Tom and Jerry.

"They'll all be back soon," I was told. The matter was dismissed out of hand. Perhaps my awakening was not such an earth-shaking event as I'd imagined.

The evening was balmy and Mama decided we would eat outside. Only later I learned that eating outside was the norm, not an exception. I was looking forward to my first real meal in ten years. So far, in spite of my rebellious comments, I have been allowed only a special concoction that offered little taste, less aroma, and virtually nothing to bite into.

"So what happened to the rest of the world?" I asked during dinner. With the speed at which changes occurred before I lost consciousness, they could have been both, catastrophic and/or redeeming. I was ignored. Perhaps they were not used to having me around.

"Tomorrow you can have anything you want, darling," Ambrosia tried to cheer me up. She was obviously reading my thoughts.

I was allowed no wine either. I almost decided to go back to sleep until I remembered our little session on the beach with the birds. Recalling my family's ability to read my mind, I quickly dismissed those thoughts, but not before Papa gave me a quizzical look while Ambrosia, in spite of her dark complexion, managed to generate a slight blush.

Then we all looked up at Mama. Apparently she was the only one capable of answering my previous question.

"It was different everywhere," she began, a weariness underlying her tone. It must have been a difficult subject for her. "About four years after we all arrived here, the level of the oceans rose by close to four feet. This wouldn't have been completely tragic, but it was accompanied by category five hurricanes, cyclones, typhoons and climatic aberrations for which we do not have words in our dictionaries."

There was utter silence while she talked.

"Water spouts seemed to appear with suddenness of a gust of wind. They swirled with such force that large ships had been lifted completely out of the water. There was no question of air travel, of course. In fact, with the power plants down in most places and no alternate sources of energy, travel became a thing of the past."

I didn't have to ask for more. It was evident that the world as I knew it ten years ago must have changed beyond all recognition. No power, no travel, lower landmass under water, hurricanes and their eastern cousins making havoc on land. The world would never be the same.

In all those climatic upheavals, Milos, the island of the gods, remained a haven of such serenity that it seemed almost indecent to talk of hurricanes and inundations.

"And here? Why is it so balmy...?" I blurted, looking at

the lustrous sea stretching towards the horizon.

They all looked at me as if regarding a wayward child. Again. I was getting tired of being treated as a retarded black sheep of the family. Again. Yes, again.

I'd have to snap out of it. All I saw on their faces was surprise.

"Look towards the east. The Mediterranean to the south, where I've been facing, was a picture of serenity. But as I turned to face east, perhaps a little northeast, the horizon showed distant signs of unrest. Partially obscured by the rising terrain of the island, yet I could see that progressively the azure turned grayish, then darker, until at the extreme distance of my vision I could see lightening cutting across the dark blue, almost black sky. For some reason, yesterday, I hadn't noticed it. Obviously I had been so preoccupied with my own awakening that all else became secondary. Now my mouth fell open and stayed that way till I heard Mama's voice.

"Don't worry, Simon. It's like this most of the time. People there must be used to it now."

The far, far horizon must have been over Turkey. Or, perhaps, what once was Turkey? I no longer knew what to expect.

"So it's not over yet?"

This time Mama's voice carried a note of sadness. "No, Simon, it is not over. But it is necessary." And, at least at that time, she wouldn't say any more.

I was alone, again. Back in Montreal, the children had spent most of their time in boarding school. I only saw them on weekends. Here, finally, I was hoping to spend more time with them. To see them grow. Mature. To tell them stories. And now, here I was again. Ambrosia in her lab and children all grown-up. And I? I was alone, again.

Whatever incomprehensible Gordian Knots someone

twisted with the concept of time, was of no consequence.
What did hurt me, hurt me a lot, was that I lost the growing
up of my children. A little girl becoming a woman is
probably the most enchanting period in her life.

And I?

And I was asleep at the time. All the time. Throughout
her teens. I, her father, didn't see a bud opening up to become
a rose. I even missed worrying about her.

Were there boys around? Did anyone approach her
without my permission?

How dare they?

"Sorry, sir. You were asleep at the time."

I supplied my own scenarios until I realized that there
were no 'boys' on our small island. None that I've ever seen.
At least not close-by. And had there been any they would
have had to face Papa. Frankly, I suspected with only slight
embarrassment, if I were them, I'd rather face me. One bear
hug from Papa and their ribcage would need orthopedic
adjustment.

Good 'Ol Papa.

And then there was Amadeus, of course. He wouldn't let
my little girl come to any harm. No siree. Not my son. Not
my Amadeus. Quite a man he's become. Quite a man.

My boy!

And yet, I still missed being a father.

***

2
Mavis and Jerry

Once again I had to find my way around in the little community of the island. Apparently, here, little has changed. Some days later, as I came out to have my breakfast on the terrace, I saw two heads bent forward across the table, apparently lost in deep conversation. They hadn't moved as I approached.

For a moment I had an idea that I could listen in to their talk by entering their minds. I know that this was a no-no among the gods but, let's face it, I had a long way to go to divinity of any kind.

But what if they find out?

I don't know how I knew, but I felt that this must have been a man talking. I had no idea who it was. It didn't sound familiar. My memories were still hazy.

But it's our baby!

A woman?

But there are no babies here. No doctors, no nothing...

I stopped peeking. Into their minds, I mean.

I cleared my throat, which made both heads swing in my direction. They were unmistakably Jerry and... and Mavis? Only it wasn't the Mavis I knew. There was nothing girlish or shy about her. She was a woman who measured me with her eyes before getting up from her chair, then rising in an agile leap and running towards me. She threw both her arms around my neck, her body pressed against mine. Even yesterday I had been so preoccupied with my waken state that I completely forgot to look for Tom and Jerry, let alone Mavis.

"We only just got back, Uncle." She hugged me as one would a long-lost friend. "How are you?"

How is a man after a ten-year sleep? Ask a polar bear after an ice age, I was about to say. I didn't have to. From the expression on her face, she must have guessed. Or was she listening to my thoughts? I vaguely remembered that that was why she'd left her family home in London. She called them dead—those who couldn't read thoughts.

Wasn't there something about reading thoughts that brought us closer to 'divinity'? Actually, there was. It was that by reading each other's thoughts it cut psychological barriers. It brought us closer to oneness. To feeling the omnipresent unity of all life. Or was I just imagining things? It's been ten years...

But this was not the Mavis I knew ten years ago. She remained as tiny, hadn't grown physically, but there was an air of maturity about her. She was no longer a lost soul. She's found herself. If she could read other peoples' thoughts way back in London, then by now she must have been very proficient in the art of telepathy. Was it an art? I was just a beginner. Yet, she didn't really look any older. Just, well, as I said, more mature. And more, much more confident. As though she came into her own, whatever that was, or may have been.

"Mr. Jackson?"

A man only inches taller than Mavis cleared his throat. I recognized him immediately. This was Jerry. Tom was the tall one, a mountain of a man. Suddenly it all came back to me at a flood.

"Jerry!" I exclaimed with real pleasure. Contrary to Mavis, he hasn't changed a bit. Not one iota.

It was my turn to embrace the man; short, yet probably broader in the shoulder than I was. Still am, of course. Then I turned again towards Mavis.

"You only just got back?"

"Yes, Uncle. Tom, Jerry and I are the scouts for the surrounding islands. We bring help wherever it is needed."

That's right, I was the uncle—ever since she absconded from London without permission. It seemed like ages ago. The mystery of their appearance, or lack of physical change after ten years, had to wait for later.

"We're sorry we weren't here for your, ah, your…"

"Awakening?"

"I was going to say arrival. It was as though you weren't here for a very long time. We all missed you, Uncle. We really did."

There was a tear forming in the corner of her eye. I hope it was of joy at seeing me. I certainly enjoyed looking at her.

"You've, ah, grown?" I formed it into a question.

"Actually people say I haven't change a bit. Mama taught me to soul travel. It's such fun. And it sort of rejuvenates you." Then she looked embarrassed. "But you know all that…"

"Not as much as you might think," I put in, remembering the troubles I had in the past entering the alpha brain waves. Of course, I haven't tried it since my waking up.

I glanced at Jerry, standing by, stepping from one foot to another in vague discomfort. I perceived it had something to do with his relationship with Mavis. They are adults, I told myself. It's their business, whatever it is. Yet Mavis saw my badly concealed scrutiny.

"Until six months ago, he was in…" she was looking for the right word.

I heard the thought for coma in my head.

"…in Limbo," she finished, yet apparently still dissatisfied with her choice of word. "That's what Mama called it. "Coma is essentially just physical, whereas Limbo includes mental and emotional activity of the entity… of Jerry. When he first came out for a day or two he was like a baby…"

Evidently she couldn't resist stepping closer to him and stroking his hair. A very large, very powerful babe, I mused, smiling.

"He only came out about six months ago. I've been looking after him since he came out," she added, maternal love mixed in with her tone of voice.

I took another deep look at my niece. She definitely hasn't changed, rather like Ambrosia, but there was an air about her that wasn't there before. And then she stumped me.

"Did you hear what we were saying, Uncle?"

I did and I didn't. I had no idea if I ought to admit to my indiscretion. On the other hand, I did not 'hear'. Not exactly.

"No, Mavis, I did not *hear*."

Perhaps I stressed the word *hear* too much? She looked at me with a little doubt showing in her eyes. I tried to cover my tracks.

"Was it confidential?" I looked at Jerry this time.

"We'd better tell Mr. Jackson. He ought to know," he said looking sternly at Mavis.

"I'm pregnant," she offered, without any preambles.

"And I'm the father," Jerry added with a mixture of pride and embarrassment. Yet having confessed his authorship, his hands fell flat against his sides, palms out, as though he had nothing to do with this.

"We're in love," Mavis added, redundantly. I could see that at first glance. Didn't it all start back in Montreal, years and years ago?

At this Jerry nodded vigorously. Probably at her assertion of being in love, rather than my reminiscences.

"It looks as though I am going to be the first to congratulate you. Both of you."

Believe it or not, they did make a lovely couple. And they most definitely were in love.

Last night after supper I had been so tired that only now fragments of my past began returning to me. Wasn't there a cat, Lazarus—we called him Lazy, and later a Golden Retriever whom Ambrosia called Goldie? Where were they? Surely they must have lived past my ten years of hibernation, particularly after the rejuvenation resulting from using the quantum-tunneling mode of travel through Ambrosia's gizmos.

Ignoring for a moment the joyful news of Mavis' pregnancy—after all, the young lady has come of age in my absence—I asked them about the pets.

"Lazy is wherever Ambrosia is, and Goldie is looking after the sheep and goats, out yonder," she pointed towards the hills on the south of the island. "He certainly earns his keep," she added with apparent admiration in her voice.

"And what of Tom?"

"Wherever Mr. Milos is," Jerry answered at once.

"Mr. Milos?"

"Papa," Mavis cut in. "Jerry still finds it awkward to call him Papa."

Ah, yes. Wasn't there a connection between Papa and Tom going way back to when Papa was Paul? To Saul even before he became Paul? Doesn't time fly, I mused vaguely amused. It really was all coming back to me.

Memories. Sometimes I think that all our life is made up of memories. As we plod along, we create new ones, more and more, and when our storehouse is full we die. And then? And then we start again.

Mavis looked at me in a strange way.

"Sorry..." she whispered.

I guessed at once. She was peeking, perhaps inadvertently, into my thought-stream. I have not learned, as yet, to guard them—my thoughts, I mean.

"I have no secrets from you, Mavis. That's why you joined us, remember?"

"Yes, Uncle. Thank you." She smiled, relieved.

That day also came back in my memory, when we left London, my old home in UK, the remains of my family, and

Mavis had decided to come with us. At the time I wasn't even quite sure if she was old enough to leave under her own cognizance. Later I'd learned that she was. She just looked so very, very young. In a way, she still did, although she was into her late twenties. Jerry, by now, must have been pushing forty, if not more. He did not look it though. No more than she looked her age. There was something very strange going on around this island. I was determined to find out. From Ambrosia. If necessary from Mama.

I left the two lovebirds—they seemed to be doing very well on their own—and made my way to look for Ambrosia. As was to have been expected, I found her in her lab. I peeked through the Judas peephole. She was bent over a table, making something move up and down, without touching it. The door wasn't locked. I walked in as quietly as I could.

"How do you like it?" she asked, without turning.

I smiled. I loved her long hair cascading over her shoulders.

"The gizmo, not my hair, silly!"

"Sorry," I muttered.

"No, you're not. But I am referring to the antigravity I am playing with."

Antigravity? For crying out loud, what was she going to invent next?

"Cold fusion," she replied, putting down what looked like a thin pencil and turning to face me. "And how are you, my husband?"

"Do we need it in this island?"

"So you've given up on Montreal altogether?"

"I stand corrected… It's been a while…"

"Yes, darling. Strangely enough, our penthouse seems to be safe and sound."

"You've been back?"

"I and Tom. Dad wouldn't let me go on my own."

"Cheers for Dad. I mean Papa."

"It's all right. He would love you to call him Dad. He always wanted a son, every man does, and you're as close as he can get to one."

Somehow this sounded nice. My dad had died so long ago that a surrogate father would be nice to have. I often needed advise on things only experience of age could provide.

"So what's all this cold fission?" I asked instead.

"Fusion, darling, not fission. And it has to be cold. Hot fusion takes place in temperatures in the millions of degrees, as does fission, for that matter.

"And the difference is…?"

"In fusion two nuclei join together to form a heavier nucleus. That's how our sun and the stars get their power. Fission is the exact opposite. It is a process, in which the nucleus of an atom splits into two or more smaller nuclei. That's how we get energy in our nuclear power stations."

"And…?"

"The principle difference is waste. Fusion energy would also produce some waste material, but it would decay much more quickly. And the only by-product would be helium."

"And that's harmless?"

"Pretty much."

"So just why are you working on it, or intend to?"

She took off her gloves and swung her chair to face me. I missed just looking at her, just looking at her face.

"Sy, we are here only about ten years, but the Age of Aquarius lasts a total of about two-thousand one hundred and sixty years. I want to make sure that during that time people do not pollute our planet as we did in the first six segments of the Zodiac?"

She was about a thousand years ahead of me.

"And the antigrav? It sounds like science fiction."

"At the moment it pretty much is. But if I can take it a step farther, then Paul's people could get intra-planetary travel on their own terms."

"Papa's people?"

"Simon, darling. You know that this reality is based on imaginary assumptions. We can travel in our dreams, lucid dreams, to the edges of the universe, but the masses cannot. They? They must work hard to get as far as the moon. And they are the people Papa cares most about, you know that?"

More and more was coming back to me. Mama submerged in a reality in which she could dismiss time and space with a wave of her delicate hand, and Papa working his fingers to the bone to help the ordinary men and women. To help the masses. To help those that are many by choice, or don't know, as yet, how to be called to be among the few.

I abide in a very, very strange reality...

"And you, darling, you straddle the two realities. You are this link between being and becoming."

She looked up at me, her eyes filed with laughter.

"That's why I missed your body so much for so long..."

"And my pristine soul?" I asked.

"Your not so pristine soul is immortal, I can have it any time. But your body..."

She was capable of most lascivious looks of any women I'd ever met. Could I blame her? She waited for ten years to take advantage of my almost divine body.

Could I blame her?

This time she heard my thoughts as though I'd said them out loud. She got up and melted into my arms. I liked that. I liked that very much. Perhaps Papa's people had a thing or two they should hold on to. For a while. Like a million years or so. Maybe longer?

An hour later we went for a walk. I had to exercise my body, she said, which sounded ridiculous after the exercise I had for the last hour.

"Seriously, darling. As a matter of fact, it is I who has to move more. This constant sitting in the lab is not doing me much good. I might have to do some QTs to rejuvenate myself."

QT was our well-established abbreviation for Quantum-Tunneling.

As far as I could see she needed no rejuvenation, but you know women. If they don't look seventeen coming on eighteen, they begin looking for gray hair. We walked.

As a matter of fact, those walks were practically the only time I had Ambrosia to myself. With the obvious exception of you know what, but that was usually relegated to just before going to sleep. At least ten years ago, it was. Now, we were catching up. It seemed to have had beneficial relaxation for me, particularly as when I'd attempted OBE. That's Out of Body Experience, for those who never tried it. For now, we just walked. I had a lot of questions for Ambrosia. I didn't even know if she took any time off. Hibernating time, I mean. I also didn't know what was new with the rest of the family.

"I looked for Amadeus all over the house and saw nothing of him."

"He's circulating, QT wise, between dad and his own interests, which he refused to tell me about. I peeked and peeked, even in his sleep, and couldn't get anything from his gray cells."

"What do you think it might be?"

"I don't know, but he also spends some time in my lab, working on some computer patterns that are strange to me. Also for some reason he wouldn't divulge, he acquired fluency in Mandarin."

"Chinese?! That's my son," I said, proudly.

"Yes, darling, he can be just as difficult as you sometimes."

"And he won't tell you why?"

"There could be a thousand reasons. Close to two billion, if you count them individually. And most of them speak the Beijing dialect."

And then I asked out of the blue. "Was Tom also in Limbo?"

"You were talking to Mama?"

"No, Mavis, actually."

"Mavis made great steps in your absence. She didn't sleep, at all, I mean not long term, yet her OBEs seem to have maintained her in what I can only call prime condition. She hasn't aged, has she?" Ambrosia looked up at me, trying to read my face. Perhaps she wondered what I really noticed about my niece.

"Matured," I said. "Quite beautiful, also," I added glancing at my wife sideways. The only time I saw my niece lately was at night, gazing at the stars. Quite romantic, I thought.

"Watch it," she said threateningly.

Actually, there was humour in her voice.

"Do you think she'll be happy with Jerry?"

"Definitely. They both love children. Jerry did already in Montreal, remember?"

I did. Jerry was probably the best babysitter we've ever had. As well as a bodyguard.

..and lab assistant… he and Tom… of course.

This time I read her mind. She didn't mind. We really had no secrets from each other. It was as if we were a single entity occupying two distinct bodies. Perhaps that was why we had such need to unite, at all levels of perception.

"It's Tom I am worried about," she said after a moment of silence. I waited for her to continue. "He is dwarfed by dad. Literally. He doesn't seem to have a mind of his own."

Dwarfed by a man half his size.

…exactly…

I smiled. This verbal and non-verbal communication seemed to be growing between us.

"Papa is one of the strongest personalities I'd ever met," I tried to console her.

But Tom has a right to a life of his own…

I sensed her concern. Ambrosia looked deeper into things than I. She was her mother's daughter, in more ways than one.

"Did you talk to Mama about it?"

"You think she doesn't know?"

Of course. If anyone knew, Mama did. Mama knew most things.

We reached the bottom of the path that wound its way, gently, toward the sea. Waves lapped the rock outcroppings, leading to a narrow strip of sand, which used to be a broad expanse of beach, where we once had our wedding.

We sat down listening to the silence. It is amazing how much you can hear when you learn to listen. Just listen without inner commentaries. I could hear every single beat of Ambrosia's heart. We looked at each other. Our thoughts drifted to that day when plates had been flying over the sand. That's what Greeks do at weddings. It took hours of sifting the sand to pick up the pieces.

Not much has changed. In my eyes, she looked exactly the same as she did then. On that glorious day. A day I'll never forget.

She put her head on my shoulder. We stayed like that for a long time. At least, it seemed like a long time. In moments like that time stopped, and for a fragment of eternity we were one.

And then the earth moved. No. Not as in a romantic novel when a lover kisses his beloved. The earth really moved. It wasn't like an earthquake. It was like a wave that lifted us gently, in slow motion, perhaps a meter upwards, and them carefully placed us back, where we were, only about a half-meter higher. The lapping waves retreated some fifteen meters, then returned in a small surge that almost touched our feet. Finally they settled as much as twenty meters farther away from the shore.

We watched, speechless, in utter fascination.

We didn't have time to become scared before all things reverted to normal. Of course, I still had no idea what was normal, these days. Did things like this happen all the time? Was the whole world in geological upheavals? A *dance macabre* of some underground demons? Were we supposed to be scared?

Yet soon things reverted to normal as though nothing had happened. Except for the change to the coastline.

"It started," Ambrosia whispered. "Only a week ago Mama said it would. How come she knows those things?"

The newly exposed sand was already drying. A moment later I wasn't sure if anything had happened at all.

***

3
Cleansing

"**I thought it all happened** while I was asleep," I said. I couldn't keep a tinge of accusation from my voice.

"It did. Most of the horrors that man can perpetrate on man already took place. Hopefully the unprecedented blood-fest is over. At least, I hope so. Mama Milos assured us it wouldn't last past ten years."

It was evident that Mama's statements were perfectly satisfying to my wife. Not quite so for me, however.

"So that's why I've been…"

"…spared the worst of it," Ambrosia whispered in my ear. "Mama really loves you, you know?"

If I didn't before, now it was becoming obvious. Yet even as I, like a spoiled child, was about to raise more objections, we heard the distant roar of Papa's twin engines. Mama ran out of the house, her eyes lit up, as she searched the sky for the airplane. It seemed as if she wasn't quite sure if Paul would really come back. "There are only probabilities in this reality, one can never be sure, not really," I recall her saying. Ten years ago? She must have read my thoughts.

"These are still times of transition," she said. "Events are even more uncertain. We must have faith," she added, a smile returning to her face. Evidently she'd sensed Paul presence, even up there, in the air. She sensed that Paul was all right. She visibly relaxed.

Do gods also worry, I wondered? I thought they were almighty…

Mama smiled.

"I see you are back on your theological pursuits, Simon. Welcome back."

I wasn't sure if this was a complement or an insult. I've been a professor of Comparative Religion for so long that I could not help myself questioning events with a sort of philosophically-theological bent. Or maybe I had the Jesuits to blame for that, in my old school, back in the Old Country. No, not in Canada. In the UK, at the St. Stanislaus Kostka College. The place where I'd once broken my ankle, remember?

Ambrosia smiled. She remembered, and Mama read all our thoughts. She just didn't show it.

I had to smile, too. What I remembered most from the old days was having played rugby. Rugger, as we called it. And the ensuing recalcitrant ankle. On the other hand, it was almost thanks to the game ankle that I met Ambrosia. Don't all things happen for a purpose? For a reason? In a way, if it hadn't been for rugby and my twisted ankle I'd never have met my wife, never walked through walls, hence never found myself in this heaven on Earth. Nor would I have met Mama, learned OBE... and, let us not forget, I would have been at least ten years older. I still found it hard to believe that I wasn't. At least, they've all said so.

The list could go on.

"Yes, Simon," Mama smiled. "Everything does happen for a reason. Only it is up to us to figure out what that reason is."

The sound of jet engines died down and, for a brief moment, there was total silence. It was the sort of peace that one cannot experience in a large city, in Montreal, or previously in London, UK. It was silence born not from the absence of sound, but of inner and outer serenity.

A state of balance?

Peace on earth for men of good will. Didn't Luke write something like that? Luke the Evangelist. Funny that. He wrote it more than two thousand years ago, and only now the meaning has reached me. Time seems to slow down, when that happens. Maybe they were right. Maybe time is relative, like everything else.

And then we heard Papa's old Fiat pulling in at the front door. Papa stepped out and made his way up to the terrace. He moved like a young man. I wondered what was his secret. He ran up to Mama, lifted her up in the air, swung her around and put her back on her feet. Only then he turned to face us.

"Simon! You're back!"

He knew I was back for some time. Didn't he give me a lecture on the relativity of time?

"I mean, son, you are back on your feet. All there. Feeling good?"

It was the first time that I was greeted before he embraced his daughter. His *mikro koritsi*. This time my ribs have been spared his power-hug. Almost spared.

"Mama tells me that you're still in a fragile state," he smiled, glancing at Mama who hasn't said a word.

I felt like a pregnant woman—too fragile to be hugged.

"I'm fine, Papa, just fine," I assured him.

And yet, later that day, I still felt the echo of his 'gentle' embrace. Papa didn't know his own strength.

By the time he put me down, Amadeus, Athena and Jerry were on the terrace to greet Papa.

"And where's Tom?" I asked.

"Rolling the Cessna into the hangar. It's going to rain today," Papa replied, dismissing the matter.

"And just how do you know that," Mama asked, I suspect mostly for our sake. She must have already known. For a moment I imagined Tom pulling the twin-engine aircraft with one hand tied behind his back, before Mama's question had reached me. Papa ignored Mama's question. To gods, such things as forthcoming rain were apparently obvious.

"Well, I took a slight detour on the way back. Gibraltar is

closed. The Tell Atlas Mountains and the Saharan range all the way to Aurès Mountains were pushed up, at the expense of the Salt water Lakes which are now an open sea. Farther down south, most of Sahara desert, the Erg Igoudi, the Great Western, and Eastern Ergs returned to their original geological formation."

"Erg?" I asked. I must have sounded stupid, but I never heard of some of those places.

"Erg is the name they have for the fields of sand dunes in the Saharan desert. They had the Grand Erg Oriental, Eastern, and Western. Well, no more. They are all under water now. The Atlas Mountains must have been pushed up by a good two or three thousand meters to balance the geological changes. I don't know what happened farther south."

Papa said all this in a conversational tone as though he was describing most natural events. A sort of… "A funny thing happened to me on the way to work this morning…" But his face was deadly serious.

"That's a lot of water. The Great Eastern Erg alone is more than 100,000 square kilometers, and some of the dunes had been as high as 300 meters. They're all under water now. Ah, there you are," Tom added. He'd just joined us, but must have read Papa's thoughts from a distance.

"I just looked it up on the map," he added, as if he'd just pulled a fast one. As a matter of fact, I soon learned that Tom had learned a great deal in my absence.

We welcomed Tom. We were all so taken up by Papa's report that none of us heard Tom's motorbike approaching. A super-souped up by himself, meticulously reconstructed, Vincent HRD. The original frame must have been at least 100 years old. Perhaps a lot older. Tom was very good with his hands.

The mountain of a man smiled shyly until he saw me.

"Professor Jackson," his mouth stretched from ear to ear.

I got up to embrace my former bodyguard. Well, mine and Ambrosia's of course. Now? Now he was Papa's right hand man in a dozen diverse jobs.

"So good to s-see you, S-sir," he almost stammered.

"Simon," I corrected. "If I remember rightly, after all these years you're a member of our family."

"Yes, Sir," he exclaimed. "...ah, Simon?" he added in halftone as though my name bestowed special privileges on him.

"Louder," I said. "Louder, Tom!"

"Simon?" he said louder, yet my name sounded like a question.

"That's me, and don't you forget it," I commanded, looking sternly upwards at this head towering over me. I was only a little over six feet. He was pushing seven.

He took turns to shake hands and embrace the rest of our family. Then, he fitted his frame on a stone ledge overlooking the garden.

"Papa was just telling us what happened to the Sahara Desert, Tom. Were you impressed, too?"

"I've never seen the desert, Sir'ah'mon... Simon," he corrected, smiling. "But the sea was very impressive as were the mountains. I've never seen any that tall."

"We were lucky that most of the upheavals took place mostly on the western part of Africa. Otherwise we'd feel considerable aftereffects right here," Papa added.

At least now I knew what enlarged our beach, if only by a few dozen feet. Papa remained for a while, then retired for a little nap. He'd just spent a good few hours piloting the plane. He deserved a rest.

We remained on the terrace.

Amadeus leaned back in his chair. He was looking at the map of Northwest Africa on his miPad. It used to be the ancient iPad of the early part of this century, until Ambrosia and Tom did things to it, and to all the other computers around. They all became miPads, miBooks, and even miMacs, which hopefully didn't offend anyone.

"What I find amazing," he said, pensively, "is that the inundated terrain had hardly any population. There must have been hardly any lives lost..."

"The Pluto Effect, Amadeus, is not for replacing people only for replacing their state of consciousness," Mama spoke slowly, making sure her grandson got the message. I wondered, at the time, why she appeared to have directed her words specifically to my son. You might even say *at* my son.

"And yet," he mused aloud, "millions have lost..."

He must have been referring to the ten years when I was 'away'. I looked at Mama.

"Those were tough years, Simon. Even before you retired into your protective cocoon, more about that later, there were sociological upheavals all over the world. The reason, as we now know, was the economic disparity between the very rich, and the rest of the world's population. Democracy, even in the Greek ancient or primitive sense, gave way to the rule of plutocracy. To the very rich. And again this disease has spread all over the world. Innocent people suffered the most. As for the rich, they completely lost their sense of oneness. They stood apart from the masses, from nature, from earth itself. Money, and the attendant power, was the sole motivation for all their actions. They even destroyed their own families for their personal financial gain."

She stopped, perhaps waiting for comments. None came.

"So the millionaires had to pay their dues?" I asked.

"Millionaires, Simon, were a dime a dozen. There were no members of any world parliament who made less than a few millions from public coffers. They were just the henchmen. The *vendus*, they used to call them, those who cooperated with the enemy. Your Jesuits friends would say that they sold their souls to the devil. No one worth less then three or four billion counted at all. The millionaires, if smart, managed to stay away from politics and big business. Those who did not have been little more than henchmen of the few who amassed enormous wealth, invariably through fairly or completely nefarious means."

I resented a little having Jesuits defined as my friends, but I let that pass. After all, they did let me play rugby.

"Were there none honest?" I asked. I had to catch up on ten years. All this was new to me.

"Of course, there were. Papa is not quite a billionaire, but in pre-crash market he would count among the very rich. Yet not for a moment did he try to take advantage of his acquired wealth to control others. Quite the reverse. He fed tens of thousands of people in your absence. Tens of thousands... There were others."

Mama looked fondly towards the villa where Papa was taking his well-earned rest.

"The very few?"

"Not many, but a few. Less then a dozen. As for the other gods? Those who lost their way counted in hundreds— perhaps little more than three or four hundred in the whole world. But with their personal henchmen their ranks swelled to hundreds of thousands. Still no more then one percent of one percent. About a million at most."

I looked at Mama with growing understanding. She turned her head away.

"They are all gone now. Eliminated by the masses," she said, hardly above a whisper. "They were the gods that lost their way."

I could only imagine how many of the masses must have died to affect the revenge on the few. It must have been a bloodbath on unprecedented scale. I suddenly felt grateful to Mama for making sure that I slept through that period of history.

Papa woke up in high spirits. He came to join us on the terrace. He seemed as cheerful as I ever saw him. Tom followed him like a dutiful guard dog, only much, much bigger. I don't mean that Tom was servile in any way, but I had a feeling that if anyone intended any harm to Papa, he or she would have been torn apart, chopped up into little pieces and fed to Goldie. Or the fish. Or any carnivore.

Yet there was another impression that seemed to emanate from Tom. He acted and looked like a most caring father, protector in the gentlest possible way. There was a paternal feeling about him, towards Papa, a man at least twice Tom's age. A paradox that came easy to both of them, as Paul seemed quite unaware of Tom's protection.

And then I remembered. Back in Montreal, neither Ambrosia nor I ever felt the presence of his protection. It's just that his very presence discouraged any unsavory thought that might be directed in our direction. He had that air of invincibility that only men who believe in human goodness possess. I've never met a man like him before.

Tom checked if all was as it should be, and left us to do whatever was on his mind. I wouldn't be surprised if he wouldn't go to ask Ambrosia, still in her lab, if he could be of any assistance. He and Jerry still took their part time jobs very seriously.

"I'm told that Tom also had spent some time in Limbo?" I asked quite innocently.

After all, Tom also didn't look a day older, and I was very much interested about this Limbo 'thing'. According to the Roman Church it is the place where children who died before being baptized go. Supposedly, in a state of 'original' sin, they could not enter the Kingdom of Heaven. So, unless their God was a psychotic monster, He wouldn't punish children before they could acquire cleansing from a sin they have never committed, and thus Limbo couldn't be that bad.

Even as those thoughts passed through my mind, I saw Mama's face changing from surprise to amusement.

"It's amazing how logically you can explain all sorts of nonsense," she remarked, her smile taking the sting out of her words.

"You mean I am full of it... or the Church is?"

"I am not here to criticize either, but I can tell you my version."

Which was precisely what I was hoping for. Mavis gave me the outline, but hardly sated my hunger for details.

"Uncle, once and for all, it's all in the stars," Mavis had said. She always began most things with the stars. "The only reality is that which originates from pure consciousness. Everything else is transient, ephemeral, and certainly not real. It is what the Eastern Gurus call Maya, which we know as illusion. Whatever explanations you find for any of those terms must conform and agree with that first premise."

She told me that some days ago. Today, now, I leaned forward to hear the juicy part when the terrace surface began heaving up and down, then sidewise. Not much, but enough to lose my train of thought, let alone to keep balance perched on the edge of my seat. The next moment I slid down bumping quite hard on the paving stones.

Quake number two?

Sitting now in the floor, I was facing the south end of the island. Even as I wondered about the force of the quake, I found that I could now see much farther, in fact, beyond the previous horizon. We were moving up in the world. Up by a good seven to ten meters. Yet, for reasons unknown to me, it all happened seemingly in slow motion, gently, one might say ponderously, without subjecting my behind to any more bumps.

I was grateful for little mercies.

"Well," I heard Mama's voice, "I'm glad that's over. At least for now," she added. Her voice sounded quite unconcerned, practically amused by the geological upheaval that was having quite a profound effect on me, let alone on my behind.

"How can you remain so calm, Mama," I asked, still perched on the floor.

"Of the countless possibilities, there are four probable futures," she replied, "and in all four of them we remain safe, as will our villa. What is there to worry about?"

It's easy for you to say," I murmured, picking myself up from the floor.

"Chairs, Simon, are intended to be sat on, not perched on the very edge," this time her remonstration was accompanied by a big smile.

But it wasn't over. For once, Mama has been mistaken.

Before we retired there were tree more geological movements, which hoisted our whole island by a good 50 or 60 meters, yet, strangely enough, without any tremor being noticeable. It was like going up in an extremely slow elevator, which included the whole island.

The only scary parts of this tectonic exercise were deep, raspy groans, which seemed to emerge from the very bowls of Earth. Those were accompanied by sounds of water cascading, murmurs as though conveying something secret, and a distant gaseous plume of smoke, which erupted, according to Papa, in the west facing the bay of Santorini. As Santorini was located southeast of us, of Milos, with the prevailing western winds the acrid smoke was blown directly east.

We were OK.

Once again I gave thanks to the Greek gods, particularly Aphrodite, who had chosen so wisely our island for her private domain.

It was then that I heard the gentle pearl-like notes of the piano. Apparently, rather than being scared, Athena began playing on the piano in the Main Hall. The double doors were wide open and the music, it sounded like one of Chopin's nocturnes, washed down the steps, crossed the lawn, and surrounded us with its magic.

For a while we remained still, as finally so did nature.

Perhaps nature wouldn't dare to interrupt her own goddess playing her music. And it was her music. Even as Chopin's nocturne was finished, Athena's fingers continued to caress the piano, until slowly, very slowly it died in a gentle *diminuendo* tempered with *rallentando*. The music flowed softer and slower until it lingered only in our memory.

What a strange daughter I had. What an incredible gift from Mama. We sat, silent, listening to the echoes that still reverberated within us.

"Thank you, Athena," I whispered.

Next morning Papa and Tom, invariably together, took off in the Cessna to reconnoiter if there was any major damage on adjacent and even on the farther out islands. If necessary, Jerry and Mavis would motor over and offer such help as was necessary. There was only one medic on the island, but he had no means of transportation. Jerry took care of that. The boat engine was powered by solar batteries, and so far we were not running out of sunlight.

Luckily, the airplane, the airstrip, and the boat were all intact, although Jerry had to swim out some fifty feet along the shore to bring the boat in to a new anchorage. Obviously, at least to me, someone "up there" was looking after us.

Papa and Tom were back by early afternoon. Papa looked cheerful, fired up, as though he'd finally found something useful to do himself, other than constantly teaching others to take action. Papa was only happy when he was busy. He and Tom found us waiting on the terrace for the latest news. Even the guests from adjoining houses had been invited. They spread themselves out all over the lawn. They looked like a happy bunch, although the occasional salvos of laughter were not preceded by audible sounds. It was obvious that they communicated at some sort of telepathic level.

I didn't mention, that one of Tom's jobs was to scan the skies with his powerful shortwave radio, looking for signs of intelligence still functioning on Earth. What kept the Internet and a few electronics semi-operational must have been a few Chinese communication satellites, which continued in their orbits. Most western communication satellites had long burned out in the upper atmosphere. What didn't quite burn out, invariably splashed in the oceans, or in some uninhabitable areas. We were reminded that water covered about 75% of the surface of our planet. Perhaps more, after recent tectonic adjustments.

Tom's job wasn't easy. There may have been other radio signals, and they had to be analyzed for possible attempts at dialog.

Later that day, a screechy radio buzzing sound had been interrupted by a short, repetitive signal. It stated in Morse code, that 74 atomic missiles exploded in Hawaii in an extensive chain reaction. Hawaii was no more. It was wiped from the face of the Pacific. Tom managed to isolate the signal and respond with questions. Apparently it came from another sanctuary, hidden in the outer reaches of Peru, well beyond the semi-accessible Machu Picchu in the Andean Mountains.

Tom had learned that most people had long been evacuated from all the Hawaiian Islands, for the lack of potable water. What was once considered a life threatening condition had saved their lives. Large percentage of our bodies is made up of water, and people cannot survive without almost constant replacement.

We all took the news with a mixture of dread and amazement. No one was aware that what used to be USA would have stored such extensive armaments on the seemingly peaceful islands.

Papa cleared his throat. His cheerfulness seems to have evaporated. He looked depressed.

"They say that no news is good news, particularly these days."

He seldom displayed his feelings but now he allowed

himself a deep sigh. Papa always cared for the common man. For the many. Their pain was his pain.

"There is no more what used to be called Arab Spring either," he announced in a subdued voice.

He looked around to see if there were any people present who might be of Arab origin. For them it would be particularly painful.

"The new sea that formed over the inundations which I reported yesterday has now spilled over to what used to be— relatively speaking—lowlands, covering most of Algeria, Libya and Egypt. I could not even distinguish where the Nile was, it seemed… it seemed…" he couldn't continue.

We heard the rest by direct perception. I've never heard or experienced Papa being so sad. Not even when The *Vouli ton Ellinon,* the Greek Parliament, had gone up in flames. Papa really loved his people. He also loved the concept of democracy. While being one of the "chosen few", he dedicated his life to "the many".

I wondered if similar inundations were taking place elsewhere. No doubt, in time, Tom would also learn about them. These were times of physical changes—times of restructuring of water and land for the new Age. A great, unrelenting, cleansing process?

Hopefully time of improvement.

Or was it just a time that would present new challenges for the new generations?

I recalled an old, old proverb from the book of Ecclesiastes: *…a time to be born and a time to die, a time to plant and a time to uproot.* It seemed that most of us have already been uprooted. Perhaps a time would come to plant…

Apparently we were here, in this phenomenal reality, to learn. If so, then those of us who survived would have ample opportunity.

***

4
Tom

The swell, which until this morning was quite considerable, has stabilized. The sea looked quite calm again. It almost looked as if nothing had happened. Strange, I thought, how the sea could create an image of utter fury and perfect calm with hardly any condition in-between. Looking into the far distance, I wondered which part of Africa, or of the Aegean Islands for that matter, might have risen again above their previous elevation. There was no doubt that the world was in upheaval for some time now. I knew that things like that have happened before, in historical past, but not on such a vast scale. Apparently not just human consciousness was to undergo a drastic change, but also the environment, in which that change was to take place.

Nevertheless, or perhaps because of all this, I grew restless. I needed something to occupy my mind. I looked around.

Ambrosia came out of her lab only to quiet, or quieten as we'd say back home, Lazy, who was making an unholy racket outside her door. Now he was sitting on her lap, pouring his heart out. Mama and Papa were nowhere to be seen, while Tom was probably fiddling with his radio. That left Jerry and Mavis, who were most probably on one of their missions of mercy, assuming such was needed. After the considerable ups-and-downs we experienced yesterday and some more last night, it was more than likely that some people on the adjacent islands might have forgotten to take precautions.

I needed to do something. Something exciting?

Before my extended snooze, I tended to a few acres of vineyard. Then I had occasion to meet a number of villagers, or perhaps islanders is a better word, who had given me a hand with tending the grapes. To be quite honest, they'd done more actual work than I had. They were nice, quiet people, ready to smile at the slightest excuse. I decided to take a trip down the winding paths and pay them a visit.

It wasn't an easy walk. In as much as the top of our hill, or mountain, remained in a fairly stable condition, the slopes made up for it with an abundance of loose stones. Nevertheless, I was determined to visit my old friends.

I knocked on the first cottage close to the old vineyard. There and then I had my first shock. In as much as in the villa the appearance of people remained either stable or just a little more mature, here the stress and strain of the last ten years was unmistakable. I was facing a man, stooping under the low threshold, squinting into the bright sun.

I only just recognized him.

"Giorgios…?" I wasn't quite sure.

"Professor Jackson," the man almost smiled. He added something in Greek I did not quite understand. Probably some form of a greeting.

The smile that I still remembered seldom left his face was replaced by a scowl, almost one of enmity. I had a feeling that he was ready to blame me for whatever befell him in my absence. During the years of my hibernation.

Nevertheless, he stepped aside and let me into the house. It was quite dark inside. The curtains were half-drawn. I had a feeling that they wanted to keep out evil spirits. People on the island tended to be quite superstitious. After all, up there, on the top of the hill, strange things happened. Very strange things. Some said, I recalled, that gods lived up there. Real gods of yesteryear.

Ten years ago those words brought laughter to my lips. Today, I wasn't so sure.

The woman raised her hand. She, too, I also recall was full of vigour. She looked tired. There were no children; must gone out to work? They had to be in their early twenties now. Tending the fields?

The parents seemed to have aged at twice the usual rate. It must have been a very tough decade.

I stayed a few more minutes, exchanged a few pleasantries in my broken Greek, and made my excuses. I decided to remain in my villa until people's nerves stabilized. I began to understand why Mama had put me to sleep. I could have looked like that, both physically and emotionally. I climbed back to my haven as fast as I could.

Yet my resolve to remain still didn't last.

Next day I decided to try and pop over to Montreal, even if just for fun. I felt like a little boy who had all his toys taken away from him. It just wasn't fair, I thought.

"How often does Tom QT to Montreal?" I asked innocently, looking out over the expanse of Aegean that was just beginning to turn dark.

Papa cut short Tom's stay in Limbo to assure that Ambrosia would have a bodyguard on her trips to the Montreal lab. Now she had all she needed right here, on Milos. Since my snooze, I haven't been back even once. Why should she have all the fun?

"We stopped QT'ing some time ago. You don't intend to go there yourself, darling, do you?"

"The thought had crossed my mind."

"But why, don't you like it here?" Ambrosia looked at me with those dark eyes that threatened to suck me into a condition of non-refusal. She knew I couldn't resist that look.

"That's cheating," I said.

She knew what I meant and smiled.

"All right then. Why do you want to go back...?"

"To see if I can contact my old friends."

She looked baffled.

"My regression group," I added. "The telephones from here don't work. Perhaps the local might. My friends are only ten years older and many of them had been students when we left."

I could see from her expression that she'd given up.

"You must promise me that you will not take a step without Tom being there, right at your shoulder." She looked at me expecting an unnecessary confirmation. "And anyway, I'll set the miniQT for one hour."

MiniQT, if you remember, is my wife's portable tunneling device that can take one "there and back", like a boomerang, to any destination on earth. The only problem was the magnetic interference since some of the satellites were down. GPS was not as accurate and reliable as it used to be.

This was not the right time to be *l'avocat du diable*. Ambrosia was worried. Before leaving I'd make sure she'd reset the quantum-tunneling device for at least a five or six-hour return. After all, I'd have the man-mountain with me.

What could possibly happen?

I haven't seen, nor contacted my old hypnotic-regression group for ten years. Now that that was settled, I asked Tom if he had time to take a walk with me. Before QT'ing.

No, not for safety's sake, but I still haven't recovered all my strength after ten years of relative immobility, and there was a fair amount of climbing to do. I might fall down some crevice, and not be able to get up or out on my own. All this to say hello to Goldie. I wondered if he'd recognize me. After all, he was my dog, as much as anyone can own anyone. Were we not all free spirits? OK, Mama would call that "individualizations of the Single Consciousness." And, let's face it. Mama was usually right— especially in such matters.

Tom was happy to assist me.

Being cooped up in the lab, pressing buttons and listening to white noise was not his preferred cup of tea. He was essentially an outdoors man. I mean, one with nature—almost a force of nature. We left just after a light lunch.

The narrow path took us along the ridge of the island in a semicircular arc to where Goldie's charges, this time the goats, were grazing. Actually, the goats could hardly run far, but Goldie also seemed to prefer the outdoors. Perhaps having experienced the loneliness of the deserted streets of Montreal, where I found him half-starved, he felt safer outdoor with the goats. I suppose if he was really hungry, he could eat one, although I'm sure he was too much of a gentleman, I mean gentle-dog, to stoop to such subterfuge. He was fed daily, at home, where he returned for most nights and often during the day. I made a mental note to try and find another dog for him on my Montreal trip. After all, two's a company, one's nothing much at all.

We got there in about ninety minutes of fairly fast walking. At least fast considering my semi-decrepit condition. Goldie galloped towards us from afar, and jumped at Tom as though trying to bring him down in a single tackle. Tom grinned, caught the large Lab in both arms, and they went through the dog-men greeting that must have been specific to the two of them.

In time Goldie ambled towards me, gave me a careful sniff, before activating his wagging device at his rear end. He recognized me, but only just.

We sat down to rest.

I didn't realize how very weak I still was. The human body is made for movement, not for hibernation. Somehow, Tom's and Jerry's Limbo experience didn't seem to have affected them as much. On the other hand, I expected to get back to my previous condition in two or three weeks. And then I sat up stunned.

"I'm sure you will, Simon."

Was Tom reading my thoughts?

"Where I've been for almost ten years, this was the only communication possible. My physical body and all my senses were dormant. Completely dormant, as in a coma. The only problem was that I could only listen, but couldn't reply. I couldn't even make sense of what was being said to me or about me. It's like being in Limbo," he said, this time a smile lightening up his large features.

I looked at him with surprise. Even with the children, back in Montreal, Tom was a man of very few words. Almost taciturn. Tom was never so vocal, and most certainly not about himself.

He smiled again.

"Things change," he asserted, seemingly to himself. Then he turned towards me. "But there is one thing that was, still is, incredibly baffling. In as much as I could not react to whatever took place all around me, now, now that I am fully awake, the memories of all that took place then, in my dormant state, in a state of absolute mental and physical stupor, they are all coming back. It was as if I was a recording machine that had been turned on all the time, and there was no one to turn it off. Now, finally I am playing it all back."

The man has changed. From being a nice, innocent but powerful bodyguard with some computer training, he became, what I can only call, a thinker. He analyzed events, concepts, tried to solve the human equation. For the first time I felt his closeness, a kinship that wasn't there before.

And then, quite suddenly I realized that I don't even know his name. His real name…

There was that smile again. It seemed obvious that Tom, quite unwittingly, was peeking into my thoughts before I could vocalize them. Or could it be that he was only privy to thoughts that have been directed at him?

Was this true of all telepaths?

"It's Barbeau he said," answering my unasked question.

"Its Greek origin was Barba, but my mother adapted it to the language of Quebec. Father didn't mind, so she made it sound more French."

I was still taking a well-earned rest on a flat stone, while Tom towered over me, seemingly counting the goats.

He then looked down at me running his hand down his chin. "It seems," he added, "that my ancestors sported rather a large hair-growth."

And then he let out a prolonged chuckle. If I didn't know him better, such deep-throated sounds would scare the hell out of me. A chuckle is supposed to be a quiet inward laugh, not something resembling a not so quiet inward rumble of an impending earthquake.

I was beginning to suspect that if most people in our extended family were distant descendants of Greek gods, then surely, Tom Barbeau, or Barba, must have rubbed shoulders with Hercules, or Heracles, before his mother Francified his name. I was very glad that in those uncertain times Tom was on my side.

It was time to go back. Tom offered me a hand to get up. My knees still needed more exercise. As we turned towards home, Goldie decided that he'd had enough fresh air for the day. He decided to follow us home.

For a while we walked in silence. Then I heard that rumble inside Tom's throat. When I looked up at him, he shrugged his shoulders.

"Mom called me Herc, for short," he said. And this announcement was followed by another rumble.

For a while, I wondered why. Then it hit me. No, it couldn't be, I mused.

Mama said it probably was... I heard in my head.

Tom never addressed Mama as Mama. It was always Mrs. Milos. Yet I knew exactly where that idea came from.

The next day Ambrosia fitted us with her QT gizmos, which she hung on our necks, under our shirts.

"If you lose these, you'll never get back here," she murmured. "There is no other transport…"

She waited for the very last moment to set the GPS on both our instruments. Recently, the magnetic pole was performing a veritable dance. Luckily, this form of travel took less than a second. There was an excellent chance that we'd reach our destination before the pole would play tricks on our positioning systems. Also, the remaining satellites were in unstable orbits. Outside our little island, everything was going haywire.

Ambrosia kissed both of us on our cheeks, wished us Godspeed, and let us press our buttons within seconds of each other. The next moment I was standing in my study, with the big shape of Tom looming behind me.

"So far so good," I grinned.

We didn't have much time. I reached for my cellular and started dialing. Cellular mobile phones are little more than portable radios transmitters and receivers. My voice was converted to an electrical signal, then transmitted as radio waves and converted back to sound at the receiving end. In order to remain portable, the mobile phones have compact antennas and use little electric power; hence they only work over a very short range.

On my fifth attempt I got a response. It was George, who at the time we were leaving for Milos has been already running his own group.

"I thought you got lost in the riots," was his response. "God, it's good to hear your voice. You sure you're alive?"

"No, George, I'm speaking to you from the never-never land. Are you still keeping up the good work?"

"Not much, it takes practically all my time to rustle up a living for Jean and myself."

Jean was his wife.

"Sorry to hear that. Is there anyway I can help?"

"How good are you at growing potatoes?" he asked.

Somehow I knew that he wasn't joking.

"It's that tough…"

"Could be worse. We are lucky we live in NDG." That, I recall, was the western part of Montreal. "Most people moved out to the country and we inherited their gardens. We grow our own food, chicken, and four goats included. The milk's alright once you got used to it, and the cheese is just great."

It all sounded unreal. George had been a lecturer at McGill University, making no worse a living then I had some years ago. Now he was an urban farmer, if there is such a term. It was another time, almost another lifetime. Yet, he sounded almost cheerful.

"You sound cheerful enough," I said, my voice filled with admiration.

"I have you to thank for that. If it weren't for the regression, I would be mentally dead. Your ideas gave my life meaning. Something to do with my mind."

It was really good to hear that.

"There are only six of us within walking distance. Close-by, I mean. Straying too far from our place would be too dangerous. People do not take kindly to strangers. We meet every fortnight and we've got some interesting results. God, it's been a long time," he added.

"All of ten years. I tried to call from, ah, from my new home, but there was no way to get through."

"Yea, I guess so. Is there anyway you might be able to come over? It would be quite a treat for Jean and me."

I looked up at Tom who seemed quite happy stretching on my settee, admiring the view of Mount Royal through my wall-to-wall window. God, how I loved this view. The mountain was still the *raison d'être* why I loved Montreal so much.

Now Tom looked up. He must have been listening; inadvertently or not was of no consequence. He got up and disappeared through the door leading to the escape stairs. I was still chatting when he'd got back, holding up one enormous thumb.

"Yes?" I encouraged.

"There is a motorbike in the garage," he said. "The tank looks pretty full. I took it for a spin inside the garage..."

Then he smiled. "I checked out eleven vehicles left behind, and managed to siphon off enough gas from three of them to make the motorbike operational."

He wiped his mouths as he said that. Obviously the tube he used wasn't clean.

"Apparently the bike must have been in use not so long ago, as the battery was still working. For some reason they left it behind. Probably one cannot refuel it outside the city, or within the city for that matter."

Tom was a marvel! He must have worked fast. The calls I made took hardly more than a half-hour. Good 'ol Tom.

I turned back to my cell phone. "Tell me how to get to your place."

The instructions I got were not as direct as they would have been ten years ago. Apparently some streets were to be avoided. They were known to have marauding bands of men, still angry, still hungry, still unforgiving for the real or imagined wrongs done to them.

"Even in NDG, can you imagine? Notre Dame de Grass... Our Lady for Christ's sake... even in NDG they are willing and able to rob and/or kill anyone who'd step into their territory!"

George sounded deeply disgusted. I remember him as a rarity—as a practicing Catholic.

Apparently the only thing in abundance in Montreal were firearms, which drifted north from the USA which, some years ago, manufactured more of them than a dozen or two countries put together. Then they'd lost the markets. They'd also lost means of transportation. Here, George said, they still made deliveries on horse-drawn carriages, fortified with metal domes for partial protection. Horses were also covered with bulletproof blankets, made up from old police vests.

Things changed. Even Tom's size would not offer
protection against bullets fired almost point blank. However,
I mused with ants crawling up my spine, as we said in
Quebec, *qui ne risque n'a rien.* And I was only risking my
life. And Tom's. That last made me a little uncomfortable.

We left ten minutes later. Tom sat in front; I clung to his
massive back. His very presence gave me a feeling of safety.
The streets were deserted. There wasn't a single shop window
that hasn't been smashed. That also went for lower floors of
office building, where most probably angry mobs vented their
spleen. Twice I saw bushes growing in the middle of a paved
street.

It was a horrible sight. Avoiding the main streets, in less
than 15 minutes we pulled up at my friend's house. He
emerged from behind a fence, half-crouching, and opened the
gate for us.

"Quick, this way," he pointed to us to move. "Must hide
your bike. It's worth a fortune, if it has any gas."

We hid the motorbike in overgrown bushes, which no
one seems to have trimmed for years, and followed George
inside. Jean waited for us with open arms, which she
withdrew at the sight of Tom.

"It's all right, dear, he's on our side," George said, a
weak smile not quite certain of his ground belying his words.

"It's my best friend, Tom. Tom Barbeau," I added,
which in turn made Tom smile.

I suddenly realized that if there was one thing more
frightening than Tom's size, it was his smile. He looked as if
he was ready to eat you. To swallow you whole.

"I haven't been called that for some twenty years," he
murmured. "It's sort of... nice," he added, after searching for
the right word.

We were served tea made from some strange concoction
that was surprisingly good. We both refused food, knowing
that it was a precious and scarce commodity. Soon George

and I were in deep discussion about the hypnotic regressions, which he and his friends continued after my departure.

I scanned through volumes of pages, hand written, as in the old days. And then came the first shock. Every single regression went back to some sort of religious occurrence. Nothing political, nothing scientific. His pals regressed to witness a dozen or more saints, and an even greater number of people quite unknown to me, but apparently of great religious significance. How I would have liked to have had those files when giving lectures at McGill. It was original, unprecedented material that, I could see at first glance, confirmed my own conclusions regarding metaphysical concepts. It seemed like ages ago, well... over ten years, yet my subject of Comparative Religion surged back into my mind as though it were only yesterday.

George watched me with obvious pleasure.

"Would you like to keep some of these?" he asked.

"But it's your work, George. I couldn't possibly..."

"There is nothing I can do with any of this stuff. There are no publishers, no printers, and... no buyers. Perhaps they will be of some use to you...? He sounded sad yet hopeful.

I glanced at my watch. In spite of my pleas, Ambrosia refused to set the miniQTs for more then two hours. It had something to do with the GPS. As it was, we were likely to return to any part of the island. She'd set the return destination for the middle of the front lawn of the Milos villa.

I thanked George profusely, and tucked four of the six files under my shirt, right next to the QT. He and Jean saw us to the garden, peeked in both directions of the street, and signaled us to move quickly. The relatively small roar of the 500 cc engine sounded twice as loud in the eerie silence. In seconds we cleared the first corner, so as not to endanger George and Jean.

Halfway down the next street I heard a bullet ricochet against the curb with a distinctive 'ping', even before I heard the sound of firing. Tom turned the accelerator to full. We charged at close to 100 kilometers an hour through the deserted streets. I heard two more shots, though they may have been aimed at someone else. Tom only just managed to slow down before running back into our garage. Only then I noticed that he'd blocked the door open. Now he jumped off, swinging his leg over the handlebars, and pulled the overhead door shut. For now we were safe.

Papa certainly knew his business when he'd chosen Tom and Jerry as our bodyguards. They were so much more than that. And now, after Tom's stint in Limbo, he became also a friend.

Wonders will never cease, I mused.

We had about ten more minutes before the QT would spring us back. I spent my time looking down the street just in case there was a stray dog requiring saving. No luck. Nothing moved outside. As I looked up at the building across the street, a venetian blind snapped shut. So there were some people in town, even if just few and far between. Somehow they found a way to survive. Like they did during periods of war. Somehow this gave me pleasure. I used to love my Montreal. I didn't want it to die.

I returned to my study.

The mountain looked as beautiful as ever. I was glad there was something people couldn't destroy. Not that there were many people. Apart from George and Jean, and a few of their friends, and the venetian blind across the street, we saw no sign of life.

Ah… yes. And the people taking potshots…

This was once a two million strong city. More than that before some separatists scared many English speaking people to move west. And now? We, the super race, at the very top of the food chain, managed to destroy that which others have built. I wondered if any rats survived this sinking city. Sinking into oblivion?

…the lord giveth… the lord taketh away…

I swung round to see Tom smiling at me. I recalled the

day when we were leaving for Milos. He and Jerry stood empty-handed, ready to go, taking nothing with them. They were free. Free of the fetters of this world. They carried their wealth within them. Deep in their hearts.

I had so much to learn…

The next moment we were facing each other on the lawn of the Milos Villa. We were in a different world.

***

5
East is West

Rudyard Kipling, the Nobel Laureate, once wrote:
"Oh, East is East and West is West, and never the
twain shall meet..." Well, they may not have met,
but they certainly must have passed each other on the way.

Ambrosia, my personal goddess and the resident genius
in molecular physics, announced this morning that while east
may remain east, and west would continue to be west, north
was no longer north.

"And south ain't south?" I smiled, throwing in a bit of
British slang.

"Precisely," she said, smiling enigmatically.

"Would you care to explain, Ma?" Amadeus was
unusually polite. Most of the time he was a know-it-all.
What, with eidetic memory and now a good facsimile of
Apollo's features and Ares' physique, he was darn close to
that distinction.

"The poles have reversed," Ambrosia replied, with a
shrug as if she was talking about yesterday's weather.

As so often lately, we were taking our lunch on the
terrace. In fact, the way the weather has stabilized, we ate all
our meals there, right on our private agora. It wasn't a market
place but it served as our gathering place for chats, meetings
and, such as it was, social life. There were twelve of us. After
speaking to Mama, Ambrosia had invited a few of the
'special' guests. As always, Ambrosia had her reasons.

Mama performed the introductions.

"May I introduce Dr. Deng," she began. "Until quite recently he was engaged in lecturing in the University of Beijing in the Department of Geology."

At last someone who also was at, or at least from, a University. I already felt less lonely. Dr. Deng rose to his feet and offered us a polite bow.

"And this is Professor Wú, who specializes in climatological studies, which so far had proven extremely accurate. The other honoured guests you've all met before. Welcome all."

Professor Wú waved his right hand in a regal way accepting the applause. However, as did all the other guests, he remained sitting.

There was, nevertheless, a murmur of approval accompanied by nodding and bowing in a seated position. Finally the rustle down died down, and they looked expectantly at Mama.

"I'd like to introduce to you, once again, my daughter. As you know she is an accomplished physicist, and today she needs your help. Ambrosia, the floor is yours."

Ambrosia was already standing, looking left and right, as though uncertain how to begin. She was that rare combination of being both, theoretical and experimental physicist. A rare accomplishment for anyone. The fact that she was also experimental kept her grounded. Kept her practical without escaping into ever-widening horizon of multiple universes. Her feet were still firmly planted on Mother Earth.

"We might have a problem, ladies and gentlemen. My last three measurements confirmed that we are very likely to experience an event, which is said to happen only once every few thousand years. Some say millions, of course, but that can hardly be verified."

I wondered why she chose to speak out loud when they could surely all read her thoughts. Could it be politeness or just a habit.

"We knew that should there be a rapid pole shift, in which the Earth's crust and mantle moved in one piece, we would not be here to tell the story."

She glanced at some of us, trying to read if we had any idea of what she was talking about. Satisfied by our expressions of utter ignorance, she smiled and continued.

"Pole shift might send both poles sliding towards the equator. North America," this time she glanced specifically at me, "would slide towards the poles, completely changing the climatic conditions."

I've been dreaming of buying a little cottage on the balmy shores of the Hudson Bay, at least had been until I discovered Milos. Millions of Canadians would be spared having to drive to Florida, to escape the winter doldrums. Of course, that used to be true only when an abundance of gas made such travel possible.

"However, while there is a considerable shift in the drift of the north and south poles, we haven't experienced cataclysms, which would surely have resulted from such a condition. Of course the magnetic reversal has been preceded by pole gyrations on a unprecedented scale for more than ten years…" She finished on a weak note, her voice drifting away, as though lost in the magnitude of the problem.

"I would have thought that practically overnight flooding of Sahara and then East Africa lowlands were sufficiently cataclysmic by any man's standards," put in Professor Wú, tugging at his wispy beard.

"I agree," Dr. Deng supported his colleague. "It is evident that the pole shift was spread over at least a decade, although abnormal gyrations of poles have been noted more than fifty years ago. That is of course, a very short time by global standards, but it helps to explain the relative placidity of the upheavals."

"Also," Professor Wú jumped in again, "it may have spared us the loss of our atmosphere."

All eyes turned towards him. He cleared his throat and

got up to his feet, apparently ready to deliver a fully-fledged lecture.

"We don't have just our private little magnetic field," he smiled a thin smile still tugging at his beard. For some reason he must have imagined that we also found this funny. "Our dipolar magnetic field is deflecting most of the solar wind, which carries charged particles, which accelerate to speeds of 200 to 1000 kilometers per second."

This time he looked around with a grave expression in his elderly face. "Per second," he repeated. "They carry with them the interplanetary magnetic field."

"About which we don't know too much about," Dr. Deng butted in.

"Except that Mars lost all its atmosphere..."

This was way over my head.

By now I was completely lost. My field was as far from the climatic aberrations as anything could be. Even Noah's flood for me represented a flood of thoughts, negative thoughts, which were subjected to cleansing, a bit as our present events were cleansing the previous, erroneous mindset, to prepare it for new ideas.

For a while I lingered behind, just in case Ambro needed my moral support. Not so. She seemed to know exactly what she wanted, and sounded as though she might actually be in position to do something about the impending catastrophe.

Impending doom?

I shrugged inwardly.

I saw no reason for staying on the terrace. I had absolutely no influence over whatever did or might happen. It was like crying over spilled milk. Or over spilled ocean for that matter. Quietly I sneaked from the terrace, and returned to my study. Well, not study exactly, but the nook in our bedroom, which I appropriated for sitting quietly and engage in my own, private, mental acrobatics.

An hour later Ambrosia joined me. She seemed flushed but relaxed. She kissed the back of my neck and collapsed on our king-size four-poster. Two of the actual posts have been covered by a layer of carpet, and used by Lazy to perform various acrobatics.

To each his own, I mused.

"Are we going to survive?" I asked, looking up from George's files that were of much greater interest to me than solar rays.

"We shall soon know," she replied. She sounded both, exhausted and elated. As if a great rock has been lifted from her delicate shoulders.

"And just how soon is soon?"

"Well, according to Professor Wú in less than two or three hundred years."

"That sounds about right to me," I replied, breathing deeper. "So in about two hundred years we should start worrying?"

"If not later," Ambrosia nodded. Yet I could see that having discussed the matter with a number of experts in the field, she was visibly more relaxed. Then her voice changed. "All the same, I think we ought to use every chance we've got…"

I knew that tone of voice. Very slowly I spun my chair to face her. She was lying on her stomach, wearing only the scantiest panties. Her long, almost black hair, with just a glint of fresh, springtime chestnuts, formed a semicircular fan, hiding her head. I suddenly realized that having just gone twice through the quantum tunnel, my body has been rejuvenated by some 20 or 30 years. She knew that, of course. After all, she invented the QT. Not for the first time I wondered if that was her real motivation. Not that I cared. Just looking at her rejuvenated me quite sufficiently.

Why don't you come over and find out… I heard her evocative thoughts in my head.

I did. I'd put 40 years at a minimum.

We went through a few months of relative peace. Geological peace, that is. And then all hell broke loose. We felt as though the tectonic plates had a mind of their own. For some reason known only to Mama, we have been spared a real earthquake. As were presumably other sanctuaries spread over strategic places around our globe. The only scary event we experienced was a gradual lifting of the whole Island from the surrounding water. This increased its landmass considerably.

Jerry and Mavis reported that other islands in the Cyclades Archipelago were likewise rising from the depths of Aegean. They cruised day and night, as apparently Mavis had great knowledge of the stars. She must have been a sailor in her previous life. As of last week, we could cross what used to be albeit a narrow expanse of water to Kimolos, an island northeast of us, on dry land. Ambrosia immediately took a rusty mountain bicycle to say hello to her beloved 'monsters' that turned out to be monk seals. It turned out that she had to pedal some 10 extra miles to make up for the difference in elevation. She hardly realized that going up and down without so much as a pathway was a challenge almost beyond her ability. She had to walk a good part of the way.

On her return she performed a little dance of joy. She was accompanied on the piano, by a tune composed and obviously played by Athena. We all shared in her pleasure, clapping and swinging our hips to the music. Papa, the uncrowned Prince Consort to Mama's equally undeclared realm, who joined us for a whole week of rest, declared Kimolos Ambrosia's personal preserve for exclusive use by monks and other wildlife. For some strange reason this made me think of the Jesuits sauntering in their black robes along their august corridors of my ancient school in England. I wondered how they were faring after all these years.

Here, apart from the periodic lifts to a new elevation, all

was quiet. It was as Mama had predicted.

"Nothing is certain," she assured us repeatedly, "not within the confines of the phenomenal reality, but there is up to 90% predictability factor if you know what to look for."

I didn't. Apparently no more than a dozen people knew, and that was, according to Mama, the number of sanctuaries around the world.

Hence, the human race would survive, although the total number was beyond any probability factor. Not even for Mama.

On the other hand, I had to keep reminding myself that nothing on Earth, nothing in the phenomenal reality, was real. It was mostly empty space shifting around by the overflow of energy from the inner worlds. From the inner realities, which still very few of us accepted as real.

What a strange twist of fate. None of what we witnessed with our senses was real. Sometime later, an idea struck me. What if I were to examine the events from the inner perspective? Could I experience them with heightened senses of my Astral body?

Now this was more like my cup of tea.

I spent the next week trying to enter alpha brainwaves to achieve an OBE and then direct my vision, my perceptions, at what was happening in the phenomenal reality. After one week I gave up. Obviously I wasn't up to it. Instead, I began performing the relaxation exercises to be able to enter the alpha brainwave state at will.

I vaguely remembered the Jesuits' admonition of my youth: "*Keep on knocking, and the door will be opened to you.*" Was it Matthew, or Luke? How come people two thousand years ago knew so much? Is this what they'll say about us two thousand years hence?

Ambrosia updated me on the next series of meetings she held with the learned scholars.

"Should a large pole shift happen suddenly, the

redistribution of land and water on global scale would be cataclysmic. Climatic aberrations would be followed by earthquakes, and the resultant tsunamis could wipe out whole continents, without a moment's notice. The ocean currents would alter drastically, causing global weather shifts. You'd probably finally have your subtropical climate in Hudson Bay, if you survived to enjoy it."

"And don't forget new icecaps to replace the old ones," I added, just to make my own contribution to hell on earth.

This went on for a while. I was too happy where I was at present, there and then, to dream of other places.

"Will this destroy the efficacy of your QT?"

"Well, I do rely on GPS to reach my destinations. I don't know how else I can direct..." and then she looked up at me with eyes shining like two stars. "We did it without GPS to start with, remember?"

I'd never forget Lazy landing on my chest. We certainly didn't use any GPS in those days.

"We might have to go back to first principles..." she mused aloud. "It was fun, in those days, darling, wasn't it?"

It was a rhetorical question. It was also fun ever since.

Such speculation was enough to send Ambrosia back to her beloved lab, leaving me, as so often lately, alone. I wondered about the possible if not actually probable cataclysms. Having been brought up by the Jesuits, I was honed in the stringent philosophy of carrot and the stick. Of heaven and hell. It seemed to me that there ought to be someone we could blame for whatever might or might not befall us. God and Satan were good starting points. On the other hand, in the past we could have blamed the governments, perhaps industries that created pollution, or perhaps just our apparently uncontrolled sex-drive, which may have been responsible for the absurd overpopulation of our planet with its attendant consequences.

I spent the rest of the day browsing through the remnants of the Internet, in hope of finding some sort of confirmation of my suspicions. I was in need of attaching blame to someone. Anyone. Surely the Jesuits wouldn't approve of attaching blame to an All-Loving Deity who placed us here, on this planet, only to destroy us; or at least, most of us. After all, according to them and their colleagues in the Vatican, it all began innocently with Adam and Eve. Except for the apple, that is.

Except for the apple…

Only a few people appeared to have access to the remnants of the Internet these days; a few thousand at best. Yet occasionally, I came across a tidbit that tickled my fancy. What I found there and then was a strange fragment confirming my own suspicions. It had been posted, obviously, to enlighten all who came across it. It certainly enlightened me.

"Before you judge others or claim any absolute truth, consider that you can see less than 1% of the electromagnetic spectrum and hear less than 1% of the acoustic spectrum. As you read this, you are traveling at 220 kilometres per second across the galaxy. 90% of the cells in your body carry their own microbial DNA and are not "you". The atoms in your body are 99.9999999999999% empty space and none of them are the ones you were born with, but they all originated in the belly of a star. Human beings have 46 chromosomes, 2 less than the common potato. The existence of the rainbow depends on the conical photoreceptors in your eyes; to animals without cones, the rainbow does not exist. So you don't just look at a rainbow, you create it. This is pretty amazing, especially considering that all the beautiful colours you see represent less than 1% of the electromagnetic spectrum."

(signed) *Anonymous*

The spelling suggested British or Canadian authorship. I reread it a few times. I had no idea how accurate it was, but I was not prepared to dismiss it out of hand. It just felt right. It felt like the sort of truth that none of us liked to hear. It would certainly not be liked by the Jesuits of my youth. And yet...

I closed my miBook and went for a walk. The day was bright, sunny, hardly a cloud in the sky. Even the Terns hung suspended in the sky without a single worry.

There was peace in the air. Peace before the storm?

Was I becoming neurotic?

In my ten-year induced absence, most governing bodies of the world had collapsed. Judging by what Tom's scanning of the others told me, what remained were much smaller groups, the largest probably in China, yet even so no self-governing body consisted of more than a few thousand people. Only in what used to be the USA, some cities managed to hold onto their surrounding terrain, to grow their own food. They retained a semblance of municipal governance. Their communities may have been counted in one or two million people, but those enclaves were also braking up. There was no question of an army, nor even a police force, nor any other body of men organized to enforce order. Yet, there was no real anarchy. People seemed aware that they were left on their own and acted in the best interests of individual survival. Was this the model for the future?

Yet I still felt that someone must have been responsible for all that. The oligarchs? The democratically elected governments? The churches of various affiliations? Surely there were men of power and influence who might have saved humanity. From whom? From each other? From themselves?

Why, I wondered, are we so tempted to judge others?

Were we not given sufficient warnings? *"Do not judge, or you too will be judged."* Yet we continued to judge. *"Vengeance is mine, saith the Lord."* Yet we extracted vengeance. Could it be that we, the common man, are the instruments of the Lord? Of some Higher Power that was set to restore balance to the human equation?

Would we ever know?

Although we'd never admit it, most of us imagined ourselves "more equal then most of the others". A little superior, perhaps? Surely, we thought, we couldn't possibly be all equal. There was abounding evidence to the contrary. There was most certainly ample evidence that we were not all born equal. The truth was, still is, that we were all born equipped to overcome our particular and completely different shortcomings. But that was all.

Also, such privilege applied only to individuals. I remembered from my schooldays, that 'individual', in Latin, means 'indivisible'. The moment we lose our connection with the Intangible Infinite Potential—some call it God—we can no longer draw on our birthright. Perhaps the Jesuits were right, although they, too, liked to rule. At least over us, schoolboys. To us they were all-powerful. We lived at their mercy. Later, we also grew up to be the rulers or those being ruled. The rulers judged others to be inferior to them. Not just in potential, but, well, in all things that mattered.

And this was true the world over.

People were looking for a way out. Yet, there was only one way to free oneself from being subjugated to the will of dictatorial plutocrats of whatever hue or persuasion. And those masters of manipulation existed with equal abundance in the so-called western "democracies", as they did in eastern, northern or southern dictatorial or semi-dictatorial systems of government. Those who diminished the freedom of any individual that was trying to find his or her true place in the phenomenal reality was guilty of the most vile act that can be committed against the true nature of man. Whether they were the Roman Emperors, the Tsars of Old Russia, or the modern day Presidents, Prime-ministers, or their henchmen—the senators or members of various parliaments, if they indulged in diminishing the freedom of growth of an individual they were guilty of treason against the nature of man.

Against humanity.

The plutocrats of all nations abused their power in meting out unwarranted justice to maintain their position of power. And now they were gone. According to Mama, people, those less-than-equal masses, took their bloody revenge.

And yet the manipulators of human fate had all been given a chance to stop—to stop in time. They must have forgotten that power corrupts. The plutocrats thought themselves invincible until they used up their credit. Only by then it had been already too late. By then the Universal Justice took over from Universal Benevolence. It seemed that, rightly or wrongly, the consequences of abuse have come full circle.

Only now it also seemed that the wayward children who have freed themselves from the fetters of the plutocrats were lost. For too long they have been told not to think; not to take responsibility for their actions, until they lost the ability to make judgment. Not over others but over their own actions, or lack of them. They had been stopped in their development. They were adult children set free in an unforgiving world. At long last they freed themselves from their wayward parents.

And now... they were starving.

For generations the oligarchs trained their serfs, the quiet, unassuming masses, how to press buttons on an endless supply of electronic devices on which they, the rich, have made ever more billions. Lately this stupefying pastime of button pressing has been taken over by giving repeated verbal commands to machines to perform functions that until recently have been performed by men. By humans. Up down, left right, start stop... these set the limits of their expertise. It was as much as they could handle. This removed the need for the last vestiges of creative thinking. In the meantime the oligarchs continued to line their pockets, but they gave enough food to their serfs to keep them functioning in service.

Now, within a mere decade, the world has collapsed. There were no more oligarchs. In a way, they drowned in their own greed. In the blood they sucked out of the obedient masses. Yet masses could not win. Freedom came at too high a cost. There was no more food, no more factories, no more items of everyday use, no more energy.

It was time to start all over again.

I hardly noticed that I had covered some considerable ground. I was only vaguely aware of the surrounding beauty, of the charm and serenity of the island. It seemed completely untouched by the death throws that the world was going through; or at least the people, nature's favourite children. I just cleared the top of the eastern hill when I almost tripped over Amadeus. He was sitting alone, apparently deep in thought. I never took my son to be a loner. I always imagined he would grow up to be a gregarious sort of a man. Surrounded by people, filled with laughter, perhaps song and dance, and ladies looking admiringly at his masculine silhouette.

Yet here he was—all alone.

"Hello, son," I said softly.

He didn't answer. I sat next to him and waited for him to come back from wherever his brilliant mind has taken him. I didn't have to wait long.

***

6
Amadeus

"**C**ome with me, Dad," Amadeus said, a whimsical smile playing about his lips. "Come and see…"

This he said out loud and then he flooded my mind with such a plethora of ideas that even with direct perception, a sort of melding of minds, I could hardly follow. His memories stretched back for thousands of years. I had images of old Greek civilizations, of practically prehistoric times when people lived in abject poverty, fighting to keep their body and soul together on a daily basis. It was a kill or be killed civilization, with only the strongest surviving. Rather as stags fight among themselves to become alphas and impregnate the best, if not all females of the herd. Power was all. Nothing else mattered.

"Until recently it could have been said that we've come a long way," he muttered at last, breaking a prolonged silence. He didn't sound overjoyed by the social upheavals that swept the world. "Gods will always remain gods, and the many will take generations to rise above their present level".

There was neither pride nor condescension in the tone of his voice. If anything, a lingering touch of sadness.

"Are you telling me that the oligarchs were doing the right thing?" I couldn't believe my own words.

"No, Dad. I am not saying that. What I am saying is that they lifted masses to a higher level, and they kept the world going."

This time there was a mixture of resignation and

annoyance in his tone. His words seemed accompanied by subliminally projected anger at the destruction of s*tatus quo* and yet, simultaneously, a strange, evocative plea for help. In direct, subliminal communication emotions cannot be easily set apart. They flood the receiving mind in a single instant, even as they left the sender. I sensed that my son needed help.

But help in what, in supporting his unspoken ideas?

That sounded almost ominous. My mind touched on the secret that Ambrosia shared with me. It was something to do with Amadeus's past. Far, far distant past. Something to do with Greek mythology. I couldn't put my finger on it. It has been years since she and I spoke on the subject.

Perhaps, although he was now speaking aloud, the remnants of his telepathic communication were still playing havoc with my own concept of the order of things. You don't argue with ideas transmitted from mind to mind. You receive them and dissect them later.

Even as I looked at my son's smiling face, for some reason that I couldn't explain, I felt a certain disquiet, a certain trepidation. His previous thoughts were all gone. He was again a wonderful, caring smiling, handsome young man. A son I could be proud of. And I was.

"It had to happen. Nothing can survive without a degree of balance. Nothing," he added, clenching his fists.

I wouldn't like to face my own son in a boxing ring. Such an event was most unlikely. And yet that disquiet lingered.

"Come, Dad. Let us join the others. It must be close to lunchtime, and a little drop of wine wouldn't hurt."

I couldn't agree with him more.

I've been told that during my 'absence', Amadeus had spent a lot of his time in Corfu. Ambrosia told me that he watched his grandfather like a hawk, supposedly learning how to inspire people to take care of themselves.

Of course, Papa was not concerned merely with peoples' physical bodies. Perhaps there lies the problem. In order to become independent physically, one must become aware of one's individuality on, what Ambrosia called, the inside.

"How can I convince people," Amadeus once asked me, "that they are not what they seem?"

I have no idea why he expected me to have the answer for him. Perhaps he regarded me as one of the 'people'. This hurt my pride a little, since I've been told, years ago, that I'd joined the ranks of the immortals.

God, how time flies. That was still in Montreal. The years must have been taken from St. Thomas Aquinas's God's domain; from the time he called *aeternitas*. I noted there and then that for entities that are supposed to be immortal we spend an awful lot of time thinking about time.

"Is there a way to show them, to illustrate the truth, in such a way that their senses could experience it?" I offered.

Amadeus was deeply preoccupied with his, or was it his grandfather's, problem.

"It's been tried before," he replied with just a touch of scorn in his voice. "What do you think, Dad? What do you think such events as Our Lady of Pillars, and of Lourdes and La Salette, and many other similar visions were all about? People looked, fell to their knees, prayed, then went home and continued as if nothing had happened. They called those events 'miracles', and beyond the reach of any mortals."

My son was actually more sad than angry. I've never seen him so involved in any cause, although he always seemed to have jumped in his preoccupations with passion. He'd jump in up to his neck.

"Amadeus," I tried again, "you're young. Perhaps they have to spend a little more time learning, studying..."

It was at that moment that I realized that neither of my children would ever experience life at a higher institution of learning. There were no universities still functioning anywhere on earth. At least not to my knowledge. And I'd never give another lecture. On any subject.

Poor Athena. Poor Amadeus...

The next moment I realized that my son was probably reading my thoughts.

"I couldn't help it, Dad. Your emotions are such that you are almost screaming out loud." Yet he smiled even as he said it.

I was a little embarrassed.

"There is no need to worry, Dad. By the time I'd left Montreal I've read just about every book worth reading. You remember speed-reading? They were teaching it some years ago. Well, on the Internet you can do twice as fast again. Maybe faster? And now it's all still here," he tapped his head.

You and your eidetic memory... I mused.

You're right there, Dad... I sensed his answer.

We both laughed. But it didn't bring us any closer to solving his problem.

"Of course, not all attempts to awaken men were inspired by religious people," I returned to our discussion. "There was Marks and Engels, some Chinese leaders, others in Africa and South America. So far they didn't seem to have succeeded very much either. Could there be still other ways?" I mused aloud.

"That is more or less what I just asked you..." was his cryptic answer. Then he murmured as if to himself. "There must be a way... There must..."

He was getting morose again.

"Relax, son..." I tried.

"How can I, Dad? Even after five or more billion people dying, there are still an incredible number of units of intelligence, souls they call them, looking for a host in which to advance their becoming. Could it be that the human body is overdeveloped? That the brain produced a subsidiary self-awareness, an ego, that cannot be overcome?"

What a strange way of putting it, I mused. And then his numbers hit me. "Five billion?"

"That's a rough estimate. The best we can assess with Tom's data is that about a quarter of heavily populated areas are under water. Other, less populated lands are harder to determine..."

"Five billion dead?"

I couldn't accept such figures. That was more than the total population of the world at the time when my father died. I felt my head spinning. Amadeus caught my arm and slowly lowered me to the ground. I needed rest. I needed something normal. Something everyday. Something ordinary? I thought that having taught Comparative Religion, having studied the Crusades, the Spanish Inquisition, the horrors perpetrated by extreme factions of Islam, I would be immune to inhumanity of man to man. Yet this was more than man. It was nature turning against us. Has the human kind sinned that much?

"It's only the bodies, that died, Dad. Only the bodies..."

I heard my son repeat those words before they began to have an effect on my.

"Only the bodies..."

Thank God my son was not 'ordinary'. After playing with my concept of reality, he restored my sanity. For a while there the illusory reality, the Maya world, the reality that was little more than empty space, had taken me over. It seems to have taken, again, too strong a grip on my mind. On what I thought was real.

"...almost empty space, Dad. Almost empty space, remember?"

Yes, it was a question of remembering.

Just remembering who we were, why we were here, what was real... How easy it was to forget, to live this absurd illusion. And yet it affected not just our minds but also our emotions. Perhaps even more so? We knew we were wrong, but we felt otherwise. After all, our physical bodies belong to this illusion. Perhaps they had to have priority here or else how could we live inside them?

We had to make them real. We created our visions. Is

this what the ancient prophet meant when he said that we
were gods?

I shook my head. Lately, all too often I seemed to give
way to memories. They flooded my mind, pushing out the
present, the here and now, to a second Plane. Perhaps I have
not been living to the full. I made a mental note to ask Mama
to assign me permanent duties. I had too much free time on
my hands. I had to do something to earn my keep. Otherwise
I might as well go back to sleep for another ten years.

I turned my attention to my son.

"Trust me, Amadeus, when the time comes for you to
act, you'll know exactly what to do."

Amadeus looked at me with wide-open eyes.

"Did you speak to Mama," he asked, scrutinizing my
face.

"No, son, why do you ask?"

"Because last week she told me those exact same
words," he replied, still gazing into my eyes.

"And," I continued with unabashed pleasure, "as you
very well know, Mama is always right."

My son smiled knowing that there was nothing he could
add to such indisputable words of wisdom.

We quickened our pace.

They were all on the terrace already. I could see that Papa
was in seventh heaven. He'd finally run out of gas—out of
the jet fuel gas. There was enough left for emergencies, but
he could no longer enjoy his monthly trips to Corfu, with
occasional weekends back home, on Milos. His storage tanks
were near empty. Of course, he could resort to QT, but there
was something holding him back, not just the unreliable GPS.
He, like Mama, may have been rejuvenating their physical
bodies through OBEs for so long, centuries for all I knew,
that he couldn't face the prospect of breaking it down into

neutrinos, even for seconds. OBE was different. It didn't use the atoms from which our bodies were made.

Luck had it, that Papa's self imposed deadline for driving changes in Corfu was fast approaching, and his deadline coincided with an almost complete exhaustion of our fuel reserves.

People of the previous era would find it difficult to understand how little interest the gods had in technological, let alone industrial innovations. They used their brains the way we, 'normal' people use our computers and industrial devices. The difference was that computers were the product of the last century, whereas brains have been developed over a few million years. They, the gods, used them for the purpose for which they have been developed: communication, travel, altering the characteristics of physical reality. We all had this inherent capacity, we just lost the ability to use it.

Yes, lost.

There was a time when ancient people exercised their innate powers to a much greater degree. Then? Then, over millennia, the human race drifted away towards materiality. The centrifugal force took its toll.

Ambrosia developed the QT and other gizmos not for her personal use, but for those who didn't yet know how to use their brains. For gods, Internet, telephones, miPads and other technological 'advances' were little more than toys. With the exception of Ambrosia and possibly Papa, I've never seen a god use any technological gadgets. They evolved beyond them.

My wife's interests were a balancing 'act' to my preoccupation with myths. And Papa, well, Papa just loved all his children. He loved the human race. Hopefully, thanks to him, for the second time in the history of Greece, the new generation of citizens would advance the cause of democracy on their own.

The new version. The Papa Milos's version.

And now, for the first time since *Vouli ton Ellinon* went up in flames, Papa had time to spend with all of us, just enjoying the view. At long last the reserves of jet fuel, which the defunct Greek government had stored in such abundance on Corfu had run out. His eyes followed his beloved *mikro koritsi,* his little girl, as though tied to her by some invisible chords. I think those chords are called... love.

I vaguely recall how I first came across this name, *mikro koritsi,* which Papa bestowed upon his daughter. "Little Boy", with a yield of 12-25 kilotons of Trinitrotoluene or TNT, was the payload of the a-bomb Americans dropped on Hiroshima. At the time we thought that dropping Ambrosia's temper on anybody would be much more destructive. That was why we felt that the name "Little Girl" that Papa used when addressing Ambrosia seemed so apt. Of course, in Greek, it is *Mikro Koritsi*, but it is just as dangerous.

Or something very close to it.

It all seemed such a very, very long time ago.

Over dinner Papa told us, I suspect mostly for my sake, a little more about the ten years, during which he'd spent most of his time on Corfu. He was determined to prove that democracy was the only way in which the "common man" could retain control over his own future.

"No system is perfect," he said, nodding his gray head. "Nothing is perfect in this reality. But people must assert their individuality by having a say in their own lives. And democracy offers them a greater chance to do that than any other system of governance."

He went on to say that the only way to kill democracy was to buy votes. "While it might reflect the will of the rich, it destroys the privilege of making mistakes by the many. And it is only on mistakes that one can learn."

I recall a saying attributed to Einstein that "*Anyone who*

has never made a *mistake* has *never tried anything new.*" I strongly suspect that Einstein, as so often, was right again.

Corfu is an island almost touching the coast of Albania, which has long descended into, what Papa called, a state of disrepair. Being an island it had been spared most of the general malaise that swept the rest of the country. With radio stations out of energy, out of electric power, the 'islanders' were forced to make do on their own. Perhaps Papa knew that when he'd chosen Corfu for his experiment. He'd never pretended that his Corfu would rule over Greece. His experiment was limited to the island only, which could, later, if successful, serve as an example for the rest of the country.

And the island had a long and rich past. Papa was determined to write a new chapter of history on the same island. I hoped history would show that he'd succeeded. We all did.

"Balance," Papa said after long pause. "I must restore balance."

He had nothing against the rich, after all, he was well to do himself; nor did he feel compelled to help the layabouts, of whom there were many. But he insisted that whatever befell any of the Corfu citizens would be a consequence of their own individual choice, and not someone else's. Not imposed on them from outside.

Amadeus gave me a look from under his long, almost feminine eyelashes. A vague smile was playing on his perfectly shaped mouth. I suspected that had there been girls on the island, they'd all have fallen for my son. In droves. They would be standing in a queue... in many queues.

I shook my head.

For some reason images of my son being admired by the opposite sex didn't make me feel any better.

Papa finished sharing his thoughts with us, downed the rest of his wine and rose to his feet. "Come," he said to Amadeus. "Let's see what Tom came up with."

Tom had left some minutes ago. Papa was continuously

nagging him to scan the sky for radio news, if any, which might bring him up to date with the rest of the world.

"Call me," he'd told Tom repeatedly, "if any news came from Corfu."

Tom would, of course. Papa was definitely a peoples' man and Tom knew it. Also, Tom remained grateful to Papa from the day Papa hired him to look after Ambrosia in Montreal. Him and Jerry—and they were both still with us, now members of our extended family.

Jerry and Mavis had heard Papa's story before, and so took their leave to visit Goldie. As soon as Papa finished, Athena returned to her beloved piano in the Main Hall. I was left with Mama. As a matter of fact I was waiting for just such opportunity. More often than not Mama was busy visiting various guests, assigning tasks and, particularly in Papa's absence, generally running the island.

I felt that only Mama could help me with my problems. It seemed obvious that Mama was suspecting just such a session with me. Mama knew such things ahead of time. Perhaps all mothers do?

"Why is it so difficult for me to get there, you know, to the other side?" I began without any preambles.

Mama regarded me, as so often lately, as one would a slightly retarded son-in-law, who nevertheless had some redeeming features. Or it could have been just my impression, fuelled by my inferiority complex. She leaned over and looked deep into my eyes. At least I think she did. I found myself in a semi-waken state, then gradually coming back to my usual bright, intellectual stupor.

"It's coming back," she said. "It's not going there, it is coming back."

I looked at her not knowing if I am to understand her words, or if she was just testing my sanity.

"When you want to go… ah, there, to the… well, people call it the Astral Plane, don't think of going there, but rather as coming back."

I knew I was supposed to make sense of this. Mama sighed and stopped talking. The rest came to me at the subliminal level.

...ultimately... we are all one...

I knew that, it's just that these were just words limited by concepts we all associate with physical reality where it's not really true. Not true at all.

Mama sighed again. Sighing was as close to criticism as she ever allowed herself to get.

...think of entering a hot tub... first you test the temperature... you put your finger in and your finger becomes aware of the warm water... here... on earth... in the phenomenal reality... you are a finger... you are aware of what is immediately affecting your perceptions...

It came to me like a continuous stream of thoughts. I smiled. At least that made sense.

...when you submerge a whole hand... your perception of water is much greater... you are becoming aware that there is more water... that the warmth is vast... inviting... almost compelling you to enter the tub and experience the warmth of the water on your whole body... on all your physical perceptions...

I was beginning to enter into the spirit of her concepts. They seemed more real, more tangible, when received directly from her mind, before they became limited by words that were just symbols for the "real thing", so to speak.

This time it was Mama's turn to smile. She felt that she was getting through to me.

...and now you submerge your whole body in the tub... imagine that your body is completely permeable... that not just your skin but every single cell of your body is equally aware of the totality of that warm water... and now the tub is expanding until it fills the whole universe... and you are experiencing the totality of...

This is when, I was told later, I lost consciousness of my surroundings. Apparently I just lay there, like a lug in need of waking. Was this how Mama had put me to sleep ten years ago? I wondered that only after I came to.

I felt beautifully relaxed; floating on a warm white cloud without a care in the world. Life was beautiful, I thought. At least, I think that I thought that. For a moment there things got a bit hazy, and incredibly beautiful...

When I opened my eyes Ambrosia was bending over my body. Luckily I was listening to Mama on one of the padded *chaise longues* that cluttered the terrace, and no harm came to me. Well, to my body anyway. As for my mind, my sanity, it was still to be determined.

"You all right, darling?" Her eyes looked worried in spite of her unconcerned smile.

"Too much input..." she whispered.

"What happened?" I pleaded, not quite knowing what the fuss was about.

"You had a wisp of Oneness."

This is what Ambrosia's lips had said. But I was still partially in the receiving state. What her mind said was, *you touched the hem of God.*

This second realization nearly knocked me out. Again.

***

PART TWO

Second 40 Years

"....and power was given him that sat thereon
to take peace from the earth,
and that they should kill one another:
and there was given unto him a great sword."

The Revelation
of Saint John the Divine

7
Second Awakening

What I didn't realize was that between the time Mama had put me in the hot tub, and when I became aware of Ambrosia bending over my body stretched out on the deckchair—something in the order of 40 years had passed. I didn't care if it was St. Thomas Aquinas's 'temporal', '*aevum*', or '*aeternitas*' time. I sensed almost immediately that something very strange had happened, but only the next day Ambrosia confessed to me the extent of the duration.

I was hungry.

As for the type of time that passed, it would have been difficult to guess which it was, as Ambrosia looked exactly the same as she did this morning. It's just that "this morning" was 39 years and some days ago. You can believe it or not, but I was very hungry, and, once again, I was given a concoction that I wouldn't give to my worst enemy. I wondered how my children looked.

For all I knew I have been in some sort of suspended animation, like a frog that can be frozen solid and then awaken as good as it was before.

I wasn't frozen but they did things to me that seemed equivalent. I also didn't age, didn't think, and apparently didn't have any metabolic functions. If there is a difference between being and becoming, and in being time stands still, then I was in that state in which no change of any nature occurs. A state of being. A stasis, like the Infinite Potential. Isn't that where gods really reside? Outside time?

What was even more misleading was that the furniture,

the planting, the lawn itself, the views left and right, and the villa itself looked identical to what I remembered. Surely, after some 40 years there ought to be some signs of wear and tear, shouldn't there? Add to it the appearance of most people, particularly Mama's, Ambrosia's and even my own, and you would be as confused as I was during those first few days. Perhaps the whole of Milos was, at times, subject to the laws of being, and not becoming. Perhaps this is what made it a Sanctuary. It was protected not only from the ravages of geological upheavals but also of time.

Gods were becoming more and more enigmatic. On the other hand, so were frozen frogs, when first discovered.

On yet another hand, I would swear that Papa did have a few extra gray hairs. Not that he never changed the colour of his hair in the past. Just for fun? I remember him as a redheaded, long bearded, "Viva Zapata" mustachioed gentleman.

That was way back in Montreal...

The mystery grew a little less obscure when I learned that both, Tom and Jerry suffered from the same memory loss of the last, purportedly, 40 years. Only what I can refer to as *bona fide* gods, at least gods in my estimation, retained their awareness of the passage of time by whatever definition.

There were, however, one or really two very sad items that nearly broke my heart. Before my second stint of hibernation I made it a habit of visiting Goldie on a daily basis. I needed some exercise, and Goldie and I played all sorts of games to while away the time. Now, I've been told, Goldie was no more. They tried passing him through QT periodically, but the rejuvenation didn't work quite as well on animals as on humans. Something to do with alpha waves. One day I hoped to understand how it works.

...goodbye my friend... sleep well...

I wiped tears forming in both my eyes. They made my eyes sting even more.

Lazarus also refused to wake up from the dead a second

time. Actually, way back in Montreal, when we first passed him through the QT he wasn't really dead, just in terminal death throes, but this time he died of natural causes. He finished his stint on Earth making Ambrosia very happy while he was here. Would I be able to say as much when it it's my time to go?

I wondered.

Later my wife told me that she visits them both, regularly, on the other side of the Great Divide. Yes, cats and dogs do have a subconscious; hence they have Astral bodies that survive after death. Learning this I was determined to improve my OBE techniques to visit Goldie. I really missed my hairy friend.

I don't know how anyone else would react to all this, but speaking for myself, it hit me on the emotional Plane. I accepted the evidence of my eyes, but my emotions went haywire. I wanted to have been there when Goldie died. I wanted to hold him so that he wouldn't be alone.

...he is alright Simon... he is really all right...

This came from somewhere, I don't know from whom, but I was grateful. For some of these people, my very own family, there was no distance setting us apart. In their minds, perhaps in their hearts, we really were all One. Yes, with a capital 'O'.

Another thing that bothered me in the first few hours of awakening was the sun. It was hurting my eyes. I closed them and kept them shut for most of the time since seeing Ambrosia bending over me.

Only later I learned, hours later, that my body had been moved, vibrated I suppose, from time to time, by electrical impulses. Also, that it had been fed intravenously. Only now I was really lost. Did the time stop or didn't it?

I gave up.

How would you react?

I wanted to scream only I couldn't. My throat was almost shut down. It was dry as the sand in the middle of Sahara desert.

For a while I remained inert. I pretended that I was a frog—aware but still frozen. I pretended that I was not there. Or here, on the terrace.

Then, with relatively little pain, I sat up. It was all beginning to come back to me. I remembered that there was no dry sand in Sahara. The desert was a raging sea. Or was, 40 years ago.

What the devil was going on?

...*you were very lucky*... this came from Ambrosia the old-fashioned, subliminal way.

Then my awareness moved elsewhere. When I heard that my body had been jerked by electrical impulses, I was stumped. Standard procedure, I've been told. I'd heard of dance of St. Vitus, which apparently chickens performs after you cut off their heads—but for a few minutes, not 40 bloody years! My head was firmly attached to my neck, and my neck to my body. I checked. Yet apparently I 'danced' to the tune that Mama had commanded without batting a feather.

While Saint Vitus is considered patron saint of actors, comedians, dancers and epileptics, I did not associate myself any of these groups, hence I probably found it difficult to be jerked around for 40 years without having been aware of it. No doubt, in her own good time, Mama would explain. Or not. You never knew with Mama.

I was lucky, my wife had said. Why? What was so lucky about sleeping like a baby until adults wake you up. I was tired of being treated like a baby. Tired as hell.

With this I sat up and looked around. My stinging eyes grew larger until I collapsed back on my deckchair. I, the terrace, the villa... we were all sitting on the top of a mountain that cleared all surrounding islands by a good kilometer. Probably more. We were overlooking the Aegean as birds do. We were sitting on the top of Olympus.

My God, I whispered, perhaps these people really are gods!

A day later I actually walked, if slowly, from the villa to the terrace, a good thirty paces. I felt wobbly but reasonably safe. For some reason no one offered to hold my hand, or elbow, and any other portion of my anatomy. Not even Ambrosia. I have been diagnosed healthy in mind and body. As far as I was concerned, nothing could have been closer to the truth. Or anything? My mind wasn't working so well. I needed more practice.

I looked around.

Once again, other members of my family were already gathered on the terrace. The easterly breeze made this place heaven on earth. Balmy, warm, yet with a refreshing touch of zephyr. It was like a place of eternal spring—of constant rejuvenation? Who needs to go to heaven, I mused. This was as good as it got. As good as it could get.

Nobody looked up when I approached my reserved deckchair, though I noticed, just as surreptitiously, that everyone stole glances in my direction, and then followed my every step as I approached them. There were also some conspiratorial subliminal whispers. I couldn't detect their substance, but I sensed they concerned my person. This sufficed to placate my injured ego.

Apparently they were all waiting for me.

It seemed that Mama was about to share her thoughts on her concept of Infinity, or on what most people still called God.

"The Infinite is always neutral," she began in her usual quiet voice.

Just for a moment I had a flashback to my studies in Montreal. I had been reading Tao Te Ching. *"Tao is always neutral"* it said, *"It is always on the side of the just man."* It sounded like a contradiction in terms, yet, in Lao Tsu's eyes—it wasn't. I think I noticed a smile on Mama's face as she momentarily glanced at me. There was approval in her eyes.

"Beyond time, beyond space, beyond good and evil," she continued. "We, you and I, Simon, and all of us are the only gods. We and only we, and all who evolved to the level of understanding their potential, are the only gods. Good and bad. Christs, Archangels or Lucifers. Whenever we stray from the straight and narrow we pay for the consequences. Yes, both Christs and Lucifers.

Wasn't there but one Christ?

"Yeshûa was just one. A magnificent one. Christ is a state of consciousness, Simon. Not a person. It is often referred to as Christ Consciousness. Just as Lucifer mentality is not limited to a single entity. Lucifer is as far, and as high, as your ego can take you. Regrettably it is a state of consciousness of utter alienation. In sheer power, it is not that far from Christ," she was searching for words, "only facing the wrong direction."

...yet... even so... necessary to maintain the balance...

These last words reached me directly from her mind. I detected a deep sorrow within them.

"Yes, Simon. The Saviours and the shining ones, the Morning Stars—Lucifers. Now and again our emotions are so strong that they dwarf the memory of our origins."

Lucifers as gods? My mind rebelled. Mama smiled.

"Simon," she resumed speaking in her quiet almost conspiratorial tone of voice. "Genghis Khan, Hitler, Stalin, Mao Zedong, known to most as Mao Tse-tung, had been all responsible for millions of deaths yet they all had their vast followings. Many, many more than Yeshûa had in his day. More then most religions at their outset."

"So gods are defined by their following?"

"No, Simon, there are not. But most people define them by the power they wield. And don't forget, we all come from the same Source. Just one, single Source.

...beyond time and space... beyond good and evil... I heard Mama's thoughts repeating her previous words. *Beyond...*

So much to learn, I sighed. And then I snorted. Not so long ago, I was teaching Comparative Religion. What a joke!

"Not so."

This time I heard Mama's voice blended with the wind that seemed to rise from afar, as if to make up for the moments of absolute stillness. Are we again beyond time and space, I mused?

"Not so, my friend," Mama smiled her most serene smile. "All religions contain a minute trace of truth. If people would only search deeper, they would all point the way in the right direction."

Mama never called me a friend before. Yet I felt to the depth of my bones that she was by far the greatest friend I ever had. Even as those thoughts formulated in my mind, I felt surrounded by enigmatic yet very real warmth. Not so much of heat but of love and serenity. The next moment, if but for a single instant, time stood still, again, and then it once more took up its eternal journey. Yet from that moment on I regarded it from outside, as though I was no longer carried by its currents, but rather as an observer.

I felt an inexplicable sense of freedom.

When others dispersed each to his or her duties, Mama waved me to come closer. I moved up to the table at which she was sitting.

"Sit down, Simon. I have a favour to ask."

About time, I thought, before I remembered that she read all my thoughts.

"You must learn not to broadcast them, my friend. You

really must. Whenever you join us here, on the terrace, you sound like a beacon in the middle of a desert."

"One can control one's thoughts?" I had my suspicions but I was never certain.

"Ambrosia will tell you. She's very good at it."

"You mean not everyone can do it?"

"All that we know, Simon, had been learned at one time or another. When you first arrived here you were no more than an amoeba."

I wasn't that pleased about the way Mama referred to my ancestry. As though to placate me, she added with an amused smile. "We all did, Simon. You're in good company."

For a brief moment I saw an ocean with countless amoebas frolicking to their hearts' content. Again I had to shake my head to lose that image.

"There, you did it again. Broadcasting. You have a good sense of humour, Simon, and great imagination. That is why I asked you to join me."

At this I sat up.

"You have been determined to find something useful to do. To earn your keep, as you called it."

Broadcasting?

"Yes, my friend. You do it all the time. Anyway, I thought that you might help the next generation avoid the errors of the past."

That sounded like a very tall order. Not for the first time, I felt humble. Surely I was the least likely person to offer substantive help to anyone.

"To avoid willful, and some not so willful, misinterpretations of ancient scriptures," Mama continued, "I want you to write history of events that were taking place for some time, and still do, while they are still fresh in your mind."

I never wrote a book in my life, but I did write innumerable reports, innumerable notes, to be able to deliver my lectures at McGill.

"You think I could do it?" I was not nearly as confident as Mama appeared to be.

"You have all of us to check up on your facts."

"What of the decades when I was, ah… absent?"

"I'll tell you about them. There is not that much to tell. In fact, isn't that why you agreed to go inside until a more propitious time?"

"I agreed?" This time I sat up even straighter.

"We read your thoughts, remember. Broadcasting?"

…I made a mental note to ask Mama to assign me permanent duties… I had to do something to earn my keep… …otherwise I might as well go to sleep for another ten years…

I heard my own voice in my own head repeating those words. As far as I recalled, word for word. Mama only smiled.

"I said ten…"

"Time is flexible. I thought a bit longer would spare you the mountain going up and down like a yo-yo."

"This mountain? Milos?" When I first got here, Milos wasn't nearly a mountain. More like a hill sticking out of the sea.

"Yes, dear Simon. We had to do quite a lot of mental acrobatics, as you'd call them, to save our buildings, our roads, even the flora and fauna. We were all quite busy."

"You can control earthquakes?"

"No, Simon. But when we all got together we could influence them sufficiently not to allow them to do us much harm."

"I might as well have been asleep…" I mused.

Mama smiled again. I was beginning to relax. I was obviously in good hands, and Ambro was right. It seems that I was lucky. Very lucky. I might have gone stark raving mad!

I allowed myself a deep, grateful sigh.

"How would I call the notes on history, Mama?"

"How about 'Aquarian Trilogy'? You could describe

your life in Montreal, then the first wave of physical, sociological, and even political upheavals. You could call them the Pluto Effect. And the present changes I leave to you. I'm sure you'll think of something."

"Of Gods and Men," I said. That was as close as I could get to define the difference about man's present state, or condition, and his ultimate potential. Of Gods and Men," I repeated.

"If you like. Only neither ultimate nor infinite," she added, obviously peeking into my thoughts. "Infinite lies in the future and future is infinite. As is the past... Your notes would help to dispel the myths that people make up about gods."

I still wasn't sure if they were all myths. Right now, I was right in the middle of one. Or at least, of what in time would become a myth. There were moments when I wasn't sure if any of this was real. Perhaps I was still asleep and just dreaming. For 40 years? It seemed that I had my work cut out for me.

"Good luck, Simon. I rather think that you'll enjoy earning your keep."

This time we both laughed. I even heard joyful chuckles coming from the direction of the villa. I was among friends. They shared in my pleasure. It must be fun to be gods, I mused.

...*you should know*... I heard.

I swung my head around but there was no one there. Except Mama right in front of me, and she wasn't laughing. Not any more. I suspected that she considered the commission she gave me quite seriously. I was determined not to let her down.

A week later, Mama told me that as far as she could see the geological upheavals were at an end. We had little idea what might have happened in the rest of the world, but our Island

Milos has grown, one might say expanded, to unite all Cyclades. The nine provinces have been united under a single roof, so to speak, and the land area has grown more than a hundredfold, allowing only a relatively narrow strip of water running north and south. This strip was well protected from the Meltemi winds, which could reach force 7 in the open seas. This main canal, rather like the Grand Canal in Venice, was connected east and west by smaller, narrower arms, which multiplied what Papa called 'waterfront' properties.

It looked like Papa was ready to start building a brave new world. Hopefully it would be nicer than that envisaged by Aldous Huxley way back in 1932.

All we needed now was people, but those were the most scarce commodity around. It would take a few generations for the beautiful land to be colonized anew. For now, our 'guests' were busy transplanting trees over land recovered from the sea. Others were planting corn which Jerry and Mavis found, abandoned, on one of the islands before the final upheavals.

From an administrative point of view, not that there were many citizens to administer, Papa moved the capital of the Cyclades from the deserted Ermoupoli, which didn't fare so well in the earthquakes, to Milos. The few dozen survivors from previously independent islands joined us, on foot, to be closer to our little enclave. We had a welcoming party that lasted into the early hours. Apparently, gods like to have fun. Even with us, simple folk.

It was hard to believe that little more than 40 years ago, the Cyclades which comprised around 220 islands, were now joined by nature into what some called, with a broad smile, the Milos Kingdom. Originally, most of the smaller islands were uninhabited. Now, had nature not joined them together, even the larger ones—some 40 or more of them, would have also remained almost deserted. Most people escaped to the mainland, not knowing if the islands would rise in elevation, or be swallowed by the Aegean Sea.

According to Mama, this particular exercise of the Pluto

Effect was over.

As I already mentioned, I was determined not to let Mama down. I decided to put down all my memories, and secondary research, on paper, actually in my computer's memory, in more or less chronological order. Only later I intended to cut out of the superficialities to make it more into a historical document. If I didn't manage to write a serious historical document, then at least, whoever took over from me would have a good base to work from.

"I love to see you work," I heard a whisper behind my back.

Apparently Ambrosia was watching me, unwilling to interrupt my work in my study. Yes, I have been assigned a spare room as my personal study, to protect me from... I have no idea what. Probably from the intrusion of people who constantly milled in and out of our grounds, in search of advise or just to reassure themselves.

Anyway, the solar batteries provided all the juice I needed to keep my miBook going. I had two spare ones, which Tom had scavenged from Montreal some years ago, by QT, just in case. Tom and Jerry have also upgraded the one I was using for work to be twice as fast, although the old, old version was perfectly sufficient for my needs. In addition, Tom collected all the old computers left behind in the Milos Kingdom, and used them as spare parts to refit mine. Our Tom and Jerry were two very smart guys. Needless to say, Ambrosia kept a close eye on their work.

I smiled and leaned forward. I raised my hands as I've seen concert pianists do in *Place des Arts,* in Montreal. Then I struck the first chord:

AGE OF AQUARIUS
HISTORY OF THE WORLD
THE ZODIAC

PART ONE.

I spend the next ten minutes staring at the computer screen, deep in thought. I had no idea how to write history. Didn't one start with dates, famous personages, with Kings and Presidents and Prime Ministers, and other important people? I haven't met any of them. How on Earth was I supposed to write history?

Another ten minutes past.

I leaned back and closed my eyes. Our life in Montreal, Mama had said. Mama knew what she wanted. Our life in Montreal, eh? *Pourquoi pas*? I wondered if I could write with a French accent. I erased the pompous title and let my fingers dance on the keys.

WALL, I wrote, A Tale of Love, Sex and Immortality.

That was more like it. At least it wasn't pompous, and I'd write about something I knew something about.

Then I leaned back admiring the title. I wondered if I should write "by Simon Jackson", but then I realized that this would be a very communal effort. I needed all the help I could get. I needed input from all the people I've met over the years.

Chapter One, I typed next, and sat back waiting for inspiration.

"I can help with that," Ambrosia said. She was still standing behind me, by now gently rubbing my neck. "Shall we go…"

I knew that tone of voice. We went. She was one hell of an inspiration. I also knew that I'd write a hell of a book. To hell with history. This was going to be a hell of a lot of fun!

***

8
Visitors

At long last I learned to enter the alpha brainwave at will. It is that state of consciousness that serves as the departure lobby for Astral travel. After countless years of trying, it happened almost accidently. Not that I knew what to do once I was in it. That, apparently, was quite another story. I could fall in and out of it in a blink of an eye. And that is, I suppose, why I was not supposed to blink. Literally—I was supposed to keep that still.

Our villa was now sitting atop quite a high mountain. I wanted to see something just around the corner, and the next moment, without moving my feet, I saw it. It was something quite inconsequential. A bird was flying over the edge of a reef and I wanted to see where it landed. After all, the last time I looked, the reef had been under water. This was new. I was curious. It was as silly as that. Apparently a god can be as silly as the next man. Powerful but silly.

I had to laugh.

I went back to my study to test the theory. I closed my eyes, relaxed, and thought of my other study, in Montreal. The next moment I was looking out of my study widow in my penthouse, staring at the green mountain. I was glad there had been no earthquakes in Montreal. Everything in my study was shipshape. Except for a layer of dust.

Funny that, I thought. All windows closed, nobody stirring up anything from the floor, yet—a layer of dust. Or could it be that in alpha state we made up a reality as we expect it to be?

The dust was gone. In an indefinable instant all was spick and span. Ship shape.

So that's the game... We don't really go anywhere, we just imagine we go.

I looked again through the window. The trees were moving in a slight breeze. Mount Royal was just as I remembered it. Beautiful. A cloud was drifting, forlorn, in an ocean of blue. Did I imagine that also? The beauty, the green, that particular cloud.

Something didn't fit.

I opened my eyes and the image was gone.

With the geological adjustment complete, there was nothing to stop me from coming here by QT. I mean going there. Admittedly this was more fun, but I could check out what was real and what was imagined.

I had a lot to learn.

I've spent the next six days in my study. Athena brought me food and drink, and obviously I spent the nights in our bedroom, but other than that, I remained sequestered. I had to get things going, I told them. To gather speed, or direction? Once I knew where I was going with my book the rest would surely unfold itself as it should. Isn't this what happens with all things. Even the world? It continues to unfold itself with all of us all just playing catch up.

On the sixth day I had it. I'd already described my success with my recalcitrant ankle. I knew that I struck gold. Things, in my notes, began to unfold by themselves, as they should. Slowly I emerged from my memories.

I came up, almost gasping for air.

Ambrosia joined me on the steps leading to the garden.

"Hello, stranger," she quipped, "do you come here often?"

I skipped the normal response about restricting my visits to the mating season. By now, it was just too trite.

Things have changed. The terrace furniture has been rearranged in a semicircle. The chairs were facing the villa, not the magnificent view as they normally did. I wondered what was about to happen.

"Mama invited people," Ambrosia said, a whimsical smile playing about her lips.

"From where?" I asked. As far as I knew, there was no transport available. "QT?" I asked.

"No, my husband. God's don't use QT."

"Gods from where?"

She was barely stirring my interest. I lived amongst gods for years. This was getting just a mite annoying.

"From all over the world, Simon. Really. From all over the world," she repeated, herself apparently in a daze of admiration.

For some reason I realized that she wasn't kidding. For a minute or two I remained flabbergasted. Then I had to ask, "...b-but how?" I almost stammered.

"You would call it the Father Pio technique. It still works, you know? It is essentially an emotional response to desire implanted through the usual channels."

"Thank you, dear," I retorted.

I felt sure that her response should have made things perfectly clear, but most certainly not to me. Were we all going mad, or was it just me, I mused.

...just I... darling... just I not me...

...who is the writer... you or me... I mean I...

...ha ha...

...to you too...

The silent exchange took less than two seconds.

"You are perfectly sane, darling," she added seeing frazzled expression on my face. "Mama will make it all clear for everybody. Soon."

Ambrosia knew that I must also be tired from the last six days of virtually continuous work on my computer. "Just relax, and let things happen," she said softly. "You are among friends, you know that."

I knew that. I had proof enough. Ambrosia knew exactly what buttons to press to make me relax. After all, she was my personal goddess.

"Thank you, darling. I know. It's just that occasionally I need reminding."

"We all do," and this time her smile became quite carefree.

We descended the steps and walked around the villa to the garden at the back. I always thought of it as our private domain, yet we hardly ever went there. No time, I supposed. We strolled the narrow pathways. I was amazed that after all these years, this was the first time ever that Ambrosia and I walked the labyrinth arm in arm, silent, just enjoying the aromas generated by a variety of plants and flowers. I was still trying to see any sign of a single gardener taking care of the intricate flora.

"We all do it, Simon, there are no servants here."

"Do what, trim the hedges?" I was just kidding.

"Precisely. Mama says that working in the garden for ten to fifteen minutes a day has therapeutic effect on your nerves. Have you never tried it?"

"No one ever told me..." he said defensively.

"You are not a child, my husband. We don't usually tell adults what to do. We try to be self-motivating. That is the meaning of true freedom."

So I had to observe and learn. After all, this was precisely what I did when I was teaching. Only now, it seemed, that it was supposed to apply to all things, not just a narrow band of my expertise.

...precisely...

Once more, I had to smile. Ambro was too polite to agree out loud. It would have sounded patronizing. Somehow at the subliminal level it didn't. At the subliminal level we were much closer to that elusive oneness that gods liked to talk about.

...we are all gods... I heard.

...in the making... long time coming... I countered. Long time coming.

...*love you*... I heard her sweet voice caressing my mind.
...*love you*... the voice repeated.

I was a very, very lucky guy.

...*me too*... I managed through a constricted throat, before I realized that one doesn't use one's throat to pass subliminal messages.

"Me too..." I repeated anyway. My throat didn't hurt at all. Isn't it funny, I mused, how we continuously create reality and don't even know it?

We walked on in silence. Hand in hand, like we used to on Mount Royal.

When we reached the terrace through the most roundabout way, Mama was sitting in the middle of the semicircle with Papa at her right side. Amadeus and Athena were one place removed on each side. There was an eerie silence. We stopped, I held my breath. And then it happened.

First one, then the second, then three all at once, figures in different clothing, different dresses and head gear, shimmered over the chairs facing the two generations of my family. Only the middle generation was missing, Ambrosia's and mine.

"Those are the two empty chairs between Mama, Papa and the children. Hurry, they are almost ready," Ambrosia whispered.

She led me to the left of Mama, and sat herself on Papa's side. Then we waited in silence as some ten or more figures appeared out of nowhere. It struck me that Father Pio of Pietrelcina would have enjoyed it. These were his kind of people.

I had to use all my self-control not to cringe in disbelief. Things like this just didn't happen. Not since... not since Father Pio supposedly turned up in South America while simultaneously saying Mass in his monastery, just south of Rome. Only now it happened in droves. And to my knowledge, none of Mama's visitors were even of sacerdotal fraternity.

I closed my eyes.

...I want to welcome you all...

This was Mama's voice, as clear as bell in my head.

...we have entered the second phase of adjustment... the emotional phase... we must be ready for absurd behaviour of our charges... we must show great understanding...

Why was I here? I didn't belong among these spiritual giants. Judging by their attire, these people came from all parts of the world. From China, South America, Australia, Mongolia and Tibet. There may have been others that I didn't recognize.

I should have been listening to Mama, yet my mind kept wondering. Why couldn't those people come here like ordinary people. Then I remembered. No airplanes, no ships... and even if the sailing ships could get here, how would they have reach us at some 2500 meters above sea level in bare feet. That's right. Some of them arrived in bare feet, would you believe it?

When I followed that bird coming in for a landing, I saw the cliff. It rose thousands of feet. Meters. Almost a sheer drop. I know that the terrain descended more gently towards southeast, but that was miles away. Miles. We were no longer a tiny island basking in the sunshine of the Aegean Sea. They could hardly jump up to reach us. In time roads would be built, landing strips lengthened, Papa would see to that, but now...

It's been a while since we could use QT. With the magnetic poles dancing a fandango, the GPS was useless. Now we were stranded. Except for the gods. They could reach us anywhere. And they did, at Mama's command.

And then a strange thought struck me. I recalled that Machu Picchu had been built at 2,430 meters, some 8,000 feet about sea level. Was there any connection? Was this a magic number of some sort? I wondered how high the Tibetan Sanctuary was located. Perhaps I could ask after

Mama finished...

... when people finally realize what they have done there will be mass hysteria... we must protect them...

Mama's voice continued invading my mind.

So this was a briefing session. It seemed that Mama was in charge. I wondered who had elected her. Then again, as though through a dense fog, I remembered something about the Chinese Immortal Woman. Hé. Or Hé Qióg. Or was it He Xiangu? Perhaps the Immortal Woman had many names. Was Mama...

... we must not impose... just help when needed... they must find their way on their own... yet we must always help...

Mama's inner communication sounded like a voice that was alternating between pleading and commanding. Apparently we must not impose our will on ordinary people, but this did not apply in equal measure to gods. Sometime gods had to be told.

Suddenly I felt very tired. I closed my eyes and the semicircle before me dissolved into darkness. Some time later Ambrosia told me that it was time to go.

"What? Where?" I did not feel like going anywhere.

"To bed, darling. To bed. The visitors are all gone. You looked so tired I didn't want to disturb you, but you'll be more comfortable in bed."

Isn't she wonderful? She had to help me to my feet. Minutes later I slept like a log—although I've never seen a log asleep.

From the moment I woke up, the question of bilocation bothered me. I clicked on the Internet and browsed till I found what I wanted.

When the Incas disappeared from Machu Picchu, were they bilocating? I didn't forget that we are all 99.999etc% empty space. If we are mostly empty space, then when bilocating there wouldn't be much left behind. They, the

Incas, departed from the mountain peak and only dust lingered behind. Almost like the Cheshire cat's smile.

Bilocation would be a very useful if not favoured form of travel. Several Christian saints, monks, and Muslim Sufis practiced it. According to Spanish tradition, in the year 40 AD, *Nuestra Señora del Pilar*, later known as Our Lady of Pillar, appeared in Zaragoza, in Spain. From that moment on people witnessed strange appearances of St. Anthony of Padua, Ursula Micaela Morata, St. Gerard Majella, Charles of Mount Argus, St. Severus of Ravenna, St. Ambrose of Milan, Maria de Agreda... the list went on and on.

Then how come I'd only heard about Father Pio? What was so special about him?

I gave up trying to figure it out on my own and went in search of Mama. She was about to leave the villa on some errand, but I persuaded her to give me five minutes. I told her about my problem and Father Pio.

"Well, he also carried stigmata, and many unexplainable events, such as healings, have been attributed to him. Events people call miracles."

"And there were others, other practitioners of the, ah, art?"

"I can count a dozen others..."

"The select few..."

"Many are called, Simon. Very few choose to be chosen. After all, there was a time when such ability would lead one to be accused of witchcraft. Many didn't advertise their gifts."

"Gifts?"

"Abilities. But don't forget that life here, in the phenomenal reality is a gift, as is everything that issues from it."

"Everything?"

"In everything we do, we alone are all co-creators of the phenomenal reality. In that sense, we are all gods. Or, at the very least, creators or potential gods."

I remembered that, in fact, I'd once given a lecture on the subject. In ancient scriptures gods are referred to as creators. Even the Torah refers to them as *Elohim*, which is Hebrew plural for gods, and assigns creative processes to them.

"And such gifts are given to saints only?"

Mama stopped and... sighed deeply, then smiled as though looking at a wayward child.

"Vladimir Ilyich Ulyanov, later known as Lenin, has been seen in his Kremlin office, in the very heart of Moscow, shuffling through his papers in October 1923, while he was simultaneously lying critically ill in Gorki, some ten kilometers south of Moscow. To my knowledge no one ever accused Lenin of being a saint."

"So it's just... power?"

"No, Simon, it is the consequence of power. How you use is up to you. Always."

"So how do you explain all this, Mama? All that happened yesterday?" There was a plea in my voice that I just couldn't hide.

"A teacher does not excuse himself, or herself, for assigning his or her homework to his or her pupils. They call them students, nowadays. It is up to us to derive such lessons for our growth that we feel are necessary. All that our permanent I AM can do is to create conditions which are most propitious for our advancement."

This sounded like a lecture that I might have given some ten, or now fifty years ago. Have I forgotten so much?

"Truth is one, Simon, but it must be continuously rediscovered." She must have peeked into my mind. "Also, everything that is in harmony with Infinite Consciousness, with Oneness, is the Truth. That makes the Truth infinite, too."

Now, that was deeper than I have ever dived. Mama was something else. She smiled, pated me on my shoulder and ran like a young lady trying to catch a train. She was amazing. I wonder just how old she was. I don't mean just in this body but as an individualized consciousness. If she really was the Hé, the Immortal Woman, than that would place her in the category of infinity, and I never forgot the lesson I learned long ago: Whatever has no end, it also has no beginning. That's the only definition of infinity that makes sense. On the other hand, in one sense, aren't we all immortal?

I returned to my study. For a long time I looked through the window trying to discern a pattern in the clouds forming on the far horizon. Perhaps there was no horizon. It kept retreating each time I raised, or expanded, my view of the world. I needed to empty my mind of the invisible, the intangible, which seemed so natural to a certain group of people. For me it still remained on the border of black magic, or some other sort of mumbo-jumbo.

And yet those gods seemed so eminently sane. Perhaps the most balanced group of people I'd ever come across. In addition, they seemed a happy lot, an equally tangible trait that appealed to my hedonistic convictions.

Yes, they were most definitely a happy lot.

Yet, the cloud patterns notwithstanding, my mind returned to the bee in my bonnet that continued to stir my neurons into a frenzy of activity. Mama's cryptic comments about bilocation helped me to broaden my view, but hardly answered all my questions. As with most other enigmas I encountered since I stopped teaching Comparative Religion, sooner or later I'd turn to Ambrosia. It is not that she had all the answers, as I suspected Mama might have, but she was more apt to speak the language I'd understand. After all, first and foremost, my wife was a physicist with a string of scientific accomplishments to her name.

...you have a problem... I heard in my head.

It wasn't a question. It was a statement of fact. I didn't even hear the door open. Ambrosia sensed my conundrum and came to join me. "Two heads are said to be better then one, although…"

"Darling…" I bit my lip. I almost said, 'speak of the devil' before realizing that nothing could possibly have been more inappropriate. If not a goddess then the least she could possibly be was an angel, coming from above to help a guy in distress.

"It's still the bilocation, isn't it?" It sounded rhetorical.

I nodded.

"Don't try to dissect everything with a scalpel. That's the dualistic way. The more you enter the inner reality, the essence of who you really are, the more all things are interlocked forming a singularity. I mean that all things, abilities, talents emanate from the same Source. The same Single Source is manifested in or through all attributes that you discover within yourself."

This did make a sort of sense. I nodded.

For some reason I couldn't put my finger on, the words "*I am a jealous god*" came to my mind. A single Source that would not tolerate or recognize other gods. Other sources? Was this what Moses was trying to tell us in Exodus? But none of this got me much closer to understanding the enigma of bilocation.

I heard Ambrosia sigh. She was still standing behind me, gently massaging my neck. She was doing this more often lately, and I wasn't about to dissuade her.

"Think of QT. Remember how we started? There was the alpha state, then the patterns, then the computer…"

"Yes, darling. I do recall the basic premises. We went a dozen times through it in Montréal."

"Well, all you need do is to substitute psychic energy for the electronic impulse and you've got bilocation."

"But in QT we transport the whole bag of tricks!" I almost shouted in frustration. "And here…"

"And here people leave 0.0000000000001% of mass behind and then pick it up again on the way back."

She counted her zeros on her fingers and had 3 left over.

There were 13 of them. After the decimal point. That is the percentage of our body that has actual mass. The rest, ever assuming that our bodies were made up of all those very invisible atoms, then the rest—we had been assured by many scientists—was empty space. I often had to remind myself that we don't see atoms or atomic structures but at best we see photons reflected from the electrons whirling in wild abandon. A most uncomfortable scientific fact, which reminded me, once again, that my wife was first and foremost a nuclear physicist.

"And they reclaim the dust on their return…"

"Which in the meantime has been supported in its original shape by residual energy for a limited time."

"Why limited?"

"Energy tends to dissipate over time."

"Bingo!" I said, with more confidence that I actually felt. In the context of quantum tunneling it was easier to accept such a premise than now. Yet the way she put it, it did make sense. She was one clever lady, that wife of mine.

I was beginning to relax.

"Miracles of today are little more than self-knowledge of tomorrow. Remember that nothing can ever happen contrary to universal laws. They were developed over countless billions of years, and they cannot be contradicted. That's why I love physics so much. There are no contractions."

"Not to you, darling. Not to you. But you are a genius, it's easy for you to say…"

But Ambrosia was already gone. She only left her beloved lab to help me out. She did. I'd be able to sleep that night. Right next to her. Wasn't I lucky?

It was Tuesday. For some reason we had our dinner early. Even before we finished, I noticed an unusually large number of people walking slowly up the winding serpentine road leading up to our villa. They didn't approach the terrace but distributed themselves, seemingly at random, over the lawn. By the time we finished eating there must have been upwards of 400 people sitting tightly, next to each other, with an air of expectation.

"What the hell's going on," I asked Ambrosia. "Is Mama going to give another of her lectures?"

I was going to add "why wasn't I told?" but thought better of it. I was so busy lately making notes for my book, and, yes, working in the garden at least twice everyday to make up for years of my abstinence. Hence, I didn't know that anything was being planned.

"Wait and see, darling. I think you are going to like it."

Within minutes of my asking this question I got my answer. The double door of the Main Hall opened, and almost immediately a joyous Mazurka filled the air. I knew that touch. It was unique. It was my own daughter, Athena.

She played a half-dozen pieces before she emerged on the steps to acknowledge an uproarious applause of her audience. I joined them with equal passion.

I didn't see or hear any announcement. Then I guessed the reason. I've been really busy trying to write the history of the events in Montreal. I missed the subliminal whisper that must have spread far and wide, which mobilized people to come and hear Athena.

Apparently this was to become a regular weekly, Tuesday night, performance.

My daughter's gift to the people.

Athena was a concert pianist by any measure. And now some 400 people confirmed my opinion. They all loved her, even as did I.

The moon was high by the time her last chords were absorbed by the silence of the night. Yet the night continued to be filled with her music.

I love you, Little Girl.

***

9
Hysteria

At long last, thanks to Tom, and at least in part due to Mama's session with advanced members of our race—perhaps species is a better word—we reinvented communications with different parts of the world. A total of twelve sanctuaries have risen to the occasion, and guided by Tom and Ambrosia's instructions, installed equipment, which gave us audio and visual contact without resorting to
the semi-defunct satellites.

When the magnetic poles began their tantrums, there had been some 1,300—both government and private—active satellites. Close to 3,000 more were spinning around that no longer worked. Now we could count on some 200 to 300 satellites that were still functioning, yet which could not assure us of an uninterrupted service. Still, with a lot of patience, we did the best we could.

After the first few reports, which Tom has received from our distant friends, we were almost sorry we asked. No news is good news, they say, but these were depressing to say the least. This time the news did not concern the select few, only the remnants of humanity scattered all over the realigned globe.

In recent times, at least since my second awakening, most of us have been so wrapped up with our own plans that, at least for a while, we seemed to remain completely oblivious of what was happening in the rest, of what used to be, civilized world. We knew about most of the cataclysmic changes brought about by the polar readjustment. Parts of old continents descended into the oblivion of the deep. Others emerged, in our case slowly and ponderously, all waiting to be populated, civilized and probably, given time, polluted by man's greed if not by man's inhumanity to man. I often thought that we need a few million more years to become at least a partially civilized.

We were still in kindergarten.

Throughout known history man has been given instruction manuals, which greedy sacerdotal fraternities have quickly usurped for their own ends, twisting them sufficiently to make religions out of them. They usurped wisdom telling us how to live, how to advance more quickly, how to evolve beyond our primitive barbaric proclivities. To this day we hardly rose about the rest of fauna, an unavoidable consequence of individualization and the attendant separation from the Source.

The wisdom, the priceless knowledge acquired over thousands of years, was lost in the musty halls of temples and churches. Later religious leaders invented tithes, which made sense thousands of years ago when it enabled a few to study man's advancement, and became total nonsense when the population explosion made millionaires out of priests, who lived head and shoulders above the standard of those who supported their need to sample the latest *Beaujolais Nouveau*.

There were exceptions. There always are. The Few.

Alas, over the last few decades the donation boxes had been emptied by the poor, the starving, and the temples and churches fell into disrepair, loosing the magnificent works of art which various religions accumulated over many centuries.

Such is the immutable Law of Karma.

And talking of kindergarten brings me to the subject of John. John, the baby born in my 'absence' who was now 40 years old. I've never seen my 40-year-old grandson; or, at the very least, my 40-year-old grand nephew.

How come some of us age and others don't?

For some reason only now I've been told about his 'arrival' on our scene. I've already seen both Mavis and Jerry, yet no mention has been made of John. Admittedly he spent his time outside the sanctuary, outside the villa grounds, but still, surely, they should have mentioned something. After all, wasn't I the maternal grandfather? Maternal granduncle at the very least? Or something like that? After all, I had adopted Mavis as my very own.

Only then I remembered that it was I who'd stayed in my study for weeks at a time, not even coming out for meals. Perhaps it was my fault. I have been completely consumed by the commission Mama had given me. Still, it hurt.

Mavis had been pregnant during my 'first awakening'. I must have "gone to sleep", again, before she'd given birth. Hence, I couldn't have been around for more than nine months, in fact less. And now? I've never witnessed childbirth—not that I'd want to be present at the actual event. But I'd enjoy a cigar, if only I smoked.

But also, with both my children adopted, I've never held a newborn baby in my arms. Don't men do that? I never looked deep into their eyes to perceive the remnants of infinity sill lingering behind... Refusing to go? I never witnessed remnants of divinity before it became imprisoned in a corporal body.

Is this why newborn babies cry?

I missed that.

I missed a chance to find out for myself. Yes, yet again, I missed being a father and a grandfather. I missed having an ordinary family, like ordinary people the world over have. The world that now was mostly under water?

And today John, once again, was away on some mission of mercy. They told me that he was like that. Contrary to me, he adopted the whole kingdom.

"He is like that," Mavis told me. "He once saw a bird hurt. A tiny sparrow. He carried it with him for three days. Fed him, protected him, until it was well enough to fly off."

I was beginning to like my grand nephew, no matter how old he was.

"And you know what?" Mavis's eyes were growing larger. "That bird comes to see him whenever he's in the villa. Would you believe?"

There are many even stranger things I had to learn to believe here. John surrounded people and birds with love. He probably loved everyone he'd ever met; and every bird.

I would have liked to meet him. I did. Later on.

We met for lunch, as always, on the terrace. After we all sat down and Mavis poured Sangria into all the glasses, perhaps for the first time ever Tom was the first to speak.

"The world is drunk," he looked around. "Smashed," he added. "Inebriated," he said just to make sure that we all got the point.

He made this announcement over the rim his glass only half-full after the first 'sip'. "Cheers," he added raising his glass for the second time. I think we all got the point.

His glass was empty. Perhaps this accounted for the absence of the *perron* carafes. Some of us may have tended to take slightly too long swigs from them for our own good. Apparently, so did the 'world'.

Yet, this wasn't like Tom. He never drank wine, not even Sangria, until after he first ate something. Not that a glass of wine could have any effect on his bulk.

"I just finished putting together my daily report. It's in the main hall on the table, as always," he continued looking around, making sure everybody heard him. Obviously, there was something very special about this report, at least in his opinion.

The Main Hall round table was our news centre for the

distribution of news not just for us, but also for all the guests who frequented our villa. We were the only source of news for the immediate vicinity. Later, those who came by would pass it on through the old-fashioned grapevine. Some of the islanders still had distant relatives scattered around the world. Apparently I wasn't the only one who had already read all the bulletins Tom had produced. After all, I have been commissioned to record the history of current events.

We stopped talking when Tom told us about the content of the latest news.

"It's mass hysteria," he said. "I looked it up. In the past it has been associated with slave revolts, also Salem witch trials, but those were usually local occurrences. Now we have the hundredth monkey effect which threatens to sweep the whole world."

Tom has done a lot of reading these days. He described briefly what he found out. Below are my notes:

Laurence Blair and Lyall Watson had observed the "hundredth monkey effect" in mid-1970s of the previous millennium. They both claimed that a new behaviour could spread rapidly by totally unexplained means from one group of monkeys to another, without physical contact between the groups. And now people's pathological behaviour was little more, and sometimes less, than that of monkeys. Mass hysteria had spread across continents, old and new, throughout the world. Such symptoms were usually assigned to moral panic. People may have suddenly realized how low they'd fallen, but were helpless to pull themselves up by their own bootstraps.

"I suppose, my friends, this is where we come in…"

Mama, looking regal in her long blue dress, a tiny diamond tiara holding down her long jet-black hair, was celebrating the end of physical turmoil to which the Cyclades had been recently subjected.

"It's all over," she assured us before Tom came and ruined all the fun. "It is time to celebrate."

Yet now, following Tom's announcement, for the first time ever I detected a touch of hesitancy in Mama's voice. I recalled her statement that we can only predict probability, not certainty. It seems that even Mama has been caught by surprise.

"The whole world..." she whispered. There was pain in her voice.

"They said it has been caused by fear, and unmanageable emotional distress..." Tom added, this time without a trace of humour.

The sanguine Saturnalia was over.

"The King is dead, and there's no king to take over," Mavis whispered. There was an old English saying: "The king is dead, God save the king". Now, there was no monarchy in England either.

That left the remaining masses, still some five billion of them, without guidance, without anyone telling them what to do, how to earn their keep, how to feed their children. Those close to farmlands survived. The others were close to starvation. Suburban gardens, deserted parks and robbery were their only sources of sustenance. Not much to live on. And, on the top of that, no future. Yet they continued to breed, like animals. Perhaps now they, the people, were very little more than animals. At least the animals were not starving, those that hadn't been eaten.

Yet, like all good things, such lackadaisical existence had to come to an end. Thousands more died from diseases, from swallowing inedible items that destroyed their digestive systems, or from elements, which completely lost their predictability in various parts of he world. People were beginning to realize that things cannot continue in their present form. Yet, generations of abuse of their gray cells by the rich, by the oligarchs, and by religions, left them helpless.

It was then that the Sanctuary in Peru reported the first signs of hysteria. This was followed by reports from other parts of the world. It was like the "hundredth monkey syndrome" that makes people react in a similar manner, regardless of how far apart they find themselves from each other.

Yet there was even more.

To cut the story short, people have learned to ferment almost anything that grew in the wild and distilled alcohol from it. Some of their concoctions were poisonous but most of them simply exacerbated their already prevailing mental stupor. Millions upon millions of people got drunk. Simultaneously. Almost everywhere.

We all looked at Mama, who remained motionless, silent, as though descending into a trance.

I also sat, silent, helpless. There was no such thing as a medical profession. Frankly, nor any other profession. If there were one or two shamans, here and there, they would hardly be in a position to help people succumbing to the malaise in such numbers. The pharmaceutical conglomerates were all gone. There was no one who could possibly produce a pill or any substance that would negate the effects of mass hysteria; or help to reduce alcoholism, for that matter, although the latter was merely a symptom of the first. A deadly symptom.

Mama remained motionless.

When Mama was that still, none of us dared to move. Not even Papa, and he knew best what Mama was doing. I made an effort to read his mind.

...she is reaching back... generations... the origins...

That's all I got. Mama was searching for an antidote. From the corner of my eye I saw Tom slipping away from his chair and tiptoeing back towards the villa. Whatever Mama was doing, he too had a job to do. Mama kept in touch with the heads of sanctuaries by her own, inimitable, subliminal means. Tom had to keep in touch with the whole crazy, chaotic, hysterical world in a more pragmatic, down to earth way. The gods had little interest in worldly affairs. They were concerned with the state of men's consciousness, not their physical wellbeing. He also had to make sure that the news traveled throughout all the sanctuaries. Only they had the means to keep in touch.

Some minutes later we all followed him, each to his and her particular duties. Only Papa remained at Mama's side. He'd know what to do. He knew Mama and her needs.

I sat down at my computer. Ambrosia came with me, uncertain what to do. Usually she was the strong one, but on that day, perhaps for the first time, she looked worried. I remembered way back when the CIA or some other ungodly characters were stealing her research papers on QT. She wasn't nervous then. Angry, but not nervous. She wasn't worried when supposedly some other low life had been supposedly threatening both her and my lives. She was always too busy looking for solutions to worry. But this was different. This concerned the whole world.

For some reason I felt exhausted. I got up and we both sat on the small settee facing the lawn and the hedge labyrinth at the back of the villa. She leaned her head on my shoulder. I thought she was about to take a nap.

"What do you think she'll do, Sy?" She sounded worried. "I never saw Mama quite so still. It was… it was…"

She couldn't finish the sentence. I read it in her mind.

…it was almost as if she died… as if she was not here any more…

There was little I could say to consol her. We sat, quietly, saying nothing, trying to send positive thoughts towards Mama. To surround her with light. She probably needed all the help she could get, only we had no idea how to help her.

The whole world...

How do you save the whole world? And she had only days, perhaps hours to do so. To find a solution. People were dying all the time. The sanctuaries reported that they only spotted the symptoms when people had already produced masses of alcohol. Must have been barrels of it. Everywhere, like a hundred monkeys multiplied by a million. According to Tom, confirmations were still coming from the other side of the globe. We didn't even know how that side was called now. Everything has changed.

Ambrosia put her fingers on my temples and moved them in circular motions. Moments later, all was still.

I came to some hours later. Tom knew that my study faced the lawn on the garden side, away from the terrace. As I looked out, I saw Tom waving his arms. He looked frantic. I nudged Ambrosia who found solace next to me. She was also asleep; her face relaxed looking almost like a child's. An induced sleep, nevertheless restful. Perhaps more so.

I signaled Tom that we were coming down and pulled Ambrosia to come with me. On the way out, I passed by the window overlooking the terrace at the front of the house. Mama was still out there. Seemingly she hasn't moved since we left the table. Nor had Papa. They looked like two people linked into a singularity born of a trance. I've never seen them like this. I wouldn't dare to disturb them.

When we came out on the lawn, we had to calm Tom down. He was waving his arms, apparently going frantic. And then I froze. Tom was hysterical. When a man Tom's size goes frantic, it is not a safe place to be around. Ambrosia held on to my arms or I would have sat on the grass, there and then.

Not the hundredth monkey, I thought. My legs were still going weak. Surely, the malaise couldn't have reach Milos as well. And Tom...

"I'm all right," he murmured, apparently trying to catch his breath. His mouth twisted in a strange grin that hardly resembled a smile. Tom was always a mountain of stability, of reliability and peace. In a way, his size alone commanded that.

"It's just w-what they are s-saying..." he blurted out at last, haltingly. "And nothing came through on the video... nothing at all?"

This last sounded like a question, expecting us to confirm or deny his statement. Tom was definitely overwrought. Like an enormous babe with nowhere to go.

"Sit down, Tom," Ambrosia commanded. "Right here, on the grass.

To illustrate this complex request she lowered herself and pulled her legs under her skirt. I followed suit. Tom, unwillingly, joined us. He was too exited to sit down.

"Now tell us, slowly, what happened."

For a change Tom was speechless. His mouth opened and closed in quick succession, probably looking for the right words. I hoped to God this wasn't really hysteria taking hold.

...no Simon... he is all right...

This reached me in silence from Ambrosia. Obviously, there was no one else here.

I took a deep breath. Thank heaven for little mercies.

At long last Tom swallowed and opened his mouth without closing it again before he uttered a word.

"I got it from seven sanctuaries. Peru, Tibet, Alaska..."

"Never mind, Tom. We believe you. Just tell us what you got."

His eyes got larger as he faced Ambrosia. He crossed himself as if entering a church and continued in a shaking voice. "It was Her," he said at last. "Our Lady," he repeated. "She was there, everywhere, all over the world, in Peru, Tibet, Ala..." his voice cracked again.

And then to my amazement, with apparent

embarrassment, he crossed himself, again, touching his forehead and both shoulders with the extended fingers of his right hand. He did it three times, rather as American footballers had done ages ago when entering or leaving the arena. I mean the playing field.

Tom's behaviour was strange to say the least. In all the years in Montreal he'd never expressed any desire to go to church, let alone any Catholic church, to pray or express his allegiance to the cult of Virgin Mary. And now this? It didn't make any sense. The reputed vision of Our Lady in different parts of the world must have made a powerful impression on him.

So some people had a vision. Others... I wondered if others merely reported the same image due to the hundredth monkey syndrome. Could that be possible? If sufficient number of people had the same vision, as they did in Fatima, would others follow suit?

I was getting excited. I wanted to share my idea with Ambrosia. She shushed me.

"Tell us more," she asked Tom.

"Well, it began in Peru. Then, according to the broadcasts I picked up, it spread all over. Each time I picked up any radio waves from any sanctuary the same news were broadcast. As I was saying, the world over.

"And just why did they imagine it was, ah, Our Lady?"

"Some remembered Fatima, others Lourdes, still others La Salette. You know? A tall lady in a blue dress, with a diamond tiara on her dark hair... And golden slippers, they said. Standing on an Earthlike globe in golden slippers. It had to be..." And there he stopped.

I had no idea how to react to Tom's announcement. The story sounded too absurd to be true. Perhaps Tom was overworked, or someone was playing tricks on him. I glanced at Ambro. Her face showed no expression, and Tom sounded pretty serious.

I looked at my watch. It was supper-time. I waved Tom

to come with us. He declined.

"Must go back…" he pointed behind him. He sounded in control now.

We got up without a word and walked around the house to the terrace. Mama and Papa were still there, motionless. I took Mavis and Jerry aside and told them what had happened.

"They saw images of Madonna. Everywhere. It was like Fatima and Lourdes and a dozen other places, happening simultaneously. All sanctuaries reported the same thing," I told them.

Jerry was flabbergasted; Mavis took it without a word. She looked almost as if she knew. She was a very strange niece of mine. Very strange indeed. Then we all waited some distance from the table.

Only minutes later Mama opened her eyes and smiled at us, as we all stood in silence, not to disturb her. Papa took a deep breath.

"What must one do around here to get some supper?" she asked. This was the old Mama speaking. With her old, gently smile.

 Mavis and Jerry ran to the house to bring the stuff that has already been prepared. We now had a cook and an assistant, who insisted that working here, at the villa, was a privilege and an honour. Papa was a very important person, they knew. We all continued to chip in of course. And there were other volunteers in and around the house, of course. It seemed that people just like being close to where Mama lived.

We ate in silence. Parenthetically, I noticed that one chair next to Mavis's was again empty. I guessed who's it was. For whatever reason, nobody wanted to raise the subject of hysteria, monkeys or even alcohol, although Papa did raise the toast to the Kingdom of Milos.

"May it rule over us in wealth and serenity."

That sounded good enough for me.

Papa outlined plans to convert the Kingdom into a center for all men of good will as a permanent sanctuary. There were other proposals regarding making the smallest kingdom on Earth self-sufficient.

We all liked the idea. There was absolutely no reason why it couldn't be. The first test carried out showed that most of the land recovered from the Aegean was arable, but only for new species of plants, similar to old mangroves that turned out to be edible. With a little work it would be suitable for planting. It was quite rich, and relatively free of salt. It just needed turning over.

The arguments and counter arguments went on for quite a while. No one was in a hurry. What Tom had told us had a calming effect, though we weren't quite sure why.

Finally we decided that an early night would do us all good. We were about to get up when music reached us from the Main Hall. Athena must have slipped away from the table when we were having a heated discussion about the future of Milos.

The doors to the Hall were wide open. The music was soft, somewhere between piano and pianissimo. Athena had a very gentle touch.

I recognized the melody. My daughter was playing Shubert's Ave Maria. When she finished, she floated down the steps in her multihued chiffon, down to the terrace, seemingly hardly touching the ground, and threw here arms around Mama's neck.

"That was for you, Grandma. Just for you."

...I hope it will work... darling...

...I know it will... Grandma... I know it will...

For once I managed to catch the wisp of their non-verbal exchange. They were very close those two—as would be a real grandmother and granddaughter.

And then, a funny thing happened. A sparrow alit on the back of John's empty chair. Soon two more came and all three chirped their tiny throats off. I was beginning to guess.

It was the welcoming committee. We all turned to the ever-open gate. There, walking slowly was a man in a long brown coat, or something between a coat and a robe.

I got up and hurried down the steps to meet my grand nephew.

"They should have called you Francis," I said. "He also loved birds, you know?"

I realized it was a funny way to greet a grand nephew I have never seen. It was too late. We embraced like two old friends.

"He was nice, wasn't he," John replied and started laughing. As we approached the table the sparrows sang one last trio and flew off.

Since, I found that John spent a lot of time laughing. In fact, most of the time. The others already left the table to allow John and me to get acquainted. Only Mama stayed behind. Apparently she had a soft spot for John.

After about two hours we got up to say good night and made for our bedrooms. As I turned to go, I looked back at Mama. She wore a blue dress and her hair was held in place with a tiny diamond tiara.

I looked down at her feet. She was wearing yellow slippers that people must have seen as golden. Yet... there was no globe beneath her feet. Just beautiful white Milos marble.

***

10
Athena

Nobody noticed when Athena had left the table. She often managed to slip away without being seen. As in the distant past Mavis, now Athena was becoming her esoteric double. She seemed to specialize in invisibility, or at least in not being seen. This contrasted strongly with her past behaviour, when she danced as though to attract attention. Now she floated like a butterfly moving from flower to flower, or a ballerina in an enchanted forest.

But she remained as beautiful as ever.

And her music remained enchanting. Since that wonderful day when Mama bought for her a surprise birthday piano, and she played her own arrangement of "happy birthday" which she made up on the spot, she'd composed dozens of pieces, each as joyful as the first. But at her Tuesday concerts, attended by hundreds of people who often came and stayed overnight, sleeping on the grass, she liked to improvise. After playing a few well-known pieces that she's heard through her miPad, she'd improvise on any subject to do with nature. She played joyful fantasias to spring, and quiet sonorous adagios to honour the doldrums of summer. On special requests thunder and lightening struck the air over the lawn from a cloudless sky. And once or twice she played reminiscences of her winters in Canada, where pristine flakes descended on all who listened to her impromptu variations.

She loved to improvise, to hear the music within her and then to share it with others. In that sense, she was a prolific giver.

But there were consequences.

While Mavis grew in confidence and self-expression, asserting her presence, Athena retreated into her inner personality, as though her real world wasn't here at all.

She was a strange one.

Strange… yet the moment you saw her, she had the power to sweep you off your feet, inveigle you with her music, sometimes by just humming a song, and pull you into her enchanted world that made you forget what you were doing. The Sirens in Homer's Odyssey came to mind. Even knowing her insidious yet benevolent charms, they were nearly impossible to resist.

And then it happened. If I were a religious person I could only describe it as a miracle. I was sitting in my study having just finished my notes of the latest developments resulting from visions people had all over the world, when I felt a presence. I swiveled my chair to see Athena standing behind me.

"Hi Papa," she smiled at me.

Her lips moved but I didn't exactly hear her words. I heard her inside my head, as if she was communicating telepathically.

"The Gate is open," she said next, again silently yet clearly as a bell.

"The gate?" I looked at her wondering if this was some sort of a joke. The only gate we had was the main entry to the villa grounds, which hasn't closed since I first came here. Ages ago.

"No, Papa, the Gate."

For some reason I visualized the word Gate with a capital G. Athena must have been playing tricks on me. She did so in the past, back in Montreal, but those were childish games. Not like this at all.

I decided to play along.

"And just where does this "Gate" lead, Little One".

As in Papa's eye Ambrosia was *Mikro Koritsi*, namely a Little Girl, I reserved Little One for Athena. She seemed to like it. Her next answer made me sit up. Just a little, but I decided that there was more to it than just a game.

"Home," she said. And then as if to make sure I understood she repeated, "Home, Papa."

Just then I also realized that she never called me papa. I was always dad, with or without a capital 'D'. And now, for some reason it was Papa. I was still pondering this new revelation when she whispered another word.

"Come," she said.

"Come where, Little…"

But she was already gone. Was she playing tricks on me? Am I imagining things? Surely this had nothing to do with the monkey business. They were imagining things but I spent half my life unveiling what was thought to be religious mysteries to prove that there are no religious mysteries.

Or it could be that I was going just a little mad…

For quite a while I have been rubbing shoulders with people who were head and shoulders above my present evolutionary level. I have been told that what appeared to be magic today would turn out to be science tomorrow. It is an old adage, but they were proving it. OBE, telepathy, bilocation, space and even time travel… all have already happened to me. It is hard to dismiss or deny what one has experienced oneself.

Yet I was still a beginner.

Unfortunately, speaking for myself, my faith in science was not much higher than in religion. Except for Ambrosia's science but, let's face it, she was something else. As was her science.

I wondered what she'd say about what just took place.

I didn't have to wait long.

A quiet knock on the door was just politeness. My door

was always open, to everybody. But my wife never failed to knock, gently, in case I was taking a nap, I suppose. It did happen once, actually, and she didn't wake me up, although she did spend the next three days calling my study my bedroom.

"Where shall we sleep tonight?" she'd ask me, with a straight face.

Ambrosia came in with a broad smile.

"You called, Master?" she bowed low.

I ignored that. "Athena just left," I announced without any preambles.

"That's funny, she and I have just been taking..." There was a mischievous expression on her gorgeous face. Those full lips always drove me to distraction. I could never be angry with her when I was looking at her. Although, right now, I was fairly close to it.

"You were, were you?" I replied in kind.

Ambrosia looked left and right, peeked under my desk.

"Well, she's certainly not here," she concluded in a very serious voice.

Obviously, by some nook or crook, she was onto Athena's antics, if such they were. I kept quiet and waited for my wife to enlighten me.

"She was giving you a bit of Father Pio," Ambrosia said, studying my face for my reaction.

"I suspected as much," I replied.

"You are not a very good liar, my husband."

For a little while there was a slightly embarrassing silence. Then I swallowed and asked contritely if she could explain. I even added, please, at the end.

I didn't have to ask twice.

"Your daughter was trying to help you to visualize what you still refer to, in your mind, as Father Pio's technique. She did it by demonstrating and telling you that the method is always available to you and to everyone who wishes to use it."

"…the Gate is open," I murmured.

"Precisely," Ambrosia nodded. "All you need is to walk through it."

"Don't you think if it was that simple everybody would do it?"

"Almost everybody does, only they do it in their dreams."

"So it's all lucid dreaming?" Lucid dreaming was a gateway to OBE techniques.

"Not quite, but the principles are the same. What changes is the intent."

"That's it?" I couldn't quite believe it.

"Well, that and commitment. The slightest doubt will whisk you right back into your body. Your physical body, that is. The other body remains always there, until you bring it out, so to speak."

Now, once again, I was getting confused. She sensed that.

"Simon, each reality needs a means through which to express itself. The physical, emotional, mental, and what is referred to as spiritual, which is little more than individualized pure consciousness. Otherwise all those realities would exist but no one would be aware of them. Wouldn't make much sense, would it?"

A scientific mind had to make sense of everything. For once I was grateful. And apparently my daughter, my sweet Athena knew all that. And as the inner turmoil that fulminated within me was impossible to hide from more advanced people, Athena became aware of it and tried to help.

…in some areas… she knows more than I do… this came over on the inner, and I found it a little hard to believe.

"The only difference is, Simon, that I have a trained mind in physics and mathematics. The latter gave me the ability to think in sequential patterns, in which events follow each other in a logical way. Otherwise I'd be talking in religious lingo, using symbols to represent events which are not part of our everyday reality."

I took all that with *bona fide* gratitude. But something still bothered me.

"What I don't get is..." I had to put my thoughts together, "...is how on earth, or on whatever is out there, can we create bodies that can be sustained here, in the phenomenal reality."

"Oh, that's the least of our problems," she laughed with genuine amusement. "Here, on Earth, you are not in the least bit bothered by the scientific fact that you inhabit and sustain a body that consists of almost exclusively empty space. Yet there, where you have an infinite number of photons at your disposal, you think it's harder to put them together into a pattern."

She looked at me, as though still disbelieving my inherent obtuseness. I was beginning to feel like a congenital idiot.

"But... but..."

"But don't worry, darling. You don't have to do it. It's all done by your subconscious mind, which has billions of years experience of just how to do it. Yes, sweetheart, billions upon billions of years..."

If that was supposed to cheer me up, it didn't. Not yet. Not until she suggested that we try to relax and generate alpha brainwaves. I had nothing to lose, and anyway, I really needed a rest from these concepts. My head was beginning to pulsate from overload.

"So it's possible..."

For the first time she interrupted me. "Perhaps I should have mentioned that there are neutrinos, that fill the gap between the two realities. But that happens automatically. You don't have to worry about it."

Thank heaven I didn't have to worry about something!

We sat on the settee and I, for one, closed my eyes.

"Hi Papa, I'm glad you came."

Athena was sitting in the middle of the lawn, surrounded by a sea of flowers. Even grass seemed to be in full bloom. Most unusual, I thought. But certainly beautiful. I was glad that my daughter surrounded herself with beauty.

"Isn't she clever?" Ambrosia asked, her voice filled with admiration. "She created all these by herself. I've never seen grass in bloom, have you?"

"No darling, I haven't. But somehow it looks good all around her."

It did. Athena herself looked like a beautiful rose, her smile lighting up the whole place.

I looked around me. "Just where are we?" I asked.

"It's her place," Ambrosia replied. "Ask her."

Before I could ask, I found myself sitting on my settee back in my study, Ambrosia looking at me with a slightly worried expression.

"That will be enough for the first time." Her smile lit up the room, matching Athena's, although Athena was nowhere to be seen.

"What happened?" I asked, with my usual lack of perspicacity.

"You did a Father Pio," she answered, smiling.

"You mean we OBE'd, together?"

"No, we can't do that together. We each create our own inner realities. You bilocated with me to the other side of Milos, the south side, where Athena has her private garden. Or it may have been Athena's and Mavis's."

"With blooming grass?"

"Beargrass is a member of lily family. It is a tall, sensuous wildflower. According to Athena, its stalks can reach five feet. Unfortunately they are said to bloom only once every five to seven years. Athena was lucky she found them. That is, by the way, why she goes there. Bilocating, of course. She pops over to see them two or three times each day."

Gosh, I had a lot to learn…

"Don't our goats eat them up?"

I had to ask a down to earth question. Something real, tangible. Ordinary. Sane?

"Well, bears don't eat beargrass, which is just as well since we don't have any bears around. But, Athena told me, bighorn sheep and elk eat the flowers and our goats nibble on the leaves." Then her eyes grew misty. "Athena tells me that to walk amid those tall, luxurious flowers is an unforgettable experience. I did it only once but Athena keeps coming here for more."

And who could blame her?

"And she does it by bilocating? Always?"

"A walk would take more then two hours each way…"

That made sense, if you know how to do it.

"You did it?" Ambrosia showed genuine surprise.

Again she read my thoughts. As for the trip, it still seemed more like a dream than reality. My reality.

"Ask Athena if she saw you there, even as you've seen me. And then tell me how three people could experience exactly the same dream at exactly the same time."

She had me stumped. I suddenly realized that I bilocated without even knowing it. Ambrosia must have relaxed me to a degree in which I was in no position to disbelieve it. We did tricks like that with hypnosis. I read some years ago that even under self-imposed hypnosis a man operated on his own appendix without feeling any pain. Things were beginning, just beginning, to fall into place. I wasn't crazy. Things really happened. Inexplicable things. Things, which until a few minutes ago I considered to be interesting myths.

There was one other thing that made me wonder if I lived in a real world. Just before Athena's garden disappeared from my awareness, I had a strange vision. I could have sworn that I saw Mavis sitting there, among the five-foot tall blades of beargrass, being virtually invisible. What I really saw, or thought I saw, was her smile. Perhaps it was also her secret garden. Perhaps that was a place where people went to dream amongst the wonders of nature. Perhaps I also would learn, one day, to hide amongst the gently swaying blades of grass.

When I found myself back my study, a single phrase from my Jesuits' days kept nagging at the periphery of my awareness. Something that Ambrosia had said about the slightest doubt... I couldn't catch it, and then, suddenly, it became clear.

"...if ye have faith as a grain of mustard seed, ye shall say unto this mountain, remove hence to yonder place; and it shall remove..."

Or to your body... and you'll find yourself in an enchanted garden...

I needed air. I needed air to fill my human, physical, very ordinary lungs. I took Ambrosia by the arm and led her to the back lawn. I didn't want company, other than Ambro's. No such luck. Athena was sitting next to bougainvilleas, which threatened to rise about the roof if not overrun the whole house. A sea of red against the white walls of the villa.

As we approached, Athena burst out laughing.

"What so funny? I asked innocently.

"Amadeus was telling me a funny story."

Amadeus was nowhere to been seen. Apparently my children were so close that they were as one even when far apart. I wasn't sure that thought made sense, but it came to my mind anyway.

"And you're just lazing around?"

"Come on, Dad. I've just given him the Alleluia chorus for his Requiem."

"To Amadeus? I didn't know he could compose too."

"He can't. The other Amadeus. Wolfgang. He was so miserable writing Requiem that he just couldn't snap out of it to write something joyful. He's all right now."

"Correct me but didn't Wolfgang Amadeus Mozart die

some centuries ago?"

"Dad! No one ever dies. We just translate to a different reality. And as for time, you know that it is imaginary? We only use it…"

"…to stop all things happening all at once."

"Right."

And then I had an idea. "Talking of nonexistent time. When did you last visit your beargrass?"

"Are you being silly, Dad? You were there, minutes ago." She turned towards Ambrosia, a worried look on her face.

My wife smiled. *…it is all right… he is just testing…*

Athena nodded and relaxed. "So how did you like my private little garden, Dad?"

"I loved it, Little One. I just loved it," I assured her. Surely, I thought, why does she ask when she can read my thoughts?"

"She's polite, darling. We all love you, you know?"

I knew. On the other hand, I wondered what happened to Papa. It seemed that in this reality I was 'dad'. Elsewhere, I'd take whatever I could get.

And then, politeness notwithstanding, the two favourite women in my life started laughing. I gave up on my pride and joined them. I had little to lose.

I needed a day or two of sanity. My type of sanity. Ordinary, everyday, uneventful, even boring sanity. I needed sanity that had nothing to do with paranormal, or esoteric, or even with religion, which for many years filled most of my time. I wondered if McGill University would ever open its doors again. If people would have enough time to study, instead of just trying to rebuild the civilization they'd lost, let alone find enough to eat.

I wanted to walk the beach, to feel sand under my bare feet. There was a slight problem. The beach was some 3000 meters below us. Way down. There wasn't even a path that would take us there. Not yet.

"Papa has some parachutes," I heard behind me. "We could jump?"

Dear Ambrosia. She'd actually jump down the mountain just to let me get my feet wet.

"There is only one little problem. How would we get back?" I mused half aloud.

"Antigrav," she said. "We could test my antigravity gizmo. I don't have a name for it yet."

She has been working on it for some time. She has been working on many things for some time. She spent 90% of her time in her lab. We had beautiful views, amazing weather, glorious flowers around, and she'd spent most of her time in the basement Papa has built for her. To make her safe, he'd said. Not from the 'ungodly' but from electronic noise which some years ago filled the air to overflowing.

I often suspected that apart from food and sleep, she only came out from her den to baby me in my juvenile tantrums. Hardly juvenile though. If time had any meaning at all any more, then I've been born around 100 years ago. Perhaps time really was just imaginary. Perhaps everything was.

"I'm serious," she assured me. "Only it wasn't tested yet." She sounded hopeful and apprehensive at the same time.

"So who's jumping first?" I asked.

"We could test it right here, on the lawn."

"You mean bouncing up and down?"

"Well, yes, I suppose so."

I looked at her, making sure that she was being serious.

"I couldn't test it yet," she confessed.

"Why?" My wife very seldom used the word 'couldn't'.

"Well, you see, darling, I don't know how far I'd rise if I switched it on. I might end up in orbit..."

This announcement produced extended silence. A moment ago I wanted something ordinary; something everyday, even boring. And then my wife came into the picture. Wasn't I lucky?

"Couldn't we test it on some object? Something we wouldn't be sorry to lose?"

"I've only got one prototype." Evidently she was not ready for testing yet.

Well, so that was that. No swimming in the sea today. No wet sand under my feet. Nothing ordinary would happen today.

...you could tie it down with strong ropes...

Amadeus much preferred subliminal communication. As we turned we saw him leaning out from an open window of the upper story where his room was. He must have been listening for some time.

"Don't lean out so much," Ambrosia waved him back.

"Would ropes do?" I asked.

"I suppose so. It's funny how the most simple things escape me," she mused aloud.

"You scientists are all the same," I declared. "If it isn't really complicated and incomprehensible then you don't believe it really exists."

She smiled, but I knew that she was weighing Amadeus's idea in her mind. I wondered where we'd get enough rope to tie down whatever she'd use for the test run. Test rise? Whatever.

Just then Amadeus came out of the house, a length of thick rope slang over his shoulder. He had a smug expression on his face. I prepared this warp for the boat I was going to take out before Milos jumped up a few thousand meters. He threw the rope on the ground at Ambrosia's feet.

"Your wish in my command, Ma," he bowed deeply.

Ambrosia smiled but she still looked preoccupied.

The thing's darn heavy," he said. "You might try tying one end to something and sending the other end into space. Or orbit," he added, a smirk on his handsome feature.

He was quite a lad, I thought. Quite a lad.

We decided to try it all bright and early tomorrow.

That evening I tried to sort out the problem of time, or more precisely of the aging of various members of our family and some 200-300 original residents who remained on the island.

This business of time really got on my nerves. I knew that first time, I've been 'under' for more or less ten years. On that first 'awakening', I discovered that some people have aged normally, in fact quite substantially—that went for the majority of 'normal' people, as I referred to those who were outside our immediate circle—compared to Mama's special invited guests. Among those guests, not that I've seen all of them, I did not detect any sign of aging, although ten years was little to go by.

Others aged just a little, like Papa, and to a lesser degree Tom and Jerry, though in their case it was hardly noticeable. Their visible aging was limited to some slight touches of gray at the temples, which could be seen on many people of their age, whatever that was, before the present temporal cavalcade. Papa, of course, alternated between red, black and gray hair, depending on the mood of the day. Over time, I've met all three disguises, and I'd never been sure which was real. For Papa, a no-nonsense businessman, this was, in my eyes, completely out of character. Still, Papa was Papa. Perhaps this was his only diversion?

As for Tom and Jerry, I already knew that they had spent most of their time in 'limbo', which reputedly is a sort of induced coma, which slows down biological functions to near zero, and also stops emotional and mental activities. That is hardly surprising if we consider that in relation to our potential, our brain is functioning at somewhere between very slow, and hardly at all.

All this I learned mostly by observation but also by certain comments made by the select few who didn't seem to age at all.

Contrary to all of the above, my children Athena and

Amadeus seemed to have progressed into the stage of young adulthood, but as they have been quite incredibly precocious children before my ten-year 'sleep', I was aware only of their physical maturity. The same applied to Mavis, who changed incredibly not only in physical terms but also in the mental acuity and character. From a frightened teenager she matured into a self-assured young woman.

All of the above I could tolerate taking into account my relatively short 'absence'. What got under my gander was my second awakening. This time I've been told, and I had no real means of checking other than trying to find the date on the semi-defunct Internet. It confirmed that some 40 years had passed, although I also had no way of checking if the date was correct. For all I knew, some other gods in some other sanctuaries may have fiddled with the data for reasons to which I was not privy.

The sole exception to the rule was Mavis and Jerry's son, who looked somewhere between 30 and 40, and confessed to being around forty…

"But, it doesn't really matter, Uncle, does it?"

Apparently he was already poisoned by the lackadaisical approach to time by my betters.

And here is the punch line. Whatever I surmised about all other people after my first hibernation, applied equally to my second stint in the no man's land; in the no man's reality. In a ponderous, frequently or periodically half-interrupted coma. I hoped that Mama or even my wife would enlighten me as to what was going on, without my having to wait till my next reincarnation into a smarter body.

After prodding Ambrosia repeatedly, she made a statement that was supposed to explain it all.

"We are protecting your physical body, darling, to make sure that you reach the white horse."

After that she wouldn't discuss the matter any further.

***

11
Papa's Parliament

Papa **was reaching a state** of frustration most unbecoming to a god. He fidgeted at the dinner table, interrupted Tom when he was giving us the latest news, and appeared to have lost his grandfatherly tolerance for people around him. It was obvious that he was a man of action, of vigorous action, and extended periods of inactivity was destroying his equanimity.

Papa was angry.

It was also evident that he was hurting. He had no way of knowing that the almost ten years of work he'd put in on Corfu was not being wasted. Ten years which by normal, human standards had run their course almost 40 years ago. Yet, for Papa, it all felt as though it happened just yesterday.

He was determined to make sure that people wouldn't fall into the trappings of power, which destroyed his previous, ancient attempts at installing a sense of liberation, when as Paul he had tried to inspire a reconnection of people to their heritage. The heritage of immortality, of virtual omnipotence, all derived from absolute faith in one's own abilities.

"Not all people are equal," he announced when 'young' John complained that he couldn't do something or other. "We all have our particular, individual talents, and our job is to

contribute to the Universe in our particular expertise," he
assured his new great-grandson. A 'new' great-grandson that
was nearly 40 years old.

As Papa looked at me I could almost hear him saying:
"I'm sitting here not doing my job..."

John was convinced that given enough love and
compassion, all would be well.

"Action!" Papa stormed at John's serene assurances.
"We are here to do things. To act. To create. To build. To use
our talents to the full." Day by day, Papa was becoming more
excited.

"Couldn't you try to organize something on Milos? Right
here?" For once Mama's calm voice had an adverse effect on
Papa.

"Here? Here? Here they have you, and Ambrosia, and
Tom and Jerry, and... There? There they had only me. Just
me. And now they have no one. No one at all..." his
thunderous voice died down to a mere whisper.

And then news started pouring in.

Tom's eyes got bleary. He spent almost 16 hours a day
scouring the ethers for the details of latest events. It seemed
that changes were accelerating. Not in global upheavals, but
in peoples' actions seemingly motivated by emotional
outbursts.

For me, writing this part of history was the hardest. I
owed Papa a great deal. In a way I owed him my wife. I most
certainly owed him my penthouse in Montreal, the security
provided by Tom and Jerry, and indirectly through his wife,
Mama, the wonder that my children provided. That's a debt
of gratitude that could not really be discharged. And now?
Now I was supposed to write about his emotional outbursts?

Shame on me, I thought. Shame on me.

And yet, Papa himself had said that we are all given a
particular talent that we are supposed to explore. Perhaps I
went through so many periods of emotional turmoil that I

used up my allotted portion, and now, at long last, I could make notes on events in a placid, unbiased, dispassionate fashion.

Only history would show.

At this last reflection I heard a chuckle behind me. It was Amadeus who came to ask me if I was ready to try Ambrosia's antigravity gizmo.

"Sorry, Dad, but you are writing history and you said that only history will show... I found it a bit funny." He still tried to stifle a deep-throated chuckle.

I wondered how long he was standing there peeping into my thoughts.

"It's only because I learn so much, Dad. You don't seem to realize what an incredibly organized mind you have..."

I didn't know if he was serious or attempting flattery to make up for his peeping, so I decided to take his complement in good faith.

"With children as smart as you and Athena I have little choice," I replied in kind. This time we laughed together.

Ambrosia was waiting for us outside. In her left hand she was holding her mini-computer, no larger than a fairly thick mobile phone. It did not have a keyboard, but I noticed a number of buttons and some sort of sliding scale on one side. The thick rope, Amadeus's contribution to the experiment, was lying coiled on the grass. Next to it was a black plastic bag.

"It's exactly one hundred kilos. For you, Simon, that's around 220 pounds, or 'lbs' as you call them." Ambrosia always pulled my leg about my British imperial preferences. "The weight of a good, hefty man," she added, looking at her son with undisguised pride.

"You mean I can't go first?" Amadeus pulled a crestfallen face.

"All in good time," my wife replied. "All in good time... Now attach the end of this rope to the bag, make sure it's well tied."

She left Amadeus and me the task of attachment, while she started looking for a suitable anchorage for the other end.

"Wouldn't just anything do?" I asked.

"Not if you don't want it to rise up together with he bag," she warned.

Then she looked at me with slightly worried expression on her face. "Simon, there is a tremendous difference between theoretical physics and experimental results. Some stuff that Einstein came up with had only recently been proven—many decades after his death."

...I thought you do not die... I thought...

She gave me a dirty look.

"You know very well what I mean. Now tie the other end to that rock over there," she pointed with her computer.

The rock had a nice overhang that might be just enough to attach the end of the rope. There was a problem though; the rope was too short. Amadeus picked up the 100-kilogram bag with one hand and carried it nearer the rock. I decided never to pick a fight with my son.

Five minutes later the rope was wound around the rock projection and we were ready for the first test. For the first time in my life I saw my wife nervous. Her lips were tightly closed, and the knuckles of her hands were white. I didn't know what she had to worry about. If worse came to worst, we would lose the bag, or the rope, or the rock would be sheered off. No great harm either way.

For some reason Ambrosia was delaying pressing the right button. Or sliding the notch on the scale; whichever was necessary to activate the antigravity gadget. Sorry, antigravity instrument? Amadeus and I waited expectantly. Then, at long last, she did it.

Nothing happened.

Then, very slowly, the black bag began to rise up in the air. It rose slowly—ponderously—the word unwillingly came to mind, as if it was opposing the laws of nature with a great effort.

Moments later the bag began to accelerate. Within seconds the rope was stretched to its limits. Then, with a sound of a thousand violins it snapped as if made of thin twine. The bag continued to accelerate until in no time at all it disappeared in the blue of the sky.

"I suppose what goes up must come down?" I offered. "Shouldn't we take cover?"

"Hardly. The higher it goes the smaller the gravitational pull. With the geocentric kinetic pull and the angular momentum it will soon join all the junk swirling in our upper atmosphere," Ambrosia said, frustration evident in her voice. She'd worked hard on her antigravity idea.

"... and then, slowly," she continued softly, "it's orbit will decay and it will splash into the Pacific. Only, I understand from Tom, that since the Hawaiian atomic debacle, the new crater it has formed spewed enough lava and ash to form an island at least the size of our Kingdom. Let's hope it's still unpopulated."

None of this made any sense to me. Seeing my face, Ambrosia took pity on me. "Action creates an equal and opposite reaction, Simon. I irradiated the black bag with anti-gravitons, which act as a mirror. And then I activated them. The rest happened automatically."

Ambrosia didn't look happy with the experiment. It was my turn to cheer her up. I tried to change the subject. Or at least redirect the point of interest.

"How would Tom know? Did he take Papa's jet and fly over the crater?" I thought I was being funny to cheer up my wife. She was looking positively depressed.

"Some satellites are still up there, Dad. They are holding on to their last breath, so to speak."

That hardly made things much clearer.

"So..." I began, "no swimming today?"

This unloaded the tension into an explosion of laughter.

When Amadeus laughed, everyone laughed. His roar was that contagious.

At dinner, we returned to Papa's problems. This time Mama took the bull by the horns. Papa was the bull.

"The Age of Aquarius, darling, will not repeat the mistakes of the past. At least, I hope it doesn't. Enough changes already took place to make such repetition difficult if not impossible. People will gradually find a different ladder to climb. Hopefully one that will avoid the previous errors."

Papa listened, but he didn't relax. I saw concern on Mama's face. It seemed that she was dealing with a problem that didn't have an equitable solution.

"Papa," she began again. "Democracy is a wonderful system, but it belongs to the previous age. Now people will not rule over each other, by whatever means or systems."

"But they are lost, Mama. They are lost. I know my people. They need me..." his voice trailed off.

Just then I stole a glance at Amadeus. The intensity on his face was almost frightening. I sensed that he was determined to help Papa whatever it took.

Mama was still concentrating on Papa. It was evident that he really was the love of her life. He was that rare man that never gave up, that was always trying, always willing to help total strangers.

"Papa, hierarchical world has already fallen apart. There are no nations, no political unions, no dictatorships, nor even functioning democracies. You know that?"

Slowly Papa looked up at Mama. There was emptiness in his expression—such as I have never seen. For the first time ever Papa looked lost.

"Then what am I to do, Mama... what am I to do?"

...*remember Peter*...

This was a silent response, yet there was a command there also.

...remember Peter...

At long last, Papa's face relaxed. He sat back and closed his eyes. Even as we watched, a suggestion of a smile began to soften his face. His dilemma, almost anger, was replaced by a strange, inward serenity.

I think I knew what just happened.

Mama asked Papa to go back in time. To go back to when he was Paul, organizing the early church, based on his idea of democracy. People elected administrators from their midst and called them bishops, who had considerable power to make decisions. This was going back more then two thousand years, close to the beginning of the Age of Pisces. That was the Zodiac Age of the Fish, which for some reason symbolized wisdom—a perfect amalgam of knowledge and love. Speaking for myself, I've never met a smart fish, although many managed to get away...

My mind was wandering.

Later, I imagined, the essence of the Age had been intended to apply the golden rule to find balance between science and religion. We now know that it failed. Peter didn't trust it even then. That's St. Peter, officially the first bishop of Rome.

According to Ambrosia, only just before losing his life, Paul asserted that Peter was probably right. That ultimately every single man and woman embodies infinite potential, and had to rise by his or her individual effort. One could help but not impose a system, no matter how noble the intentions. Peter knew that even then. After all, his Master, Yeshûa, later known as Jesus, never created any religion. He merely tried to clean up Mosaic teaching. Apparently, he failed in that, except in leaving a heritage through people like Peter. Paul had learned that only just before being beheaded—too late to have the knowledge firmly embedded in his subconscious. He was paying for his mistakes ever since.

"Peter..." Papa's lips formed the word. "Dear Peter, such compassion..."

Papa remembered.

"Such incredible compassion… I should have listened."

Hopefully Papa was spared the memory of horrors that the Roman Church had perpetrated over the ages. I knew. I was teaching history of religion as part of my professorship at McGill. For the first time since I came to Milos, my own memories flooded my mind. Corruption. The Church wielded virtually absolute power over it's faithful. It claimed to wield it even after its followers' supposed death, after the faithful had left their bodies. It aspired to sentence people to eternal damnation. Surely, that was the Church's greatest crime.

The Roman Church was a unique example of absolute power corrupting absolutely.

There have been many members of the Church that tried to restore balance, but the scales of the Church itself, of the organization as such, weighted heavily on the material, selfish, dictatorial and punitive side—greatly overbalancing the side of compassion. At least they left behind, what was thought at the time, immortal works of art; that, and perhaps surprisingly, a string of *bona fide* saints. Today, I suspect, we would refer to at least some of them, as gods.

Alas, nothing is immortal in this reality. Even the greatest works cast in, or chiseled out of, stone are transient. All is transient; in time, all turns into dust. After all, everything is made up of atoms, and atoms are mostly empty space. Even the pyramids of Egypt are slowly, yet inexorably reverting into sand. As of late, they are not even showing above the water.

A slow smile of understanding was replacing the frown on Papa countenance. It was all coming back to him. He knew. He remembered. He'd tried so hard to forget…

He was beginning to understand. Mama was visibly relaxing. And then, just as serenity was returning to our gathering, a strange thing happened.

Amadeus got up, his chair flying behind him, hitting the ground with impact. The noise brought Papa back from his reveries. Amadeus without a single word stormed out from the terrace. We would not see him for days.

...*Ouranos*... Papa's lips were twisted in a mirthless smile. ...*he has not changed*... ...*he has not changed at all*... That's all I heard. Later I'd learn more. Much more.

In my study I clicked on the miPad. I had to learn about Papa's subliminal words. At the time they meant nothing to me, until I remembered having been told, years ago, not to mention the name Ouranos in Amadeus's presence.

It was too late now. Papa has brought it forth to our minds.

I typed the words "Chronology of Greek Mythology". It was all there, from Atlantis forward: way more than four thousand years back, and counting.

The Internet offered mostly dates, but a pattern emerged. If reincarnations for advanced people are few and far between, spanning 1000-2000 years, then Papa may have dated back to Khronos, also known as Chronos, who was said to have brought the concept of time into human awareness. He is said to have lived around 1880 BC. He was one of the first immortals to inhabit the Earth.

Could this have been when Mama and Papa had met? In the misty past of yesteryear?

If Papa and Khronos had been responsible for the concept of time, as a means of measuring the duration of and between different events, then this ability would predate his need to be an organizer. Imagine, four thousand years and still carrying his initial traits. Talk of immortality...

Papa remained an organizer to this day!

The play is complex, and the dramatic personae had been probably mixed up by historians looking for some sort of sense in the myths presented to them.

In 1834 BC Ouranos, or Uranus, bursts onto the scene,

apparently emerging from an egg created by Khronos. Even in myths, Ouranos was quite a guy. According to ancient records, Ouranos fathered twelve sons and six daughters. Ouranos enjoyed absolute dominion over heavens, yet tried to dominate the Earth also. Apparently being in charge was important to him. It seems that things don't change that much over just a few thousand years. Amadeus still liked to do things his way, or not at all.

It was a long, long story, which doesn't concern us. What does concern us is that, allowing for reincarnation, Amadeus had a previous bellicose life on Earth, which must have left its scars on his present personality.

Enough said, all this happened before Zeus came on the scene. I am tempted to say that the rest is history, but it will only be so if anyone ever regresses in time sufficiently to verify the facts as they actually happened. I even read some notes in which Ouranos precedes Khronos. It is also possible that the pre-Zeusian gods have been disembodied entities, in the process of acquiring physical properties.

We shall probably never know.

What matters to us is that the personalities of Khronos and Ouranos, or of Papa and Amadeus, have been interlocking in the misty past, and that they share some sort of desire for dominance or cooperation. Whatever it was, they were obviously trying to join forces in their present life.

Of one thing I was certain, and that was that the story of Papa and Amadeus would continue to unfold in a manner in which none of us could expect. They were both aware of being immortals, of being gods, and I've been told that gods, good or bad, are defined by the power they wield. I hoped, even then, that the two people so dear to me would find an amicable arrangement.

I didn't notice Ambrosia standing behind me. As I leaned back, I felt a gentle touch of her hand on my shoulder.

"They are just people, darling, like you and I…"

"Perhaps like you, sweetheart, most certainly not like me," I replied, and most certainly I meant it.

She smiled her gorgeous smile.

"Your problem is that you are a professor at heart. You have to arrange all events and things to be just so. You must place them in historical order and expect them to conform to your kind of logic. But…" she swung my chair and looked into my eyes, "…but life is not like that. We are here for a reason. And the reasons manifest through our physical, emotional, and intellectual bodies. You are in the physical stage with intellectual overtones. You completely forgot about the emotional."

"Are you saying that I don't have any feelings?" I felt this was a most unfair accusation.

"No darling, I don't mean that at all. What I am saying is that you don't allow for other peoples feelings. And even people more advanced than you and I will be for millennia, for as long as they are embodied in physical envelopes, here on Earth, they have to deal with all three of their bodies."

I sat back and let that sink.

And then I had an idea. I now faced her, with the computer forgotten behind me. When I faced her without any distractions, she continued to take my breath away. I was deeply convinced that she was not 'just' a human. Nobody that perfect can be.

…*I love you too*… I heard inside my head.

"Is this what love is?" I muttered like a teenager struck by lightening.

"Love is being one."

That's all she said. Just being one. Inseparable. Indivisible.

"Isn't this what they say about our consciousness? About it being indivisible from the Omnipresent Oneness?"

"Yes, darling. It is precisely that."

And then she gave me a look of such beguiling power

that I felt sure that she must have practiced on luring Greek sailors onto the rocky coast of their island.

"Sure I did," she replied to my unspoken suspicions, "shall we go?"

Soon she transported me to heaven with very earthly overtones.

***

12
Lackadaisical Anarchy

As far as Tom could assess, within weeks of the miraculous visions that occurred all over the globe, the drinking stopped. Not altogether, but the number of people who experienced the "Second Fatima" was astounding. Strangely enough, "Our Lady" had not spoken a word to anyone, did not communicate any revelations to "innocent children", nor did she threaten anyone with wars or echoes of wars. She did not even promise anyone eternal damnation if they didn't change their ways. On the other hand, those men and women who had experienced the visions and had been contacted by members of various sanctuaries, spoke of experiencing inexplicable warmth that could not really be expressed in words. I could only smile—I knew their problem all too well.

They'd touched the hem of god.

For a while, all was quiet on the western front—or on any front, for that matter. Of course, we weren't quite sure if East was East, and West was West. The sun continued to rise and set, but admittedly from slightly different directions. As we now regarded the world from the regal height of more than 3000 meters, we couldn't be quite sure if East has remained East. As for our compasses, they were pointing towards what used to be South. Straight down towards what also used to be Africa.

No one was sure what was there now.

I asked Ambrosia what exactly might have happened with regards to people's visions.

"You know, darling, that in moments of stress the mind is weakened. It is much easier to influence a mind weakened by hysteria through a telepathically induced equivalent of post-hypnotic suggestion. In fact, everyone saw whatever they chose to see following Mama's subliminal message..."

I could guess the rest.

And yet a certain malaise lingered. Papa called it lackadaisical anarchy. Of course as much as Tom could gather from his near-constant radio watch, there were no governments people could blame for their fate. Those were gone long ago. I suspect what kept people going a little less astray were the repetitious visions, which people continued to experience, periodically, in various parts of the world. No instructions, neither threats nor promises, just visions. And that strange warmth. That intangible, enigmatic, emotional warmth.

By now I strongly suspected that Mama had dipped her fingers in these phenomena, although I had absolutely no idea how. There were still many things I didn't understand about Mama. Perhaps I never would. If I was right, then neither did the 'people'. The masses. Habits die slowly. They marveled, waiting to be told what to do.

Papa was right.

The vast majority of people needed to be told what to do, how and when to do it. And yet this was the onset of that Age of Aquarius, during which people were intended to step out of kindergarten and stand up on their own feet.

"It will come," Mama assured her husband, stroking his gray temples gently with her long fingers.

Of course, we were still going through the last stages of the Pluto Effect. We still had close to 2000 years to go. It might be enough even for slow-learners. Such as I was.

I glanced again at our hosts. Mama's gentle fingers were still giving Papa visible pleasure. His eyes half-closed, he seemed submerged in Mama's ministrations.

Sometimes I thought that that was why Papa allowed himself such emotional outbursts—just to have Mama massage his temples. Perhaps, after years of work for so many people, after years of helping by giving so much of himself, he now needed to replenish his reserves. Lately, he was running on empty. Mama knew that. She was glad that Papa could not fly his jet to Corfu any more. Not for quite a while, now. The last dozen times he'd returned exhausted. Papa expected immediate results. He seemed to have forgotten that there was no hurry, that we were all immortals.

Only not here, not on Earth, I mused. Not even on Corfu... On the other hand, what did I know?

Even so, it appeared that Papa was more likely to accept Mama's ministrations with equanimity, than Amadeus did with her kind words. My son seemed even more frustrated than Papa by the condition of inaction. We had enough food, great climate, and even sufficient amount of wine to relax anybody. Amadeus wanted more. His youth made him impatient.

And by the way, whatever age he was will remain a mystery for me. He looked, moved, and behaved like a man in his early or middle thirties. I suspect that gods measure age by some divine metronome, incomprehensible to us, mortals.

Yet when all was said and done, since I'd last spoken to Ambrosia I began to notice more and more emotional reactions to various events, even as they have been filtered to us by Tom. Many such events had neither rhyme nor reason, yet apparently had been accepted by the broadcasters as reasonably normal. Others, screaming for a logical analysis, remained ignored, as though there was no need for such scrutiny. For some reason I have been exempt from the assault on my logic, though I have no idea why. I could only suspect that, as always, Mama must have had something to do with it all. Of course being a 'historian', I had to keep an emotional distance from all the news, or my notes would suffer from unexplainable bias.

Even Athena and Amadeus suffered from strange reactions, let alone Papa. Tom and Jerry remained reasonably immune, while Mavis's son showed signs of frequent tears. A most unmanly behaviour. He was past forty, or looked this age, when I'd recorded this. He was the only person in our immediate midst that, although still well below usual expectations, aged more than others. He looked as if he wanted to age, if not to die, and return to his haven. Or heaven. Or, perhaps, in his case, both.

On the other hand, they say that only the good die young. Surely John displayed all the attributes of goodness—of unconditional compassion towards his fellow man. And he was happy. Must have been. Smile seldom left his face.

No matter, I enjoyed my work.

Outside our sanctuary evidence of the lackadaisical anarchy continued. While people stopped drinking to visible excess, they remained lethargic, getting up from their recumbent position only when hunger forced them to do so.

Yet there were a few who began to take risks, as though to prove that they were still alive. Being deprived of means of transportation, and with very few radios finding power to operate properly, they took up, almost *en mass*, the ancient art of sailing.

Frankly, it was one deviation from normal of which I thoroughly approved. Not the way in which it was done, usually in a most haphazard way, but the principle of sailing to develop contacts among new settlement along the new coastlines, appealed to my sense of adventure. It seemed that for many the telepathic ability still remained dormant. People settled close to the sea for the simple expediency of food. It seemed that the only living creatures that had not suffered severely from the prolonged global cataclysms were the creatures of the sea. Fish, shrimp and even octopi were easy to catch and available in abundance.

By that time Papa, in need of useful occupation, organized some people from our, and until geological unification, adjacent islands now reachable on foot, to straighten out the terrain sufficiently to be able to drive a car, which he and Jerry converted from the old gasoline driven motor to electrical. Whatever climatic changes took place elsewhere, we were blessed with all the sun we needed to light all the bulbs, cook our meals, run the computers and now run our one and only automobile.

Until three more vehicles were successfully converted, there was a waiting list for the use of the single car. Finally Ambrosia and I managed to get hold of one. We immediately drove down from our Olympian aerie to the very end of the mountain, where the terrain descended more gently towards the sea. Athena, who was next in line for the use of the car, told us about the place. You've guessed it. She found it by frequent bilocations, which she practiced daily. It seemed that she knew the whole Kingdom better than anyone else. Amadeus suggested that she sketch a map, to help us all. She did, although she refused to guarantee its accuracy.

It was a shame that Ambrosia still couldn't control her antigravity gizmo. Until she would, we had to wait our turn for the wheels.

I drove first. Slowly, carefully—we only had four cars— but it didn't help. The road was little more than a mountain trail, more suitable for mountain goats than wheeled vehicles.

The road was so bumpy that Ambrosia suggested that we follow Athena's example and bilocate the rest of the way. However, I had different plans, which I managed to hide from her peeping mind. I was learning not to broadcast my thoughts by removing from them emotional content. It didn't always work, but I was getting better at it.

"Wait and see, darling. Don't you enjoy your gorgeous

body any more?"

She smiled.

I wondered if my thoughts had remained hidden. I drove slowly down the sloping trail, and in little more than an hour the road began to descent quite steeply, revealing a secluded cove with sand that has never been touched by a human foot. Officially the trip was to find a place where we could organize a pier or some sort of protected cove, in which to hide a sailing boat. We assumed that eventually we would find one on a dozen ex-islands that were now completely landlocked. We assumed that the boat would be in a reasonably ship shape condition.

Having been born in England, I had sailing in my blood. Love of the sea is hammered into British boys, until it becomes second nature. Already as a youth I'd sailed the Solent, off the coast of Yarmouth, and later on my friend's sloop on Lake Louis, in Montreal. Not the same as an open sea, but it kept me abreast in the use of lines, shrouds and stays fresh in my mind. I even remembered which was port and which starboard.

But that, I promised myself, would come later. Right now, I had slightly different plans.

As we neared the cove I became excited. We descended the last 100 meters or so on foot. Then I took off my shoes and touched the sand. It was just as I remembered it—cool in the shade, hot in the sun.

I glanced behind me. Ambrosia stood still, transfixed by the beauty around us. It was the most virginal, most pristine cove she'd ever seen, which was also true of me, of course. No, I wasn't pristine, the cove was. Still looking at the sea, she began removing her skirt, then her top, finally panties and bra. For a while she stood naked, enjoying the breeze caressing her body.

I must have been crazy. I felt jealous of the wind.

Before she could reach the water I was running after her,

shedding my clothes on the way. We reached the water simultaneously and both dove headlong into the oncoming waves.

She swam out with strong regular stroke. Having been born on the island, she was an excellent swimmer. And then, I trembled in my skin. A dark shape emerged from the sea, no more than a few meters in front of us. We were at least 200 meters from the shore. There was no escape. And then I heard it. A terrifying sound, yet, for some reason I heard no malice in it.

Ambrosia, instead of rushing for the shore, swam towards the dark monster. Moments later the monster dove under, and emerged with my wife sitting astride on its back.

It was a monk seal—an enormous beast that acted like a kitten. Perhaps a steed is a better word. I trod water in place waiting for what was to come next. Moments later I was sitting atop another beast, staring open-mouthed at Ambrosia.

"You met my friends before, darling. Say hello to them. They remember you!" Ambrosia assured me.

The only time I saw her and the seals together had been many years ago. They couldn't possibly remember me.

"Racial memory," she assured me. "They never forget."

For a short while we just sat there, on the broad monk seals' backs. Ambrosia looked euphoric—I felt near a nervous breakdown.

"Lift your heals up as if you were racing on a horse, and then lean forward, as flat as you can, on her back." Ambrosia sounded as if she'd done it before.

My beast was at least two and a half meters long. There was plenty of room to stretch out on its silky body. The only problem I had was that I might slip from it when it moved. Sorry, when she moved.

The moment I assumed the position Ambrosia had indicated, my beast started moving. First slowly, then gathering speed. They managed to keep both our heads above water.

"Where the devil are we going?" I screamed, hardly expecting an answer.

"They came to thank us. We managed to keep the Kalamos Island, their home, from rising as did Milos…"

"You managed what?" I interrupted.

"Never mind. Now they want to show us that everything is really safe and sound. In their home, I mean."

We got there in no time at all. The seals carried us with a smoothness of luxury car. No bumps, no swerves, just a smooth sale. Swim? I'm not sure which it was. They slowed down to a mere crawl as we neared the shores of very sharp crags jutting from the sea like a defense structure, discouraging anyone from getting near. Our steeds moved up and down along the shore, then turned and took us back to the cove where we met them.

…thank you… …that was very beautiful…

I heard that over the sounds emitted by the beasts. Ambrosia was thanking her friends for the excursion. Feeling like an idiot I also tried to express my gratitude subliminally.

…I thank you very much…

I tried to put as much gratitude into those thoughts as I could. This provoked a veritable fanfare of oinks and barks, squeaks and other sounds for which I had no name.

"They like you a lot," Ambrosia shouted over the noise. "They like you a lot!"

At this my seal accelerated and lifted herself and me bodily out of the water to a height I hardly imagined they could. I came down with a splash, not more then ten meters from the beach.

"Yippee!" I screamed.

I couldn't help myself. Quite unwittingly I entered into the spirit of festivities. Even as I was collecting myself, Ambrosia landed a meter away from me.

"So how do you like my friends?" she asked, her eyes filled with laughter.

"That's the most incredible ride I ever had in my life, on

anything or anybody," I said. "We must do this again."

I must have sounded like a little boy whose favourite toy has been taken away. I felt like saying "please, pretty please".

"Me too," she said.

We waded ashore. With no towels we had to let the sun dry us. It took a while. It also allowed me to do what I intended to do from the moment we'd left the villa. I waited a very long time for it. The last time it was ages ago, when we had come here to celebrate our tenth wedding anniversary. I had no way to work out, exactly, how many years had passed since then but, it turned out, I didn't forget how to make my goddess happy.

When we were perfectly dry, we went for a quick dip. It was the only thing I could think of to dry ourselves again. I don't know what they did with my body while I was hibernating, but obviously they've done me no harm. On top of that I was glad I took that QT trip to Montreal. It was after my second awakening, wasn't it? For a guy writing history I sure didn't have a good recollection of time passage. It's amazing what it does to your body. Or had it been the hibernation? I guess I'll never know for sure. In fact I felt like a young man on a first date. I was discovering Ambrosia and even myself all over again. There is nothing like a naked swim. It's incredibly refreshing.

Isn't life beautiful?

We got back just in time for supper. In fact Mama, Papa, Athena, Mavis, Jerry and John, and Tom at the end of the table, were already sitting in their usual places. For some reason Amadeus was missing. They were all sipping Sangria. Lately we only drank wine with food, and Sangria as an aperitif before the meal. Any meal. We tasted it before lunch, or dinner, and sometimes before 'high tea', which apparently Mama introduced in my honour on Saturdays. Funny that. I haven't had high tea in Canada even once. Or it could have been that it brought memories to Papa of his good old days in

England. After all, High Tea is a strictly English custom. Or
was. Who knows what they drink there today… Are they still
above the water?

We run up the steps and collapsed into our allotted
places. We were both exhausted, not so much by you-know-
what, but by the bumpy road which had shaken all my bones
to the quick. I felt exhausted, painful, almost fragile. If I had
my choice, I would have forsaken dinner and gone straight to
bed. Then I remembered that we have had no lunch, and I
decided to stay.

"Did you enjoy your trip?"

This was Mama. I had a strange feeling that she not only
knew if we enjoyed it but also how. If it were possible for a
man my age, I'd have started blushing.

"Yes, Mama," Ambrosia replied with a relaxed voice.
"Thank you."

Boy… she was good, I thought. I'd probably have
stammered. For some reason, I really felt like a boy. A very
tired boy. I also wondered why Mama was smiling while
avoiding my eyes.

"Did you find a good place for mooring?" Papa wanted
to know.

"Yes, Papa. All we need now is to find a boat. A sailing
boat." Ambrosia said, again with a straight face.

She wasn't really lying. Although we hadn't really spent
any time actually looking for a good mooring place, that little
cove we found was protected on three sides from what used
to be prevailing winds, and with just a single wave-breaker
on one side, a boat could easily survive a gale there on short
anchor. I had no idea if Ambrosia thought about that, but
she'd certainly sounded as if she had. Did gods, or goddesses
for that matter, lie?

I suppose they did, or do, whatever they jolly well want.
Isn't this what makes them gods?

I finished the salad and took a deep swig of wine, for
purely analgesic reasons. I needed painkillers for most parts

of my body. My feeling of youthfulness was evaporating from me fast. I wondered how Ambrosia was doing. Physically, I mean. She looked OK, but I learned long ago that she was an excellent actress.

"We met some of my old friends," she said with equal innocence.

"Monks?" Mavis asked. I told Mavis about them when we first came here together.

"Yes, darling. Monk seals. And they remembered us. Both of us. Isn't that just wonderful?"

We all agreed that it was.

"So what else did you do?" The next ten minutes my wife was describing in great detail our ride to Kalmos. No one thought it unusual or unlikely. It was as if they all took daily rides atop monsters emerging from the deep. I don't know if it was the wine, or just general fatigue, but my eyes were beginning to close. I was about to excuse myself to go to bed, when Amadeus appeared out of the blue.

"My apologies," he said, bowing to Mama and Papa.

"Did you find one?"

He nodded. "A 46-footer," he said. "Room enough for all of us."

It transpired that Amadeus went looking for a yacht, hopefully abandoned, that could be put in water again, and give us a chance to visit other parts of the Kingdom and the adjacent islands. There had been only one difference between his trip and ours. He visited more than twenty places, and, obviously, he used bilocation. These people never ceased to amaze me.

I kept listening to his story, even though my eyes were closing. I made a special effort to keep them open, only to feel my upper eyelids collapse under their own weight. It couldn't have been the sex. After all, we've made love on a regular basis, probably at least once a week, and yet the experience I had in the cove was very special.

And now, everything felt special. I was overcome with

an abundance of emotions which filled me with a feeling of love and gratitude to all present.

Then Papa started talking, again, about lackadaisical democracy. Something about it being necessary, at least to start with. He didn't explain the start of what. But it must have been important because nobody else was falling asleep. Except for me, of course. But I've been on a trip today. A long trip to a cove and sea monsters and then, and then…

The last thing I remember was Ambrosia leaning over me, and planting a lingering kiss on my lips. I liked that. I liked that very much.

After that, I don't remember anything any more.

***

PART THREE

Third 40 Years

*"....and he that sat on him
had a pair of balances in his hand."*

The Revelation
of Saint John the Divine

13
Third Awakening

"**A**re we dry yet" I asked. Only after a minute or two I noticed that I was lying flat on the same deckchair on which I sat down, after dinner, when we got back from the swim. I must have napped. After all, it was a tiring, bumpy road.

There was a stifled giggle.

"He doesn't know yet."

That was a whisper. Why are they whispering? "I'm awake already," I said to no one in particular.

Only then I recognized it. That was Mama's voice. It reached me from a far, far distance. I wonder if she guessed what really made me so tired…

"It must have been a beautiful dream, he's still grinning," Mavis put in her penny's worth.

After another moment or two, Ambrosia started giggling again like a teenage girl. "It's not a dream, Mavis. He's remembering…" And she giggled again.

I heard all that, and opened my eyes wider.

"Welcome back, darling. We missed you."

Ambrosia was bending over me. Mama, Athena and Mavis were standing close by, as if waiting to see what is about to happen. I didn't see anything interesting nearby, and tried to sit up to see. And then I realized that I am incredibly stiff.

"It must have been that bumpy ride," I said, turning painfully towards my wife. "I ache all over."

"It will be better soon," she smiled her angelic smile. "I promise," she added.

Only then it hit me. I felt exactly that sort of stiffness sometime ago, when they brought me out from my last hibernation. Apparently no amount of induced walking in your sleep keeps your body in good shape. Actually, I don't believe I've done any physical walking. They must have been referring to something else. Weren't there some electric shocks involved? Stimulation of nerves?

"How long?" I asked.

"It's been a while out there, darling." She waved her arm in a broad gesture. "But time is of no consequence. You already recorded all that really mattered."

I remembered. I was the historian. A historian who slept through most of history.

"That's not quite how it works," Mama said. "You are doing just fine, young man."

Young man? Apart of stiffness I felt like a young man. I looked at my hands. I remembered the skin of men seventy and older. It was old, dried up, shriveled, with aging spots all over. My hands were young.

"How long," I repeated.

Ambrosia sighed. "By your reckoning about four decades. By ours a few minutes. Well, a day or two. We all jumped time to be with you."

"You what?"

"It's got to do with quantum theory. There is time and there is negative time. It's… it's complicated."

I've heard that expression before. Ambrosia evidently decided that explaining negative time to me would be an abortive endeavour. Whenever she hit a brick wall with me, she used "it's complicated" as an excuse to change the subject. I learned long ago that she was right.

Finally, after about ten minutes, I felt that blood was returning to the outer parts of my body. Little baby ants were crawling all over me, particularly over my legs. Not that the circulation wasn't there before, but is seemed as though my cardiovascular system was working at a reduced pace. Just enough to keep me alive? Not enough to feed sufficient energy for me, or to my brain, to allow me to remain conscious. I have no idea how they did it.

Paradoxically, at that particular moment I had a vague memory of reading, back in Montreal, about a Hindu holy man named Prahlad Jani, who claimed to have not eaten or taken any fluids for several decades. According to the fully accredited doctors, he was in perfect physical and mental health.

As Ambrosia has said, it complicated.

I shrugged, and even that was painful.

Later, in our bedroom where Ambrosia took me for a 'real' nap, I tried to pump her for some idea of this negative time business.

"Think of it this way, darling. Imagine that Mama and Papa and myself were already in the present, and we only went back in time to experience your becoming. All we'd have to do would be to remember what already took place and relive it, so to speak. It is like remembering in four dimensions. In fact, in physics, there are many more than four. Does that help?"

She actually looked concerned. In everyday life we never really discussed her expertise in quantum physics, with accent on 'string theory' to which, I believe, she was alluding. I was getting ready to give up, but it was too late.

"Surely, Simon, you don't want me to delve into string theory and explain all sorts of elementary particles using the quantum states of those strings, do you?"

Mumbo-jumbo. I was careful to hide my thoughts from her. I thought mumbo-jumbo quite dispassionately.

Anyway, hers was a rhetorical question. I didn't want her to drag me into her invisible world of invisible particles, dangling on invisible strings, presumably all full of empty space.

Not for all the tea in China.

I had enough invisible mysteries to solve already. Things we shared had nothing to do with theoretical physics, nor with comparative religion. We left those subjects in the office, so to speak. Long ago.

The next day I had it confirmed that for ordinary mortals, such as I've always regarded myself, some 40 years had passed since Ambrosia and I made a concentrated effort to remember our tenth wedding anniversary on a beach.

Forty? Or had it been eighty? Or one-twenty?

I didn't care anymore. I was here, in the present. Alive. Isn't that what really matter? As for the beach you might say that we did it in four dimensions. Physically as well as back in time. Maybe there was something to this negative time business, but it would take a lot to convince me that it was real, and not just the product dreamt up by theoretical physicists reclining in a hot bathtub. It seems that a hot bath was a frequent source of inspirations for Ambrosia's colleagues. At least it had been at the time when she and I both had colleagues.

How time flies…

Or perhaps our whole life here was just an illusion; Maya—as they called it in the East. Or was it West these days? After all, with the so-called solids being little more than empty space, could the concept of time be any different? Any more real?

I decided to leave it to the gods to figure it out.

"So what's for breakfast?" I asked instead.

"For you gruel, darling, just for a day or two."

Apparently 'gruel' was the only digestive that could activate my peristaltic movement, after years of dormancy, without killing me.

"I might as well have remained asleep," I muttered. Can you blame me? After 40 years…

"It's not that bad. I've put some salt in it…" she looked really sorry.

And then an idea struck me.

"For how long have I been awake?" I looked up at her. It was much better than starring the hideous concoction I was supposed to eat. "I mean since you last woke me up?"

"It's not as simple a that."

"What isn't?"

She placed another pillow behind my back and handed me the bowl of gruel. Trying hard to hide my disgust I poured it down my gullet, spoon by spoon. Ambrosia turned her back. Evidently my facial contortions made her queasy also. She sat down facing the window.

"It's complicated, she began…"

Here it comes, I thought.

"There are four parts to this story—to the story of evolutionary cycles in every segment of the zodiac. Then even those are divided into segments. In Esoteric Buddhism they call them ages, with some 'kalpas' lasting millions of years. But really there are ages within ages. As you can see it's all to do with time, yet time remains liquid, malleable, adapting to the needs of any particular stage of our development."

I almost finished my gruel. "You can turn now," I said.

She remained facing the window as though avoiding my eyes. "You see, darling, for your sake we are going through the four segments consecutively—one after another. But in fact, they all happen simultaneously. It's… you know?"

I knew. Complicated.

Thank God she'd left her beloved physics behind. Listening to her talk like this made even gruel more palatable. OK. Not exactly palatable, but less revolting. I cleared the bowl and put it on the bedside table. Ambrosia turned to face me. I expected her to say 'good boy' when I realized that by 'my' standards I'd probably turned about 130 years of age. A bit much for a 'boy'. I kept quiet.

"You can think of these stages as kindergarten, primary school, then secondary and finally the university. Although they are all very separate methods of teaching, they are subdivided into classes or years. The same thing applies to our evolutionary cycles."

To my utter amazement I could live with that explanation. When she tried, she could be quite logical.

...thank you darling... I heard on the inner. It seems that ages notwithstanding, I was still broadcasting. I was determined to put a stop to that.

...you will in this cycle... I heard. I felt? Somewhere in-between? I didn't bother to ask how she knew. I probably wouldn't understand it.

"To return to your question. By accepting Mama's commission of writing a brief history of the period of transition, we had to make sure that you would be around to see all four of them. Hence what you call hibernation."

"But *you* don't sleep...?" I countered, stressing the pronoun. She got the point.

"I don't regard my body as myself..."

I knew that, although she made a magnificent facsimile of it being herself. I remember as if it were only yesterday... or some 40 years ago, but for a while there, in the cove, I could swear that she was her body.

"...anymore than you regard your outer clothing as you."

This, again, was getting to be complicated. "Let's go back to ages," I asked.

"Basically we have the physical, emotional, mental, and what people call spiritual age, or what it really means is complete acceptance that consciousness is the only reality, which can nevertheless use illusion for its learning process."

That wasn't quite as simple as I thought, but I got the gist of it. As I understood it, we had to adapt our bodies, our emotions and finally our intellectual understanding to be able to accept the truth as it really was. Or is. Pure Consciousness. Wow!

"It's as simple as that," Ambrosia murmured.

It was time for my first walk. I thought we'd stroll around
the garden, in the mini-labyrinth of passages among the
closely trimmed hollies. Not so. Ambrosia led me to our
terrace, our beautiful agora, which offered a view that took
my breath away. It did so, just about every time I stood on it.

No, mother earth had not lifted us another thousand
meters towards the eternally blue sky. What I saw was a
stretch of the road that we crossed, it seemed like only
yesterday, towards our secret cove. Only now the road looked
smooth, or nearly so, and extended into the distant hills like a
gray ribbon painted on a canvas of green pastureland.

So time has passed, I mused.

By some means Papa, as I suspected it had to have been
him, contrived to build roads in his Kingdom. I recalled that
the late Roman Empire managed to build more than 400,000
kilometers of roads, of which more than 80,000 kilometers
were stone-paved. They did it without a single bulldozer,
without modern machinery. Perhaps Papa remembered the
technique from his Paul days. There were few things Papa
couldn't do. After all, wasn't he a god, too?

We sat on the terrace admiring the passage of elusive
time. Just catching up on what I missed.

And then Ambrosia's words began to catch up with me. I
had to reach back more than a hundred years. I remember
teaching the probable symbolic meaning which John, Saint
John to many, had written in his Apocalypse. I wondered how
or who passed on to him the knowledge that now, according
to Ambrosia, was a matter of fact and not of religion. If you
really know things, you no longer have to believe them, or in
them. Belief or faith is only necessary as a motivating force
to drive us towards the unknown, towards that which we do
not as yet know.

Also, I remember saying that faith is necessary to give us strength in adversity. Any adversity over which we do not have control. That's what makes gods gods. They have the power to overcome, sooner or later, all adversities.

Saint John had a revelation, which he tried to share with people of his day. Whether it came from within, or from a time traveler, such as some of my friends here on Milos appeared to be, we might never know. Although never is such a long time, which it seemed to me was becoming just as imaginary as the solidity of matter.

The revelation became known as the Apocalypse of St. John. What it did was tell people what had been told, over countless years, many times. It affirmed that we, humans, perhaps all intelligent beings, are endowed with fourfold nature. That our true being is pure consciousness, but that to become fully aware of it we have to conquer our lower natures first. He called those lower forms of expression as the Pale, the Red, and the Black Horse. Only when we managed to harness those steeds would we be permitted to ride the White Horse, the body that dropped all its limitations and gave us power over the true reality of the universe. The four horses represented our physical, emotional, mental and spiritual nature. I thought that we've just entered the phase of Black Horse. We had this one to go to gain our freedom; to overcome all our perceived limitations. I wondered how many of us would make it.

It was a long haul. For some reason, gods allowed me to take shortcuts. They could do whatever they wanted. That's what made them gods, after all.

And then I remembered. Gods could be both, good and bad. Manifest divinity meant just power. Potential divinity was the source of it all. Truth lay in the middle. It was forever neutral. Like Lao Tsu's Tao.

I wished I could eat something that didn't taste like something that someone has already eaten, let alone, digested. To use a William Chandler's literary expression: "Like a half-digested meal in a greasy spoon joint," although Chandler referred to how he felt. Well, I was pretty close on this count, as well. I read Chandler as a boy, and still remembered the line.

This took me back to Old England and English cuisine... Never mind.

I had to shake my head repeatedly to clear the cobwebs. If this was the Black Horse then I ought to be riding it in a waken state. I'd better shape up.

It's not that easy to wake up after a 40-year nap.

"When you fully recover, I'll take you on a little trip," Ambrosia said, a wink accompanying her promise. Apparently she was still keeping a close eye on me. Good-old Ambro.

I decided to exercise daily no matter how many gruels I had to eat.

The following day, the third of the Black Horse era, we celebrated 'my return' at dinner. Yes, I was allowed to eat with the others. I studied them for signs of aging.

Mama and Papa remained identical as I remembered them. I may not have mentioned it, but so did my wife, of course, as did Athena and Amadeus. It seemed that once gods reached their desired physical age, they stopped there and remained that way for many years to come. I strongly suspected that when they eventually shed their physical bodies, they emerge from their chrysalis and simply metamorphose into their higher nature. After all, butterflies do it, why shouldn't gods?

Only gods do it by an act of their will.

I wondered if I could ever do it without resorting to hibernation. Not dying, but remaining my youthful, irresistible self. Or would I have to go under, whatever that meant, wherein I wasn't my usual lively, gregarious self.

I heard a slight chuckle from Amadeus. I must have improved masking my thoughts. Or the others might have been too polite on my first official day out. Out to dinner with the adults.

That brings me to Tom. He must have been in Limbo again. He looked even larger then before, but somehow less frightening. Not that he ever scared me, but I've never met him at night, on a dark street. Perhaps he'd softened with age, although he didn't show his advancing years.

Advancing years? He'd advanced as much as I had. We were both old. Bloody old. Only neither he nor I showed it. The gods were having fun with us.

Tom was still looking after communications. He was an expert now, apparently keeping up with the latest progressively dwindling sources. Even Ambrosia had said so.

As for others, well, Mavis began to look a little matronly. She was a widow now. Jerry had refused to go under again.

"I won't go under, again, just to retain my good looks," he'd said. Ambrosia smiled when she told me that those were his last words.

Mama and Papa made sure that his transition was an easy one. Later I discovered that Mavis was visiting him on a regular basis. Apparently, one of the aspects of the emotional segment of one's becoming was great easing of access to, what my friends referred to, as 'first heaven'. It was the reality wherein emotions and imagination were at par with other dimensions.

Mavis said that Jerry was looking to his next reincarnation in a much larger body.

"At last a foot taller," he'd said when he and I were alone. "He changed his mind when I told him that on his next stint on earth he would probably be a girl. Then he threatened to become a lesbian until he'd learned that I might turn out to be a boy."

No one seemed to feel sorry. They really did not believe

in death.

That left John. Tom seemed to have adopted him as his own, not that John needed adoption. He was definitely a mature man, although he remained an emotionally fragile person. I know of no other way to describe him. Ambrosia told me that he could shed a tear when he accidently stepped on an ant. Perhaps he was a Buddhist at heart.

I was still in no position to judge anyone, even if I wanted to. Yet it was my job to start making notes, to return to my job to justify my existence. Duty calls, I told myself and struggled upstairs to my study.

Here, nothing has changed. All looked exactly as if I left it only yesterday. Not like in Montreal. Not a spec of dust. Perhaps someone has cleaned my study in expectation of my return, but I don't think so. This was not how gods operated. They created reality, and if they didn't like it, they changed it. Not as fast as we do in our dreams, on the other side or the Great Divide, but a great deal faster than ordinary mortals. My last trip to Montreal gave me an idea how they may have done it.

Although Ambrosia used the term before, I don't think I ever asked what exactly she meant by 'The Great Divide'. She started in her usual way.

"It's complicated," she said.

I let that ride.

"There are different realities, also known as planes, which manifest different means or methods of creative expression," she began, after giving it some thought. I think she was looking for words that I would understand.

"The Great Divide?" I nagged, just a little. She was very concise in her physics, but tended to be verbose in metaphysics.

"I am getting there. To reach the next Plane we must cross the Great Divide. It can be entered only when your brain is generating alpha waves."

I already knew that. "And...?"

"We pass through the Great Divide to get to the other side. The problem is that we have only control of entry. We slip to the other side automatically, like going down a shoot. However after a while we get snapped back into our body."

"And that makes it 'great'?"

She ignored me. "The problem is that once you leave your physical body permanently, it is extremely difficult to find your way back. Of course, your physical body deteriorates, so there is nothing to come back to. But the pattern you had once created has a much longer shelf life. You can recreate a body out of neutrinos that are flying around all the time, all over the place. But most people can't do it, hence one could say that "the dead stay dead", only they are not dead, of course. They also have problems finding the entry into the Great Divide from the other side."

This was getting a little more interesting.

"However, there are some extraordinary people who can. Find their way back, I mean, from the other side. Hence the visions some people have."

Hence the visions... I repeated silently. That explains the visions as well as their rarity.

"Thank you, my love. I think I am getting the idea."

It is the people who find their way back that make it great. It is their greatness that gives it its grandeur.

"Thanks again," I repeated. And I thanked also my lucky stars for giving me Ambrosia for my wife.

I sat at my desk and clicked on the miPad. I looked at the date. It advanced almost 40 years. Forty years since when?

I wondered if it mattered any more. What's a few years between friends? I wrote down my observations of the last few days, just to have something to go on. A start. I left out my memories of the past that still lingered on. I didn't mention our trip to the cove. That was personal.

I guess it always will be.

But I spent a lot of time trying to put down the words that Ambrosia had told me. They might turn out to be of great help to people in the future. No more miracles, no more mysteries. I remembered Luke's words in the Bible, *'For there is nothing covered, that shall not be revealed; neither hid, that shall not be known.'* These words were responsible for my first battle with the Jesuits who insisted that I must rely on faith, not on knowledge. Funny that, I mused. They, the Jesuits, are all dead by now and yet... here I am.

By that time I thought I knew why gods descended to Earth; to the phenomenal world of physical pseudo reality. They wanted to be human. They wanted to err, to make mistakes, to know what it's like to hurt someone and then to make it good again. Human life was exciting. It was an expression of contrasts. Of good and bad, of beautiful and ugly.

Of love and hate?

But mostly of love. Of ordinary, human, physical love, before that love became unconditional. And also of love of constant, irrepressible change. Of every morning being different. Of life with all its pains and sorrows, with the rewards for the work well done. But mostly of being alive in all four realities at once. A great gift that, from the Infinite Potential.

And even if one slept through some of it, the wondrous gift of life persisted in all its glory.

Perhaps for... ever?

***

14

Milos Kingdom

I t took me a few days to find my bearings. The winding
road, which Ambrosia showed me on that first walk
since my third awakening, was just the beginning.
Perhaps there were many more years than just 40 since I last
trod the earth. Perhaps the years they counted were stretched
on the scale of a divine calendar that only gods used and
understood. Now that I looked around, I was facing a new
world.

There seemed to be also a different way that I was
looking at my surrounding. I became aware of relationships
of various things to each other, detecting an underlying
pattern that I have not been aware of before my extended nap.

What changed were not just physical things, but what
they represented in a new reality. What reality? A reality of
inherent order and harmony? Perhaps. A reality that I was
still to discover.

What was missing was traffic. No cars, busses or any
evidence of any form of vehicular transportation. I scanned
the horizon. The winding roads leading down the hill from
our Olympian heights were the only evidence of the return to
civilization. I know we had four electrically powered vehicles
before my snooze. Now, I saw none. Perhaps they were far
away beyond the many hills… What I saw were roads devoid
of traffic.

I went back to my study and fetched my old field glasses,
which I last used to gaze at the verdant glory of Mount Royal
in Montreal. The glasses had spent innumerable years lying
on the top of the high cabinet in which I kept scores of

printed notes of the many lectures I'd given at McGill. The
cabinet was the sanctuary of my past. It was a sanctuary
where I kept a few items of personal memories. As I reached
for the glasses, I also found a medal I'd won, a million years
ago, in England, playing rugby. At long last I found
something that gathered some dust.

Another time, another lifetime, another dream?

I wiped the lenses and directed them at the terrain
stretching before me.

Staring at the vast landscape had given me an idea.

As I gazed at the distant hills bathed in early morning
rays with just a trace of fog hanging on to the lowest vales, I
began to doubt the evidence of my eyes. It wasn't just that the
sun was shining with much greater intensity but it came from
a sky that changed the shade of its blue. Only later I put it to
clarity of the air. I strongly suspected that over the last 80 to
120 years, due to the reduction and later complete elimination
of industrial and vehicular pollution, the colour of the sky had
to change. There obviously was neither coal, nor oil, nor gas,
and possibly not even atomic power to ruin our planet. We
seemed to be reverting to the days of our forefathers, when
the only vehicular transport would be horse-drawn.

I thought wistfully of a tour I once took Ambrosia on in a
single-horse *calèche*, as it clip-clopped over the cobblestones
of Old Montreal.

Yes, it was definitely another era. Almost another
planet? Most certainly a different reality. Until that day I've
only seen such skies in my lucid dreams, on the other side of
the Great Divide. In my OBEs.

Alas, the *calèches* were also missing from the Milos
roads. I was beginning to suspect that Mama had been
playing a trick on me. I was growing convinced that by
means known only to herself she kept me in some form of
suspended animation, an induced sleep if you will, and that
the events of the last few days were still part of a dream. I

suspected that any moment I'd wake up to see all of them, all of my family, sitting on the terrace, laughing, as they watched my surprise on waking up.

This scenario was more likely to justify what I saw next. Sliding my field glasses along a distant stretch of the road, I saw a shape, seemingly a man, standing on a platform. They were both suspended about a foot above the road, and moved along the road at a pace equal to a quick run. I remember a movie from my youth, "Return to the Future" I think it was, where a young hero was gliding on small surfboard, supported on a cushion of air.

Perhaps the man I saw moved faster than that. Not faster than the movie star, but faster than a man could run. Even as I looked, the distant shape accelerated, then slowed down, and finally turned at right angles to the road and disappeared between the trees.

This must have been either magic or a dream. Nothing else explained the evidence of my eyes. Then a thought stuck me that there had been something resembling what I saw in my days, in the days when sanity was not a dirty word. The conveyance was called a segway. Segway was two-wheeled vehicle consisting of a platform mounted above an axle and had a post supporting handles. It moved forward and backward, and sophisticated tilt sensors controlled its movement. It had a motor, of course, and a computer that controlled its stability. And it stood on two wheels.

"Aye, there's the rub," as Hamlet would say.

What I saw had no wheels. Surely, this was proof enough that I was still dreaming. The next moment I heard the giggle. Somebody was reading my thoughts again.

"You're wide awake, darling. Wide awake," she repeated.

As I swung round I saw Ambrosia standing just behind me, a broad smile on her face. If this was a dream I lost all desire to wake up.

"How long were you standing there?" I asked.

"It doesn't matter. When you don't make a conscious effort, I can hear you from a distance." She continued to smile.

"And you guarantee that I'm not dreaming any of this?" I was perfectly serious.

"Your observations are very accurate, darling, as becomes our resident historian." This time her face and her voice matched the seriousness of my tone of voice.

"And what of the segway?"

"I admit that it inspired me. Only my lighter is run on antigravity. It's cleaner, silent, and it doesn't need wheels."

"Laiter?"

"Lighter, with a 'gh'." Her fingers squiggled two commas in the air. "That's what I call it. A 'lighter'. It makes you lighter than air. I could call it 'weightless', but I thought that would be presumptuous. After all, you continue to weigh exactly the same as your mass has not changed in any way."

I was awake. I couldn't possibly make up such stories in a dream. On the other hand, Ambrosia seldom deserted my dreams. She filled all my realities.

"Thank you, kind Sir," she replied with a deep bow.

I must stop this broadcasting, I mused.

...*not necessarily*... she smiled.

I let that pass.

"Were there many, ah... technological changes during my hibernation?" I went back to the old term.

She pursed her lips. "Not really. Mama says that with few exceptions, technology would not be necessary. It tends to spoil us. It stops us from using our inherent gifts. That's what happened towards the end of the Age of Pisces."

That made sense, especially from Mama's point of view. After all, Mama was a living example of what magnificent possibilities were available to us. There was Leonardo da Vinci, there was Shakespeare, there was Mozart and there were mystics and philosophers. And there was Mama, and surely, she was in a class of her own.

Ambrosia smiled.

"Architect, engineer, painter, sculptor, musician, mathematician, anatomist, geologist, cartographer, botanist, writer and inventor. Not bad for one man... Mama can't do any of these things..."

Ambrosia enumerated some of da Vinci's talents. And yet Mama stood alone.

"Except she could, should she choose to," I murmured. Mama never ceased to amaze me.

Ambrosia nodded. "Mama has quite a different mission to fulfill, I suspect. Leonardo would have had considerable problems with doing her job."

We both laughed.

We were skimming over the terrain at a good clip. I judged it to be between 40 and 50 kilometers an hour. Good enough to get anywhere within a tiny Kingdom, if your legs didn't get tired. For some reason Ambrosia didn't seem disposed to fit the platform with a seat.

Driving this thing, this 'lighter' thing, was actually quite simple. As Ambrosia had admitted, it was based on the segway principle, only instead of handles, all control remained in the legs. In the feet, really.

"Point down with your toes, and you'll move faster. Lean back on your heels, and you slow down. The same applies to turning left or right," she instructed me before we took off.

I was a little nervous, but looked forward to the experience. I suspected that it would be similar to a surfboard I once tried in Jamaica, oh... a thousand years ago? Only, well... you didn't need a wave and you floated on air.

I found it great fun. And I was very proud of my wife.

It was fast enough to feel the warm air whistling past my ears. We drove, or skidded, if that's the right word, side by side, little different than we would be, had we been walking.

Only we covered a lot more ground.

Let's face it. I loved it.

After some twenty minutes we sat on a rock to rest our legs and admire the scenery. Ambrosia was brining me up to date, filling the gaps of my absence.

It seemed that while I was not consciously around, Papa was instrumental in making the whole of Milos Kingdom economically independent. He no longer dreamt of a democratic structure of society, where the chosen few control the lives of the many. People continued to make mistakes, but they did those on their own, and seldom made the same mistake twice.

Within the first ten years every family had their own vegetable garden with bi-annual crops. During the second ten years, Ambrosia's 'lighter' enabled people to visit each other and exchange goods to mutual advantage. Six people were working full time making the 'lighters', until the market was reasonably filled. People paid by offering other services in exchange.

During the third decade people had enough time left over to visit the Olympus on a regular basis. This illustrious name, Olympus, was the name given to the highest point in the Milos Kingdom. It was also the small plateau where our villa stood. And the last decade was still in full swing. People came once a week to hear Mama give instructions on the power of the mind. She not only gave lectures but also backed them up with demonstrations. I soon learned the old adage that magic of today is the science of the future. Mama gave evidence that the future had arrived.

It was here, now.

"Always look for patterns," she invariably repeated when the expression on peoples' faces suggested they were lost. "An idea must form part of a pattern of the rest of reality, or it will not work, and if it does, it will not be sustained."

...*it is pure mathematics*... I heard her add.

Pure mathematics, I repeated to myself. Next we would get the theory of numbers. Then... I preferred not to think. It will all come at the right time. Whatever time was in this reality. Or any other reality for that matter.

So far I heard Mama speak only once, and I use the word 'speak' advisedly. There was a fundamental difference between Mama's lectures and those I'd once delivered at McGill University. Mama seldom spoke. Seldom spoke aloud that is. Her ideas were mostly conveyed subliminally, where they reacted with the mindset that was receiving them. It was a very different kind of teaching method. If you were ready, ready and receptive, then her ideas would become part of you. You'd never have to make notes to remember.

For a moment I had an image of the biblical story of the descent of the Holy Ghost, or was it the Holy Spirit? I remember the Jesuits at St. Stanislaus calling it the Pentecost Sunday. Ten days after the Ascension, forty days after Resurrection. I remembered that way-back-then I thought that the Jesuits were teaching me their version of magic. Perhaps it hadn't been magic at all. Perhaps it was just a little ahead of its time.

A Catholic Magic?

I vaguely recall that it was there and then that I'd decided, that when I grow up, I would study the ancient myths to find out if there was any truth to them. I've been doing it for years, and I wasn't getting much closer to the truth—to an intellectually verifiable truth. Now, with Mama around, I wasn't so sure. Magic wasn't so magical any more. It never is when it happens to you, directly.

No. I wasn't sure at all.

The villa itself was much as I remembered it. I am told that a few years ago some of the citizens of the Kingdom had offered to repair some walls, and replace some of the external stone facades. Mama's esoteric abilities must have saved the building, but a crack or two in stonework were evidently beyond even her incredible powers. Let us never forget that this particular island has been pushed more than 3,000 meters upwards. This may seem like nothing much compared to flooding the whole of Sahara desert, but by my standards it was as close to a miracle as anything could be.

The whole front facade certainly looked brand new to me. Not that I didn't like the old masonry. I'd have just covered it with bougainvilleas and be done with it. However, evidently in the restoration department, Papa was the boss.

Papa needed order. He also needed to act. To be useful. Papa remained a man of action.

In addition, on the north side of the plateau, behind the villa and just a bit lower than the labyrinth garden, Papa supervised the construction of a strange looking dome, which could house up to 400 people during inclement weather. I said strange, because it wasn't there until needed. When the weather demanded protection for people gathering for Mama's lectures, the dome rose slowly, like a balloon filled with compressed air, until it reached the required height. It took me a while to realize that Ambrosia's antigravs had something to do with it. Strategically placed 'gizmos', I still don't really know what they are, were activated to lift the roof of the domelike structure.

When no longer required, the dome descended to the ground, so as not to interfere with the view. Papa insisted on having visual access to all of his Kingdom.

He actually chuckled when he told me about it. Papa was long past taking himself too seriously. But he still cared about 'his' people, whoever they might be at any particular time. Papa loved all people.

For a while the dome bothered me. It contradicted my understanding of how our reality worked. Then I gave up. This was definitely a different kind of reality than I have been used to.

I had to record all of this for posterity. To earn my keep, remember?

The garden behind the villa was as enchanted as ever. One could easily get lost on the paths that entwined or intertwined themselves in mysterious ways. No matter which direction one took, one always arrived at the same spot, while taking an entirely different route. Or could it be that I was just imagining things? Perhaps this world was finally becoming as unreal as it really was...

While I kept my fingers on the keyboard of my computer, Ambrosia was reading a book on the settee behind me. Since I'd been resuscitated she'd spent more time with me. I was beginning to suspect that she really missed me. A lot.

I rather liked that.

I began describing the garden and its complex arrangement of passages. The labyrinth while not designed to hold the Minotaur, the mythical creature or Greek mythology until its eventual demise at the hands of Theseus, was nevertheless a work of art. Yet, while Greece was famous for its many labyrinth designs, this particular one, at the back of our own house must have been exceptional. I still could not figure out how it worked.

"No, darling, you're not imagining things. It used to be, well... quite usual. Complex but usual. Then Athena redesigned it as an expression of her music. She called the paths "*Rondo Capriccioso*". You can well guess what that means. The result is exactly as you described it," Ambrosia offered, apparently aware of my consternation.

"Capricious?" I asked, hopefully.

My wife only smiled. I knew I had a very special family, but its peculiarities were growing more fascinating by the day. Also more baffling.

"Rondo what?" I knew that rondo meant going around in circles but this?

"You were right, *Capriccioso*," Ambrosia repeated. She

said that she'd been inspired by Saint-Saens. A strange choice for a garden, I thought. But you know Athena. She has a mind of her own."

And just who doesn't in this family, I mused. Yet I had to admit that 'capricious' seemed to match the way the various paths interlocked. Perhaps Athena was right. As usual?

...*thanks Dad*... reached me from not very far. I looked through the window. Athena was dancing on the lawn below. Solo, though seemingly with two or three invisible partners. I gave up.

"She is teaching dancing in various part of the Kingdom, you know?" Ambrosia said, standing beside me. "She has hundreds of pupils. They all love her."

That didn't surprise me at all.

That very evening Mama was giving a general lecture. I risked not being able to understanding most of what she would be saying, but, *qui ne risque rien, n'a rien*, as we used to say in Quebec. Here we say, nothing ventured—nothing gained, but it doesn't carry the same *je ne sais quoi*.

Mama was sitting on a simple straight-backed chair, facing more than 300 people. Some were sitting, some standing on the front lawn. They were all silent, as though expecting something special to happen. Perhaps Mama's lectures were as special as anything would ever be in their lives. These were simple people, the original inhabitants of the island. Many have travelled on foot for hours to be here. While practically every family owned at least one antigrav, this hardly sufficed for everyone who wanted to hear Mama talk.

Mama looked up from her hands resting on her lap.

"We are not trying to go forward, my friends, we are trying to remember where we came from. We are trying to recall how to get back. We start as indivisible parts of the

Whole. We are perfect, hence we are gods. But gods are endowed with power and power, as we all know, corrupts. The rest is history. When we regress sufficiently to remember whence we came, we regain our power, but we must learn not to allow it to corrupt us again. If we don't learn, we shall sink into materiality. On, and on, and on. Hence the Wheel of Awagawan. The wheel of rebirth. Luckily we are immortal."

The rest of her lecture was delivered subliminally. I remained mesmerized as apparently was the whole audience. Mama had that effect on people. We felt wiser and, at some level, filled with love. Not just for Mama but for each other.

Mama made us feel the force that held us in an indivisible, if still only subliminal unity; an all encompassing, irresistible Oneness. Mama had that effect on every single one of us.

A week later I saw people coming to another of Mama's lecture. I stayed in my room but was determined to listen to her. At least the inner part. I probably missed a great deal of vocal instruction, but later I heard something that left a lasting impression on me.

...some of us think that we are gods... ...there are many things we can do that ordinary people think are miracles... ...we know they are not... ...we know that every reality can be manipulated if one knows the rules that control that particular reality... ...that it is all pure science...

Each thought, each idea was set apart by period of silence. Then there was an even longer pause.

...but which of us can turn a star into a nova... ...which of us can create a solar system out of a cloud of interstellar dust... ...remember my friends... ...becoming a god is not the end... it is the beginning... ...the end lies in infinity... and infinity has no end...

And after that there was only silence.

***

15
Once More Amadeus

A madeus showed unmistakable signs of frustration. On the outside he was his old, almost boisterous self, but when observed from a distance, when he was not aware of anyone's scrutiny, his face took darker shades of an inner struggle. It was my job to observe—sometimes without being observed. After all, I have been warned many, many years ago that in the hoary past Amadeus acquired traits that might make his present life difficult if not actually challenging beyond a normal humans ability to overcome.

I remembered that his reincarnations reached back so far, that most people regarded his previous life on earth as wrapped in mythology. It was a past so distant that without accepting the concept of periodic rebirth, it wouldn't make any sense.

When I detected his inner turmoil I did the unthinkable. Very surreptitiously and with considerable trepidation, I began peeking into his mind. I have been told that among gods this is a profound no-no, but in spite of frequent assurances to the contrary, I refused to accept membership of the elite circle of the illustrious Olympians. I kept forgetting that realization of divinity means essentially the acceptance of indivisibility of one's self from the Universal Oneness. You are god because you are indivisible from God. The two gees, the individual and the universal became indistinguishable. Every single drop of water in the universal ocean carries the same characteristics, embodies the same traits, possesses the same attributes. It is the degree to which we've learned to use them that distinguishes us from each other. Nothing else.

No matter. I was no longer giving lectures. I became Mama's student like most people on Milos. On a good day, when Mama spoke, they covered the lawns surrounding the house like mushrooms that spring up after a drizzle. Many could not even see her, but by some nook or crook they gave an impression that they were all in individual contact with her.

I breathed deeper when I saw that Amadeus was so preoccupied with his own thoughts that he hadn't noticed my mental probing.

Yet this seemed what distinguished Amadeus from the rest of us. He seemed preoccupied with what he could do, rather then what can be done. There is a great difference between seeing oneself as an instrument of the Universe, and as an instrument that decides in what way the Universe is to unfold.

Amadeus was beginning to show signs of ego. Not in his outward behaviour, but in the struggle, which I managed or contrived to observe. My consolation was that if I managed to become aware of it, then surely Mama and Papa did even more so. After all, I was but a beginner in this group that resided on the Olympus.

It was only later that I understood what motivated my son. He was determined to help Papa. I began to suspect that he carried some sort of karmic debt, which he was deeply committed to discharge in his present life. We all do, but only some of us seem aware of it. For me it would take a miracle.

"Why do you, and so many other people always think in terms of miracles?"

Ambrosia was standing behind me. I didn't hear her come in. I wondered if she'd read more of my thoughts.

"We don't. We only do so when the unexplainable happens," I replied defensively.

"But there are thousands of things which you find unexplainable," she replied. "Can you explain my antigravity platforms? Or even my old quantum tunneling? I'd explained it to you in the past, but can you really say that you understand it?"

I couldn't.

"There are no miracles, darling. There cannot be. A miracle as people think of it, would be denying the laws of nature. Even worse, it would be denying the Universal Laws. And those, Simon, cannot be broken. Not one iota..." she said, looking deep into my eyes.

I knew why. She was digging into my past, my lectures on Comparative Religion. *One iota or one tittle may not pass away from the law...* Mathew wrote it in his gospel. They knew the truth 2000 years ago, why do we keep going in circles?

"Why indeed," was Ambrosia's cryptic comment. And then she left my study only to return in less than five minutes.

"Sorry," she began.

She took my smile as absolution.

"You're still broadcasting. It doesn't matter when I hear you, but it wouldn't help if you were overheard by Amadeus." She sounded very serious.

"So you agree with me?"

"About karmic connection between Papa and our son? Of course. We all knew it."

By 'all', I presumed, she meant Amadeus himself as well as Mama, Papa and Athena. "Simon, we all have karmic connections. That's why we are all here, to help resolve them."

I was a little stunned, but not completely.

"Including you and I?"

She looked at me with those dark, probing eyes. Her lips didn't say anything, but her eyes shouted: *What do you think?*

"Is it as bad as that?" I couldn't believe her eyes.

"Not for you," she murmured.

Two weeks had lapsed before she hinted at her and my secret past. Or, perhaps, only secret to me. I sat back and listened. It was quite a story. Apparently when she was in the "upper classes" of ancient Greece, she'd repeatedly taken advantage of my prolific charms. She refused to say what those charms were, or may have been but, apparently, I could have advanced much faster on the evolutionary scale if I hadn't met her. She was determined not to make the same mistake again, although she refused to comment on my present endowments in the charms or any other departments that I may or may not have possessed.

"I thought you ought to know," she finished, her eyelashes lowered down to her cheeks.

Way back in Montreal, I recalled studying some goddesses, who were reputed to have taken advantage of some Satyrs or other members of male fraternity to satisfy their divine hunger. On the other hand, I thought that one's reincarnations alternated between male and female.

And then it hit me like a ton of bricks. Ambrosia's and my karmic connection may have been lesbian. If so, no wonder she was reticent to admit it. On the other hand, if our sexuality alternates with each embodiment, then... then we might have been both homosexuals. Lastly, she may have been a man and I an innocent virgin beguiled by 'his' irresistible charms.

I preferred not to elaborate.

"And by the way, you have a job as a historian, not as a buttinski into other people's business."

She was on the attack, which, if she was again peeking into my thoughts, only served to confirm my suspicions. How about 'all three in different bodies?'

"Karma," I said. "Karma not business. And I have no

desire to butt into Amadeus's karma other than to protect my son, which is a father's job, not a historian's."

She gave me one of those long, penetrating looks.

"You are getting very good at this."

"This?"

"Well, as you know, we are now in the penultimate phase of the mini-cycle of the Age of Aquarius. The Mental Segment, if you like. Your logic is undeniable. You might even get away with it."

"With what?" I asked. She was talking in riddles.

"Karma is exacting. If you have a negative influence on Amadeus, regardless of reasons, you'll have to restore balance either in this on in your future stint on earth. It cannot be done on inner Planes."

I think I was beginning to get the gist of the idea. That also must have been why neither Mama nor Papa, nor even Ambrosia ever pushed me into inner understandings of any kind. It seemed that to advance on the evolutionary scale one had to find out about those things all by oneself. One could offer help, but not do any thinking for others. It also struck me that here, on the Olympus, we were past kindergarten. We paid our dues. I strongly suspect that Amadeus knew that.

And yet... and yet I was his father. Father of a 120 year-old lad.

"So it has nothing to do with good or bad?"

"Not really, darling, not unless you define 'good' as a state of balance, while allowing that only upsetting such balance allows you to learn."

"A paradox?"

She only smiled. What a gorgeous smile she had...

"Dad, may I speak with you?" Amadeus's head was inside my study, the rest of him waited for permission to enter.

"You don't need permission to speak to your father, son," I replied.

My heart missed a couple of beats and then my pulse played catch-up. Could he have heard the discussion I had Ambrosia? That was three days ago but time was funny up here.

"Come in," I added, as he remained standing at the door.

I clicked the computer shut and waited. Amadeus never suffered from shyness. I could but wonder what I had to offer to a man with eidetic memory that carried the world's wisdom in his head.

"I was just wondering what you would do, Dad," he began, still standing on the door.

"Sit down, son."

During the last 120 years, I do not recall Amadeus asking me for advice. This would be a historic first.

"It's China," he began. "I don't know if you know, Dad, but they suffered relatively little loss of life during the global geological adjustments. After it was over and done with, they still boasted more than a billion people. Probably a lot more. They even retained some of their technology."

This was new to me. I waited for him to continue.

"Well, Dad, they already started fighting among each other for material goods. A sort of semi-primitive civil war. Yet since they have little if any energy, and lost most if not all of their industrial capability, the war seems to be conducted on a purely technological basis, with increased use of nanotechnology."

I felt less and less competent to get involved in Chinese problems.

"And what exactly do you want me to do, son?"

Even as I asked him the question, I felt icy fingers down my spine, saying, Sy, stay out of this. Mind your own business. This is way over your head.

I must have been broadcasting again. Amadeus got up, smacked his forehead and charged for the door.

"Just remember, Dad. I'll be back!" He threw over his shoulder.

But he didn't come back. Not for quite a while.

The next day was something of an occasion. While my family favoured bilocation for visiting far away places, Ambrosia thought it unfair to limit frivolous travel to just the few who could use the esoteric means. With considerable trepidation she mounted a larger platform and rose some fifty feet in the air. She sat cross-legged, seemingly in reasonable comfort. She then activated a propeller, which was attached to a rucksack on her back, and the platform began moving forward. After inscribing a large circle, she landed at our feet on the front lawn. She dismounted the contraption and parked it some ten feet above the ground.

"Any child can fly it," she announced, wiping sweat from her forehead. Apparently she hasn't been that certain when she'd began.

"You looked like you were flying a magic carpet, dear," Mama commented, nevertheless applauding her daughter's effort. "How fast can it go?"

"That depends on the wind, Mama, and on its direction, of course," she said with a straight face. "But I am sure…"

Before she could complete her answer, Amadeus ran down towards us from the house, holding the communication tablet in his extended arm. His expression was in stark contrast to the usual stoic behaviour of all people with the exception of Athena, who usually danced wherever she went. We all looked up.

"They are asking for help!"

He held up a tablet, which we all recognized as Tom's communication bulletin. It was good to have Tom around again. Apparently they all missed him when he was taking his nap in Limbo. Telepathic contact was great, but it seemed to concern mostly the exchange of ideas, not to keep up with the everyday affairs of the world. It used to be on paper, until we ran out of this common commodity some years ago.

"Imagine," Athena once said, "cutting down trees to

make paper. How barbaric!" She loved nature.

"What's up, Amadeus?" I reached out for the tablet but he held onto it.

"It's the Chinese. I must help them. They are falling back into... There are quite a lot of them. They built flying machines, based on your antigravs, Mother. I told you it would come to no good. You can't give people toys and expect them not to use them."

"The antigravs must have been produced in a Tibetan sanctuary. Have they done anyone any harm?" Ambrosia looked just a little worried, but mostly her facial expression showed disbelief.

"Maybe not yet, Mother. I don't know. But you know people. And..."

"And what, Amadeus? Is that all there is? They're flying around?"

"Well, I don't know. I'm told that they are flying all over the place, dropping some sort of stuff from their magic carpets. That's what they call them, Mother. Magic Carpets."

"How quaint," Athena clapped her hands. "I must fly one, I must, may I, Mother?"

When she acted like that she looked like a girl of twelve. Not a mean feat for a 100-year-old maiden. Incongruously, right then I wondered how come she hasn't married, or at least had a boyfriend.

"Amadeus," Ambrosia sat up straight in her chair. She spoke quietly, only just above a whisper. "There is something you don't seem to understand. Everything I produce, every new idea I have, comes from within, from the Infinite Potential. It is not mine to keep it away from others. All my ideas belong to all who can read my mind. Surely, you know that?"

It was at that moment that I began to get a glimmer of what they meant when they said that we were all One. It seemed so obvious, yet it never came to me before.

Mama raised her hand and immediately there was

silence. For a while no one spoke. Mama sat very still, with eyes closed. Her facial expression hasn't changed, but I immediately guessed what she was doing. I'd bet my life that she was communicating with the Head of the Tibetan sanctuary.

Finally she opened her eyes.

"Amadeus is right. There may be a problem with the Chinese. We need more facts."

I was trying to figure out what was going on. We were all one. In a way, we shared all that we possessed; all knowledge, but not necessarily all that resulted from it. It was as though Einstein had kept the equation $E=MC^2$ to himself. Even if he did, he couldn't do it for long. The same applied to the teachings of the great Masters of the past, the great composers, great artists. For a while people have tried to maintain a 'copyright' to make money, I supposed, but even that expired after a while.

The gifts we received from within were universal. I wondered why I didn't see it before. The only question remained who would be responsible for abusing such gifts. Could we hold Einstein responsible for others producing an atomic bomb? Hold Yeshûa responsible for the Crusades? For the Spanish Inquisition? It would hardly seem fair.

Hence, whatever the Chinese did with Ambrosia's invention would remain on their conscience, not hers.

And then we all heard a rumble, like a deep, sonorous, smoldering volcano. I knew immediately where it came from. Though his lips were tightly closed, we all looked at Amadeus. And then I heard the lava exploding. It was more horrifying as it was delivered to us in utter silence.

...and no one can blame him who built the nuclear bomb as he never dropped it on anyone... ...nor can we blame him who offered the means of delivery... nor those that didn't pilot the plane... ... nor can we blame him who dropped the bomb... as he did not invent gravity... ...we are all innocent... ....

"Then what are we all doing here?"

That last was said in a reluctant whisper, but the hurting was still there.

What preceded this final question was the most poignant silent scream I ever heard inside my head. It was painful. It was throbbing in my head an hour later. It was obvious that it was tearing Amadeus apart.

My son was hurting.

The silence stretched. One by one we all turned towards Mama. Did she know the answer? Would she offer help? Surely, she'd not impose her solution. That was the one thing she warned us against. Not against solutions but about imposing them.

"We are all free agents of the Universe," she said at last. "But let us never forget that it is an Infinitely Benevolent Universe. It is that benevolence that we carry. It is due to that benevolence that we are here. Most of us could just as easily remain behind the Great Divide much longer. We have chosen the challenge of coming here during the time of great transition. We shall all make mistakes. All we need do is to make sure we leave a better world for having been here."

She did not take the sting out of Amadeus's poignant cry. Nor did she offer a solution. But she reminded us why we were here. Now it was up to us, up to every single one of us, to find our way. It was the only way to earn our place in the Benevolent Universe. There were no shortcuts, no easy answers. There was only hope. And faith. And most of all there was an abundance of love.

Slowly, almost reluctantly, people were beginning to leave the table. When Ambrosia got up, I followed her. At that moment I heard a silent whisper.

...*stay*...

It was Mama. I saw that we were alone. She patted the chair next to her.

"Sit down, Simon. I must explain something. You alone

amongst us have been brought up in the Christian religion. My explanations to others might not be as clear to you. You have been raised to believe in the Son of God."

I nodded, lamely, though I have freed myself, if not wholly from my Jesuit conditioning.

"The Son of God is nothing else than consciousness. It is that within us that makes all the decisions, passes all judgments. It is the sole arbitrator of what used to be called good and evil. It and it alone can decide on your future, on your potential."

Mama was right. My conditioning was still strong. In part I still expected some celestial power to do my thinking for me. As for the Son of God, surely, wasn't there only one? But if so, why did the scriptures call us all children of the Most High?

Mama smiled.

"And don't forget that there is only one, single Consciousness. It is omnipresent. It chooses to individualize itself through each one of us. We are all called to bid its will. It is that within us that assures us of our immortality. It is that within us that is indivisible from the Source."

Slowly the weight of Mama's words was getting through to me.

"And, my dear Simon, from amongst the countless billions of biological life forms on Earth alone, we and only we have a vague awareness of our heritage. That, my friend, is an enormous responsibility."

Her last words were hardly above a whisper.

It was getting dark. I didn't notice that rare clouds began to gather over the eastern horizon, and now were approaching with increasing speed. It was the East that brought us lately the prevailing winds. There was little protection from them. We were the highest point over the vast era of the Aegean Sea. It was time to go indoors.

It was too late for us to return to our duties. Each to his and her own individual, crucial function, necessary for the smooth operation of the Universe that we have been destined to perform. No matter how great, no matter how small. They, and hence we, were all indispensible.

Tomorrow will be soon enough.

Some minutes ago, we'd all risen from the table with our heads bowed, helpless to help Amadeus. The knowledge that he had his own Karma to discharge was of little consolation. We all loved him, hence we all shared his anguish. We all did so in our own, individual way.

Only one of us didn't drag her feet.

Before Mama had asked me to remain, Athena jumped up from her chair, kissed Amadeus on both cheeks, then Mama, Papa, myself, and finally Mavis, Tom and John on the other side of the table. And then she danced away, down the garden paths, performing a couple of pirouettes on the way. Perhaps she was practicing for the next lesson she was going to give, somewhere in our tiny Kingdom. Or perhaps right there and then, she was doing her own individual, crucial function, necessary for the smooth operation of the Universe. She was spreading joy. On that day, her function was perhaps more important than any other.

***

16
The Yellow Dragon

The problem with China did not go away. Problems, I found, seldom if ever disappear on their own. They were here for us to solve them, to learn from them, to rise above them. And apparently Amadeus decided to do just that.

I could see that Mama and Papa remained worried. It was evident that they considered all people on Olympus, if not in the whole Aegean Kingdom, as their responsibility. When I asked Papa about it, his response left me baffled.

"If you cannot inspire a tiny Kingdom, what of the rest of the Earth, or of the solar system, or a galaxy?"

To this day I have no idea what he meant by that. Nevertheless, they remained worried. I thought that acceptance comes with the territory of becoming a god. Not so, I was repeatedly reminded. Becoming a god was the beginning, hardly the end of the journey. Infinity applied to all things divine. To the absence of time and space limitations, it seemed, and to the elusive benevolence. And to the irrepressible Oneness.

A week after Amadeus came to see me in my study, he did return, after all.

"I still need your help, Dad," he began.

For some reason I found his request flattering. As I looked up from my computer where I'd spent about 60% of my waking hours, I saw that his brow was furrowed, his face very serious. Tom and Jerry, later Tom and Ambrosia on their own, were finding it increasingly difficult to keep the computers operational. They were running out of spare parts, and still had few means of making new ones. Thank God, Ambrosia's lab had some machinery which made that, at least in part, possible.

"I want you to go with me to China," he said.

I was right about my son's character. There was neither verbal nor implied 'please' in his request. It was at best a neutral expression of his will. Needless to say there was also nothing comical in his tone of voice. Nevertheless, I chuckled.

"I can't fly, son," I replied, thinking my response a perfectly reasonable to an inane request.

"I am serious, Dad. I know that I am recognized as having eidetic memory but I need a witness."

He was serious after all. There must have been more to his request than I previously thought.

"We shall bilocate," he explained.

Again, there was no 'by your leave', spoken or implied. Just a *fait accompli*. I decided to ignore the form and concentrate on the request.

I'd only done bilocation once, and that was with Ambrosia to see Athena's private garden. In spite of all the evidence, I still had problems accepting that it was real. It is one thing to accept something at an intellectual level and quite another to do so emotionally. I remember many years ago, watching a big Boeing 747, affectionately known as Jumbo Jet, taxing down the runway, accelerating, and becoming airborne. I knew exactly how that happened, but emotionally I remained ambivalent. Those birds were just too big, too heavy, and even too unwieldy to fly. Yet they did. They didn't even flap their wings. That's roughly how I felt about bilocation. I did it, but I couldn't quite believe it.

"I'd be there with you, Dad. All the time." Amadeus was

obviously trying to reassure me.

"Why do you need me?"

"It's complicated," he began, then bit his lip. Then he took a deep breath and continued. "God's can't lie. Not really, Dad. It is not that we couldn't if we wanted to, but as everybody can read everybody else's mind, it would be rather abortive, don't you think?"

Now this was the kind of logic I appreciated.

"But there is another side of it. We all regard reality in a subjective way. Seeing something differently is not lying. It merely means that we all perceive reality in our own particular, you might say individual way. I need your dispassionate presence, your dispassionate observation to witness and assure me, or deny if need be, that my judgment is sound."

That was becoming more arduous. Sound judgment is based on knowledge of facts, and Amadeus's knowledge was vastly greater than mine.

"But our emotional bias is exactly at par..." my son added after a pensive moment.

"...and emotions affect our judgment?" I asked.

"Don't they?"

He was right, of course. I just made my point. Already his judgment was sounder than mine. This time we both laughed which helped to lighten the gravity of the discussion.

"So you want me as a witness, that's it?"

"Essentially yes. Do you mind? I don't want you to get involved in case... in case..."

"...in case I pick up some unnecessary Karma?"

He smiled. "You read me, Dad, the way I used to read you."

I rather liked that. Also I took it as a complement. They are a rare treat among the gods. Yet, in spite of all this, for some reason I had cold feet. It was almost as though I've been afraid I might cross over to China, and not know how to get back. It was then that I was struck by an idea. I needed someone to hold my hand and, let's face it, Amadeus's mind would be on different things.

"I have an idea," I said, quietly, as though sharing a secret. "I'd like Mavis to come with us."

"But why?"

His surprise was genuine. Which meant that he hasn't read the reason in my mind. Good!

"Do you object?" I asked instead.

"Well, now…"

"Then that's settled. Arrange with her when she's free and I'll make myself available. And don't worry. She'll be virtually invisible," I added. It was my turn to afford a spurious grin.

My son left my study shaking his head. He kept his hair short yet curly, which gave him a look of a Roman warrior, not that I've even seen any Roman warriors, but some statues I'd seen long ago gave that impression. Or it could have been the statue of *Discobolus* that I've seen in the British Museum in my youth. I remember deciding right there, after seeing that statue, to become a disc thrower. It was a painful shock to me that, at St. Stanislaus College, there were no discs. Not even javelins. I was told that after one Padre had his cassock pierced, Jesuits thought them too dangerous for boys to fling around.

My god… my youth!

It almost sounds obscene. How come I still remember such details?

I am sure that my son left my study deeply baffled. Finally, after all these years, I managed to baffle my genius son. I felt very proud of myself.

I also remember Mavis's behaviour in London. I recall her unique ability to remain inconspicuous, almost invisible, when she chose to do so. She still retained this singular trait. Now and then I virtually missed her presence, even when she was sitting at the same table during dinner. She matured, of course, particularly since becoming a mother. But other than that, she remained her old, or should I say 'young' diminutive presence. As all the gods of our little gathering, she didn't appear to age. Even her matronesque tendency of some months, or had it been years, ago seemed to have disappeared. She was the original, ageless, semi-invisible Mavis.

There were some very strange people at Olympus. Conversely, Olympus bestowed on people very strange attributes. Even I was amazed at some things I did. And now Amadeus was asking me to perform another.

Wonders will never cease.

I wasn't cognizant of anything around me, let alone of myself, when Jerry died, or translated, as they called it on Olympus. Translated to higher vibrations, they said. To the first heaven, which they said was what others call the Astral Plane. I think it had something to do with our bodies, there, being made up of photons and not atoms. It didn't seem to make them any less 'solid'—ever remembering that here, on Earth, our bodies were essentially empty space.

Mavis came to see me moments after Amadeus left. She was already sitting on the settee when I turned. I hadn't heard her come in. Perhaps my son had left the door open.

"Are you busy?" I asked.

"No, Uncle. I am never busy for you."

That sounded nice to hear. We didn't speak that much lately. In a way, Mavis seemed busy being Mama's unofficial yet apparently very welcome if not indispensible assistant. They visited some houses together. Mama obviously liked her. Perhaps it was Mavis's inherent humility—or the very fact that she was so inconspicuous. Her presence did not detract from the import of Mama's work.

"Amadeus asked me to go to China with him. Tibet, really but on Chinese business."

She sat there, quiet as a mouse. I felt a little guilty asking her to leave hers and Athena's secret garden. Not that I even admitted to her that I've seen her there. I presumed she'd still visited it daily.

"Would you come with us?" I expected an argument, an excuse of some sort.

"Of course, Uncle. I'd be happy to."

I'm so glad we took her with us, that day in London, when she claimed that all her family was dead. They weren't, of course, but they couldn't hear each other's thoughts. That made them pretty dead by her standards.

"Thank you, Mavis. You're a true friend."

Was there anything more to say? She obviously assumed that we would bilocate. There was no other way to get there. And bilocation was as good for an hour as it was for a few days. Nobody knew exactly what was the limit, but Mama once told us that eventually our physical energy would pull us back. A little like Ambrosia's miniQT, only we could set the QT, whereas when bilocating the return was unpredictable. Perhaps it differed from body to body.

"Think of it as an elastic band. You can pull it only so far, and only for so long. It pulls you back when you reach spatial or temporal limits," Ambrosia had said.

That was supposed to make it clear to me.

Seeing my vague consternation, she offered, "Would you rather I gave you mathematical equations for positive and negative electromagnetic properties of subatomic neutrinos and other particles?"

I declined with as much dignity as I could master. The only thing I gathered from her words was that our projected bodies, if such they were, consisted of particles and not just pure energy. For reasons I couldn't explain, this fact had given me a degree of comfort, or perhaps reassurance, that I didn't imagine it all.

And on a parallel course of my abysmal ignorance, I still wasn't quite sure why Amadeus insisted on going there.

Taking into account the thought transfer abilities of Olympians, his explanations left something to be desired.

In those days, China was an enormous Yellow Dragon. While Europe, the two Americas and Africa have been chopped up into smaller, if not actually islands then a series of subcontinents, China remained the same monster housing more than one billion people. Of course, we've only learned of their populations many years later. Even the Indian Subcontinent broke up into five or six mini-subcontinents, each the size of a good two or three pre-holocaust European countries. While the western coast of North America was no more, and Mississippi grew into a sea that split the rest of the continent in two landmasses, which linked the Great Lakes with the Gulf of Mexico, China was the sole exception. It alone retained its approximate geographical contours. We still had no news about what happened to Canada, although there was some talk about the Saint Lawrence River becoming many times wider. All this was fairly hypothetical, based on reports from various sanctuaries scattered around the world, which produced enough energy to broadcast their findings. Once such radio messages arrived at Olympus, they were supplemented by subliminal contact, to fill in the gaps.

China, having escaped the fate of other parts of the world, retained a great deal of their past industrial resources. About a year later, their still operating satellites supplied some photographs, which confirmed most of previous geographical reports.

China was the only nation that wielded some power.

On my second meeting with Amadeus I'd learned that they were using nanotechnological implants, to make their people subservient to the dictates of the ruling oligarchs. It was on learning this that Amadeus had decided to try and subvert the oligarchs' efforts to turn the clock back to pre-apocalyptic times.

Amadeus, thanks to Ambrosia, had enough understanding of physics including of nanotechnology to put the spanner in the Chinese works. That's an expression I brought from England. It means to do something that will upset the plan from succeeding.

My son confessed that, as of yet, he had no idea how to go about it, but that he relied on inspiration to free the Chinese masses from the control of the few.

"It will come, Dad. It always comes. You just must open yourself to the unconscious," my son told me.

"You mean subconscious, don't you," I countered.

"No, Dad. Subconscious is what already happened. Unconscious is what could be," he replied, making things perfectly clear. At least he thought he did.

...and conscious is the present...

I heard that last as though it was too obvious to mention. Perhaps it was.

Elsewhere the political, religious and industrial oligarchs had filled people with overwhelming frustration brought about by centuries of exploitation. They brought the long suffering masses to the point of no return. A little less than a century ago, in little more than two decades, they took care of the problem themselves. Outside China there were no more oligarchs, no more ruling classes. No more governmental hobnobs living off the toil of their obedient servants. Neither were there any sacerdotal fraternities living off other peoples' backs.

The ground has been cleared for a new way of life.

Before our trio's bilocation, which consisted of sitting down and keeping still for an extended period of time, I decided to find out more about Mavis. I thought that apart from Mama, only Ambrosia was likely to be able to enlighten me about her past. I don't mean her past in London, in the lackadaisical lap of my long-gone family, but her real past, as the direct result of her previous stints on Earth. I could have tried to ask Mavis herself, but somehow I found it embarrassing. My slowly diminishing, or was it retreating, inferiority complex was showing its ugly head again. I wondered why we were all born with an ego. It seemed to have made life so much more difficult.

...*it helps you to survive*... I heard in my head.

It was Ambrosia. Having sensed my qualms, she was on her way to see me. She came in before I could analyze her answer.

"To survive in the phenomenal reality," she added, even as she pushed the door to my study open.

"How come?"

"While as we enter the inner world the sensation of Oneness becomes self-evident, one of the reasons why we are here is to learn that separation is not in our interest. And to survive apart, we have to have sufficient ego to live, at least in part, at other people's expense. Once we fully appreciate that, we shall free ourselves from the necessity of coming back to the dualistic worlds."

"Worlds? Plural?"

"Countless numbers of them. Worlds without end," she said, knowing that I associate this expression from my Jesuit days, although in those days it carried a very different meaning."

"That many, eh?" I put in with my best Canadian accent.

She smiled. It was time to be less serious.

"That reminds me, my darling, you never told me about Mavis's ah, you know... origins?"

She laughed with her usual, joyful, a little rare of late, laughter. "Darling, isn't it obvious? You mean which one of them, don't you?"

I had a peculiar feeling of sinking deeper and deeper into abysmal depth of my ignorance. But, I had no choice, I was completely baffled.

"Of course," I lied, having absolutely no idea of what she was talking about.

"Well, I must admit, at first sight it is not easy to tell..."
Ambrosia admitted. "What do you think?"

I was working full time to hide my thoughts from my
wife. Of late, I was becoming progressively more
embarrassed at my ignorance. I really couldn't tell why, but I
suspected that all people at Olympus had instant recall of all
the memories accumulated over the last few reincarnation.
They were not born with them, but they managed to work
them out. I didn't.

"Cm'on, dear... there were only nine of them?"

Nine of them *what*, I could have said? But my ego
wouldn't let me. And then it hit me. Nine of them... Nine
muses! I studied them all in Montreal. It seemed so long ago,
but... what's a century or so between friends, I mused? I
closed my eyes and counted: Calliope, Clio, Erato, Euterpe,
Melpomene, Polyhymnia, Terpsichore, Thalia, and Urania.
Damn it, why did she have to be last? Mavis loved stars. She
sailed by night, she...

"Urania!" I almost screamed, triumphantly.

"Of course, wasn't it obvious?"

Everything is obvious once you think about it. And then
it hit me again. Perhaps that was why the Olympians knew so
much more than other people. They trained themselves to
think better. To use their acumen to the full. Is this what gods
also did? Thought deeper and better?

As I mulled those thoughts in my mind, I detected waves
of pleasure washing over me. I knew who it was, although
she'd already left the room.

That's another thing gods could do. They were capable
of enveloping people with pleasure. Pure, unadulterated
pleasure. It must be good to be a god, I mused,

...*you are*... reached me from afar.

More pleasure.

Amadeus knocked on my door and came in. He wasn't

rude. He simply knew that he would be welcome. Normally he was practically an *arbiter elegantiarum*. A paragon of refinement. A picture of elegance. Or something like that. I've never seen him in shorts, except for swimming, of course. His trousers were always perfectly pressed, his white shirt spotless, his shoes polished unless he was wearing sandals. I have no idea whom my son took after, as I have never been accused of being excessively elegant. An absentminded professor, but not an arbiter of anything.

Amadeus was as good as he could be.

"Yes, son, what is it?"

"They are expecting us, Dad. Whenever you are ready."

Things move fast when you don't have to book your flight or get your train tickets.

"How soon is soon?" I asked, just a little nervously.

"I spoke to Mavis. She's ready too."

"So what do I have to do?"

"Will you let me help?"

I remember the pleasant feeling of relaxation when Ambrosia administered the pre-bilocation regiment. Or whatever it was that gods did before they did the impossible. I nodded. I was about to say, go ahead son, but it was too late. Amadeus appeared to have even greater powers than Ambrosia. Once again I saw that power is what defines gods. I also realized how incredibly easy it would be to abuse such power. To abuse powers that remained totally invisible.

I looked at the man in front of me. He looked like a monk. A Buddhist monk. He bowed deeply.

"Welcome to our humble abode," he said. He then spread his arms to include all three of us.

Just for an instant I was stunned. I looked at Mavis and relaxed. She was still wearing the same light, butterfly-like chiffon I saw her wearing around the house. Both, Athena and Mavis seemed to like this ephemeral disguise. They really did look more like butterflies than women.

She nodded.

...hello uncle... it is nice to see you again...
Now wouldn't you relax if you had a butterfly smile at you?

We arrived in a room, almost a hall, which could accommodate some 30 to 40 people in relative comfort. The walls were solid stone, and judging by the temperature, with little or no insulation. Our host looked like a man of about 40, which probably made him between 100 and 200 years old. Those were the Tibetan gods, that matched the Olympians in every respect, with the possible exception of Mama.

The man clad in a red robe and a broad smile welcomed us. He motioned us to the balcony, where we were served tea. It was all very strange to me, as not a single world had been spoken, yet I understood all the sentiments expressed by the monk.

The last thought set me back. The monk implied that the walls had ears, a phrase well known to imply listening devices planted by civilian or military authorities. Once on the balcony, the monk addressed us in near-perfect English.

"We are honored, Madam and Gentlemen."

Soon I learned that that was the limit of his command of English.

While Mavis and I sipped tea, Amadeus and the monk engaged in communication that was conducted at such incredible speed that only occasionally I caught what may have been a word. Even at subliminal communication I found it astonishing. It was as though they both spoke at once, yet their facial expression suggested complete mutual understanding.

Once more I was reminded how far I still had to go.

I learned later that the Sanctuary was not strictly a part of the monastery, but it overlooked the hilly terrain where a number of buildings officially comprised the Ganden Monastery. It was one of dozens of monasteries peppering most of Tibet. It was situated at the lowest level of the built up settlement, which, I later learned, reached up to 4,300 meters, a lot higher than Olympus. In spite of its high elevation, it did not compare with the beauty that enhanced Milos. The hills surrounding the buildings looked barren, with little more than shrubs for vegetation. In fact it was as different from the relative opulence of Milos as one could imagine.

So these were the Himalayas, the Abode of the Snow, which is what the word means. We were lucky that while we were there, there still was scant vegetation softening the austere landscape.

Minutes later I was standing in my study, with Amadeus and Mavis smiling at me.

"Why did you ask me to come," I asked. "I didn't understand a single word of your exchange."

"Perhaps, Dad, not at your conscious level. But your subconscious recorded every single nuance. It is there in case I need to support my conclusions."

With that enigmatic assurance he thanked me, Mavis kissed me on both cheeks, and I was left alone. I shrugged and switched on my computer to record the event. There was very little I could write, although according to my son, a great deal remained to be revealed should necessity arise.

As I keep saying, I have a long way to go.

***

17
Karma

For reasons that have not been made clear to me, I have been invited to the meeting that Amadeus had with Papa. Soon Mama joined us. For my son, Papa was the absolute authority on how to proceed with the protection of ordinary people, of the masses who have not yet learned to take care of themselves. This taking care had little to do with their physical survival, but rather with the freedom of growth and development of their human potential.

Soon I learned that, once again, my presence had been required only in my capacity as a historian. I was to keep records for posterity, which record was intended to forestall the repetition of mistakes of the past.

I learned a great deal.

In the West, by the beginning of the present millennium, children received up to a total of 50 doses of more than a dozen vaccines, before they reached the age of 6. Within 20 years China caught up with the West. Their children had been treated to the same chemicals interfering with the natural immune system as we've been doing in the West. Only in China, as indeed most things, vaccination had been more or less compulsory.

Recently, in China, under the same plan, a vaccine that made children more docile, hence more obedient and easier to control, had been added to the already existing list. This new vaccine was similar to the one that a century or two ago had been injected into bulls that exhibited just a little too much fighting spirit in the *corrida*. After all, murdering bulls was pure entertainment. The actors, the professional *toreros*, particularly the *matadors,* had been treated as long-gone Hollywood stars, and thus were a valuable commodity. They had to be protected.

Hence, instead of injecting bulls to make them more docile, the same principle has been applied to children. Nanotechnologically enhanced vaccines had been used to produce virtual automatons, endless ranks of unquestioning, obedient workers. The monks in the Tibetan sanctuary just weren't quite sure how they did it.

In as much as protecting the human body was not against the moral or ethical code of Olympians, nor to my knowledge of any other gods, when such interfered with the functioning of the mind, it became a powerful no-no. It was counter to the attribute of freewill that enabled man to rise on the evolutionary scale. The same, of course, applied to brainwashing of any kind, which was regarded at par with black magic.

For once, Mama and Papa were helpless.

"There is nothing you can do, son," was Papa's announcement. "We cannot interfere with the natural development of a nation. I cannot even impose democracy on them," he added, in visible distress.

He looked at Mama for support.

"Sad but true, Amadeus," Mama agreed.

The matter was dismissed.

Amadeus thought otherwise.

I went back to my study.

Weeks later Amadeus confessed that the offensive vaccine was controlled by a small group of people, by the select governing plutocrats, who escaped the fate of their counterparts in the West. They survived, only to continue in their nefarious ways.

I could see that my son was in considerable quandary.

"Surely, Dad, didn't the Jesuits tell you that there are sins of commission as well as omission?"

"And just how did you know that?" I asked, redundantly. By the time we adopted Ambrosia and Amadeus I'd been cured of the Jesuits' good-natured brainwashing.

"You were thinking about this some months ago…" he replied, a little sheepishly. "I couldn't help it, Dad…"

"I know, I know. I've been broadcasting."

Amadeus nodded, a boyish smile lighting up his face. I'm still wondering how can a 100+ old man produce a boyish smile.

Never mind.

"So what is your point, son?"

"Can we just ignore things that are patently wrong just because we conform to some rules?"

I mulled that in my mind. By my standards he was right. I have been brought up, conditioned one might say, that ignoring 'evil' was a bad as participating in it.

On the other hand, most of my concepts on morality and even ethics underwent considerable change. More so since I married Ambrosia, let alone since I QT'ed to join the Olympians. They seemed to conform to a different set of rules that I was only now beginning to understand.

"Frankly, Amadeus, I do not consider myself competent to answer your question," I replied, once again aware of my inadequacy.

"But Dad! For years you were teaching Comparative Religion. At a university! You must know!"

There was an amalgam of mixed feelings in his voice. There was command, but also despair tempered by a plea. It's not easy having a son who not only suffers from eidetic memory but also seems endowed with all the characteristics of a genius in a number of fields.

I remained silent.

He understood.

"Sorry, Dad, but you see, Mama refused to answer the same question. She said I have to work it out myself."

That sounded like Mama. She never interfered with anyone's opportunity for growth. No matter how painful it seemed at the time.

Amadeus lingered for a few minutes as if hoping against hope that I'd take the burden of decision off his shoulders. I'd gladly do so, if it weren't for the fact that I had absolutely no idea what it was that he wanted to do, let alone what would be the consequences of such, as yet unknown, actions. Knowing Amadeus however, I'm convinced that if it were a small matter, he wouldn't have bothered both Mama and myself with it. As a rule, Amadeus was a most independent individual—if anything, almost excessively so. Just to illustrate my point, this was the very first time in his life that he'd asked me for advice. Once or twice he'd asked me for help, like with the bilocation to China, but advice—never.

I loved my son, but there was something almost overpowering about him. Perhaps it went with the territory. Perhaps all gods become overwhelming at times.

The answer came many months later. Apparently Amadeus found his own solution to the problem. It was, he told me, or it would be as absolute and as overwhelming as I suspected it would. It would change the course of more than one billion people.

"It will change the course of China itself," he said.

"Herself?" I asked weakly.

But he was gone.

That's my son, I thought proudly, having absolutely no idea what he was talking about.

My pride was also punished. Pride is not allowed among gods. It is as big a no-no as thinking oneself superior to anyone else. After all, in a fraction of eternity, his or her achievements might supersede your own by millennia. There were only probabilities, as Mama would say, but no certainties. I wondered if Mama picked this tenet from Ambrosia and her quantum mechanics.

If there were such, if there were certainties, then there would be little point in us learning as we go. We could just wait a few billion or trillion years and get incarnated only when everything has been discovered.

There was a good-natured giggle behind me.

"Did I tell you about the 'Theory of Everything'?" Ambrosia sounded amused.

"I heard the term," I said, almost proudly.

"At one time they, the theoretical physicists, my dear colleagues I might add, thought that they had found it. In fact they'd thought so a number of times," she smiled as if she'd just told me a splendid joke. "Just the very principle of it is absurd. As you, ah... know, the Theory of Everything, the 'ultimate theory', or whatever you choose to call it, lays claim to the hypothetical single, coherent framework of physics that explains literally everything about the physical universe. The very premise is idiotic, don't you agree?"

I nodded repeatedly, mostly not to make an absolute ass of myself by questioning her hypothesis.

"Well, to my mind, we'd all have to take our toys and leave the physical universe permanently. There would be no point living here, if there was nothing here to challenge the mind."

"I'll drink to that," I said, suddenly remembering that it was past 5 PM and I haven't had a single sip of wine that day. Not one drop!

"But that's only a small part of it," my wife continued. "Those illustrious physicists didn't seem to realize that new aspects are added daily to the physical universe. Why, you may ask? Why?" She took a step towards me, her gesture threatening.

I haven't said a word but Ambrosia was on a roll. She was dangerous when she was like that.

"Because the physical universe is no more than the out-picturing of the creative process that takes place on the mental and emotional Planes. What we see here are only the results. The end products. The fun is in the creation, but we need the here-and-now, the transient, ephemeral, illusory, phenomenal universe to see how much we've screwed up!"

She stared at me, daring me to contradict her.

"Again!" she added, stamping her foot.

She must have screwed something up again, but I had no idea what. I've never heard Ambrosia so outspoken on any subject. I knew that physical laws were sacrosanct to her. In a way, they were, I suppose, but I only then realized that they, too, were no more than out-picturing of laws governing upper realities.

Will this never end, I mused?

"Never, Simon. Trust me, never!"

She was reading my thoughts again. This too, I was resigned to admit, would never end.

...*never*... I heard.

And to prove her point she threw her arms around my neck, pressed her lips to mine and held me in a tight embrace.

"Nor will this," she added, when finally she came up for air.

"I'll drink to that," I said, again.

We went to get the wine. We had the universe to celebrate. That would take at least a small *perron*. Or *porron*, as the Spanish called it. And not so small, for that matter. Somehow, whenever we went out onto our agora to celebrate anything at all, almost instantly other people appeared.

Tom, John, Mavis and Papa were already approaching our baldachin as we arrived at the table carrying our *perron*. Luckily, I noticed that they carried two more. Perhaps they were reading our thought? Or, perhaps, we were broadcasting on purpose. It was good to celebrate life. Isn't that what our

Universe personifies?

Amadeus looked tired. I had no idea what he was doing but whatever it was, it obviously took a lot out of him. I was sure that when he was done, he'd let me know. Until then I tried to radiate positive thoughts towards him. Ambrosia once told me that it helps.

"Don't forget that physically we are mostly empty space. What holds us together is energy."

I must have looked a little puzzled.

"Thoughts are energy, Simon. Powerful energy."

I believed her. I understood that the whole universe had been created through a process of thought and a few other things.

She nodded, apparently satisfied. For now.

About a week later Amadeus knocked on my door. He looked half-dead, but sounded surprisingly cheerful. I was glad to see his smiling face. It's been a while.

"I think it's done, Dad. I really thinks it's done," he began even before he sat down.

I pointed to the settee and I waited for him to tell me what was done, and what made him so cheerful. I surmised it must have had something to do with China.

"And I haven't touched anyone of them... nor any of their toys, instruments and suchlike, I mean. I really didn't, Dad."

Once again he sounded like a young lad trying to get away with something. I waited patiently although curiosity was eating me up. When the silence stretched, I encouraged him though I was still completely ignorant of what, if any, had been his achievements.

"Of course you didn't, son. That would have been wrong."

I must have scored in one.

"Exactly!" he exclaimed, smiling.

It took another ten minutes before he started telling me the story. And what a story it was.

"I knew from grandma and grandpapa, that they wouldn't let me do things my way. I'd go to China and inspire a few good men to get rid of the oligarch, a bit like they'd done it in the rest of the world. God knows there were enough firearms lying about. They were beginning to take after the old USA. I understand there was a veritable paranoia of arming themselves before the world went berserk."

I was amused by his 'God knows' turn of phrase. It was the first time I heard it since I left Montreal.

"And so, Mama and Papa were probably right. If the people were so Americanized, then so, most probably, must have been the oligarchs. In the old USA they used to carry arms. Towards the end, virtually all of them. In China, the countermeasures would have been much stronger. After all, they must have still remembered their own Mao revolution."

I nodded. No one expected what has happened in the States. No one. It certainly came as a surprise to the rich and famous. In China it must have been different.

"So anyway, I thought that physical overpowering wouldn't have worked without an ocean of blood on both sides. The oligarchs, I'd been told, had whole armies of bodyguards. And, surely, we had enough to that. Of blood, I mean."

I nodded to that, too.

"So, Dad, I did it my way."

I took a deep breath but had to let it out before my son decided to continue.

"I couldn't bilocate and do anything without Mama and Papa having my hide. So, I did it…"

"…your way."

"Right!"

At long last Amadeus sat down.

"You know, Dad, about the Eight Immortals of Chinese mythology?"

I nodded. I'd given a lecture about them once.

"Well, you won't believe it, but with the exception of Hè, they all appeared to most of the oligarchs in their dreams."

For some reason my son started chuckling, as if he'd just told me a great joke. I was beginning to smell a rat.

"And just how do you imagine this could have happened?" I asked innocently.

"I heard your lecture, Dad," he said, and when I looked up, he added, "in Montreal."

I vaguely remembered the bunch of characters, the Royal Uncle Cao, Iron-Crutch Li, Lan Caihe... They all lived, reputedly, on a group of five islands... in Bhai Sea? Around there—somewhere on Penglai Mountain.

I was amazed that I could remember all that until I saw Amadeus's face. He was smiling. Then I knew. I didn't remember them all. He did. He was creating their images in my mind. Images, even their names...

"You're cheating, son!" I remonstrated.

"You are innocent even of remembering, Dad. But I must admit that you, quite unwittingly, had given me the idea. The images of the Immortals are so deeply imbedded in Chinese psyche that when they hear any of the Immortals speak their names, in their sleep, they don't even begin to question their sanity. It was quite fun, in a way."

"And just what did the Immortals tell the naughty oligarchs?" I knew the answer before I asked.

"Well, the Immortals in their scintillating wisdom advised them to cut the program of nanotechnological indoctrination."

"That's all?" I was surprised. I expected a much more dire answer, knowing how my son felt about them.

"Yes, Dad. That was all."

For some deep-seated reasons that hovered just below

my awareness, I found the story a little hard to believe. My son was very much a man of action, and this was quite placid. Almost lackadaisical.

"Are you sure that was all?" I repeated.

"Yes, Dad. Read my mind."

I almost ducked under the table. Even a cursory contact with my son's eidetic memory was like falling into a bottomless well of whirling memories. I pulled out as quickly as I could. How on earth could he live with that, I wondered?

"When you're little, two or three years old, it's not so bad. Later, gradually, you get used to it."

It was apparent that opening his mind to me was a two-way street. All the same, as far as I could gather, my son spoke the truth. Invading the minds of oligarchs in their dreams and leaving the equivalent of post-hypnotic suggestions was all he's actually done to them. Except for one tiny item. There was an unspoken intimation of 'or else', though 'what else' remained unspecified.

My son smiled.

...*unspecified*... he confirmed.

...*left entirely to their imagination*... I heard his thoughts seemingly reaching me from afar.

"How many were there?" I asked. I wondered what made my son look so tired.

"There are more than 3000 members of the National Peoples Congress. And then there were a few thousand of billionaires who'd already made their money and left the party, but continued to exploit the masses. It kept me busy for a while."

"What? And you invaded the dreams of all of them?"

"Pretty much. I checked for their involvement first, of course."

As I looked at my son, still questioning his intentions, a smirk of a lopsided smile twisted his mouth.

"The funny thing is, Dad, that as far as we could determine, within a single week all the nanotechnological

conditioning has been suspended. Isn't that funny?"
His chuckle would have awakened the dead.

I needed a rest.

I took my son for a walk on the condition that he would
not talk about his latest adventure, unless I asked. We went
out into the garden, then walked around the house and settled
on the deckchairs on the terrace.

The view from 3,200 meters was as mesmerizing as the
story my son had just told me. It took my mind of his
escapade. I gazed into the distance, trying not to think about
it. In fact trying not to think. Not an easy thing to do. And…
tried as I might, it didn't work.

"Did you tell Mama or Papa?" I asked after a short
while.

"I never do, Dad. They always know."

Of course… how silly of me. Then I remembered.

"I understood that peeping into other peoples minds is a
no-no amongst gods?"

"Dad, we are not other people. We are family, we are
almost One."

My son said it with such ardour, with such conviction,
that I realized that until that very moment I have been
travelling on a wrong track. I was learning to hide my
thoughts, as against trying to harmonize them with every
other Olympian.

…that is exactly it… dad…

…thank you…thank you son…

We both laughed.

"Did they mention if you acquired any negative Karma
through your, you know… your escapade?"

"Neither of them are sure, but they think that my actions
gravitate towards helping, and not imposing my will, or
depriving anyone from learning," my son said, but his face
did not display his usual confidence. "The only problem
could be that I might have initiated the learning process

before they were ready…"

We sat and chatted about Amadeus's plans for the future.

"For a little while I'll just rest. This little prank took a great deal out of me. But soon I'll think of something. I always do."

I wondered about things he might have done, over the years, during the periods of my hibernation that I wasn't aware of. Whatever they were, they must have been tailored to his specific talents. That's how gods act, I mused. Perhaps, one day my time will come.

…*we all love you… dad…*

In all the years, in Canada and on Milos, this was the first time that my son had actually said so. I could not control myself. I reached out and gave him my best hug. Such as Papa would give me. I almost hurt myself!

Even as I was recovering from the my show of parental strength I heard, as though from a great distance…

…*me too… dad…*

…*and me too… dad…*

I recognized Athena's and Mavis's overtones. Then there was a subliminal giggle.

…*I told you… darling…*

Apparently Ambrosia had to have the last word.

For three weeks Tom was busy working with Papa on his new flying machine; an electrically propelled flying carpet would approximate the description. Once Ambrosia produced the design, Papa and Tom were best qualified to organize and implement the production. They had to make do with whatever materials were available on the island, which made it a challenging endevour.

I only mention this because over the last three weeks our contact with the rest of the world, which Tom maintained almost singlehanded, has shrunk to a trickle. And on that day, at last, he left a fully-fledged tablet on the press table for us to see.

There were two items that affected me at personal level. Having taught Comparative Religion for many years, hearing that the reported birth of Maitreya was a hoax, hit me hard. Not that I was a particularly strong believer, but Maitreya represented the culmination of all great Masters of the past, that, at least in theory, all different religious groups were prepared to accept as the reincarnation of their particular prophet or saviour. Apparently one of great many monasteries in Tibet had been trying to achieve hegemony over all others.

Now, or at least for now, all hope was gone.

The second item of news concerned Amadeus more than anyone else. Tom's report stated that as of last week the National Peoples Congress had been disbanded.

Kaput. Dissolved.

Not for the inability of the thousands of members to carry out their duties, only for their conspicuous absence. Except for the few who managed to escape to parts unknown, the others, and that comprised the vast majority, met an untimely death in such a variety of accidents that no sane person could suspect collusion, or blame it on any organized group of people. There was talk of the Eight Immortals being involved, yet no one presented any tangible evidence to that effect. The matter remained a mystery.

The same mysterious circumstances applied to an equally large majority of well-known billionaires, who likewise disappeared from their opulent quarters never to be seen again. Yet, strangely enough, there was no mention of any foul play. No foul play whatsoever...

It seemed that the Chinese had their own special ways of dealing with the undesirable elements, although it was never stated what was it that made them undesirable. Only later I wondered what might have happened to those administering the nanotech doses. Somehow I felt sure that my son took care of them in his own inimitable way.

At long last, Chinese people have been left on their own. A Yellow Dragon without a head. A mystery.

That's all Tom had to offer. As usual, he made no comments. He'd once said that he was only a messenger. We believed him. Knowing Tom we knew that he'd never comment on the untimely death of anyone, let alone many thousands of people. For any reason, known or unknown. Tom loved life.

**

18
Tom and John

Many, many years ago,** thanks to my little daughter called Athena, the intrepid duo used to be Tom and Jerry. At the time they had been named after an American animated cartoons dating back to 1940, created by William Hanna and Joseph Barbera. I remember this because before Papa commandeered Tom and Jerry to be our *ex officio* bodyguards, I'd bought the series of short films for Athena and Amadeus for Christmas. I thought it much better entertainment than the ongoing slaughter immortalized on vast majority of TV programs where murder, mayhem, and explicit sex have become the daily staple. It is hard to believe that by the worldly calendar it all happened around a century ago.

Since Jerry's translation to the inner reality—most people still called it 'dying'—the duo has become Tom and John. Neither of them had anything to do with either cats or mice. They have, however, become two of a kind.

The variety of individuals through which Omnipresent Intelligence chooses to manifest Itself is truly flabbergasting. I thought that over the years, thanks to my many lectures, I've met every possible kind of people, every nuance of character, every dream that permeated the people I've met.

Not so.

Both Tom and John were different, and more so, they were almost diametrical opposites of each other.

Let me count the ways.

Physically, mentally, emotionally, behaviourally, and in every other way you can think of. And yet, in a way that I was not yet able to define, they were One. Perhaps two sides of a lopsided divine coin.

Of one thing I am certain. Whatever Tom was when he'd joined us in Montreal, he has become a very different individual. It is difficult to talk with a straight face about a man nearly seven feet tall that he kept growing, yet this is just what happened to Tom. Not physically, of course. Nor could I point to particular trait. Yet he's grown in ways that changed him from a powerful man into a giant.

From a man into a god.

There are no two ways about it. He must have covered a dozen reincarnations in a single life. Perhaps the stints in Limbo enabled him to do so. I don't know. But while he inhabited the same body, he was not the same man.

As for John, he also went already through rejuvenating stints in Limbo, or whatever reality Mama had assigned for him in which to mature. And I am sure it must have been Mama. From little things she'd said, now and then, while both Tom and John have been away from the phenomenal world in every way other than physical, she seemed to have maintained contact with them. Yet instead of Limbo, where consciousness is supposed to remain static, they'd advanced by hops and leaps to their present condition.

They were already proficient telepaths; they'd both given evidence of the ability to bilocate. To my knowledge, they both were capable of momentary experiences of Singularity, which I knew from personal experience, was the experience of what most people still called God.

Yet physically and emotionally the two men couldn't be more different. Tom was a solid, stoic, immovable object, while John was slim to the very verge of anorexia yet perfectly healthy, seemingly pliant, more like a twig bending with the wind, and apt to be moved to tears of compassion at the slightest provocation. But only when alone. I espied his behaviour without his knowledge. I'd learned the trick of near invisibility from Mavis.

On one occasion however, the two had given me evidence of their unity of thought and views. The three of us stopped for a while on the terrace to relax before lunch, I asked them what they thought about the events in China, and Amadeus's involvement in them.

I asked them if Amadeus was destined to carry negative Karma as a result of the events. Tom spoke first, and then John joined, often in the middle of a sentence, to complete what I thought was Tom's idea. I found it amazing that the two men, more than a generation apart, found such harmony of thought.

"Infinite benevolence is not manifested in selective forgiveness, out of a good heart so to speak..." Tom began.

"...but in granting immortality, which allows you, over millennia to pay all your debts," John finished with a broad grin.

"The Universe," Tom picked up the discourse, "is not equipped with the human concept of a good heart..."

"...but is based on the necessity of absolute balance," John went on, "and constant, one might say eternal, adjustment of balance."

"That's it." Tom nodded in evident agreement.

Even though, I mused, on occasion, it seemed to come precariously close to upsetting the equilibrium. This thought, which I did not vocalize, caused them both to look at me with a mixture of awe and admiration. I am sure I did not deserve such recognition.

If it weren't for her absence, Mama herself could have delivered their overlapping statement. I strongly suspected that the Oneness of which I'd spoken so often was becoming more in evidence after each stint they'd spent in Limbo.

Sadly, it was equally evident that I have been intended to take the low road, to be able to eventually present to the masses the very 'human' understanding of what has transpired. This appears to have been a historian's job, lest the views of the divine, or even the semi-divine, be twisted beyond recognition, and regimented into countless religions. Which process, I had learned in Montreal, was precisely what had happened in the past.

And talking of Mavis, who was instrumental in my ability to spy benevolently on John without being seen, I asked her about her son. John was practically twice as tall as she was. This fact always tickled my slightly distorted sense of humour. How on earth could such a tall man have been born from such a tiny woman? His birth, I mused, must have lasted for hours, if not days... I pictured a very long delivery room, and then I filed this personal paradox together with my emotional inability to accept that heavy airplanes can fly and ships made of metal don't sink.

Just emotional inability. I am not totally deprived of my senses.

At the time when Mavis had joined us in Montreal, she has been by far the shyest girl I'd ever met. In fact her near-invisibility must have originated from that very characteristic. And yet it was she who became pregnant with Jerry's baby— a seeming paradox. After all, they weren't even married. In the old days this would have been considered a no-no. Today, it didn't particularly bother me. On Milos they didn't hand out pieces of paper to attest people's love for one another. At the time, at least to my knowledge, only Mavis was able to read other peoples' thoughts, and thus she knew more about Jerry than I'd ever know. She obviously knew that she could trust him. And yet she didn't strike me as a girl who is keen to become a mother. I took my time. I asked her about this.

"At the time, Uncle, I didn't know that here, on Olympus, we are likely to live for a few generations. I was afraid I'd become like my aunt Pricilla."

I only vaguely remembered her maternal aunt Pricilla,

my long departed sister, back in London, of course. She was an old maid who'd spent all her time instructing everyone on acceptable modes of behaviour.

"I had a son," she explained, "because women who don't have children, or have them too early in life, more often than not grow up to be Aunt Pricillas."

She looked up at me to seen if I knew what she meant. I nodded.

"To be frustrated teachers," she added, just to make sure. "They seem obliged, even compelled, to pass on to everyone their acquired knowledge, 'the wonders of the world' they call them, no matter how dubious or prosaic. They think they hold the wisdom of the ages in their palms and must pass it on. They become nitpickers without a class of juveniles, on whom to vent their frustrations."

I was surprised that already then, in Montreal, Mavis had been concerned about personal growth and her responsibilities toward others. A very clever young lady, even then...

"Only later, much later in their development," Mavis added sadly, "most women realize, albeit subliminally, that they have had children in thousands of incarnations, and that many of them, as well as other women's children, survived without the benefit of their assumed wisdom."

As I already said, a very smart lady, if no longer as young. Yet, I wondered, why Jerry?

She read my thoughts.

"He was very nice and I was very shy," she explained.

"And head over heals in love with you…"

…*that certainly helped*… I heard on the inner, followed by a slight giggle. And then the unthinkable happened.

With all her stints in Limbo or whatever means she used to rejuvenate herself, she, my adopted daughter, at the theoretical age of well over a hundred—blushed.

Her only slightly suntanned cheeks assumed such rosy freshness, that for a moment there she looked exactly as she had in Montréal, when she'd realized that finally she found a home among the living.

With that she got up and ran, to hide her apparent embarrassment.

Mavis hardly aged physically. Emotionally she retained her youthfulness. Mentally she was advanced beyond any man's natural lifespan; any man's or woman's, of course. Olympus did strange things to people. And now, she was the mother of equally as youthful, and perhaps as young emotionally, John. Her first and only son. A most wonderful 'young' man.

If beauty saloons in Montreal could have pickup up on the Olympus women's secret, they would have become billionaires in no time at all. Alas, there were no beauty saloons in Montreal any more. For all I knew, there was hardly any Montreal.

It's been a little while since I had a *tête-à-tête* with Mavis. The last time I really enjoyed it. There were not that many people to talk to, not in the immediate vicinity. Apparently she enjoyed it, too. She invited me to join her in her private garden.

It seemed that the seasonal changes did not hold true in the Milos Kingdom. Or else, we didn't know, as yet, what they were supposed to be in the new scheme of things. The global climate remained a big unknown. As with other items, we were only kept abreast of such in the immediate vicinity of the various sanctuaries, and climate changes were hardly at the top of our or their agendas. And sanctuaries, almost by definition, have been created in fairly inaccessible places.

Or else, possibly, Tom didn't think it worthwhile to report them.

Here, on Milos, it was a little like living on, what used to be, the French Riviera. Perhaps it still was. There were no sanctuaries in France so we had no way of knowing.

Mavis and I went out on the terrace, sat down, and bilocated together; I mean, at the same time. Ambrosia came with us. She loved Mavis's garden almost as much as Mavis. I, on the other hand, had no idea if it was Mavis's or Athena's domain. Perhaps they both used it for moments of respite. If it wasn't the same, then there were great similarities. On the other hand, I've only been there once before.

At the very last moment John asked to join us.

The next moment we all stretched out on the grass, inhaling a multitude of wild scents that permeated the whole area. There seemed to be no animals around, except for the birds and the bees; and other gnats, of course, though of the non-bloodthirsty variety. Perhaps our bilocated bodies didn't smell right to their olfactory senses. Of course, if I remember, we were of the neutrinos variety, though I can't be sure.

"I love it here at night. The whole Universe is in the palm of my hand..." Mavis sighed, remembering the beauty.

"I've never bilocated in darkness. I suppose it must be eerie?" I asked.

Mavis looked at me with unbelief in her eyes.

"Eerie at night?"

Ambrosia and I laughed. We both remembered the muse Uranus. Once again, Mavis blushed.

Ambrosia was the first to ask Mavis about Jerry. For the second time she blushed, this time not even trying to cover it up.

"He thinks I'm still with him. There. All the time."

We waited for more.

"John comes sometimes. They are good friends."

Mavis sounded as if the "first heaven", the Astral reality, or Plane, was like a beautiful island next door, in the Aegean Sea. For her, perhaps for all Olympians, it was just as real. For me it was just beginning to be so. It was taking shape, slowly whispering, then calling, as sirens called the ancient mariners. Yet it was different for everybody; both the trip and the destination. We, gods, created all realities, not just the phenomenal one. One might say that the whole Universe was our oyster.

Also, while in Limbo, others had access to all Planes of perception except for the phenomenal world. For me, all worlds were cut off, suspended, to make sure that I record the events from the human point of view. Even the privilege of aging, I suppose or, perhaps, its absence was my sole reward.

"What do you do when you get there," I asked.

"It's complicated," Mavis said.

Ambrosia smiled. Where have I heard that answer before?

"No, really," Mavis insisted. She looked up at Ambrosia, her eyes pleading for help.

"Well, Simon, you'd discover this very quickly yourself. We don't really visit anyone. We visit the person we've created in our minds, who have reality, there, according to our image of them."

She looked pleased with her answer. And she was right. It was complicated.

"We, each one of us, comprise a whole Universe. The whole of our reality is extant within us. We do not experience the Universe created by someone else. We experience the whole Universe created by us."

Her eyes asked, "...is that better?"

It wasn't. I read her mind. Her thoughts said ...*it is complicated*... I just nodded. There was no point interrupting or belabouring the point. I suspect it had to be experienced.

"This is why the concept of Oneness is so important, Uncle. It is only when we become One that our Universes overlap, then merge, and ultimately meld together. They meld into a Singularity. Ultimately we are all One. A single omnipresent, omnipotent, everlasting, entity..."

This last was John, his eyes dreamy, as though he was already there, in that ephemeral Oneness. I'd almost forgotten he came with us. Vague images of saints flashed before my eyes. Did they experience that Oneness? Didn't I some years ago? But for a fraction of a second? If it were any longer we'd surely not recover. I also recalled a biblical expression. *You cannot see my face, for no one may see me and live.* And yet… and yet isn't it the face of everyone? Of every god that chooses to lose himself or herself in the omnipresent Oneness?

Ambrosia touched my arm.

"Sorry, darling, not yet. This is dangerous. Not yet."

I had no idea what she was taking about. I didn't even know that one could faint in a bilocated body.

One cannot.

I was sitting on a deckchair on the terrace. Mavis and John were looking at me, concern in their eyes. Ambrosia was behind me, massaging my temples.

I had so much to learn.

Back in my study, I did my best to write down as much about our trip as I could recall. As much as I could put into words. Not everything can be explained in the English language. Nor in any other, I imagined. Yet my job was to try. Otherwise some time in the future, someone would come and make a religion out of all this. Create a religion that would spew a priesthood that would insert itself between the Source and the aspirant, forgetting that the only bridge between the two is I AM.

Slowly, very slowly, I was learning.

Even to me, in spite of having taken part, by then, in two bilocations, the experience seemed eerie. It was as though we were ghosts that left our physical bodies behind. Except I felt the grass below my back, I smelled the flowers, I talked and listened. It was so much more than a dream. And yet…

And yet I wasn't sure enough to be able to do it on my own. The phenomenal reality has an enormous pull on our perceptions. No matter how illusory, to us, here and now, it is real. I was beginning to envy the gods. The real gods. They seemed so sure. For them at least two realities overlapped, even if, at least for now, it was only a one way trip.

For now. I was growing convinced that for some gods few things were impossible. I also suspected that some of them were only here, in this world of illusion, for our sakes. The Buddhists call them Bodhisattvas. Enlightened beings who remain on Earth for our benefit.

This was all so different from the Comparative Religion I taught at McGill. So very different.

...*make love to me*... I smiled. I could have sworn that Ambrosia was asking me to make love to her.

...make love to me... There it was again.

I turned, yet she wasn't there. I closed my computer and went to our bedroom. Ambrosia was lying across the bed covers sound asleep. It is nice, I mused, to be in someone's dreams.

It was eleven already. We both missed dinner. We all do that sometimes. Food doesn't seem quite as important when you partake daily in the nectar of the gods. In the wine of inner reality. It is just as intoxicating, and just as sating.

And then I had an idea. There was one way to prove Ambrosia, John and probably Mavis, either right or wrong. Very quietly I lay down besides Ambrosia's perfectly relaxed, prone body, and closed my eyes. For once I had all the motivation, in fact all the confidence I needed to do something completely on my own. Something divine. Something only gods can do.

In no time I was perfectly relaxed. I felt my body rising, then hovering about two feet above the bed. Then...

When I came to she was smiling. I knew that smile—a smile of satisfaction, of abundant pleasure, of dreams fulfilled. A smile I have seen many, many times over the years, and always only in one particular circumstance. It was like a cigarette used to be. Only now it was a sated smile.

Was it good for you? I almost asked. My question was intended as a joke. We always treated making love as a game. As pure, unadulterated fun.

She smiled again.

...it always is darling...

I wasn't sure if she was smiling through her dream or if she was already awake.

Surely, we couldn't have had exactly the same dream. Not simultaneously?

...why not... I heard *...are we not as one...*

I lay there waiting until I heard her voice. With my ears, not inside my head. Although sometimes the two have come simultaneously.

"Isn't it time to get up and have a glass of wine? We've both missed supper," she whispered, as though so as not to wake me up.

...ha...ha... I replied.

One *perron* coming up, she said and was gone. She was back minutes later with a half-full *perron* of rich red wine and a tray of cheeses.

"*Bon appétit,*" she said and leaned her head back releasing a thin, perfectly aimed stream of red wine into her parted lips. I loved those lips. I waited my turn. Not just for the lips, but for the *perron*. OK. For the lips, too. Did you know that making love in the Astral world makes you just as tired as in the phenomenal reality?

I had to ask her point blank. One day I'll remember that she *always* read my thoughts.

"Did we...?"

"How dare you. You mean you didn't know who I was?"

That reaction strongly suggested that we did.

"But I thought that we, each one of us, create our own inner universes?"

"Not just inner, darling," she corrected. Her anger was remarkably short lived. I must have been good. "And anyway, what's your point? Didn't you like your creation?"

"So it was mine?"

"Don't you know?"

I was beginning to realize that I knew absolutely nothing. I was deeply confused. My reality and her reality seemed to merge. Meld, as John called it.

I took a deep breath. Maybe, just maybe I was beginning to understand.

"And by the way, you were exceptional!"

***

PART FOUR

Fourth 40 Years

"...he that sat on him had a bow;
and a crown was given unto him:
and he went forth conquering and to conquer."

The Revelation
of Saint John the Divine

19
Fourth Awakening

I was held, frozen, in a tunnel that oscillated with luminescence. All around me, disembodied light of photons that vibrated in place without going anywhere. Potential photons? Incredible silence was almost palpable, yet as though pulsating with expectancy of life. This is what the Universe must have been like before it was born. Before the big bang destroyed the silence forever splitting into the divine and the ungodly.

Here, knowledge preceded understanding. I was hovering between the two worlds. Two out of many? That would require understanding. Yet I knew where I was. Was? Not really. My inerrant, disembodied self-awareness hovered outside the confines of being and becoming. I hovered in a transient reality that neither was nor wasn't.

Ambrosia had told me that in the last stages of the transition to the new Age, the Age of Aquarius, the doors would open. All it would take would be to have the skill to walk through them. But that is not what she meant. Not really. She meant that during this glorious Age, the doors would be open both ways. One would still have to find the gates, but once in the tunnel, in the no man's world, one could go either way.

I hope that's clear. Even I can understand it. I know it.

I had to go back. I also knew that. I was not ready to move forward. I felt a gentle but persistent tugging. Like an elastic band stretched out to the limit. It was time. Time? There was no time here—and yet? The next time I'd walk through the Gate it would be under my own cognizance. As an act of my own will. Not Mama's nor Papa's nor anyone else's assistance. Gods are like socialists—self-sufficient.

That was a joke.

Gods have a twisted sense of humour. Some gods. It takes all types. At least I think it does.

I was lying on the same deckchair on which I'd woken up on previous occasions. My body felt comfortable. It felt like my own. Ha, ha! It was my own. And this time I woke up on my own. I wondered if I was, once again, 40 years older, yet virtually the same. I knew that in my absence they'd looked after my phenomenal enclosure.

Ha! Empty space… almost!

I felt a chuckle coming out of my throat.

Gods knew what to do—they know most things. Knowledge means power, I knew, and gods were incredibly powerful.

I glanced at the back of my hands. The same. No change. No aging spots, not even new wrinkles. No dry skin hanging over the edges. Thank God for gods. God? The good die young, but old habits die slowly. Wasn't the Pluto Effect supposed to have gotten rid of them? No matter. I had been in stasis. Again. The last time? And then I understood. That's what the tunnel was. Is. It is a phase of stasis, both temporal and spatial. It is where all activities are suspended until you decide which way you are going. Most people do not have a choice. Gods do. I did. I woke up on my own. At last.

"Hi," I grinned a little sheepishly. Like a schoolboy on a first date?

"Welcome, darling. Welcome back."

She could have said 'on your own'. She didn't. She had too much respect. She knew that I knew. God, I loved that girl. Woman. Goddess. My own Ambrosia. There was that God again!

She hasn't changed a bit. She was exactly as I

remembered her. Every detail, every hair on her head... She leaned down and kissed me. On the lips. Like in the old days. I couldn't have aged.

Then Mama and Papa came over. They all smiled. I detected a trace of pride as they looked at me. As if my waking up on my own was purely their personal achievement. I didn't care. I felt waves of love sweeping over me. They were my people. My family.

Athena, Mavis, John and Tom came next.

I had a feeling that I arrived. That finally, at long last, I was really home. I was an Olympian.

But there were still questions. Most of them I could probably, with a little effort, answer on my own. It was as though I gained access to the knowledge of others. Of other Olympians. Not all of them. Not Mama's knowledge. But most others. Even Papa became known to me. I even felt his emotions when I placed my attention on him.

It was a new, a little frightening feeling. *Noblesse oblige.* Gods have their own crosses to bear. Each day was the beginning of the rest of eternity. Scary and magnificent at the same time. For me it was mostly scary.

There were consequences. Responsibilities.

Only then I realized why my body has been maintained for such a long time. They, the 'other' gods, could leave the phenomenal reality at practically any time. In a way, they lived on both sides of the gates—of the Great Divide. By crossing the Great Divide, they rejuvenated themselves to virtually any time, to any age. There is no time on the other side. It is an ongoing process of creation, without any limitations of either time or space. At least, not by the standards of the phenomenal universe.

My body had to be maintained for me to witness all the changes that took place to this day. Perhaps also to see and record changes that would take place over the next few years.

In a way, the gods knew what would happen. Not in detail, but within the realm of probabilities. I had to find out the slow, plodding, 'homo sapiens' way, so that people who would read my notes one day would understand what took place from human, temporal, transient point of view.

It had to be that way.

Now, finally, I was free. Even as they were, the Olympians. Yet they remained here. It was the love they held for all who did not understand yet. They all remembered how hard it was, how hard it had been for them before they understood. Papa only reached his peace in this reincarnation. It was not easy. We all travel our own individual paths. Yet we all harbor the same incredible potential.

No wonder thousands of years ago the prophet assured his people saying: "Ye are Gods".

For the last time I have been sentenced to two or three days of gruel. Knowing it was the last time made it easier. I lapped it up a though it was of no consequence. Of course, this time I could control my body much better. I became its master, not its slave. I switched off my taste buds.

The glances I received from Mama and Papa filled me with pleasure, but most of all those I got from Ambrosia. No one could question our love that spanned centuries. Yet by then, we both knew that it also spanned realities.

A truly Olympian gift.

Three days later we were again all sitting on the terrace. This time the *perron* was passed on to me as in the good old days. Only, I strongly suspected that the new days would be much, much better than anything I'd experienced in the past.

Little has changed. The bougainvilleas were conducting a winning battle with the stone facades. Soon there would be no villa left. All we'd see would be a gigantic, two storey bush overflowing with red flowers. For years Papa insisted that it be trimmed but lately, I am told, he gave up.

On the other hand, gods must have indulged in some hanky-panky. While originally the flowers had been in their perfectly natural environment, I've never heard of them growing at some 3000 feet—at 1000 meters above the mean sea level. I suspected that being a god must have its privileges, but this was pushing the limits of fair play. On the other hand, in the Andes of Bolivia, on the slopes of the Sajama Volcano, tree line has reached 5,200 meters. I learned that when, back in Montreal, I was trying to unravel the mystery of the disappearing people from Machu Picchu and other similar environs.

No matter, the bougainvilleas were stunningly beautiful, and that was good enough for me.

And then came the first shock.

Amadeus decided that having freed the people of China from their oppressors, he'd done his job. I learned that today we were celebrating the 10th anniversary of his departure. We used to call it dying. Not any more. We lost the basso voice, the broad smile, the frequent explosions of contagious laughter. But, I have been told at that first dinner together, that we have not lost Amadeus at all. That we could all see him, daily or nightly, or in lucid dreams, to our hearts' content.

I tried it that very first night.

It was true. My son was exactly as I remembered him.

"You realize that what you see is the image created by your own mind, don't you?" Ambrosia asked, her face showing concern.

"Don't be silly, darling. I'd spoken to him. We laughed together…"

She kept looking at me.

"In a way, you are right. Once there we don't really change. All becoming takes place on this side of the Great Divide."

I was getting lost again.

"So what is the 'other side', as you call it, for?"

"Some people call it heaven. A place where you cannot be hurt, or punished, or held responsible for your actions."

"But I've been told that there are many heavens?" I was thinking of Papa's writings in his previous life as Paul. I remember the actual quotations, *I know a man in Christ who fourteen years ago was caught up to the third heaven.* I knew she'd read my mind.

"Already then, Papa knew many things that we are still only just discovering. He told me that the number of levels of consciousness is limitless. But it is not really of any consequence. There are also limitless phenomenal realities. What do you imagine the countless stars are for, with their abundance of planets? The Source is infinite. We, all of us, are only aware of the reality in which we find our becoming at any particular time."

I was discovering that being a god was not all it was implied to be. She was right, as always. Three days ago was the first day of my becoming. And today, is still the first day of the rest of my becoming, of which there is no end.

Amazing.

"Yes, darling. It is truly amazing. And if you're lucky, every day you'll discover new facets of the Infinite Potential that manifest through you."

I spent the next few hours thinking about my son. What an extraordinary man he was. Is? I don't believe you lose your attributes on the other side. You don't acquire any new ones, but you don't lose what you've earned. I decided to ask my son for the real reason for his departure. I did so that very night.

I still hear his voice…

"Mama asked me if I am interested," Amadeus had replied. "I couldn't be sure," he said. "I don't know if Papa wants to continue his work with 'the many'. I suspect that he wouldn't leave Mama. Remember, I have no wife." There was a wisp of sadness in his voice. Then he continued. "After all, Mama is still here, I mean there, and Papa wouldn't want to live without her. Not on any Plane. They are just too close; probably already are one, remember? Virtually one?"

I knew what he meant. I had Ambrosia.

At long last, relaxing and entering the alpha wave state came naturally to me. I have no idea why, but I suspect that, as always, Mama had something to do with it. Perhaps she felt guilty that having asked me to take on the job of a historian, she deprived me of the benefits of heaven, of the Astral reality, for more than 200 years. Humans are not aware that 'dying' earns them a rest, from which they return to the phenomenal reality with not only a new body, but with recharged creative energies. The expression 'may they rest in peace' makes a little sense, as long as we don't destroy its veracity by adding 'for ever and ever'. That would be utter hell. A hell born of boredom, and you couldn't even die to get out of it!

As for myself, by submitting me to long periods of 'non-existence', or suspended animation, I could "neither have my cake nor eat it" so to speak. I can't think of a better way of putting it.

Anyway, now that I could enter the alpha state seemingly at will, in no time at all I was facing my son again. I came straight to the point. I remembered that I wasn't there when Amadeus took his leave.

"What was the real reason, son, for leaving..."

He knew the rest. It was as if he was waiting for me to ask him that very question.

"It's a long story, Dad," he began. It felt a little strange being addressed as dad by someone who was not even 'alive'. Not in the usual sense of the word.

"Just before the previous Golden Age, in some ways similar to the present Age of Aquarius, certain very unpleasant things happened to me. I was not quite ready yet to face them. To forgive and forget."

I nodded, though only partially understanding his argument.

"The problem with eidetic memory is that you remember not only everything that took place in your present embodiment, your present life, but in time you learn to reach back thousands of years into history that not only is long forgotten by most, but twisted beyond all recognition by others. Let's leave it at that."

Again, I could do little but nod.

"I will assure you of one thing, Dad. In all memories accessible to me, no man, in all the millennia that I trod the dust, nobody has ever showed me more understanding, and… more love than you did. It will be my memories of you that will guide my future life on Earth. I would have told you that, had you been there when I was leaving."

The next moment I was wiping my tears. I was back on my bed, upstairs, in my own bedroom. Ambrosia was sleeping quietly, her chest hardly moving with light breath. I didn't sleep that night. Whatever privileges gods have, they are not exempt from suffering. And I missed my son.

I missed his flesh and blood, his physical presence.

I missed him more than I could ever imagine.

This time, during my 'absence' a lot had changed. We still had little idea of what was happening in the rest of the world, but on Milos, the whole of the Kingdom of Milos, or as most now called it the Aegean Kingdom, people were behaving as though they were coming out of a long sleep. It seemed that they were awakening in the Buddhist sense, as though living in constant amazement. Also, it may have been that they were no longer distracted by the superficialities of the phenomenal reality.

No tourist cars with their blaring horns, no airplanes crisscrossing overhead, no cruising ships crowding the piers of ports, islanders milling around hungry for the mighty dollars; or pounds; or Euros. Money became a useless commodity. It's value dropped to zero.

You are where your attention is—I recall an old adage.

And peoples' attention was no longer distracted by the thousand and one electronic devises, nor by TV, nor even radio. They satisfied their interests from whatever they found within their hearts. From their imagination.

And in addition, as Mama had foretold, the doors have opened. The gates that no one suspected were there. Each day more people visited their 'dead' relatives. First in their sleep. Later they'd do so at will. The power lay dormant within them. I know. I've been through it all.

After a short brake to tend to matters dealing with other Sanctuaries, Mama has resumed her lectures.

"Divinity is omnipresent," she said, even as I scrambled to get a seat, "and in every fraction of time and space the totality of divinity is manifested."

I heard her within and without. I was like listening to a stereophonic sound.

"It is not that you are the whole universe," she continued, "it is that the whole universe if within you."

And this, she told us later, is what will happen, gradually, over 2000 years, to most people. Some will stay behind, but all will have a chance to rise to another level.

Ambrosia and I had more time on our hands. At least for now, I had few notes to make. The world was unfolding exactly as it should. As Mama had predicted.

We took long walks, flew the magic carpets to our secret cove, bathed, swam, and even sailed in a 46-foot sloop that Amadeus has rigged for us before translating. Sometimes Athena or Mavis came with us. There were few spare parts, it took him years to fix it. I'll always be grateful to him for that boat. It reminded me of my first sails in the Solent, that narrow strait between the Isle of Wight and English mainland. As for Ambrosia, she reached back in her memory and soon became an expert sailor. She must have had a truly rich and adventurous past.

We did all the things that a 'retired' couple is supposed to be doing. Next to nothing.

Yet, after a week or two, it wasn't enough for either of us. Ambrosia returned to her lab, I tried to make a nuisance of myself elsewhere.

I got busy trying to help the other inhabitants of the Kingdom with their various chores. There was still land to till, gardens to peel, wine to press, and sheep and goats to milk and look after. It was a very rural society, yet some people, inspired by their interests, opened little workshops in which they produced elements of everyday use. A small army of sailing ships, the sails supplemented by electrical motors spinning homemade wooden propellers, began extensive trade with a number of waterfront settlements along the shores of what used to be Greece, Turkey, Bulgaria as well as a number of smaller islands which, over the last 100 years or so, licked their wound and began afresh.

In addition to being the official scribe, I returned, part time, to my only specialty of looking after our vineyards. The work gave me a warm feeling that I could contribute to the welfare of all, not just with my computer but with my hands, my muscles, with the body that through Mama's ministrations survived more then 200 years. I reminded myself of the purported biblical longevity. Not as impressive at that assigned to three Sumerian kings who reined, it was recorded, for 72,000 years each. Not even the more humble biblical characters such as Noah, who not counting the years preceding the flood, is reputed to have lived for 950 years. They must have had good Medicare in those days, let alone a good pension plan.

But even Moses, though he never saw the Promised Land trod this land for some 120 years. Hence, I was still in good company.

Some weeks later I looked into my 'ancient' notes, which I produced in Canada, in preparation for lectures that never materialized due to our rapid departure. I didn't have much to go on, but I vaguely recalled Mama's or it could have been Ambrosia's warning, not to mention the name Ouranos in Amadeus's presence. Likewise, Kronos seemed mixed up somewhere in Papa's life. It's been many years, and that was all I recalled.

I paged through my notes, wondering if anything would catch my eye. I knew that the myths were bound to have been misinterpreted and, as Amadeus once said, twisted beyond recognition. Nevertheless when I came across the phrase below, I caught my breath.

"The Titans fight and defeat Ouranos. Kronos castrates Ouranos with a sickle."

There may have been a different Kronos, and a different Ouranos. I didn't care. I took out my notes and burnt them. I was through with all mythology. From now on I decided to live exclusively in the present.

I sat back and pondered on my future.

Ha, ha... ...present?

Within minutes of closing my eyes to rest them from constant light of the computer, Amadeus dropped in. Obviously not physically, but his image stood before me. He smiled.

...I see you are still thinking about me... Dad...

I no longer questioned such visions as miraculous. I smiled and welcomed my son as if he were right here, in my study.

...if you look on the top shelf... Dad... you will find a file... ...it has your name on it... in my spare time I did some regressions into historical periods... ...you might find them interesting... Dad... ...I did them for you...

I was beginning to doubt the reality of my vision. Yet

Amadeus kept looking at me from his standing position.

...who can tell... ...you might resume your lectures...
...is it not what historians do...

There was a question mark at the end of that thought.

...people are interested in their past...

That last made me smile. It seemed that even on "the other side" people did not lose their sense of humour. It seemed there was only one life, and it manifested through whatever means it had for its disposal.

After this Amadeus's presence dissolved. I suspect my desire to look into my cabinet was so strong that it pulled me out of my alpha wave phase.

I got up and reached for the top shelf. It was a thick file with my name on it. Below, in small letters, I saw my son's handwriting. *"For my Dad, with love."*

That was all.

I took the file and even as I sat down to examine it a voice spoke inside my head.

...as for Titians... I do not know where they are...
...but I am still here...

This was followed by a resounding chuckle.

***

20
The Great Divide

A t long last, after thousands of years, just as Mama has foretold, the gate was opened both ways. This, she'd said, would only hold in the Age of Aquarius. If you could find it within the range of your alpha waves, you could cross from one reality to another, though only for a limited time. Hours, days at most. The pull back was the same, or of the same category as in bilocation. The dominant embodiment, be it physical or photonic, held the upper hand. In my experience Amadeus was the first to use it in our direction. In the past, the religious fraternity would call such an event a vision, or a miracle. The non-religious would refer reports of such events to psychiatrists.

Mama mentioned that there had been cases of visits from even higher Planes. Apart from the mental and ultimately what is still referred to as the 'spiritual' Plane, there are, she'd said, an infinite number of in-between states of consciousness.

I put 'spiritual' Plane in inverted commas, because in all my years on Earth, no one ever explained to me what exactly is the 'spiritual' Plane, or 'spirit' for that matter. I recall from the lectures I'd given in Montreal that 'spirit' comes from Latin *'spiritus'* which simply means 'breath'. And if you spell it with a capital 'S', then it becomes 'holy', as in Holy Spirit. Few people seem to be aware that the word 'holy' comes from Old English meaning 'complete'. Hence it seems evident that for countless generations many people used to worship Complete Breath.

To each his or her own.

Returning to Aquarius, I found that the real difference that characterizes this Age is the ability of those on the other side of the Great Divide, to locate and use the gate on their side. While Mama claimed to have done it in the murky past, she would not divulge the method.

"As with everything, all is given to those that are ready to receive it."

Apparently the concept of "The Many and the Few", the "Chosen Few", held on both sides of the Great Divide.

We knew that he would be coming. Mama already said that he would. All we had to do was wait. We all pretended that it would be nothing out of the ordinary. Certainly not a resurrection of any sort. Just Amadeus claiming his birthright. The birthright of the gods.

Of Olympians.

She didn't mean 'coming' as in appearing behind our closed eyelids, or in our dreams or reveries, but actually walking around in broad daylight. Mama had said that at any moment now the conditions would be propitious. It would be only natural for him to visit us, she'd said, looking at me.

For me it would be much more. I've never had a chance to said goodbye to my son. Never wished him Godspeed.

We also knew that the body he would be wearing would not be made up of atoms. Ambrosia said that on the way back he'd have to adapt the photons to neutrinos. I have no idea what that implied, but apparently Ambrosia knew. Perhaps Mama told her, although she was no physicist. I still had a great deal to learn.

I keep saying that. Thank heaven for eternity.

We waited for him from the day I awakened. At dinner, his chair has been left empty at the table. Every day. Waiting. Hoping. I told no one that Amadeus and I have already been in contact. It was a father/son thing. Private. I suspect they already knew. They were gods, after all.

And then it happened. Amadeus looked both shy and smug, at the same time. I always thought, or imagined, that such two contrasting expressions would be mutually exclusive. But, there again, very few things were exclusive for my son. I bit my lips to act normally. Only yesterday Mama had said that I should. "It is not a miracle, Simon," she'd insisted. "Nothing could be more natural," she'd assured me.

"Are you going to tell us about it?" I asked him, trying hard to keep the tremble out of my voice.

I thought I was referring to Amadeus telling us what it's like 'on the other side', but he chose a different route. As for my greeting, I didn't know what else to say. '*How are you, son?*' would have sounded too stupid. I held onto the arms of my chair not to jump up and embrace him. I was told I shouldn't. It had something to do with neutrinos, not being able to repel the electrons swirling around my atoms. My almost empty-space atoms. Apparently I'd go right through him. Ambrosia said he'd only solidify some time later. It had something to do with some atoms in the air combining with his body.

He looked so very alive. Perhaps more so than when he was here, with us.

For me… forty years ago.

Moments ago we were all lounging after dinner, looking at the reflections of the setting sun on rugged crests just north of us. The fleeting flames dancing on the smooth rock were enchanting, almost mesmerizing. Now that we were on the top of the Mount Olympus we were actually looking down at the fires of the setting sun. An incredible sight.

And now, as though by magic, Amadeus took the center stage. I had to remind myself to keep breathing.

It all happened so naturally. There had been no shimmering air, no fanfares, no hysterical ohs or ahs. One moment he wasn't here, the next he was sitting in his usual chair, which, as I mentioned before, we have left empty for him. I couldn't really define when exactly he appeared. It was as if he's been there all the time. Perhaps he was, in my mind. My heart?

"You remember, Dad, when you sent me back to visit my namesake?" Even his voice was perfectly normal.

Of course I remembered. I've sent my son, as a boy, back in time under hypnotic regression to visit Wolfgang Amadeus Mozart. He came back with an oboe concerto, if I remember right.

"Yes, my son, what of it?"

"Well, there was so much talk lately "of gods and men" that I wanted to find out what really happened."

"With what, my son?"

I kept saying 'my son'. Subconsciously I must have wanted to establish first claim on him. On his attention.

"Well," he started again as though he hadn't heard me, "the first time I heard of gods as pertaining to men was in that Psalm, I believe number 82 (there goes that eidetic memory, I mused). I put myself under, just like you taught me, Dad, and adjusted for temporal flexibility, using the expression 'ye are gods' as psychometric guide line and attraction. I had no way of knowing if it would work, but I had nothing to lose."

Psychometry, I remembered, was a form of extra-sensory perception, or ESP, which enables gifted people to locate and/or make physical contact with the owner of an object belonging to that person. I never heard of anyone using the authorship of words in that manner. It must have had something to do with vibrations the words produced. Knowing my son, he must have spoken them in the original Hebrew.

At any rate, my son made me sit up. Using established words as psychometric draw was a novel idea. So far we've only used objects, as we did with the manuscript, which Amadeus had taken to find Mozart.

"Well," he started again with his usual modifier, at least that's what I think 'well' is in this context, "when the words 'ye are gods' had been spoken for the first time, they had not been addressed to any particular or special people. The speaker, I wasn't close enough to see who, and anyway I wouldn't be able to recognize a person I've never seen..."

"Go on, my son..." he tended to get lost in his oratory, especially when he had captive audience. His basso voice gathered confidence as he continued.

"At any rate, the speaker was addressing a multitude. A crowd of people. Lots of them. He was telling them that they were gods. I found it rather strange."

"That's it?" Not that it wasn't a lot already.

"Well," Amadeus concluded with a much lower voice, "the man, the psalmist I presume, did add that they were all children of the most high, whoever that was." This time he looked at Mama.

We all followed his gaze, but she remained silent. There was a cloud passing overhead, and in that very moment it cast a shadow over her features. It was a strange effect. Momentarily, it removed her usual smile.

It was my turn to say 'well'.

"Well," I said, "if men were gods, then it is indeed a puzzle who was the most high. An enigma indeed." This was the sort of puzzle I tried solving when I was still teaching Comparative Religion.

We continued looking at Mama. At last she spoke. "This single statement has done more harm for generations to come than any other sentence written in all the scriptures."

There was an eerie silence when she spoke. We all waited for more. Mama was in the habit of admiring most scriptures, although her interpretations were far from traditional.

"This single statement has externalized divinity. It

created the first paradox in which gods that by definition are immortal, suddenly had their origin defined. Immortality, as we have already said, not only assumes infinity ahead, but also in the past. Hence, the paradox. You cannot be born yet be immortal."

"But surely..." I couldn't help myself, yet for once Mama wouldn't let me continue.

"Simon, how would you describe Omnipresent Intelligence with all Its attributes to men and women who never heard about psychology let alone of the concept of Consciousness permeating all realities? They had to personify It to make it acceptable to men of their day."

That worked for me.

"The problem was that the ancient speaker described the vessel that the Infinite was using, and not the Presence Itself. 'Ye are gods' refers to the immortal, unchangeable, indestructible I AM within that vessel. Yet, at the time, I suppose he had no way of explaining it. He took the easy way out."

This was the first time that I hear Mama criticize anyone. She was by nature en enabler, not a destroyer. I glanced at Amadeus. He looked as attentive as we all were. And then he wasn't there any more.

In days, months and years to come, Amadeus visited us on many occasions. Yet at that particular moment when Mama stopped talking, he was gone. Once again, no one noticed his actual departure. It was as though he existed in a reality that obeyed different laws.

I found it strange that while already practicing OBE and even bilocation, I could not accept the reality of life after death. I needed evidence. I needed proof.

Over the years, in spite of the countless stories of miracles and strange phenomena I read about in many scriptures during the years I'd spent at McGill, this was the first time that I accepted fully their reality. I remembered the phrase *"Blessed are those who have not seen and yet have believed."* I guessed, I wasn't so blessed, after all. I'd taken the long, arduous road to reach the same destination.

And yet, now, finally I've arrived. And I've arrived thanks to my son. Thanks to Amadeus. When he first arrived at our doorstep in Montreal, I looked up the etymology of his name. It means "Love of God". Now I feel like making a slight adjustment. I thinking the name really means, "Beloved of the Gods".

My Amadeus. My son.

For a long time we waited to see if Jerry would pay us a visit. He did not. Perhaps the ability came to some, even as it did here on Earth. Perhaps it came only to those who knocked hard on the door.

Jerry was as nice a guy as you could hope to find. Yet, apparently, he was satisfied with frequent visits from Mavis, not fully realizing that she is visiting her image of him. There must be some kind of link between all the images we've left behind, there, in the first heaven. I suppose he derived some sort of vicarious pleasure from them. After all, with each heaven we enter, the barrier between 'us and them' is slowly disappearing.

One day, we shall know.

Ambrosia claimed that there might be other reasons. She tried to explain to me her own observations. She was fairly convinced that in the first heaven, the first reality we encounter on the other side of the Great Divide, our individuality, our I AM, is contained in a body consisting of photons. It would go a long way to explain the feats we could perform out there in the Astral reality. There we seem to have abilities completely beyond our limitations here, in the physical universe.

"While here our bodies, in fact the whole reality, is made

up of but a tiny fraction of solid matter, and that matter consists of innumerable atomic and subatomic particles…"

"I am supposed to understand all that, right?" I interrupted. I always did when she took off on her theoretical physics horse.

"Just listen…" she said, a trace of annoyance in her voice. "I am making this as simple as I possibly can."

I shrugged the smallest shrug, which I trusted would go unnoticed—like all her atoms and subatomic particles.

"…and there, should the reality be made up of photon particles, remember they have characteristics of both waves and particles, we would have an enormous range of elements with which to build our reality."

I did my best to look intelligent. Her eyes were developing that dreamy hue, which I've seen whenever she drifted into theoretical physics, with accent of the theoretical.

"Just imagine… radio waves, microwaves, infrared radiation, visible light, ultraviolet rays, x-rays, gamma rays… all perceived with our Astral eyes… What richness, what variety, what kaleidoscope of colours… who knows what range of images we can absorb in a single body?"

She was gone. She'd come back in time the way a concert violinist comes back after the last cord of a violin concerto. It takes time to return to mundane reality; to a reality in which we all choose to conduct our becoming.

She went on to talk about hertz and megahertz, and frequencies, and flexibility such reality would offer, and all sorts of ideas that were well over my head.

I'd learned that visible light has a wavelength shorter than a bacterium, yet radio waves can stretch to 30,000 kilometers.

"Would your skin be as soft"? I asked after a while.

She ignored me.

I wondered if Amadeus has discharged his Karma, whatever it may have been. I also wondered if according to Universal Laws he would be responsible for the thousands of 'accidents' in China, following the enigmatic appearance of the eight, or in his case, seven Chinese Immortals.

"...radio spectrum..."

Or would the Immortals hold the blame. Karma is supposed to be absolutely impartial.

"...low, medium, high, very high, ultra high, and super high to the extra high frequency range. Only then comes infrared radiation and only then, finally, the visible light. Darling, you are not listening!"

Can a man be responsible for inventing a lancet that saves lives yet can also be used to commit murder?

I caught a slipper on my chest. I was lucky. Usually it landed on my head.

"I thought only Iraqis threw shoes at their..."

"It wasn't a shoe only a slipper, and you are not a president of the United States. And that was centuries ago."

"It would have been a shoe if you happened to have been wearing one, darling," I countered, forgetting that this was the wrong time to raise logical arguments. I ducked before the second slipper hit the wall behind me. "Anyway, I am very interested in photons." I was trying hard to raise my most injured expression.

"Would you like to recite the whole spectrum?"

"What here? Now? You want me to make a spectrum of myself."

This time I didn't wait. I ran from my study on the double. She caught me on the grass outside. And you know what? I'd bet my life that her skin out there, or up there, well, 'there' anyway, wouldn't be any softer, whatever it was made of. It just couldn't be.

I was lucky. She read my thoughts.

I was counting on it.

And then came a most unpleasant event. Tom, our dear bodyguard, Ambrosia's able lab assistant, later Papa's right hand man, and finally our news director as he was officially called, disappeared. Lately, in the relative absence of news, he'd become a jack of all trades. It turned out that he fell into a crevice that formed during the global adjustments, some 120 years ago. We assumed Tom was on some sort of trip, until he was missing for nearly a week. Only John sensed that something was wrong when he couldn't contact him subliminally. He then set out to look for his friend.

It was hard to believe that during the last eight decades we haven't heard of a single earthquake. We never suspected that Tom fell victim to something that happened more than 80 years ago. Even the climate has stabilized. The hurricanes and monsoons seem to have died out of their own accord.

It turned out that Tom was repairing a fence that protected others from meeting a similar fate. Alas, he served others better than he served himself.

It is hard to believe that Tom had been born close to 200 years ago, although he'd spent about a 140 of them in Limbo. He'd 'slept' less then I did, mostly because my 'services' have been less required than his. Also I was needed to record only relatively large changes, for prosperity, not news of everyday life.

Nevertheless Mama kept him close to us out of sheer kindness. She was also aware of his close link with Papa in both their previous reincarnations. Although Tom had two embodiments between the time he shared part of his life with Papa and the present one, there was a strong tie between them. At first glance it seemed as if they've become fast friends in the present life. Also, Papa was determined to take him for another trip, this time not with his trusty Cessna, we've long since run our of fuel, but through the special abilities that Age of Aquarius offered.

About those—more later.

Papa was a risk taker, and I saw Tom risking his own life to protect him even from Papa's own weaknesses. During the last century or so, we were Tom's only family; of course with his and our imposed longevity, this was hardly surprising. Towards the end, Papa loved Tom as his own son.

As for myself, Tom who began as our bodyguard, had grown, over many years, to become my closest friend. It was with him that I shared my 'non-godly' problems, ideas, which we, human beings, encounter every day. With his departure I became lonely. It was as if I lost part of my own humanity. Part of my own temporal, silly, transient, reality that he and I shared for so long.

I'll miss him more than anyone else.

Apart of my son, of course.

Apart of my son…

In all the years I've spent on Milos, we've never had a funeral. Of course I wasn't here when Amadeus translated but I doubt that his departure had followed the established protocol. None of us practiced any religion, yet, in a strange way, we all followed the teaching of the great Masters of the past. Golden Rule was the *sine qua non* mode of behaviour for everyone I ever met on the island.

The problem was that there was absolutely no way to pull Tom's body out of the crevice. Mavis had bilocated down there, into the murky scar nature had produced during those days of geological adjustments. She made very sure that Tom was dead. That he no longer occupied his body. To make doubly sure, she, Mama and Papa have all visited him on the next Plane, where he wouldn't be had he been still alive. Yet, there is a strange if understandable rule among the gods. Their bodies must be removed from the surface of the Earth.

There is a reason for it.

Throughout history, people made a habit of taking scraps of body or even clothing of those they considered saints or mystics and continued to pay homage to such relics. This, in Mama's eyes, was not only absurd, but was in danger of prolonging sympathetic vibrations of such physical remnants. In fact prolonging the inability of those who had departed from achieving complete freedom. We must remember that in Mama's eyes, our total and absolute essence, the I AM, was exclusively in the state of consciousness. By attaching attention to the vessel through which it manifested itself, we did a disservice to the Essence Itself. And that includes the physical, emotional and mental envelopes.

"By that, my friends," Mama explained, "I mean that everyone of us contributes to the totality of knowledge. In this sense, every one of us is Truth incarnate. We must not follow the teachings of another individual and imitate the way they did it, but find our own way to express Infinity. This is what makes each one of us an indispensible element of the Whole."

It took me a few years before I fully understood her words. And by then, I was already on my own. By then, Mama and Papa were gone. They've both done their individual, indispensible, jobs.

We poured the remainder of precious fuel down the crevice and set it afire. There was no need to say 'a few words'. We all shared each other's thoughts. We all loved Tom. His heart was even bigger then his body.

Tom was free at last.

***

21
Aegean Kingdom

While there were always very advanced gods who regarded next to nothing as impossible, the access to the Great Divide from within has been tightly closed. While all people who mastered controlled entry into the alpha brainwaves could visit the higher Planes, they would be snapped back by the reality in which they were experiencing their becoming within a very short time.

Such is the Universal Law.

Now, however, all has changed. While since the onset of the Age of Aquarius the gate to the Great Divide remained accessible from the phenomenal reality, those who found their being already on the other side, those on the Astral Plane, could now also visit the physical world.

Every 25,000 years or so, the configuration of Zodiac occurs that allows for a two-way traffic through the Great Divide. Not only could people visit their 'dearly departed', but those who already 'passed away' could drop in on the dear ones they'd left behind. In the past such events would have been possible only for very advanced states of consciousness, you might refer to them as gods who became aware of their divinity many rotations of the Zodiac in the past.

In the past, this ability resulted in the relatively rare visions of the so-called saints, mystics and saviours.

"But darling, aren't those miracles?"

I was still nagging Ambrosia. In spite of my reputedly advanced state of consciousness I still found it hard to reconcile the various Planes of existence on which we all find our being.

"If you define miracles as events that are at odds with the Universal Laws, then the answer is no. Universal Laws are unbreakable. This is what makes them Universal."

I had little choice but accept the evidence of my own senses. I've seen Amadeus looking perfectly normal and alive. The fact that according to Ambrosia his body was made up of neutrinos, well, I couldn't see the atoms that made up my body either. Perhaps that was because they really were made up of almost empty space.

"What you see and experience, Simon, are the photons reflected from the electrons of your body or the clothes you wear. Our reality is made up mostly of energy, as are elements of other Planes."

Spoken like a true physicist.

For Ambrosia there never was anything resembling a miracle. On the other hand, she lived in constant awe of the reality around her—both here and on the other Planes.

I went back to the original notes I made at Mama's lecture. The problem with those was that I could only record electronically her spoken words. That which she conveyed subliminally I had to write down, or others would not have access to it. While some advanced gods might be able to dig it out of my subconscious, normal people, people for whom I was making these notes, would have nothing to read. I was not granted eidetic memory like my son.

This is what she said.

"Now, though only for about 2000 years, the two-way traffic has become possible for those who only recently became aware of their potential. Those, who only recently became aware that they are gods."

That was very important to me. I was among the many who were in the process of becoming one of the few. If I were to 'die', to take leave of my body, which since my last awakening was beginning to show signs of aging, I could visit my wife, who remained as fresh as a daisy. If you knew Ambrosia as I do, you'd want to do the same.

...when we go... we will go together...

This came to me almost simultaneously with the thoughts that have just crossed my mind. I turned from my desk. I was alone. She must have left without my being aware of it.

...I never leave you... ...we are always one...

There it was again. I had to wipe a tear of joy that for a moment clouded my vision. Then I saw her through the window talking with Mavis.

How could I not believe in miracles? I couldn't resist a supercilious chuckle. I still thought that I knew better. Yet, I knew with unshakable faith that love does span death, not that there is such a thing.

Back to Mama.

"While rare individuals could always circumvent limitations of less advanced minds, only now we can all experience the truth, which will keep us all going for the next 25,000 years. In time, these events will become myths, then religions will form, and the truth will become obscured by the many who cannot accept it. Alas, we are all immortal. Every single one of us will eventually become aware of his and her potential."

I had all this written down. Mama had passed it on by direct perception. That way it was more likely to embcd itself in the minds of the listeners. Her last words had been both spoken as well as delivered telepathically. They sounded like thunder:

YE ARE GODS

That was all. Just three words. I wondered how many people would believe them this time.

I went back to my own notes, those I made ages ago, in preparation for one of my lectures at McGill. It's been many years since I'd printed them out.

They dealt with Zodiac.

The Cycles of Zodiac last about 26,000 years. 25,920 years for those who study those matters. Twelve astronomical ages correspond to 12 zodiac signs. Then the whole bundle of signs repeat themselves. On and on. Those repetitions are called the precession of equinoxes, and a whole bunch of them is called a Great Year. Plato called it the Platonic Year. Or maybe somebody else borrowed his name. Did I care?

Not yet. Not unless Mama told me that I should. And why. The scientists want to know how, while I always wanted to know 'why'?

I also often wondered what would I do without Mama. So did many people. Just about everyone I knew.

At any rate, a complete cycle of the Zodiac is also called an Astrological Age, or a period in which major changes take place in people's consciousness. They affect culture, civilization and the way the world is run; in other words at personal and social level. It is neither good, nor bad, and is intended as neither punishment nor reward. It is like the next class in a kindergarten; or hopefully, for some of us, in an elementary school. Let's face it, I've been lecturing on Comparative Religion some 170 years ago, and a lot of this stuff is new to me. And that had been an institution of 'higher learning'! I could but wonder what lower learning would be like.

And then there is the popular astrology, also known as astromancy. It consists of attempted divination from astronomical phenomena. It has been practiced by the Chinese, Mayans, and even our North-American Indians.

"Of course," Mama once told me, "everything affects us. But we are more effected by what we ate for breakfast than by the stars."

Good Ol' Mama.

"And then," Mama resumed at her next lecture, "Aegean Kingdom was born. It is called a Kingdom for one reason. Every man woman and child who live here are kings and queens of their domain. And no one else. Remember that."

There was a rare ring of command in the tone of her voice. She waited for a while for her words to sink in. When she spoke again, she sounded different, at though speaking from a great distance.

"For the first time in the recorded History of the World, a Kingdom will span two realities. It is up to you to make it true. It is up to you to experiment with the two realities. You can explore both with the abilities inherent within you, the abilities that this New Age has stirred again, and made this possible. You are blessed among the gods. You alone can make this true."

I had been standing, leaning against the wall of our villa, when Mama had said that. I remember my legs lowering me to the ground by their own accord.

"Whatsoever you do here, will be done there," she continued. "Only this time you will be able to rise in your consciousness and see the countless consequences of the choices you've made, outside the limitations of time."

I remained sitting on my heels, then slowly sliding to the ground.

"In the past, you had to leave your physical body to do that. They called it 'dying'. Now, and for the next two thousand years, you will be able to move to the next reality at will, and then return to continue rejoicing and building on the choices you've made, or… or to repair the damage you may have done."

This, I knew, would advance the rate of evolution by hundreds of thousands, if not millions of years.

"Alas, some 26,000 years ago, people had the same opportunity. You be the judges if they took advantage of it. You alone are the judges. You alone bear the consequences.

You alone reap what you have sown."

She seemed to embrace us all with her smile.

"I wish you all the best."

And the next moment Mama's image became hazy, and gradually dissolved into thin air. I began to wonder if she was ever here. Perhaps she bilocated from wherever she was? Perhaps she already visited us from the other side of the Great Divide?

I know it sounds crazy, but I even wondered, just for a split second, if my previous 170, or whatever was the real number of years, have not been a dream. Then I shrugged. After all, who cares? If the physical world is Maya, an illusion created for men and women to go through a process of learning, did it really matter if it was real? What is real, anyway? Matter isn't. Time isn't. According to our best scientists, nothing I can detect with any of my senses is. So what is real?

A little bee was buzzing in my bonnet

...love... darling... ... love is real...

I was sitting alone, apart from others attending the lecture. Bougainvilleas, hugging all the walls, were hiding me from view. I felt like Mavis—almost invisible. Yet I finally understood that only my body was alone. I wasn't, nor shall I ever be. I can't be. I can't be alone any more than a drop of water could be in an ocean that spans the universes.

I can't be because she and I are one.

...me too... I thought. *...me too...*

This time I didn't hear any echo, any answer. But I felt something better than that. I felt a smile washing all over me. For a moment I closed my eyes and just basked in the unique feeling of oneness. It was overwhelming.

I needed a break. Too much thinking never did anyone much good, not unless they were on a governmental pension—myself excluded, of course. And most of those guys couldn't think at all. Luckily, we don't have them anymore.

And yet, even now, after so many years, my early studies continued to strike a chord with me. When Ambrosia was repeatedly reminding me that she and I are one, I recalled a verse from my youth. '*So they are no longer two, but one.*' Mathew had written that more than 2000 years ago. Did he already know something we are only now rediscovering?

'*For this reason a man will leave his father and mother and be united to his wife, and the two will become one flesh*'. No matter if the flesh is made up of atoms that consist of essentially empty space; or of neutrinos in transit; or of photons on the other side of the Great Divide.

I also understood that the oneness I felt with Ambrosia was only the first step on the long journey towards us all returning home.

This Aegean Kingdom was going to be great fun. Now that people could move in and out of the next Plane, it just had to be fun. Except for one tiny detail. What of heaven and hell? Wasn't it a place we were supposed to tippy toe after we left this glorious valley of tears?

Frankly, I didn't care much where I'd go, as long as I could take Ambrosia with me. It would be nice to have Athena and Amadeus and Mama and Papa to string along. Just for company. OK. And Mavis and Tom and Jerry. And John of course. I think this little group would make me happy wherever I went. There was this third heaven Papa, I mean Paul, wrote about in one of his letters, which screwed things up a bit, but no matter. We didn't have any religions left to mix us up. Not yet. According to Mama, not for at least a 1000 years, and I expected to be long gone by then.

I expected to be long gone in 10 years. Maybe sooner? On the other hand, what was the point of going if one could be here and there at the same time? Surely, here it was like heaven on earth. Perhaps this is what made Olympians stick around for such a long time.

I decided that heaven could wait. So can hell, for that matter, even though we are the sole creators of both heaven and hell.

No one to blame anymore.

Doesn't seem fair, does it?

"Darling?"

"Yes, dear?"

For once she was snuggling on the settee with a book, a real, ancient paper book, one from our archives, instead of pouring over facts and figures in her lab.

"Would you go to hell with me just to keep me company?"

"Of course, darling. Didn't I for the last hundred years of so?" This was accompanied by a giggle. "We could have an enormous barbeque and invite the neighbours in."

"It would have to be bloody big…" I mused.

"Don't worry. I am told they have lots and lots of fire there."

"Like in Florida?" I've been there once. There were BBQs on every single balcony. The smell of stale burning fat had been too ghastly for words."

"Yea, it must have been," she was peeking again, "It must have been hell!"

This time there was no giggle. This time we both laughed outright. Wasn't hell funny?

Only then I remembered that I haven't eaten any meat for about umpteen years, barbequed or otherwise. Not because I loved vegetables so much, only because I loved animals more. After all, were they not incipient units of consciousness getting ready to take their first giant step on the ladder of evolution?

We were both on Olympus. Just the two of us. The same terrace, the same giant baldachin over the same table, furniture… views… The very same Ambrosia smiling at me, seemingly almost with embarrassment.

Yet, things were different. Everything except Ambrosia that is. She was the same. Perfect. And then I understood what happened. Thing were more pronounced. More defined. The colours were more distinct as though someone had just washed every wall, every street, every piece of furniture. But that was not all. The same was true of vegetation. The leaves, the flowers, even the grass was greener... and then, farther down the rocks, the blue of the sea...

It was the same, only it was perfect. Not really as it was but as we wanted it to be. We created this reality. We enjoyed the evidence of our creation. We shared desires, hopes, loves.

For a long while we just sat there, filled with gratitude that cannot be expressed in words. Whatever Universal Laws allowed this to be our reality, surely, heaven couldn't be any better. It might not be as good.

...thank you my love...
...thank you my love...
We both thought it together.

It was our first time since Ambrosia's Mama's had made her promise that defined the Aegean Kingdom. The place in which we found ourselves was in no way different from what we imagined it really was. Perhaps we didn't quite see it the same way on Earth, in the phenomenal reality, because there it was polluted with atoms. Just few and far between, mostly empty space, but still, it was polluted with matter. Here, on *this* Olympus, it was pure energy. It consisted of arrays of photons, of waves, perhaps countless quanta, that responded and arranged themselves in accord with our hopes, our desires.

With our expectations.

Is this what heaven is like? I couldn't help wondering, thinking in terms in which I have been brought up so long— so very long ago.

...you did it my love...

...we did... I corrected, *...we are One.*

And even as this thought formulated in my mind, the colours began oscillating in a dance of unrestrained joy.

"It must be heaven!" I exclaimed. "It must!?"

I closed my eyes. As I opened them again, all was as before. Perfect. Only... only I felt a gentle tugging. It was like a wind pressing on me, only there wasn't any wind.

"It is time," Ambrosia said.

I nodded.

We were still sitting on the same deckchairs, on the same terrace, only the purity was gone. Yet it was still beautiful. Perhaps beauty was inherent but perfection could only be born of our hearts?

I still had so much to learn...

A while later I asked her the $64 question.

"Will it always be that short?"

Frankly, I had no idea how long we have been away, but any length of time would not have been enough. Not really.

"How long are your dreams, darling?"

"My dreams? How am I supposed to know? I'm asleep when I dream, aren't I? I dream five or six times a night, that's about all I know."

"You have to stretch your consciousness to accept new parameters. What we just did was giant step beyond lucid dreaming."

I thought about it for a while. She was probably right. Of course she usually was. Always? Always is a long time.

"Do you know how long were we there?"

"How long did you sit here with your eyes closed?"

"I have no idea."

"Is time so important to you?" She smiled. "If you moved the sun from east to west while we were there, would it make you feel better?"

"Move the sun?" I thought she was pushing the argument

too far.

"You could, you know. The reality there is created by your imagination. If fact, all realities are, only here it takes a lot longer to become manifest."

As I was saying, I had a great deal to learn.

...you have the rest of eternity...

It was my turn to smile. I'd heard that before. Many times. And yet, we humans, are constructed, by I know not what, to take just tiny bites of reality at a time, and chew on it until there is nothing left. Only then we move on to another morsel. This new reality was my new morsel. I wondered how long I was going to chew on it.

"A thousand years?" she asked.

"Will you wait for me that long?"

She came over and cuddled up on my deckchair. And suddenly time was of absolutely no consequence. One second equaled a thousand years, as though both were just fragments of eternity. An eternity of bliss…

"You have to earn it, you know," she said after a while.

"I'd rather earn it upstairs," I said.

This time we walked up slowly. With a thousand years left for exploration, we both thought that we'd best begin at home. And in all the 200 years, so far, I never got tired of exploring the object that consumed all my attention. Thanks to Mama, my body was still in middle fifties. I didn't care any more how she did it. I'm just very glad that I have been chosen to be the "Court Historian"—the resident historian to the Aegean Kingdom.

When we came up for air it was getting dark. We found Mavis sitting alone in the garden gazing at the stars. She did that often. I wondered if, since Jerry moved to the next Plane, if she was lonely. She sensed my concern.

"Do you know, Uncle, that there he is six-feet tall? He has a bunch of unruly hair, and he is slim and incredibly handsome? He modeled himself after Garry Cooper, an actor of a bygone era. "

I didn't know. Jerry had been fairly bald down here.

"And do you know that the way he is now, he thinks that I will love him more?"

I didn't know that either.

"He bends way down to reach me down there, where I am, the same, tiny girl...?

I could believe that.

"And he tells me that he adores me because I am petite, would you believe that?"

They were lovers, on both sides of the Great Divide. Who needs heaven with such fringe benefits?

And then Mavis's eyes returned to the ocean of star.

"Each star has planets, and many planets have people just like us, learning. They may not look like us, but their dreams and aspirations are the same. They are searching for a way home, whence they came."

Then Mavis's voice got dreamy.

"There's an infinite number of them... After all, everything is consciousness... all things are infinite. Even people in whom it resides. This is also why we have to be immortal? And just think, Uncle, they are all on the way home."

Wasn't this what we were all doing? Only some of us have lost our way. Just temporarily. Just for a little while. Ultimately we'll all meet our destiny. And after all, what is time anyway?

It was late. I went to my study to record the events of the day. The sky was getting gray by the time I clicked off my computer. A great deal happened today. Yet it seemed that only moments have passed since yesterday. Maybe time really was illusory, after all.

***

22
Mars Here and There

I raised the Mons Olympus by another five kilometers, and felt myself covered with sweat. What on Earth, I mean on Mars, am I going to breathe at this elevation? On the other hand what on Mars had I been breathing before I raised it by five thousand meters...

She was right. Imagination is a dimension.

Mind boggles. Gods must be crazy.

I did it exactly as Ambrosia had told me to do. I closed my eyes and imagined the mountain much higher.

"If you don't close your eyes," she's said, "you'd find yourself buried under a thousand tons of rock."

Apparently what you see is what you get. You can only fool the senses you don't use. Must be very careful with that. My interplanetary trip hasn't happened overnight. I practiced in less ambitious environs: like walking through walls, jumping through second floor closed windows, and meeting Ambrosia a mile away. The other day I tried walking through a wall and got a nasty bump on my head. I forgot to close my eyes. When I did, I found myself on the other side. The bump was gone too. The mind didn't support things you didn't like. And yet, I am told, some people created a veritable hell for themselves. I can only imagine that they think they deserve it. The subconscious appears to be a very moral, or consequential. Action equals an equal and opposite reaction, sort of thing. It is a state of mind that is fueled by our inherent concept of justice and thus balance. And it seems that the reality of first heaven is generated mostly by our subconscious. Like in dreams, lucid or ordinary.

There are rules that govern every reality. I wondered what rules the next one would have. The next reality, I mean.

...learn to crawl before you walk...

This came over from Earth. Can you imagine? Ambrosia was hearing me across tens if not hundreds of millions of kilometers. It made me wonder what the Mental Plane might be like. Mars's orbit brings it to between almost 55 million and 400 million kilometers or more from the Earth. An average of about 225 million kilometers. And she can hear me!

"Am I really here?" I heard my own voice but it sounded like a whisper. No air to carry vibrations?

"Then what am I breathing...?" Do bodies made up of photons breathe?"

...only if they want to...

Hey! I can hear her again! Fancy that! She's looking after me even now...

It seemed that the rules in this reality did not take distance into consideration. At least not as far as thought transfer is concerned. I suspect that thoughts are the energy of the higher realms, such as the Mental Plane, which supersedes the Astral. Wonders will never cease.

And then finally the reason for her caution connected. I was a beginner. I was still crawling, never mind walking. Not according to what the Astral Plane offered. After all, it was only the first heaven. The first reality in which we were not lumbered with or by our physical bodies. By our physical limitations? No wonder they called it heaven. Well, at least the first heaven. I can't even imagine what the other Planes would be like.

I sat down near the peak of Mons Olympus and wondered. And then I made my first mistake. I closed my eyes and imagined my computer. In that same instant I found myself sitting in my study, my hands poised over the keyboard.

As you all know, for many years I was teaching the essence of Comparative Religions. One of the principle axioms, of the invaluable tenets I'd been teaching, and tried to convey to my listeners was that *"You are where your attention is."* This simple maxim is as true on Earth as in the upper realms. It seems that the Old Masters, the enigmatic mystics of the past, have been giving us hints of what was yet to come. Did anyone listen? And here I was forgetting about them.

I felt deeply embarrassed.

"I must remember to control my thoughts," I said out loud. I didn't care if anyone could hear me. I was past being embarrassed.

It was not going to be easy. After all, Moses had been told to go forth and multiply. He was not told to make sure that the people of Israel must become sex maniacs. The commandment was referring to the inexhaustible richness of thoughts. The thoughts that continued to multiply, yet even now I found them hard to control.

I sighed, but it didn't help. I was beginning to understand the reason for immortality. Earth was around (no pun intended) for some 4.5 billion years. Man, in spite of religious fundamentalists' assurances, as far as the analyses of our Y-chromosome DNA is concerned, has been around not for 6,000 but for more like 60,000 years. And yet, I had to face it, I was still stupid. I was a slow learner. I've learned little in the last 60,000 years.

I punched some keys. It was high time for me to start learning. Before Amadeus good-naturedly regressed China to the middle ages, their plutocrats, obnoxious though they were, managed to restore the Internet to almost pre-apocalyptic quality, even in English language. For a while at least, all knowledge accumulated by the human race would be there, up in the cloud, available, ready to multiply my thoughts. Thank you, Moses. Thank you plutocrats. Nothing is perfect in our world. Also nothing is totally bad.

I decided to check my data from my last trip.

I learned that astronomers of the past thought that the equatorial ridge on the asteroid Vesta was considered higher. On the other hand the view from Mons Olympus, the endless flat planes stretching into infinity was something to behold. The Mons rises some 26 kilometers above the Martian northern planes. Next to Mons Olympus, our own Mount Everest with a North Face of a mere 4.6 kilometers if little more than an anthill. And now, by a quirk of my imagination, I increased the height of Mons Olympus by another 5 kilometers. I suspect it collapsed to its physical size the moment I withdrew my imagination. Obviously, I wasn't thinking what I was doing. Perhaps I was drunk with power? No wonder the ancient prophet called us gods. But my juvenile behaviour wasn't necessary. Don't ask me why I did it. I suspect I was just flexing my Astral muscles.

Had I done my research before my trip, I'd never dream of raising Mons Olympus by another 5 kilometers. On the other hand, there is a good chance that, thanks to my ignorance, I sat atop a mountain higher than anyone in the last 60,000 years. Surely, that must count for something.

Doesn't it?

Anyway, I did it. I had to admit that there was just a touch of pride lurking just below the surface of my ego. Five kilometers, imagine?

Luckily, my eyesight had improved in parallel with my inflated ego, which allowed me to take advantage of the view. Likewise my lungs seemed quite happy breathing… empty space? I dare say, I'll never know.

The fact that I was looking only on endless gray, dull, uneventful desert was purely coincidental. Nevertheless, the curvature of Mars with an ocean of shimmering diamonds of stars receding into the endless void of space beyond was breath taking.

Only… I wasn't breathing, so to speak. Not really.

When all is said and done, the view from the top of Mons Olympus was beyond anything that any man or woman alive, dead, or 'otherwise' had seen, even in their wildest dreams. Well, perhaps with the exception of the Olympians, though I've never heard anyone of them bragging about it. This includes not only my family, but also all Mama's invitees, who for many years now went about their business on their own.

People were not inspired to move around physically. One day they'll probably reinvent airplanes, pollute the planet with new exploration for new fuels, and reach Mars and Venus, and the remnants of the planet that now forms the asteroid belt. After all Atlanteans did it, so why shouldn't they? The human body is a powerful instrument and is antagonistic to other means of expression. The physical god is a jealous god. Gods on higher Planes are more permissive. Down here, they act in the image and likeness of our egos. The physical consciousness wants to do things its way, no matter what the mind, often even our common sense, dictates. Hence pollution, greed, wars and suchlike. They all belong in the physical reality with misinterpreted overtones of emotions.

No matter.

For up to 1000 years we might remain free of our material predispositions. Or perhaps, just perhaps, the new generations will be satisfied with developing their consciousness and its attendant abilities?

If not, they'll at least have Ambrosia's antigravity equations to reduce the need to overcome the pull of gravity. It struck me that they must have had them on Atlantis. It's just possible that Ambrosia reached back in her memory to recapture them for humanity. After all, they produced zero pollution. The antigravs, not the Atlanteans. For all I know, the Atlanteans created the Asteroid Belt. I read it somewhere in my flamboyant youth. OK. Not so flamboyant but the Belt was pollution enough.

In the meantime, the present and the next few generations before the long descent into materiality begins anew, all gods would offer their time to teach the masses, those that are willing, how to enjoy travel without dragging their physical bodies with them.

Apart from juvenile escapades to other planets, even distant galaxies, we all had a job to do. It was up to us to inform the masses, those who by luck or perspicacity survived the global upheavals, that they didn't have to stay at home and spend their time making children. Admittedly humanity has lost about two-thirds of its previous population. It was in need of rebuilding. That's what their ancient predecessors did. And, after all, physically we are all animals. Our drives are controlled by our chromosomes, not our brains.

Also… sex is fun.

I've also learned that this was far from the first Cycle of the Zodiac. Infinity has both ends open, remember? According to Mavis, there are worlds shimmering in the infinity of the firmament that are hosts to people as advanced from us as we are above an amoeba.

"At least," she added, when she saw the expression on my face. "There are many who have shed their material bodies eons ago and now just seed new worlds with new ideas, which in time will bear fruit."

I cannot claim to fully understand her words even now. Lately, each time I met Mavis, which was at least during the three meals we shared, she was eroding the remnants of my ego. She, my adopted daughter, was becoming my teacher.

Now, at the onset of the Age of Aquarius, when the effects of Pluto have stabilized, we had to teach the survivors, that they could communicate with each other by thought, and that they could travel without taking their physical bodies with them. It took me about 200 years to learn that. I was hoping that the 'masses' would be smarter than I was. Still, we had 1000 years to go.

All was not lost.

Contrary to the Olympians, the rest of the Aegean Kingdom produced ample progeny. They would serve as chalices for returning units of consciousness. The babies would serve as physical envelopes for those who have earned the privilege to be reincarnated during this glorious Age of Aquarius.

And then I had the first quite undeniable evidence that the Great Divide remained open at both ends. As you must already suspect, Mama had left us—dissolved into thin air. Or at least, so it seemed. We missed Mama. It was difficult to mourn her departure as for the first few weeks we saw her daily in our dreams. It seems that she'd made sure that we would. We were grateful beyond measure. She'd obviously decided to stay clear of our waken states.

Strangely enough, we could almost see Mama's smile in Papa's eyes. By means known only to them, they seemed to remain as one, no matter on which side of the Great Divide one or both found themselves.

Like the Cheshire Cat's, their smiles lingered behind.

And then a thing happened that, until a few years ago, I would have been forced to categorize as a miracle. At times, I still do.

Mama, who as you know had left us some time ago, Mama who by old definition of the word had 'died', called a meeting of all her invitees. And she called them all by planting a request in their subconscious from wherever she was now. I could only presume she did so from the Astral Plane, though it could have been from any other Plane to which she'd ascended.

We sat in silence, waiting. Then it happened.

A sphere of light solidified into the contours we all knew so well. And then she spoke.

From the moment she opened her mouth, it was evident that Mama was still in charge. She probably only changed her permanent address, so to speak.

"It is time," she began. "It is time for us to go forth and teach all nations. To awaken all young minds to the gifts that are dormant within them. For so long…"

She stopped. I saw a little pain passing through her caring face. She must have really loved humanity to stay with us for so long. She really was the Immortal Woman. She was definitely the immortal Hè worshiped in China long before she visited other countries. And now, it seemed that once again she was preparing for her departure. This time, it might have been for good.

We couldn't know. Not for sure.

"We shall start by invading their dreams. Gently. Very gently. If they resist we shall withdraw and try later. Time is on our side. They must wake up with ideas that will stir the potential within them. We needn't tell them anything they don't already know. Yet… by certain Laws of the Universe that we do not as yet understand, they are not aware of them. Buddha tried to awaken them. He failed. People didn't believe him."

How true, I thought. Had she been around at the time of Buddha?

"People would rather have miracles imposed on them than perform deeds that are within their power. They would rather be told what to do than to discover most new things for themselves. It was as though they didn't want to be among the chosen few. Yet now, in this age, once in every 25,000 years, the many could become the few. We need them. Countless units waiting to be reincarnated need them to become the few among the many. It is up to us to make sure the new get their chance."

The Wheel of Awagawan. The few become the many, who help the many to become the few.

Eternity moves on...

Why did we always end up with just a few? Perhaps the others were afraid? Perhaps they remembered that power corrupts, and that their potential holds enormous power. Perhaps they know from past experience that divinity is neither good nor bad. Only we are, and we are bound to pay for our mistakes. Even gods. Remember Lucifer?

Divinity has Its being in the middle. Along the narrow path. Path invariable trodden only by the few.

A year later, we began taking the Aquarians on trips— always together, never unassisted. Adults only, of course. Soon we discovered that the young ones began to join us of their own accord. That is as it should be. When the adults tried it on their own they got scared, and snapped back into their physical bodies almost immediately. Not so the children, they seemed to know no fear. For them it was a game, like playing with invisible friends. We didn't take them far, just to whatever dreams simmered in their young minds. Some destinations they had chosen were not pleasant ones. They learned. Slowly. Yet, my ego was taking a frightful beating. They were all learning a lot faster then I did.

I put it to the influence of Aquarius.

It was then that Ambrosia couldn't contain herself.

"Darling!" she exclaimed the moment we were alone. "We are all immortal. What difference does it make if somebody learns faster or slower. The only thing that matters is that we are all learning."

"It's easy for you to say. You know it all."

"I? I've learned more from you than from anyone I've ever met, including Mama."

"Very funny. No one knows as much as Mama."

"No one has been around as long as Mama," she replied.

"On the other hand, this will injure your ego, but Mama cannot tell us, let alone show us, what *not* to do. She'd forgotten most of the negatives, what to avoid."

I didn't particularly like tenor of this complement. My face must have shown it. But for once I kept quiet wondering where she'd take us.

"Simon, darling," this time her voice softened, "every single one of us has a different and unique function to perform. You, me, and Mama. You know how hard it was for Papa to stop organizing others. To let them, 'the many' as he called them, find their own way. Don't ever forget that we are all indispensible to the Whole."

Including the many...

I knew that, but only in theory. I still had to accept it emotionally. And I suddenly realized another reason why the Olympians kept me around for so long. The added dimension in this Age was imagination. But imagination is stirred by emotions, not by a reasoning process. I had been given a chance to experience the full benefit of becoming in this particular segment of the Zodiac. The rest was up to me. Unfortunately or not, it always is.

Sometimes I wondered if freewill was really a gift or a scourge. Who wants to be a god, anyway? Over the years I'd learned that very few did. And those that did, usually gravitated towards a downward slope of corruption.

It wasn't easy.

About a week after this discussion I had with Ambrosia, a young mother came to see us for some inconsequential advice. In her arms, she carried a baby. The baby did not as yet speak. I listened carefully to the mother, giving her my full attention. And then it happened.

My attention was disturbed by a hum, then a nagging call for attention inside my head. It took me a while to realize what was happening. Then I knew.

The baby was communicating. It, I still didn't know what sex it was, has been attempting to open telepathic channels. It was asking me how to accelerate the process of growing up.

I had no idea.

It cried.

I told it that it was immortal.

It stopped crying.

I learned later that it was a boy. At the time the baby didn't know the difference between a boy or a girl. Does it really matter? It would learn soon enough.

Farther down the lawn Ambrosia was showing a teenager how to use a "magic board". Only the larger conveyances were known as "magic carpets", the smaller ones were just boards. My wife stopped the instruction and stood perfectly still. It was with her that the baby was trying to communicate originally. Mavis overheard it and passed it onto me. I was just caught in the telepathic cross-wires, white noise, so to speak.

I soon realized that even tiny babies act as hosts to often mature, advanced individuals. Those new to reincarnating consciousnesses might be thousands of years old, perhaps waiting patiently for the Age of Aquarius. And there were not that many bodies available. For once having large families could be justified. With no pollution, no wanton waste of excessive eating, and with the climate becoming more balmy than in the past century, the earth produced an abundance of fruit and later vegetables. More than one could possibly imagine. The added bonus lay in the quality of land pushed up from the sea. It, having been submerged for many thousands of years, was a repository of countless carcasses of sea life. It produced an incredibly rich soil.

And now, each baby born was a reason to celebrate. People were becoming aware of the contribution they could make to future generations.

Ambrosia, who stopped her lesson while listening in on

my discussion with the baby, returned to her flight-instructor duties. The ten-year-old stood up on the board, rose in the air, squeaked with joy, and made a perfect circle before falling down. In my early days, some people had the same problem riding a bicycle. Others didn't.

Poor boy, but he'd learn. He was already standing on the board, again, still rubbing his elbow.

Later, when we were alone, I asked Ambrosia what she told the baby. She smiled from ear to ear.

"About the same that I am telling you."

I didn't know if I should be insulted or not.

"No, darling, I wasn't patronizing. I only told him that there is no need for hurry. That he was immortal."

"I told him that…?"

"He already knew that. He only needed to be reminded."

Don't we all? I was the living example that truth must be continually rediscovered.

It happened at night. We were resting in the deep pre-REM sleep, having earned a rest after a full day of helping new arrivals with their problems. They came from all over the Kingdom, and stayed in tents they carried with them. I saw a family of five walking beside a small magic carpet, on which they pulled their scant belongings. At least they didn't have to carry them. Mavis made sure they were all fed, though many brought their comestibles with them, and we had plenty of water. It transpired that the newcomers have been discovering abilities within themselves that they were unable to recognize. It must have been like Mozart discovering for the first time that he could compose. It must have been nice, interesting, but until he saw a piano, or originally at the age of four—a harpsichord, he didn't know what to do with all those notes whirling in his head. He had no means of arranging them in order.

Such were most of our days.

And now, in the middle of the night, we seemed to have met more visitors. First I thought this was another of my lucid dreams.

Whatever it was, a couple standing at the foot of our bed interrupted our slumber. I saw Ambrosia sitting up with her eyes wide open. We haven't heard them arrive, but both of us sensed an alien presence. There was no light, yet the man and the woman emanated sufficient sheen to be seen if not recognized. Their luminescence was quite uncanny. I've never seen anything like it. For a moment I thought they were humanoid, but that must have been what I'd expected. As my vision cleared, what I really saw were two oscillating, or perhaps vibrating globes of light. The rest was just my imagination. Why I imagined them as being of two sexes I also have no idea. Perhaps I saw what I wanted to see, to satisfy my need for balance, rather than what I really saw.

In fact, when I first became aware of them, for a moment I thought they might be some sort of robots that someone had sent over from afar to scare us. We heard that in China their technology was still in full flight. Not so. There was palpable benevolence radiating from both globes hovering before us. Also, I still couldn't dismiss an aura of humanity, or at least intelligence, emanating from whatever it was that we were facing.

They hovered there motionless, as though waiting to be asked to sit down. I, being the official host, the man of the house, if you prefer, did so.

...please... you are welcome... I thought, wondering if I should have said it in English or perhaps Greek. By now, my Greek was quite fluent.

They floated towards us and remained at the foot of our bed. This was not at all what I had in mind, but it was too late. Inside my head, I still heard my greeting them. They returned the greeting at the subliminal level, which was the only way we could possibly communicate. After all, telepathy is a non-verbal form of communication.

The following moment, without warning or so much as
'by your leave', they were gone. I did, however, have a very
distinct impression that they would be back. For some reason
we didn't discuss it there and then. Recently, both, Ambrosia
and I, experienced a lot of lucid dreams of some nature or
other.

Next morning, on waking, I described the event to
Ambrosia. She confirmed that she had exactly the same
impression. We didn't dream any of this. It really happened.
As I got out of bed, I found a small shining disk lying on the
bedcovers. It turned out to be a map imprinted on a material I
didn't recognize. It was a map of the sky. The night sky. One
bright spot had a circle drawn around it. I immediately called
Mavis.

She smiled broadly.

"Uncle what a lovely map," she said. Her eyes were
shining, practically euphoric. "And who circled the
Andromeda galaxy?"

We were stunned. Not by the map as such. We were
stunned because the map had been drawn as though looking
up from us. From the Earth. Only one thing could possibly
explain this. The visitors from Andromeda must have been
here before.

I would spend the next few nights waiting for another
tête-à-tête with our extragalactic visitors to manifest their
presence at the foot of our bed. Alas, it was almost a year
before they came next. And there were three of them. But
then, Mavis took over. I'm told that they talked of galactic
dust clouds shaped like giant brains, and other phenomena
even stranger, though farther away. Mavis said that the dust
clouds were mathematical prototypes of possible neuron
configurations. Mavis was becoming a little stranger lately. A
dreamy look seldom left her eyes.

But that's another story.

***

23
Maitreya Effect

I **learned later that none** of this would have been possible without the Maitreya Effect. Most peoples, the Jews, the Christian as well as adherents of the ancient far-eastern religions, trod time in expectation of their particular Saviour coming back and sort out their problems. They forgot their heritage, their inborn and indisputable promise to be gods themselves.

The Buddhists simply forgot to wake up.

The Jews were hoping for a new king to appear at any moment, a Messiah, and beat up all their neigbours, particularly all Arabs. Of course the Holy Land was by now mostly under water, as the rift between the Red Sea had widened, about a 100 years ago, to join the Indian Ocean with, what used to be Mediterranean, and now was a broad expanse of water joining the Indian Ocean with the Atlantic. It was a wonder that there was any room left for land. New continents have appeared, of course, but even now, little was known about them. About that time people in our Kingdom and the surrounding islands have learned that Ambrosia's magic carpets worked as well over water as they did over land. The age of new colonization had just begun. Still the Jews waited.

After all, they have been told to have no other gods before them. If only they'd listened.

As for Christians, well, they were still sure that their own Messiah would also come back on a swirling cloud, and also sort things out. In the event they refered to as *parousia* or rapture, the goody-goodies would be whisked up to heaven to remain there, bored, for all eternity, while simultaneously, presumably in the spirit of infinite love, all the incorrigible baddies would be cast to hell for eternal damnation. Without offending anyone's sensibilities, I must confess that neither alternative tickles my fancy.

Even for Christians, that's a long time to stay bored.

The Moslem had a different problem. As according to Islam, Jesus, the Christian Messiah, did not die, and eventually he must, thus he also must return to complete his life and work, which he left incomplete.

Lastly, many Buddhists mirrored the Christians and the Jewish Messiah with their own Second Coming, whom they called Maitreya. At least the Buddhist version did not threaten to either beat up anyone, or to send anyone to hell or any other equally unpleasant destination. The most that Maitreya had to offer was *moksha*, meaning liberation, and thus release from suffering through *samsara*, i.e. through the need for near perpetual reincarnation.

The nice part of the Buddhist version is that Maitreya, in Pali language means 'loving friend'. I dare say, after all that took place on Earth during the last 200 years of so, we could all do with one.

Only, to be honest, during the last hundred years, we haven't met any people who practiced any religion. Those stories came over from sanctuaries referring to people who probably were not yet aware of the onset of the Age of Aquarius.

And this is precisely where the Maitreya Effect came in. Not everybody had radios, and many more still had no electric power. In most cases, communication was limited to people who became aware of whispering taking place in their heads. As there were no psychiatrists who would deem them insane, they began experimenting.

Next, people discovered that they could not only talk and listen to the 'voices', but they could do so to an ocean of thoughts, or what seemed like thoughts, surrounding the world. In time they learned to connect to it. Within two or three decades there was a veritable network surrounding the world, which put the old Internet to shame.

There, within that network, that cloud of interlocking thoughts, they discovered an even stranger phenomenon. While communication was filled with all sorts of bits of information, there was also a strange sieving effect. It took people another two decades to discover that only those thoughts that contributed to the welfare of all were sustained by the global net. The others seemed to fade out.

This was the Maitreya Effect.

No man appeared on the scene—with or without a long beard. No great king appeared that favoured some at the expense of others. The Effect came to all people the world over, and seemingly invited everyone to join the club.

Instead of teaching people what is good and what is bad, or what is good and what evil, what to do and how to do it, the Maitreya Effect showed people that that which benefits many is sustained, and that which is likely to benefit only the few, dissipates into the ethers.

"In a way, this is a trial and error method," Mama had said at the last dinner we had together. It seemed like ages ago, yet we remembered every word she uttered. "This is how the phenomenal universe is sustained. Universality sustains balance. Divisiveness upsets it."

I thought about that. It seemed evident that thoughts were the means through which ideas would eventually become manifest in our reality.

"Go on," Ambrosia butted into my thoughts.

"Well, imagine if nature, or whatever you want to call the Universal Laws which apply to nature… Imagine if they favoured only coniferous trees. Over time, all deciduous trees would die, probably for the lack of water. Or if it favoured one animal over another, or one part of the world more so than a different part. The only way nature can sustain physical evolution is by maintaining balance which benefits the greatest number."

"And you say that I don't learn from you, Simon?"

I remembered our discussion in which I felt sorry for myself for being such a dumdum. The fog was beginning to clear.

"As you said, if nature didn't like me she'd have gotten rid of me a long time ago."

"Very long ago, darling. And I don't think even Mama could have saved you."

I rather liked that. I wondered if I was an integral part of the Maitreya Effect.

"We all are. That which people used to refer to as God, as divinity, can only manifest in the physical universe through us. Only life can manifest life. If you don't discover the spark within you, you'll have big problems finding it anywhere else."

I'd have to think about that. But in the deepest of the deep, Ambrosia was invariably right. After all, she was her mother's daughter.

There were exceptions. There always are. In the past they called them murderers, mass-murders, dictators, plutocrats, or just devils incarnate. This last could probably apply to most of them, but not in the religious sense. Today they were people who tried to exploit the net for their own ends.

Almost two centuries ago, before the tectonic plate adjustment, the Greek islands have been loosely grouped into seven archipelagos. The Northeaster Islands, the Euboea, the Southern Dodecanese Islands, all seemed to cope with the new slightly larger landmass with joy and as far as human relations were concerned, with all the due decorum. Crete was the only island that lost some of its terrain to the Aegean Sea and only the Argo-Saronic Islands had not changed at all. But the greatest gains apart from our own Cyclades, occurred at Sporades. They too have been unified into a single continent. The Sporades are smaller than the Milos/Aegean Kingdom, but with almost equal population, as fewer people left their shores for the mainland, in search of security. The term Kingdom as applied to Milos was little more than a homage to the glory of Greece's past, and the kingship of every resident. At Sporades, however, when they too declared themselves a Kingdom, it became a realm for the exclusive benefit of people residing within their shores. Soon matters took a very different turn.

Little more than a hundred kilometers from our northern shores, the Sporades were within easy access by the new-age mariners. Our people were bent on establishing trade. Also, they harboured an all consuming desire to explore the new worlds. They sneered at magic carpets, the antigravity platforms, if you remember. We need a challenge, they claimed. We are men!

Actually three of them were women, but I understood what they meant.

"And there's the rub," complained one of our mariners, the masculine one. "The moment we dropped anchor at their shores, a group of men rowed up to us in a long boat, and demanded payment in gold, silver or goods, for the use of their protected waters."

Protected from what, I wondered.

"So what did you do?" I asked.

"Well, the men were shaking long sticks that had sharply pointed ends at us. They were threatening to stick them on our chests… if not lower, unless we paid up."

"And did you?"

"Sir, we have neither gold nor silver. You can't eat it, or

wear it, nor does it protect you from inclement weather. Why would we carry it with us?"

Two things occurred to me there and then.

One—the man called me 'sir'. The last time I'd been called 'sir' was two centuries ago, in the lecture hall at McGill.

And two—that having been called sir meant that whatever measures the gods in general and Mama in particular took to maintain my youthful looks were over. I haven't even noticed that my beard took on a colour that was more silver than silver itself.

"So how did you escape?"

"Well, we hoisted the sail and rammed their rowing boat. Sort of accidently, Sir. They didn't like that but they lost their sticks. Then we fished them out and asked them if they'd like to trade with us."

I didn't ask our own people if the trade negotiations were successful. It was outside my area of expertise. Not that I really had one.

"Well done, gentlemen. You seem to have acted honorably."

"That's all we wanted to know, Sir," the man said and turned on his heel.

There was that 'sir' again.

I haven't seen a mirror for years. Many years. The Olympians had no use for it because most of them could look anyway they wanted to look. I suspect they could look young and old the very same day, just for the fun of it. As for the rest of us, well, to an outsider, not that there were many, we must have looked pretty wild. Disheveled?

The real meaning of Maya, of illusion, was slowly coming to me. I finally knew, or at least strongly suspected, the nature of real gods. Not men or women with a divine potential; nor those who were climbing the ladder of divinity; nor even those who may have reached the level of apprentice gods. I'm referring to those few that already made the grade.

Those gods could do on Earth, in the phenomenal reality, what I could do within the Astral Plane.

The real gods.

My head was spinning and seemed to be expanding at the same time.

I also suspected that the only reason they were still here was to lift us to another level, to help us reach our potential. This would explain all the events and things and actions that we, mortal men, consider to be miracles. If the physical universe is almost exclusively empty space and the Astral world is saturated with photons, then once you really understand how those quanta work it would be as easy to alter reality of this world, as it was even for me, on the next plain.

"Is this how they kept me from aging?" I asked no one in particular. I was alone in my study recording my thoughts on my trusty computer. Somehow, Ambrosia managed to maintain it in a working order, even after all these years. Of course her lab had been fitted for just such contingencies but, surely, not for 200 years. Yet... she did it. On the other hand, I wondered if anyone would ever discover my notes and make use of them. I also wondered if the scribes who recorded Moses' words entertained similar doubts.

And yet...

I've done a lot of wondering, these last two centuries.

"And you invariably found the right answer, my husband."

Ambrosia came in quietly while I was still lost in my thoughts. Even as I looked up, I saw Mavis in the garden. I smiled to Ambrosia but my mind began gallivanting among the stars.

The stars, the galaxies, I mused, who made them? Did they just happen? Was a big Juju directing atoms to gather together to form a star, or the Magellan Cloud?

Or did Consciousness precede everything in the phenomenal world. And did not higher Planes precede ours?

Is not the Mental Plane, a reality that translates ideas into thoughts, and thoughts into patterns and symbols? Isn't that where mathematics was born? All Greek philosophers were first and foremost mathematicians.

And is not the Astral Plane the domain of beauty, of colour and form? It is. I've been there. So has every artist, every composer, though some must have reached even higher, to the realm of patterns, of harmony…

…I love you… I love you darling…

I turned to find Ambrosia staring at me. Her eyes were wide, her mouth pouting as if wanting to kiss me. I took a deep breath. I wondered if I'd ever find words to write down the thoughts that still fulminated in my mind.

"I'll dictate them for you. Word for word."

"And a few years from now, I shall be able to recall them myself…"

"…they are all there, in the cloud above us. All you need do is to reach up and take them. They are yours to hold, to keep, to share…"

I still had so much to learn.

"And as you know, the cloud is also part of the Maitreya Effect. It is ours to use."

I shook my head again. I just remembered. I was writing these notes for the future generations. For people not yet born who will no longer live in the Age of Aquarius. To help them along the way; along the Procession of Equinoxes. For ever and ever and…

We talked about the beauty that surrounded us. Above and below. We both lived in almost constant state of amazement. It took countless billions of years to produce such beauty. It will take billions of years for people to learn to appreciate it. And then, one day, they'll reach up and grab the crown. And as gods they'll create new universes, new beauty, new expressions of Single Consciousness.

Forever.

I wondered if reality must be the same for all people? Or, at the very least, the perception of reality.

If it is, it becomes objective reality.

But what of the subjective vision, subjective perceptions? Two people earning the same money holding identical positions: one is happy, feels rich, grateful for his lot in life. The other is miserable. Are not their realities quite different? Could not this be true of other aspects of the phenomenal world. Did I sleep five minutes, while the world unfolded some 40 years?

Could that be not possible?

For gods?

And yet, surrounded by the plethora of beauty and contentment, there were moments of sadness. We both realized that in spite of Mama, and all the gods, and all the sanctuaries scattered around the worlds, these were, and were destined to remain the few. The vast majority of people who survived the tectonic adjustments would refuse to accept the illusory nature of our reality. They would continue to worship physical items, blaming their necessity for physical survival. Nothing is perfect in the phenomenal world. And thus those people, in the allocation of their blame, also held a grain of truth.

For them even the Maitreya effect, so prolific in its impartial generosity, would not suffice. Not for those of whom the Pluto Effect did not erase the old ways of thinking. They remained drunk on the old wine.

It seems, that Papa's efforts notwithstanding, the many would remain the many, and the few would continue to be but the few. Such is our nature.

I wondered if the honcho at the Sporades 'kingdom' could prevail. After all, all kingdoms, all empires of the past have crumbled under their own corruption. Could Sporades do any better? Perhaps such disparities were necessary to teach others, many others, what not to do.

There had to be other such places on Earth. On the New Earth. Perhaps they were the rotten apples of Eden, which set the seed of corruption that seemed impossible to eradicate from man's psyche.

Yet, we had to try.

And yet, it seemed so easy. Just by following the middle path. The path the gods travelled from the beginning of time.

I missed Mama and her frequent advice, but she seems to have kept to herself lately. I mean even in my dreams. I suspect that she considered her job done. Even before she left, she was beginning to look tired. The phenomenal world is by definition transient. Subject to the ravages of time. Eventually, even on gods. Perhaps immortality in the reality of becoming is tiring. After all you have to keep changing in this reality. That is how life is defined. It is continuous, unrelenting change without a single respite. It begins in the depth of the oceans at subatomic levels and ends at the top of Mount Everest. Everything in-between, including human biological life is subject to its indomitable laws. Only being is changeless. Becoming cannot be. It would be a contradiction in terms.

I didn't see much of Papa, either.

Ambrosia tells me that he was supervising the construction of the industrial antigravity carriers. He took his work very seriously. As always. Poor Papa. He so wanted to leave together with Mama.

"Sailing is great fun, son, but this is business," he claimed last time I saw him. Almost a week ago. "In this post-technological age we need to be post-technological."

I dare say he was right.

When home, he retired early. I think the reason was that they wanted to spend more time on other Planes together. Many people they loved were already there, perhaps waiting? There is still so much we don't know.

But I feel it in my bones that our time with Mama and Papa is drawing to a close. It was as though they belonged to a bygone era. Others were just being born. It also seemed to me, that Ambrosia and I, for reasons that were still not clear to me, had our assignments in the time of transition. I hope we were both fulfilling our jobs.

We shall see.

It was time for another trip to the Plane above. We did pay cursory visits at night, but frankly we were both so tired with all the odd jobs we were doing that we slept most of the night. Only then, on waking, about six AM we would both get up, or down... actually it was 'in', not so much to enjoy what the Astral reality had to offer in terms of undisguised pleasure, but to rebuild our tired bodies as quickly as possible. Physical bodies, those we've left behind.

We found early on that if we really establish a strong presence on the Astral Plane, and decisively affirm our bodies as young, whole and hale, this model would carry down to the physical Plane.

There was another reason, though it doesn't make much sense here, on Earth. We went to the next Plane to make love. The reason it doesn't make much sense here because the intercourse, there, was not really physical. It consisted of both our bodies merging into a strange singularity, wherein I was becoming totally aware of all of her being within me, and likewise, I was totally absorbed by her. For a moment that defied time, it was as though the two of us became a single entity.

We became one.

Sometimes, in those moments, we both felt that we were sharing the reality with more than just ourselves. Cynics might call it not a *ménage à trois*, but rather a *ménage à million.* Perhaps billions of photons of other entities passing through us, wishing us well, and going on their journey across the endless universes.

Sometimes we flew with them, sometimes we sought solitude in the heart of a star. Those were strange moments— ephemeral instants of eternity.

People who experienced it were right. It was the first heaven. I couldn't even begin to imagine what other heavens would be like. A great scientist of the bygone years was right. The world is not just stranger than we imagine—it is stranger that we can imagine.

We also found that in there, in those strange moments, we were completely outside the confines of time. We could reach back to the beginning of the Egyptian Empire, go back to the Earth when it was still bubbling under the onslaught of meteorites, and then see the galaxy forming out of a dust-cloud with angular momentum just initiating its spin. And having seen all of this, we knew that a trillion years would not suffice to see it all. Neither would an eon of trillions. The world was not static. It was not stagnant nor in state of stasis. It was alive—in a state of constant becoming. Even as we were, its conscious fragments—ever changing, ever searching, ever-trying to reinvent ourselves.

The Consciousness that created it is infinite, and It would be satisfied with nothing less. We were just glad, awfully glad, that we had been chosen to be a tiny, insignificant part of it.

Forever.

***

24
Eden

"**Some people seem to forget** that it all began in Paradise. Not necessarily in the biblical sense, although we began as disembodies entities roaming in the vast emptiness around us. Gradually we developed self-awareness sufficiently to recognize the concept of relative independence. We needed to define our existence. For that a scale of comparison was necessary. We defined space in which we could continue to expand our awareness. We developed our own patterns of thinking."

People sat in utter silence. They came from far and wide. They came by boat and by magic carpet. They came on foot. And they also listened to the thoughts, which rose up and mingled with the cloud that enveloped the Earth. They all listened to Mama.

They listened to Mama who was not there. Not in her old physical body made up of atoms and empty space. If one looked closer, there was a slight luminescence radiating from her. It was evident that the light came from her. From the space she occupied. Assuming she occupied any space. Perhaps we all imagined her presence, but if so, it was a most incredible illusion.

...like the rest of the world...

Ambrosia added to my thoughts.

"This excited us so much," Mama resumed, "that we have been stimulated to find out what such patterns would look like. To do so we needed elements with which we could differentiate our identity, to differentiate one from another to find expression for different patterns. We created light. Now we had building blocks from which to define our individuality. We created our first light body. Our body made of pure light."

She sounded as though she was there and then, when the whole process had begun. They knew that Pure Consciousness is eternal but the cycles of creation moved in an endless Procession of the Zodiac.

"We liked what we saw." There was a smile on her face. At least on the face we imagined we saw. "There was such an abundance of elements from which our individuality could be made that it spilled over to other things. Yet so far, we were all the same. We were individualizations, mirror-like fragments of the Consciousness that gave us birth. We were still integral, indivisible parts of the Whole, and thus... all the same. There was nothing to tell us apart. Our creative urge continued to fulminate within us. We needed more. We needed to assert our individuality. Hence, ego was born. We began a process that could only reach its fulfillment in the infinity of time. In the infinity of space."

By now Mama's body had a well-defined image. She looked real, physically present. And... Mama looked tired— the way she looked just before she'd left us. Before she'd translated. Lately, even though she'd appeared to us in her neutrino body, the last expression she'd carried while still on Earth had remained. She looked tired more often, after a short time in our reality. Not when she'd first became visible, but after a little while. It seemed that each Plane had its laws that would not be denied.

Or it could have been a sign that it was time for Mama to take a more extended rest. It was evident that she still thought about us. That she still cared for our welfare; for the development of our consciousness along the right lines.

Perhaps she found it difficult to accept that it was time for us to stumble along the evolutionary path on our own, and that she had to relinquish her guidance. After all, for now, for the next 1000 years or so, we would benefit from the net. From the cloud of knowledge that surrounded our globe. It was there for us to use, to reach up and learn—to absorb the knowledge directly.

It was like having all the knowledge within us and all we needed to learn was to listen. And to find enough humility in our hearts to admit to ourselves that we still had a lot to learn.

Soon she might choose never to go out again. Never to come down to guide us in the successive, endless cycles. She'd earned her rest.

No one spoke. No one stirred. This was a sacred moment. For a moment it seemed that her image was becoming hazy, before it became opaque again.

"Soon we discovered that to satisfy our creative impulse, we needed contrast. We needed a means to compare elements and thus be able to tell them one from another. We needed differentiation, and yet maintain our Oneness."

She was breathing with apparent difficulty. I didn't even know that body consisting of neutrinos could breath. I remember my trip to Mars. Up there I didn't have to breath, unless I wanted to, of course. Here? Apparently here our bodies were built into images and likenesses of an illusion.

"We split our individuality in two, yet remained indivisible from the Whole. To go further we had to make a great sacrifice. We had to risk losing our sense of Oneness. Yet each one of us needed to continue, to remain part of the creative process. For that we needed knowledge. We needed to be able to compare one solution with another. We needed empirical knowledge to make it pragmatic. We needed to experience the consequences of our reasoning."

She looked sadly at people gathered at her feet.

...we left paradise to abide in a transient reality... we

created an illusion of the truth... we created a phenomenal world of illusion...

This last sentence reached us only subliminally. Her discourse was over. It would remain in the minds of her listeners for a long time to come. Then, later, people would invent stories, fables, for their children to understand. They would veer from the straight and narrow, and only the essence, the symbolic meaning would remain. In time, even that might get lost. It did the last time...

Ambrosia looked at me, a smile playing on her lips. *...and then Eve handed Adam an apple... and... lo and behold... and thus the process of evolution has begun...*

I heard her words in my head. In spite of Ambrosia's smile there was no mirth in her words, just a lingering haze of sadness. She was missing her Mama. We've all become accustomed to cherish our illusions. I, too, had mixed feelings. Eve had given Adam an apple. Mama gave us the key to unlimited knowledge. She gave it to all who dared to bite into its enticing taste.

Hé. Hé Qióg. Hé Xiangu?

Mama remained Mama by any other name.

Mama the Eternal Woman.

For a while she remained sitting in a straight-backed chair, looking like a grandmother from a different era. For some reason, during the last few months, each time she appeared to us, she has been showing signs of aging. Perhaps we were not meant to use the Great Divide in reverse direction too often. It was intended for us to move forward. To rise. To advance. And also, seemingly, to rest. To enjoy the fruits of our labour. Not to use it to return to a lower, illusory reality in which we had no discernment of what was or wasn't real. At least up there, on the Astral Plane, one knew that it was all the product of our imagination. That we were the sole creators. Here we did not know that. Here we needed to blame someone else for our errors. Yet only here we could learn by bearing the brunt of our mistakes.

The rest of us, and there were many, sat on the grass, enjoying the air as it cooled towards the evening. I was surprised when some minutes later, Mama looked up, seemingly refreshed.

"Then slowly but inexorably we descended into materiality."

She resumed her discourse. She didn't preach. She sounded as if she was sharing her thoughts, or perhaps telling a fable to her grandchildren. She again allowed her eyes to wander over the lawn, over the villa almost completely covered with the red boom of bougainvilleas, atop the soaring Olympus. No one spoke.

"Now, finally, we are retracing our steps." This time she did smile. "Backwards." The smile was both, sad and hopeful.

"In a thousand years or so, we shall achieve the wonder of the Garden of Eden. Not exactly the same as the image still dwelling deep in our memory, in our myths. After all, we shall still have some technology from the previous era, although most people already forgot what it was. Each Age brings forth forgotten science that remains forever ignored by new generations. Did you know that?"

This was no longer a lecture.

Now, Mama was just chatting with us—just a few hundred friends that gathered to hear her. I suddenly realized that there were no microphones or speakers anywhere. The Maitreya Effect enables everyone to hear her words. They came not just to hear her, but also to see her. To be able to tell their children and grandchildren about her.

To tell them about the Immortal Woman.

I could vouch for her last statement. Many years ago, still in Montreal, I heard strange stories about the pyramids and the Sphinx still hiding their secrets. Then we started our hypnotic regression experiments. Some secrets were brought forward, only to be lost, again, in the upcoming upheavals.

Now, I suppose, they are gone forever. Perhaps people of each Age must find their own path to travel. There were other stories about Mayas, and other Indians. There was also Esoteric Buddhism that abounded in knowledge. And, purportedly there was Atlantis, before that Lemuria, and even further back, the sands of the Gobi desert.

And who could tell what treasures were still hiding under the waters of the great oceans? Perhaps one day we'll discover that some of them have now been revealed?

...no Simon... you were right the first time... we must always travel our own individual path...

Ambrosia knew. She'd walked hers before.

Mama was about to leave us permanently. She'd never said a word, but we could all feel it. Mavis would say that it was written in the stars. At long last Mama reached the point in history wherein she could no longer contribute to the truth, which she sowed over countless generations. At least, she must have thought so, and she was never wrong. Never. The Maitreya Effect would take care of the rest. She didn't actually say so, but we all suspected that she thought that her job was done.

Old wine was gone, new wine has taken root in man's consciousness. In spite of the age beginning to show on her face, we felt that Mama was happy. She must have been hoping that Papa would go with her. After all, Papa had expressed his desire to do so. She told me as much, or implied it, but she wouldn't dream of imposing her wish on Papa. She was that sort of Sublime Consciousness.

I understood that.

Neither would I dare to ask Ambrosia to come with me, but that's a very different story. You can't ask someone to commit suicide unless you don't believe in death. I am close to rejecting that notion. Completely. I am very close. The idea of being immortal is growing in my consciousness. Even as the idea of being One. At the same time I am convinced that only here, on Earth, or another planet like the Earth that supported the manifestation of phenomenal reality, was suitable to move forward. No matter how illusory, it is a Plane that enables us to learn, to grow, to advance. It enables us to draw and manifest the potential from the Source. We used to call it the Creative Spirit. I still can't think of a better word.

The Potential of the Source is infinite, but it needs us to make the Potential manifest. To make it more than just an idea. To make it tangible.

...Maitreya is within us all...

...it is a high state of consciousness that offers Itself to the world but once every 26000 years...

...enjoy it while you can...

This I heard within my head, as though coming from a great distance. Another reality? Yet her voice was unmistakable. I continued to hear Mama's voice, now and then, for quite a while. Later I had to search for it.

I looked at her image with tears in my eyes. I couldn't help them. I was still very human.

And then, even as I saw her almost two hundred years ago, her contours began turning hazy for the last time. Papa reached over from his chair, and held her hand. His body also began to shimmer, to lose its definition. They were one, those two. They would travel together. Perhaps for a while, perhaps for a thousand years. Perhaps forever.

Time really did not matter. It's what you did with it. Not how long it took you.

I reached over for Ambrosia. They were her parents. She knew they were going. She would continue to see them on the other side, yet somehow, it wasn't the same. It never is. We were human, after all. Exponents of phenomenal illusion. We had animal instincts in our chromosomes, in our bodies, our bones. We were intelligent monkeys and just lucky that the

Whole had chosen us to individualize Itself through us, and at long last we gained awareness of it. You can't get any luckier than that.

One day Lazy and Goldie would also evolve enough to share in our delight. Until that time, we shall hold a warm spot for them in our hearts. Their time will come.

...as will the time for my monk seals.... I heard a soft whisper.

Yes, eventually they'll all come. And.... time does not matter. Not really. I wiped the tears from my face. As I looked up they were both gone. Mama and Papa were gone.

Yet, on occasion, there would be nice surprises.

Papa came to see us today. He looked as he always looked. People don't change on the other side. Unless they wanted to, of course. Frankly, I suspect that he just wanted to see his daughter, his *mikro koritsi.* There were not many of us left. Mama, Papa, Amadeus, Jerry and Tom were gone. Ambrosia told me that she'd stay as long as I needed her. Mavis and John moved in with us, into the villa. Athena continued to float like a butterfly all over the Kingdom spreading joy. What an extraordinary girl, or should I say women, she was. The life she'd chosen for herself would not make anyone else happy.

Always wandering... almost homeless...

That didn't sound right. Through the life she'd chosen for herself she made thousands happy. Countless thousands. All over the Kingdom.

Just the four of us, with occasional visits from Athena, kept the place going. There was a newcomer, however, I didn't mention before. We called him Socrates, because with his gravitas of appearance, his long beard and the abundant, wavy hair, he was a spitting image of the Greek Philosophers of yore. Of course, from what I could find in my old files, all the Old Masters: Hippocrates, Heraclitus, Democritus,

Aristophanes, even Plato as well as a bunch of others, looked pretty much the same.

We could do with a few of them right now...

We hoped that our own Socrates would eventually take over when we'd call it a day and take our one-way trip across the Great Divide. After all, at least for now, we could always come back, if needed, for a little while. On the other hand so could Mama, Papa and my son. They all did, but less and less often. We had to learn to cope on our own. Not to live our relatively simple lives, but to help others conduct their lives in such a manner as to derive the greatest possible benefit from this incredible gift. For a while, we travelled on our magic carpets not only all over the whole of the Aegean Kingdom, but beyond. Some people found their way back from the mainland. We had lots of room. At least for now, they were all welcome. By now, we were well over 60-70,000 people, with at least 20,000 children among them. Almost all the youngsters picked up subliminal communication from us with ease. Some also reach up to the cloud. Apparently it is a lot easier when you're very young.

Papa seems to have acquired the facility of crossing the Great Divide without any effort, though he seldom stayed for more than a few minutes. Now that we were a society, I could see that his fingers were itching to organize them.

Old habits die slow. His... still lingered on.

Yet, I learned later that only a few of us managed to establish contact with Papa. He seemed very selective whom he visited. Ambrosia and I were glad that Papa was happy. What he tried to accomplish over a number of reincarnations, Maitreya achieved without any apparent effort. He did it from within, not from without. There is only one Maitreya.

The White Horse emerged victorious.

And so, once again, this time finally we were alone. Ambrosia, Mavis, John and myself. And Socrates, of course, the resident philosopher. His job was to adapt the knowledge of the gods for human consumption. Not to twist it, not to submerge it in mysteries, not to surround it with a million rules and regulations and regiment it into a religion, but to translate it for human understanding. For ordinary humans. For the masses.

Not an easy job by any means. There was no one to whom he could run for advice, at least not in the phenomenal reality. The buck stopped at his doorstep. Well, our doorstep really—we, the few, were in this together.

"The knowledge is within you..." I continued to recall Mama's last words to me.

I often wondered why she had chosen me to be the recipient of her last message. Did I really still need this reassurance? Was I still wondering...

Don't we all?

As for the rest of us, we all had our self-assigned duties. Ambrosia continued to be the alpha and omega of everything to do with things material, let alone scientific. With physics and engineering of complex machinery. John was the shoulder people could cry on. He was replete with compassion. He helped people by just touching their shoulder.

Mavis remained the worthy successor to Urania. Her usefulness came into full play only after we began to entertain regular visits from extraterrestrials, mostly from Andromeda but also from at least three other galaxies.

As for myself... Well, I had little choice. Eventually I returned to my original profession. On the Olympus, and within about half-hour's 'drive' on my personal, souped up antigrav board, I gave regular lectures on everything I'd learned in my 200+ years of rubbing shoulders with gods. Also, once a month, I travelled far and wide throughout the Aegean Kingdom, wherever needed, or at least asked. Sometimes Socrates came with me. He spoke the language people found easier to understand. We lived on a small continent, but over the years, thousands, probably hundreds of thousands came to Olympus seeking advice.

Why me, I often asked? Why me? Am I not the most ignorant of them all?

For some reason they didn't think so.

Not everybody was able to reach up to the cloud and learn by direct perception. Many were still like me. Like I was. Willing, but slow learners.

As for extraterrestrials, well, they seemed fascinated by us. We remained the only orphans of our solar system. The Martians have long since moved on. We still had a million-and-one species relying on our guidance. On our protection. A great responsibility. And they studied us the way we study history. We were the galactic newcomers.

I sometimes wondered how come that in all the years I'd spent on Olympus, I'd never met a single physician. Nor any experts on any chemicals, which had once been claimed to offer solace to the sufferer. There had been occasional bone fractures, and simple splints have been applied by a woman who lived in a cottage close by. The bones invariably set within days.

I suspect there may have been two reasons.

First—complete absence of pollution in the air, soil or water, as well as an absence of 'unnatural' fertilizers in the soil, eliminated the vast majority if not all of the autoimmune diseases. Also, people stopped eating poisons with which the industries of the past destroyed the nutritional value of foods stored on the shelf for extended periods of time.

Secondly—the medical industry stopped prescribing poisons, which occasionally eliminated symptoms, but seldom if ever tackled their causes.

Now, for a few generations, people's immune system took care of most ailments before they could win the battle for the human body. Also, I strongly suspect that the immunity from diseases that our body developed over millions of years, and which protected our biological evolution, came under gods' conscious control... as did most other matters affecting their presence on Earth.

Parenthetically, there may have been another reason. I haven't met a single person who was afraid of death. And not being afraid of dying eliminated 90% of all fears, which create tension and weaken the immune system. But this is just my opinion. I never discussed it with anyone.

And so we remained the only orphans around.

There was a lot to do. Following Mama's departure, the garden had to be adjusted. No more meetings of many hundreds of people hungry for her knowledge. On the other hand, we were in great need of growing vegetables. Our visitors numbered in the dozens every week and they were always hungry. At least some of them lingered behind to give us a hand with all the domestic chores. Sometimes I wondered if they came to sate their stomachs, rather than for my lectures. On the other hand, they may have thought that since we lived under the same roof as Mama did, or had lived, we would be the natural inheritors of her wisdom. This very idea gave me many sleepless nights.

In spite of all that transpired, there was hope for mankind. All men are intended to become gods. As far as I was concerned, women were goddesses already. With immortality in the human psyche, no one could fail.

On the other hand, we had been told that we are gods before...

Nevertheless, we all still fend for ourselves. There are no governments but local elders are placed in charge of implementing decisions made by groups of people. Papa might have liked that.

With the exception of some Chinese, there was no travelling. No pollution. No industries or technological advancements. People were learning that they could achieve more by ESP and PK than by old means of manipulating matter with instrumentation. For the uninitiated, that's Extra Sensory Perception and Psychokinesis.

There was an air of serenity. Physical, emotional and mental repose. The world had flexed its muscles and now began to relax. There was peace in the air.

It was late afternoon.

All visitors had left. The sun was reaching over the distant hills of mainland. The view from Olympus was stunning. It reminded me daily that I was privileged to live in the realm of the gods. There was peace in the air.

Ambrosia and I went for a walk to an orchard just east of our villa. Lately, we had little time to just wander around together. Many people expected a great deal from us. We strolled around trying to collect our thoughts after Mama's *résumé* of prehistory. It made a lot of sense. It was fun knowing that we really do originate from a Singularity. From Oneness. It was also fun knowing that we shall never be alone. Be it up there, somewhere, or down there, or preferably and more likely down here, we are all looked after. By Mama and by all of them who already made the grade. She needn't breathe our air to look after us. She never interfered, but sometimes, just sometimes she would give us a slight nudge in the right direction. It was also fun knowing, without the slightest shadow of doubt, that we could always visit her. And that we would always be welcome.

"I've been thinking..." Ambrosia broke the silence.

I waited. Usually her thoughts were fascinating.

"If we were to add up all the days you've been 'awake', and add those to your age in Montreal, you'd be about fifty-seven now." And then for some reason she giggled.

Well, after physics, math was her strong suit. Ha, ha!

We walked along, slowly, enjoying the solitude. Her

hand in mine, like two young lovers. We needed to be alone. Just the two of us. It's been a while. We sat down on a dwarf wall that held the earth from slipping down the hill. The way Incas once did it. It made a nice bench.

...so we are in Eden...

I heard her voice inside my head. It did not break the serene silence. I wondered how Adam and Eve communicated.

...alone... just the two of us...

I added in the same spirit.

"...alone in the Garden of Eden..." she repeated, this time in a whisper, her voice dreamy.

Ambrosia reached over my shoulder and pulled down an apple. She bit into it and offered me the rest. Then she gazed into my eyes with a very serious expression.

"Shouldn't we be naked?" she asked.

I didn't answer. Then I thought about it.

"Fifty-seven, eh?" I gave her my best Canadian chuckle. Then I looked at her and pounded my chest.

*****

EPILOGUE

Second Eden

Gods move on in their eternal cycles. New candidates enter the paths of the Zodiac. The Masters and Minions—the near-gods and men. And, as Mama would say, animals are people too. Future people, but what is time anyway?

Devolution fuelled by egos for many—glorious evolution for the few, have stabilized. After all, in Atlantis they had reached interplanetary travel—not just in Astral bodies, but physically, in such bodies as you and I are wearing right now. We must hope that our grandchildren will not create another asteroid belt. We might run out of planets.

Slowly people are rediscovering the meaning of the expression "peace be with you". They are not talking about the absence of war, nor of any armed conflicts. They are referring to the inner peace that is *sine qua non* for achieving contact with one's potential. It is also the emotional and mental condition necessary to initiate alpha brainwaves, which in turn, as already mentioned, are the prerequisite to reaching and uniting with one's true self. That true self is ever present but it cannot manifest until contacted. That in turn is the meaning of free will. For most of us, it is a one-way trip. We can contact our true self, our I AM, but the reverse is not possible. It would violate the Universal Law or Free Will and thus of Individuality.

Within a mere 160 years of our move to Milos, there were profound signs of the Maitreya Effect. It had a marked effect on peoples' state of consciousness. People at large were becoming aware that they are more than just flesh and blood.

Father Pio could travel from Italy to South America. Some of us can now travel to the outer planets, other solar systems, even other galaxies. We do not do so physically, but on arrival we can adjust our inner senses to experience the local conditions better than we can with our physical senses here, on Earth.

It seems that in the whole universe and beyond, there are innumerable units of consciousness striving to rediscover their allegiance to their origin, and in the process translate the potential into reality. Hence, eventually, even the potential will grow in complexity. At least, I think so.

World without end?

Ambrosia and I have become titular ambassadors to intergalactic communities, some more advanced than we are by millions of years. Athena continues to spread joy through music and dance. Mavis continues to make new contacts, the world over. John infects all with his contagious love. He calls it the Inherent Oneness. We are still in contact with Mama and Papa and with Amadeus, Tom and Jerry. After all, they all have their being in the universes of our consciousness, Ambrosia's and mine.

Many have just stepped on their eternal journey in the new Garden of Eden, which this time encompasses the whole world. This time they have secret documents, in various vaults the world over, which will accelerate their growth. But most of all, they all still have the Maitreya Effect. Hopefully, none shall ever retreat to the devolutionary journey of our predecessors. Thanks to Maitreya, all human units of consciousness are irrevocably connected to the Singularity of Life.

And we all go on from there.

Finally, the name I'd chosen for my notes, the book, sounded to me a little presumptuous. After all I did write not just about people and their potential, but also about great many things and events on which we had little or no influence. Nevertheless, all my notes came from the magnificent aerie, which I'd called, as have many others, the Olympus. Hence, I decided the abode of the Gods to become my title. Enjoy.

***

The End

Before you forget
PLEASE WRITE A (BRIEF) REVIEW
Your thoughts are important to me.

Acknowledgments

I would be remiss were I not to thank my many friends who read the galley proofs and helped to make this book a success. Most especially my thanks go to Peter Walker, Moira Malone, and particularly Ronald Piecuch. Their diligent editing raised this book to an acceptable literary standard. But most of all my gratitude to my wife, Bozena Happach, who put up with being a grass widow for weeks on end and then allowed me to benefit from her insights.

Sincerely,

Stan I.S. Law

A Word about the Author

Stan I.S. Law (aka **Stanislaw Kapuscinski**), architect, sculptor, and prolific writer, was educated in Poland and England. Since 1965 he has resided in Canada. His special interests cover a broad spectrum of arts, sciences and philosophy. His fiction and non-fiction attest to his particular passion for the scope and the development of human potential. He authored more than thirty books, nineteen of them novels.

Under his real name he published seven non-fiction books sharing his vision of reality. He also composed two collections of poems in his original native tongue in which he satirizes his view of the world while paying homage to Bozena Happach's sculptures.

Bibliography

Excerpts have been borrowed from:
Visualization—Creating your own Universe, by Stanislaw Kapuscinski

http://en.wikipedia.org/wiki/Earth%27s_magnetic_field

Before you judge:
http://www.highexistence.com/quotes/view/before-you-judge-others-or-claim-any-absolute-trut/

Previous parts of Trilogy:
WALL – Love, Sex and Immortality
and
PLUTO EFFECT

ℍℙ
INHOUSEPRESS, MONTREAL, CANADA
http://inhousepress.ca